THE ASSASSIN OF GRINS AND SECRETS

K. E. ANDREWS

Sonder & Morii Publishing

THE ASSASSIN OF GRINS AND SECRETS

COPYRIGHT

AUTHOR'S NOTE

Please be aware that this book contains scenes of gore, violence, torture, physical abuse, sexual assault, mentions of rape, and gaslighting. This book might not be suitable for younger readers.

This novel has kingdoms and lands inspired by various cultures around the world. This isn't meant to fully represent an entire culture, people group, or time period, but a fantasy world inspired by many real-world cultures and places.

The main character also experiences synesthesia, which is when a person experiences multiple sensory responses when a sense is simulated. Chromesthesia, the main type of synesthesia used in this story, is when sound evokes the experience of color, shape, or texture, either outside their own body space into the world (projector) or existing within their internal mental space (associator). Synesthesia is unique to everyone who experiences it, so no two synesthetes experience commingling senses the same way. As such, the synesthesia experienced by fictional characters in this story might not be the exact same as what real people experience.

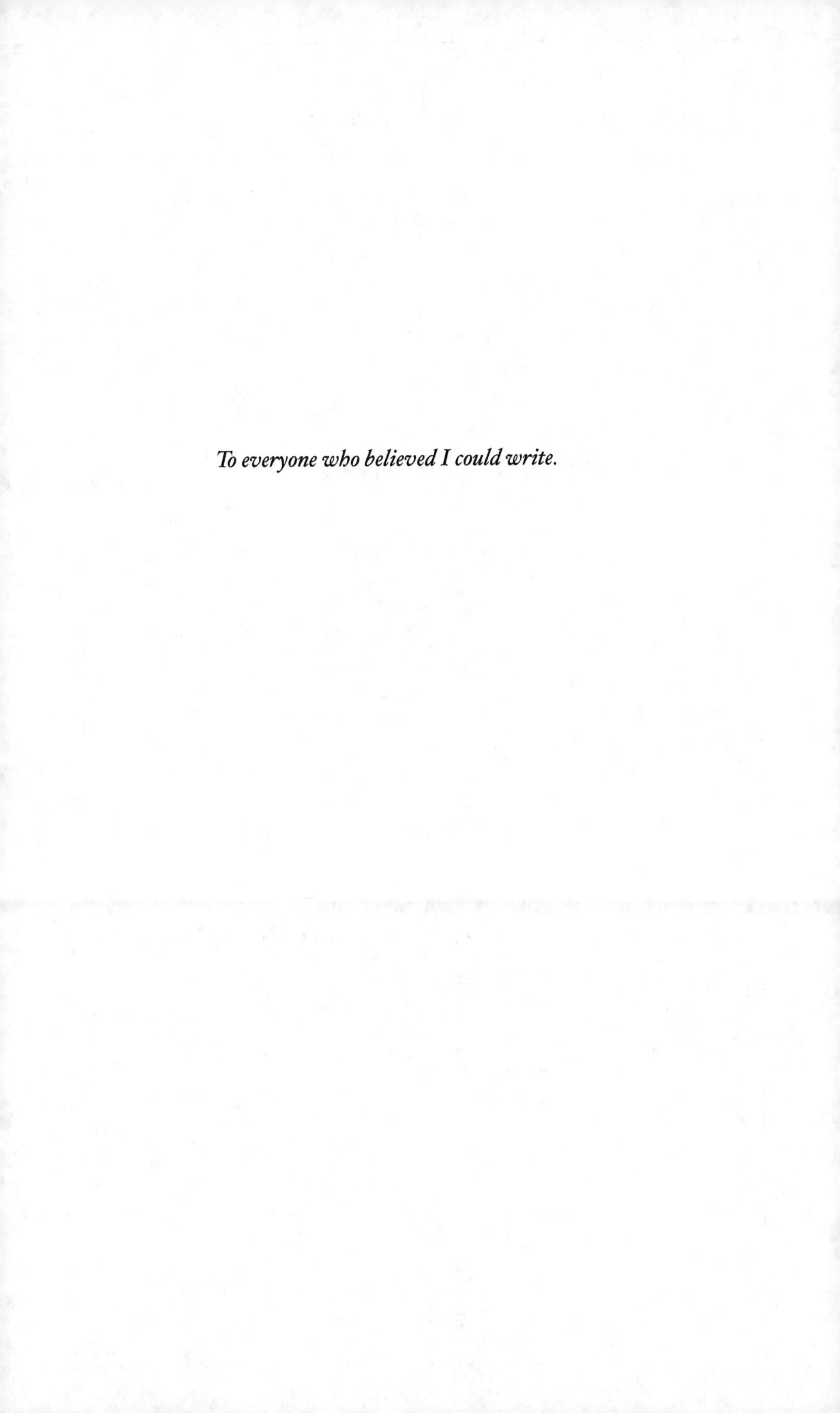

To everyone who believed I could write.

Zhao
Edolas
Plain of Queens
Olhouser
Valkyriar Mountains
Cliffs of Krieger
Silv
Fú Lián
Sky Lake
Black Isles
Edola Ocean
Sea of
Saxum
Dimidian Mountains
Ko Forests
Kona
Tenebris Mountains
Caew—im—dwinath
Marnediad's Seat
Ygris
Kannath River
Savas Mountains
Savas
The Old Kingdom
(Sarlyria)
Sea of Hestarë
Olson Desert
Plains of Dimbar
Sava Forests
Bal
Sava
Gwain M
Wendale
Idris Forest
Vinguies Mountains
Idris
Her Gorreg
Ki

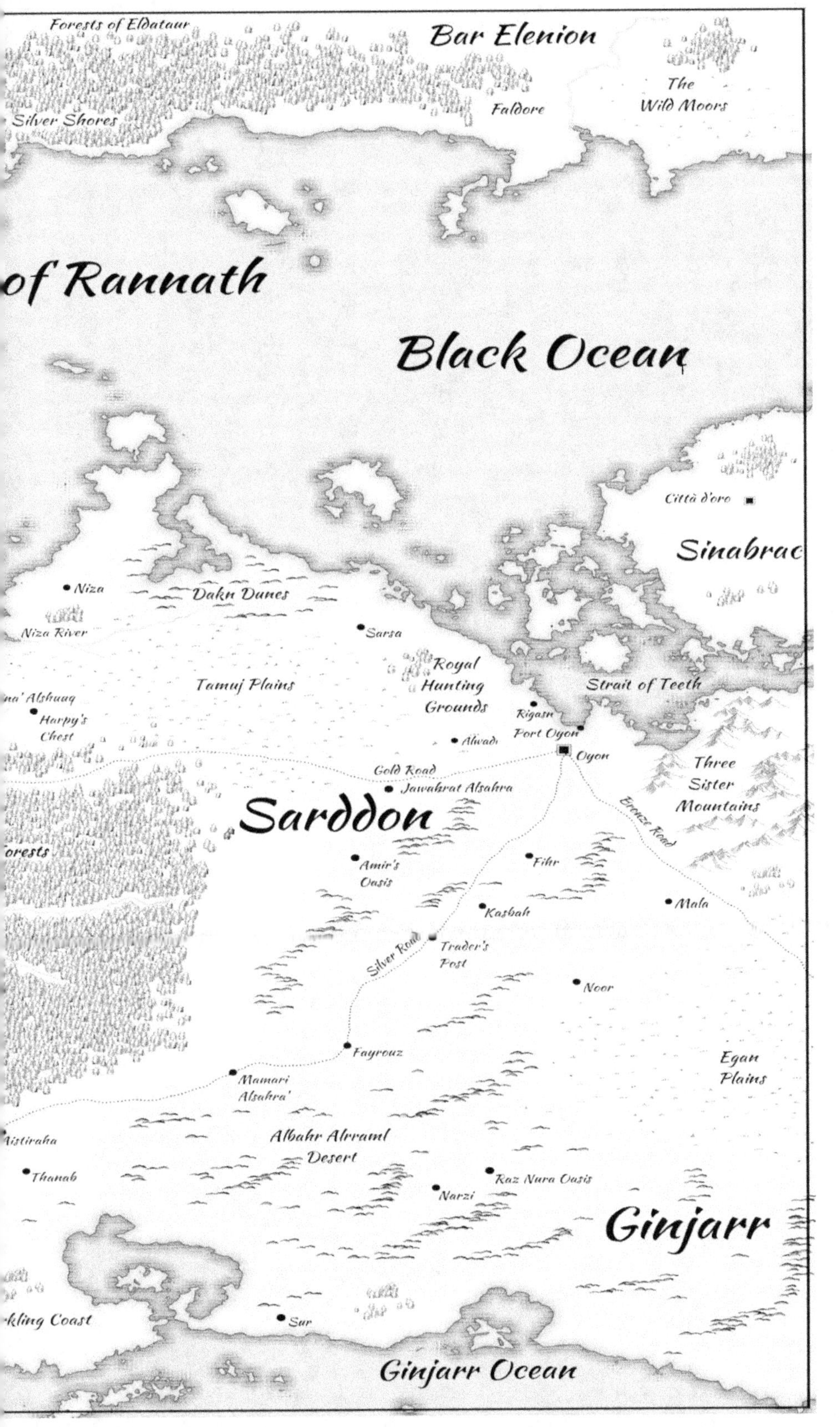

Forests of Eldataur
Bar Elenion
The Wild Moors
Silver Shores
Faldore
of Rannath
Black Ocean
Città d'oro
Sinabrac
Niza
Dakn Dunes
Niza River
Sarsa
Royal Hunting Grounds
Strait of Teeth
na' Alshuaq
Tamuj Plains
Rigasu
Harpy's Chest
Alwadi
Port Oyon
Oyon
Three Sister Mountains
Gold Road
Bronze Road
Jawahrat Alsahra
orests
Sarddon
Amir's Oasis
Fihr
Mala
Kasbah
Silver Road
Trader's Post
Noor
Fayrouz
Egan Plains
Mamari Alsahra'
Aistiraha
Albahr Alrraml Desert
Thanab
Raz Nura Oasis
Narzi
Ginjarr
kling Coast
Sur
Ginjarr Ocean

Glossary of Terms

Abaya: a long, loose robe-like dress worn by women

Abite: run

Abnay: son/my son

Accipiter: a widespread Ravanassë tribe with dark skin and white hair that live in the Idris region of the Old Kingdom

Aikhtiar: the selection competition for the Malik's muharib

Akhun/Akhi: brother/my brother

Alkhaliq: the Creator god

Amir: prince

Amirah: princess

Arak: an anise-flavored liquor distilled from grapes, raisins, or dates

Arras: a tapestry hung on the walls of a room or used to conceal an alcove

Azraq: a group of nomadic desert tribes that wear blue clothes

Badlah: the costume that a dancer wears

Bagh nakh: a weapon with four or five curved blades affixed to a crossbar or glove

Baghlah: a large ship with two to three sails

Baklava: a layered dessert made of filo dough, filled with chopped nuts, and sweetened with syrup or honey

Batbout: a bread made of semolina that cooks with a pocket like pita bread

Bazaar: an enclosed marketplace or street where goods and services are exchanged and sold

Beghrir: a small, spongy pancake with holes made with semolina or flour

Boed tân yn mynd â chi: May fire take you

B'stila: a thin, crispy filled pastry that can be sweet or savory

Caid: local chiefs

Calamor: a group of powerful Immortal mages

Carissima: dearest

Carreg cryau fi: Stone strengthen me

Carrom: a board game where players flick disks at smaller wooden disks to get them into any of the four corner pockets

Cazuela: a name used for a variety of dishes, such as stews, cooked in an earthenware pot

Chebakia: a deep-fried pastry made of strips of dough rolled to resemble a rose then coated with a syrup made of honey and rosewater and sprinkled with sesame seeds

Cuirass: a piece of armor consisting of a breastplate and backplate fastened together

Dao: a single-edged sword

Deel: a long tunic made of brightly colored silk that buttons up to the neck on the right side

Delam: my heart

Diffa: a feast

Dijil: Sarddonian currency

Djellaba: a long, loose-fitting unisex outer robe with full sleeves and a hood

Dhow: a type of ship

Effendi: a suffix used to denote respect

Falak: a giant mythological serpent

Fiat justitia ruat caelum: Let justice be done even though the heavens may fall

Gandora: a long, loose-fitting robe worn by men and women

Galu: good fortune

Ghalyan: a single or multi-stemmed instrument for smoking tobacco

Gwae: a type of elk from the Silver Shores

Habibi: my dear, my darling, or beloved.

Hammam: a place for public bathing

Harissa: a hot chili pepper paste

Haya: life bracelet

Hîr vuin: the title for the king of the Vale
Ifrit: a demon made of smokeless fire
Kaftan: a long, flowing robe-like dress
Kamancheh: a bowed string instrument
Kanisa/Alkanayis: church/churches
Keffiyeh: a scarf worn by men
Khanjar: a curved sword-shaped dagger
Khopesh: a sickle-shaped sword
Koubba: a shrine
Koummya: a curved dagger
Lacaraite: impossible
Lamellar: a type of body armor made from small rectangular plates
Lumina adiuva nos: Lights help us
Maamoul: a date-filled cookie
Maaqouda: a potato fritter
Mahia: fig liqueur
Majlis: sitting places for meetings
Malika: queen
Malik: king
Marhaba: welcome
Maqua: a group of five warriors that serve the king of the Vale
Mazar: a mausoleum
Mazarine: a deep purplish blue derived from cobalt
Mazboutah: a term used for coffee that is strong and sweetened with sugar
Mea culpa: my fault
Medersa/medersis: a college
Milcaos: steamed potato cakes studded with bacon
Moussem: a festival
Msemen: a flatbread eaten by itself or stuffed with meat
Mu'assel: a syrupy tobacco mix smoked in a hookah
Muharib: warriors of the Malik
Murrah: coffee without sugar
Mutabbaq: a thin, panfried bread folded over a savory or sweet filling
Ney: a thin wooden flute

Ogee: a distinctive pattern with two continuous S-shaped curves that form an oval before repeating out

Oud: a short-necked stringed instrument similar to a lute

Okht/Okhti: sister/my sister

Palaúlfa: small wolf

Palmeraies: palm groves

Pob hwyl i ti: Good luck to you

Qamis: a long tunic or gown worn by men

Qaris: priests who read from the holy texts during worship services

Ras el hanout: a spice blend

Ravanassë: people of the Old Kingdom with Immortal ancestry that have the ability to use magic

Rida': hooded cloak

Roc: an enormous legendary bird of prey

Sadiqi: my friend

Saifrakasas: coliseum fighters

Sahriminha: Sarddonians with Immortal ancestry that have the ability to use magic

Salteña: savory pastries filled with meat mixed in a sweet, slightly spicy sauce containing olives, raisins and potatoes

Santur: a trapezoid-shaped hammered dulcimer

Sanguis enim sanguinem: Blood for blood

Sayyidi/Sayyida: my lord/my lady

Scimitar: a sword with a curved blade that broadens toward the point

Sfenj: a deep-fried doughnut

Shafrah: a small, curved utility knife

Shahrban: governor

Shakshouka: baked egg tagine in a sauce of onion, peppers, tomatoes and spices such as cumin and paprika.

Shatranj: a form of chess that has six different pieces (shah=king, pil=bishop, rukh=rook, farzin=queen, asp=knight, and pujada=pawn)

Sidi: sir

Sirwal: a type of baggy trousers

Smen: aged butter

Sooq: open-air street markets

Tadelakt plaster: a waterproof lime plaster

Tagine: an earthenware dish used to cook food; also the name for meals cooked in the dish
Takshita: a wedding dress
Tang suit: a jacket with a straight collar
Tombak: a goblet-shaped drum
Tureen: a serving dish for foods such as soups or stews
Umm/Ummi: mother/my mother
Vade in pace: Go in peace
Vizier: advisor
Volchitsa: she-wolf
Wadi: a valley, ravine, or channel
Wali: personal guards of the royal family
Wil: fly
Za'atar: a spice blend made of dried herbs such as thyme or marjoram, dried sumac, and sesame seeds
Zellij: geometric patterned tilework

Months and Days of the Week

Months: Esta, Nésa, Ista, Kemen, Airen, Súru, Hlón, Soron, Calina, Endien, Ango, Yelwa
Days: Ennaar, Atyaar, Nelyaar, Cantaar, Lemenyaar, Mettaar

Countries of Cemiyon

Bar Elenion: the country on the northern continent next to Edolas. It's the homeland of the Immortals and is split into the kingdoms of the Vale, the Fae, and the Elves. Main language is Elpahta.
The Black Isles: a collection of islands in the Edola Ocean. It's made up of many tribes and serves as a trading post between the northern and southern continents.
Edolas: the kingdom on the northern continent between Zhao and Bar Elenion. Ruled by a queen. Capitol city is Olhouser. Language spoken is Edola.
Faldore: the kingdom of the Fae in the west. Ruled by a Fae king. Main language is Elpahta.

Ginjarr: the kingdom on the southern continent next to Sarddon in the east. Ruled by a king and a council of tribal leaders. Main language is Ginja.

Illamatras: the trading city between Edolas and Bar Elenion. Often called the bridge between the Immortal and mortal lands.

The Old Kingdom Sarlyria: the kingdom west of Sarddon. It's ruled by the four Immortal Kings. Capitol city is Caew-im-dwinath. The country has many language, the main ones being Sarlyrian, Elpahta, and Common.

Sarddon: the kingdom between the Old Kingdom and Ginjarr. Ruled by the Malik. Capitol city is Oyon. Main language is Sarddonian and Common.

The Silver Shores: the country and birthplace of the Vale located in Bar Elenion. Rule by a Vale king. Main language is Elpahta.

Sinabrac: the island nation close to Sarddon and Ginjarr. Ruled by a king. Main language is Sinabian. Capitol city is Città d'oro.

Wendale: the neutral country between the Old Kingdom and Sarddon. It's ruled by a council. Capitol city is Herr Gorreg. Language is Wendish.

Zhao: the kingdom on the northern continent next to Edolas. It's ruled by the Ascended Emperor and is made up of various tribes, each led by a chief. Capitol city is Fú Lián. Main language is Lóng Shé.

Religion of Sarddon

Alkhaliq: the creator god with six elemental children—water, earth, fire, air, light, and shadow.

The Twelve Divine Saints:

Rahat (The first Saint and Saint of Light): She could manipulate light. She divinely received the word of Alkhaliq under an olive tree and defeated a horde of ifrits plaguing the city of Noor.

Shukri (Saint of Nature): He could make plants grow. Created a forest to protect his village from a horde of bandits that hid his people and used the plants to kill the bandits.

Hafiz (Saint of Illusions): He could create illusions. He stopped

an invading army with an illusion of thousands of soldiers and
monsters.

Arwa (Saint of Beasts): She could communicate with animals and
beasts. She tamed a flock of rocs in the desert to stop them from
attacking a city.

Raz (Nura Saint of Water): She could manipulate water and was
originally a prostitute. She saved a whole village by creating an oasis
in the middle of a desert.

Esmail (Saint of Earth): He was blind and could manipulate the
earth. He created the wall around Oyon that prevented the city from
being overrun.

Faysal (Saint of Earthly Knowledge): He was a scholar who
could remember everything he ever heard, saw, or experienced. He
collected great works from around Cemiyon to put in the largest
library in the world, the Library of Mala.

Aziz (Saint of Wind): He was deaf and could manipulate the wind.
He saved Oyon from a massive monsoon by redirecting the storm.

Zaman (Saint of Healing): He had the ability to heal. He went
around Sarddon, healing the sick and coming up with many lifesaving
treatments and medicines.

Alath (Saint of Heavenly Knowledge): She possessed great
wisdom from Alkhaliq. She opened schools across Sarddon and
discovered how to build the great dome of Alqamar Palace.

Basira (Saint of Fire): She could wield fire and had a deformed
leg. She fought and defeated a falak in the desert.

Zubaida (Saint of Sand): She could manipulate the sands. She
stopped a massive sandstorm from destroying Oyon.

Religion of the Old Kingdom

Mirarnediad: the creator god who dwells in Ië, the starlit heavens.
He made the twelve Lights to rule the world they created and
maintain balance.

The Twelve Lights:

Yestarë: the firstborn Light. She created the silver tree, Thavnath.
From its fruit came the Vale, and she taught them how to use magic
through song.

Malinalda: the sister of Yestarë and the second Light. She took the seeds from Thavnath's fruit and made the Elves.

Lalaith: the third Light and wife of Gwaihir. She created the animals and creatures of the world.

Gwaihir: the fourth Light. He created the Fae.

Nolmë: the fifth Light and husband of Malinalda. He filled his library with knowledge and all the events of the world.

Belegurth: the sixth Light. He controlled the earth and created the landmasses and continents.

Rannath: the seventh Light and the sister of Belegurth. She controlled the waters and created the oceans, rivers, and lakes.

Egnor: the eighth Light. He created the sun and fire.

Lámina: the ninth Light. She was the sounds present, past, and future.

Laiquassë: the tenth Light. He was responsible for the spirits of the dead.

Rauta: the eleventh Light. She cherished metal and fashioned them into objects of great beauty and power.

Vanya: the twelfth Light. She created the moon.

Dúath: the thirteenth Light and husband of Vanya. He created shadows and the night. He and Vanya created humans. Dúath betrayed the other Lights by trying to seize their power and was cast out.

Colors of Sounds

The Aanisah: dark purple voice

Afzal: cobalt-blue voice

Armor: orange-red

Arrows: yellow-orange

Astra: sunset-orange voice, lilac-colored footsteps

Bal: lavender

Baqir: topaz-colored voice, yellow footsteps

Bells: peach

Blades leaving sheaths: light green

Bones: dingy amber

Camels: turgid green

Cats: light peacock-blue
Ceramics: ruby
Chains: speckled green
Chainmail: orange-red
Charcoal scraping: orange
Clapping: bright blue
Claws: pink
Coins: dark blue
Crickets: aqua
Crows: lavender
Death: pale silver voice
Dishes: ruby
Dogs: pistachio-green
Door hinges: teal
Elephants: rosewood
Eneca: rose-colored voice, green footsteps
Fabric: magenta
Fang: opaque blue voice, orchid-colored footsteps
Fayruz: pine-green voice
Faysal: emerald-green voice
Fire: purple-blue
Glass: ruby
Hasim: coffee-brown voice
Head against stone/wood: bright blue
Hisein: twilight-blue voice
Horns: auburn
Horses: goldenrod
Horse hooves: vermillion
Ilderim: ocher voice
Il-Makah: onyx voice, light tan footsteps
I'timad: indigo voice, brown footsteps
Jabir: steel-gray voice, purple-red footsteps
Jorham: blue-gray voice
Kamanchehs: fiery red
Kamau: navy-colored voice, sienna footsteps
Karam: light azure voice
Key in a lock: tangerine

Knuckles on a door: muted blue
Kosai: raspy teal voice
Laia: currant-colored voice
Leaves rustling: mulberry
Life: bright yellow voice
Luca: sky-blue voice, rose colored footsteps
Lujayn: mauve voice
Magic: opalescent
Mansaka: saffron-yellow voice
Marcello: indigo voice
Mayte: muddy brown voice, olive-green footsteps
Metal against metal: orange
Murdag: amber colored voice
Nala tigers: peacock blue
Ney: luminous yellow
Nightjars: pale red
Oud: chartreuse
Paper: light plum
Peacocks: fuchsia
Quill on paper: amber-orange
Ragnhildur: periwinkle voice, ginger-colored footsteps
Rahim: ice blue voice
Rajiya: bright orange voice
Rameses: gold voice, orange footsteps
Rasima: violet voice, green footsteps
Rats/mice: coral
Ringing in Serein's ears: white
Rizwana: lapis-colored voice, hazel footsteps
Rocks/stones: silver-white
Sa: ruddy brown voice, rouge footsteps
Salatis: powder-blue voice
Salveig: apple-red voice, leafy-green footsteps
Santurs: marigold
Seagulls: burgundy
Serein: pale yellow voice: light blue footsteps
Serein's mother: turquoise-colored voice
Sethos: blood-red voice, dark purple footsteps

Small birds: bright coral
Stairs creaking: blue
Sword blade: orange
Thunder: bronze
Tombaks: emerald
Umar: dark orange voice, yellow footsteps
Uriah: forest-green voice, gray footsteps
Uthman: dark gray voice
The Vale: thistle-colored voice
Wagon wheels: ivory
Warden Gharib: lemon-colored voice, dark amber footsteps
Water: opaque purple
Water pump: bright orange
Whips: sapphire
Wind: amethyst
Wings flapping: pale emerald green
Wooden sword: blue
Xansas: white voice
Yasmine: ginger-colored voice

PART I

THE SCARRED WOMAN

Chapter One
Pit of Darkness

A MOTTLED RED SCREAM CLAWED THROUGH THE DARKNESS, another echoing howl from Grasdan's living ghosts. Serein heard all the colored sounds that painted her dark world. Water falling in opaque purple drips. The speckled green rattling of chains. Her pale yellow exhales.

The charcoal stick in Serein's hand scratched against the wall, dusting the ground with light orange scraping as she finished drawing a face. Other drawings marked the stones, eyes staring at her. The chains chafed against her wrists covered with pus-filled sores. Dark, lice-infested hair hung in her face. Scabs and scars riddled the faded tawny skin stretched over a hunched skeleton. A fiery itch radiated from the mass of scar tissue along her left side and down her leg.

Death was outlined in silver and shadows, his face ageless. He drew closer with each labored breath dripping out of Serein's scars. Serein ran a finger along the stone, eyes stinging with tears.

I'm sorry, my Sun and Stars, she thought.

Are you going to die here, volchitsa? *I trained you to survive!* A white voice bled through the darkness, hissing with a forked tongue.

Serein shivered in her threadbare shift and thin trousers as the pale words fell like snow.

Dark amber and gray footsteps collected outside the cell door, and she stiffened. "How about this one?" a copper-hued voice asked.

"In her state, there'd be no profit. Jabir wouldn't be interested," the warden replied, his lemon-colored words seeping through the darkness with sour tones.

"I heard he wasn't too picky about the fodder he uses in the fighting ring. With her reputation, we could make some coin."

The warden clicked his tongue. "Might as well see what we can get," he said.

A heavy pause hung in the air, broken by the orange-red shifting of chainmail and a nervous coppery breath.

"For Saints' sake, don't stand there! What are you scared of? She bleeds like everyone else."

The key jammed into the lock with sharp tangerine-colored sparks. Fragments of light flooded the dark cell, and Serein shut her eyes, recoiling. Rough hands slammed her against the ground, and a boot pressed against her back. The chains tightened as Serein's arms were jerked back. Metal cut into her wrists and blood oozed down her skin.

"Make sure those bonds are tight." A faint tremble rippled through the warden's voice.

A sack went over Serein's head as she was dragged from the cell through the innards of the once-great Old Kingdom fortress. All traces of Grasdan's former glory were buried under soot and misery as the Malik of Sarddon filled it with prisoners from across the continent.

The hard-packed dirt turned to stone. Horses snorted nearby in puffs of goldenrod, their hooves clacking vermillion against the ground. "Load them into the wagon," said a gruff topaz voice.

Serein slammed against other bodies as the guards threw her into the wagon. The hushed ocean-blue whisper of a desperate prayer filled the space on her left, a gasping green sob on her right. Rattling crimson coughs sounded across from her. Ragged light orange and soft purple breathing spread through the air like dye in water.

Five other prisoners, Serein thought, slumping against the wagon wall. *Will they kill us if they can't get anything for us?*

"All secured. Set off," the warden said.

Serein's head cracked against wood in a burst of blinding blue as the wagon rumbled forward with an ivory groan. Stinging pain bit into her wrists with each speckled green rattle of the shackles.

Don't forget the colors of their screams. May the Lights take you quickly and give you rest. The Old Kingdom prayer echoed in time with her pulse.

SEREIN'S FEET SCRAPED AGAINST THE GROUND AS THE GUARDS pushed her out of the wagon. Dirty light filtered through the burlap, hot wind sweeping away the smell of sweat and urine. Pain burrowed into Serein's joints. The ever-present hunger clawed at her stomach, gnawing on what remained of her flesh and bones. She caught bits of Sarddonian and Common Tongue, the orange clanging of metal, and voices shouting prices in the distance.

Cooler underground air. Sounds bouncing off high walls. A day's ride from Grasdan. Probably the Harpy's Chest since it's between the Old Kingdom and Sarddon. A trading den, she thought, remembering the place from her travels years before. The information clustered in Serein's mind but sloughed off instead of weaving into something tangible.

The sounds faded as Serein was led through winding hallways. A door opened with a teal creak, and Serein was shoved forward, legs shaking with each step. The sack lifted, and red light bled through her eyelids. Blurry forms of people moved past, torchlight stinging Serein's eyes as she blinked. Someone grabbed her chin and forced her mouth open. Water sloshed past her cracked lips, and she gulped it down.

"This is a sorry lot you brought me, Gharib." A steel-gray voice speaking Sarddonian appeared on her left, cutting the air like a knife. Dark amber and purple-red footsteps shuffled closer, and nervous purple breathing trickled next to her.

"These ones survived the longest in the fighting pits, Jabir," the warden, Gharib, said. "This one is an infamous assassin."

The footsteps stopped near Serein. "This Ravanassë woman?"

"Don't let her looks deceive you. She's a Bone Viper assassin. The Grinning Assassin. Killed seven of my guards. She also killed General Mansur in his tent eight years ago in Sava."

Serein felt a gaze resting on her. "A woman took down a man like that?" Jabir asked.

"I have the papers about her capture. Eighty gold dijils for her life contract," Gharib said.

Light plum-colored rustling flew like beetles as papers were moved. "Eighty gold? Saints, you're out of your mind. She's half dead," Jabir snapped. "The only dangerous thing is her stench."

"You see the scars. She also has the brand of the Bone Vipers. Look."

Gharib's dark amber footsteps moved toward Serein, and she cracked her eyes open. His sallow face and bloodshot eyes blocked her vision, lemon-colored breaths getting stuck in the brown hairs of his beard. Nails from a four-fingered hand dug into her chin, jerking her head up. Serein's mouth tightened as she tried to wrench away. Bile burned her throat as she was spun around and pressed against the stone wall. The back of Serein's shirt ripped, streaks of magenta tearing the air.

Smells grew sharper. Fire crackled in angry purple-blue hisses, and the smell of burning bodies clogged her nose. The pain in Serein's side returned and crawled across the pink burns. Her body crumbled, bones fragmenting.

No! The cool wall cut into Serein's cheek. *Don't touch me!*

"That brand could mean anything," Jabir said.

"I assure you that she's the real thing. Tried to slit her throat several months back, but she didn't die," the warden said.

"Perhaps whoever tried to slit her throat didn't know how to handle a knife," Jabir told him.

"She *bit* off my damn finger!" Gharib hissed, lemon-colored voice bristling as he released Serein.

"I don't care if she can walk through walls or survive having her throat cut. This woman isn't worth what you're asking."

"Sixty gold then?"

Serein slumped to the floor, peering through the cracks of her eyelids. The world came into focus. Death in his pale gray and silver robes moved behind the men, turning a piece of silver wood over in his hand.

Will I make it through the day, my Sun and Stars? Serein thought.

"I'm not paying that much for someone I'm just using to settle some debts," Jabir said.

"Forty then? This is a skilled assassin, not just some common prisoner," the warden went on.

"An assassin who will probably die before she's thrown in a match. I'm not wasting my coin." Anger spiked Jabir's words, the steel sharpening. "I'm sure you'll be able to find someone interested in her *reputation*."

"But think of how much you could earn with an infamous assassin in your fighting pits? Even though she's a woman, the name alone will bring people to watch and place bets."

Jabir paused, breaths even. "One gold dijil," he said finally.

"One?!" The word splattered against the wall like a rotting lemon.

"Ask for any more, and I'll end our arrangement. You may run Grasdan, but I have friends in high places here. I can always find other suppliers," Jabir said. "Some of the others might have some potential since they're in better shape. Twenty-five gold dijils for these three. Samil, take the rest to be cleaned. I want to inspect this so-called *Grinning Assassin*."

"Watch that one, or you'll lose a finger," the warden warned.

"I have experience with dangerous persons." Coins jangled in a dark blue clinking sound. "Go watch one of the matches, Gharib. Place some bets. Maybe you'll regain some of the money you were hoping to get."

The other prisoners were led away, the warden sneering at her as he left. Serein's eyes closed, the last dregs of strength ebbing away. Steel gray breaths mixed with three others nearby as she sank into exhaustion.

A rough hand slapped Serein's cheek, the bright blue sound cracking across her eyelids. "Wake up! I didn't pay for a corpse."

A pinched, bearded face glared down at her, hazel-green eyes narrowed. The man's hair was cut short, gray creeping into his sideburns. A long, dark djellaba reached his knees over a pair of loose tan sirwal trousers. An orange rida' robe flowed over his shoulders.

Jabir. Right-handed, forty-two. Serein followed his movements, the smell of hookah smoke mingling with the odor of wine. *Vices are drink and tobacco. Makes most of his money off fighting matches. Must owe money to some important people if he bought me for so little just to throw into a fight. Not to win.*

"Get up," Jabir said in Common Tongue, holding a whip in his hand.

Serein's head remained pressed into the dirt. The pulse of the earth rumbled in her ears, footsteps and voices mingling together. Cool air brushed over her collection of silver and red scars. Serein tensed as the whip snapped across her side with a sapphire *crack*, old pains raking down her back.

"Are you deaf?" Jabir snapped, spitting onto the ground. "I said get up!"

Kill him, volchitsa, the white voice said, slithering through her consciousness.

He's not here, Serein thought, shuddering. *He can't find me. He can't hurt me.*

Serein groaned and heaved herself up, wrists scraping against the shackles. Metal cut into the sores, the wounds reeking of sour infection and speckled with blood. Jabir's eyes roamed over her scars and the blue vine tattoo on her left arm and collarbone. Fingers prodded her, and she flinched. Stale breath crept over her skin as Jabir hit her chest with the handle of the whip.

"I suppose that Bone Viper brand and the murder's mark adds merit to your identity. Who would've thought that the feared Grinning Assassin was a woman?" Jabir said. "Let's see if you're worth what I paid. Clean her up a bit and have her hair cut to get rid of the lice."

Jabir stalked off as the guards dragged her down the hall, his robes swishing with dark magenta trails.

My life is only worth one gold dijil, Serein thought, scalp itching. *He overspent.*

Chapter Two
The Fighting Pit

DAYS PASSED, MARKED BY MEALS OF STALE BREAD AND DRIED FRUIT, shifting sunlight, and the fights Jabir thrust Serein into. Three times she held a sword, the exertion threatening to shatter her. Three times she had been pummeled into the dirt, new wounds opening as she curled under the blows of defeat. The new clothes she'd been given quickly became torn and bloodstained.

When the sunlight of another day crept through the dim cell, the tiny bud of hope crumpled in Serein's chest. The metal torc with a scorpion etched into the copper—Jabir's insignia—pressed against Serein's scarred throat. Nicks and scratches marred the metal, the ghost of its previous owner a weight against her bruised collarbones. Her unevenly cut hair tickled the back of her neck and brushed against the knife-mark brand from Grasdan.

Jabir's shadow pressed against the bars of the cell as he approached. The other prisoners huddled against the walls, their breaths mixing in a nervous cloud of colors. Jabir jerked his chin at Serein. A guard pulled her out and shoved her toward the fighting pit at the end of the corridor.

Will this be the fight that kills me? Serein thought, following Jabir.

Lightheadedness nudged Serein off balance. She scratched her itching scalp, nits snagging under her broken nails. The merchants and traders in the tunnel talked about her opponent, Sa—a man who didn't leave his competition unscathed. They placed their bets, the numbers stacking against her as they looked over her scarred, emaciated state.

Jabir spat on the ground, the thick smell of hookah smoke rolling off his robes. "Let's see how you fare against Sa," he said, steel-colored words tipping upward in a smirk.

A scimitar was thrust into Serein's hands, the curved blade nicked and dulled. *Seems Jabir no longer needs me,* she thought, arms bending under the weight of the scoured sword.

Death lingered in the corners of Serein's vision. He rolled the same piece of silver wood in his palm as he followed her. The guards pushed her into the fighting pit. Its wooden sides stretched up to the stone railings, holding back the roiling mass of spectators. Light streamed from the gaping hole in the cavern's ceiling.

Serein sagged in her faded skin, each breath heavy as she staggered out onto the sands. The deafening cacophony of color shoved against her, pain digging behind her eyes. Her opponent, Sa, was a muscular man with dark, swarthy skin and thin scars across his smooth face. Light glistened off his shaved head as he strutted around, the marks from previous fights etched into the torc around his throat.

Right-handed, Serein thought, watching the weapon he held. *Thirty or so. From the Black Isles, judging by his green eyes and snub nose. Has the size and strength advantage. If he gets a hold of me, he'll snap my bones.*

The match started with a ruddy brown shout as Sa charged toward her with his scimitar raised, footsteps like rouge warning bells.

Serein closed her eyes, sinking into the red of her eyelids. *It'd be easier to die. I'm so tired.*

An orange whistle cut through the noise as the man swung his sword—orange like the laughter that clung to her memories that made the two-year long nightmare of Grasdan survivable.

Serein's eyes snapped open as the blade glinted toward her. She ducked and rolled past Sa, scrambling to her feet behind him. Sand scraped against the callused soles of her feet. Shouts from the crowd flooded her vision. The man whirled around, confusion passing over his face. Serein's thoughts snapped together, and an old fire rose from dying embers.

Kill him, volchitsa! the white voice hissed. *If you don't do something, you'll die.*

Anger rose and drowned out the voice, the black beast inside her growling. *If I'm to die, I'm taking you with me.*

Sa brought the blade around, giving Serein a moment to dodge as the edge cut across her right arm. The broad curve of his sword caught her weapon as she parried, throwing out jolts of burnt orange as she staggered back. The bruises along her ribs shrieked in protest. Each breath scraped against Serein's lungs, and pain throbbed in time with her pulse.

Serein dug her toes into the sand, weaving back while keeping the sword close against her body. She spun, angling the blade at Sa's legs. Sa swung, brushing her attack aside as he rushed in to slice her face. She raised her weapon to deflect Sa's oncoming strike.

An opening. His right side is unprotected, Serein thought as Sa shifted to her left.

Sa grabbed Serein's injured arm as she moved and shoved her to the ground. His scimitar opened a shallow cut along her side. Sa pinned her down, prying the sword from her hands.

Death peered over Sa's shoulder at her. *Are you ready?* he asked, pale silver voice spreading like a shimmering pool.

Sa's fist cracked against Serein's nose. Her thoughts scattered in fractals of white light. Shouting from the crowd increased as she tasted blood. Tears seeped from the corners of her eyes as Sa wrapped his hands around her neck, thumbs pressed underneath the torc. Serein looked up into the wild, green eyes and gritted teeth.

No! My Sun and Stars, she thought, sucking in a breath. *I want to see you again!*

Serein's discarded sword found its way back into her hand. With a yellow shout, she heaved the weapon up, ramming it into Sa's side. Blood gushed out, her grip slipping as she twisted. The blade scraped against bone, refusing to go in any further.

Sa stopped, looking down as he touched the wound. The pressure around Serein's throat released, and she as air rushed into her lungs. Red painted Serein's skin and soaked through her rough shift. Sa reeled onto his back, ruddy brown breaths gurgling as he struggled to pull the weapon out.

A white ringing noise clustered the edges of her vision. *Get up! Finish it. I didn't train you to quit.*

Serein stumbled to her feet, grabbing Sa's fallen weapon. Pain twisted Sa's features as she stood over him.

"Please..." he rasped, the word melting into the sands.

The sword pierced his chest, red seeping across his muscles. The light blinked out of Sa's eyes as his thrashing ceased. Choruses of protests filled the air, clogging the sunlight with a colorful miasma. Death scooped up Sa's trembling brown soul.

Serein's arms ached, her lungs ready to burst. Her knees gave out, and she clutched her bleeding side. Death stood over her as the stench of iron and loosened bowels clogged her nose. Spots danced across Serein's vision, darkness creeping in along the edges.

It's time to rest, Death told her, his silvery words soothing as he reached out toward her.

Guards grabbed Serein and dragged her away. Jabir appeared in a wide hallway on crackling purple-red footfalls. The whip bounced against his hip next to a curved dagger, his orange rida' billowing behind him.

"You weren't supposed to kill Sa," Jabir said, hazel-green eyes narrowed. "Although now I've earned enough from that match to settle some debts. But I never ordered you to win. Now I have to deal with Sa's owner."

Jabir's face hardened into a dark mask. His fist caught Serein in the gut, the whip leaving sapphire *cracks* across her skin. Serein sank to her knees, curling away from the fiery tongues.

My Sun and Stars. My Sun and Stars. The chant echoed as hope evaporated with each new vein of pain. *I'll be going on ahead.*

"Seems this woman is more trouble than she's worth," a voice said. "Why don't I take her off your hands?"

Gold words rolled at Serein's feet before blackness came. She hoped Death had returned for her.

Chapter Three
Golden Bargains

"ARE YOU SURE SHE ISN'T TOO INJURED? SHE DOESN'T LOOK WELL." Golden words dropped into the darkness, distant in Serein's ears.

"What's your interest with this woman, sayyidi? She's a criminal," Jabir said, steel-gray voice cutting like a blade as it sharpened into focus.

"I heard the Grinning Assassin was here. I went searching for the prisoner in Grasdan, but discovered that they were not there," said the gold voice, faint peach chimes sparkling around it. "Is this the same woman you brought from Grasdan, Gharib?"

"Yes, sayyidi. Her hair's cut, but it's the same one. The Golden Jackals confirmed her identity when she was imprisoned two years ago." The warden's lemon-yellow voice hit the ground like fallen fruit.

"I didn't think the assassin would be a Ravanassë woman. Most of the reports made it seem like the assassin was a man. The description of numerous scars and blue eyes seems to match."

Colors exploded behind Serein's eyelids as Sarddonian voices drifted around her in unfamiliar hues, agitating the pain inside her skull. Footsteps resounded in her ear, the sounds lapping like waves. The smell of stale hookah smoke and burning oil hung in the air. The cold stone floor offered relief against her hot skin.

"The warden assured me that this is the Grinning Assassin. I have her life contract papers. She has the Bone Viper's mark. Shall I show you?" Jabir asked, grabbing the back of Serein's shirt.

Serein opened her eyes, the blows and whip marks throbbing along her body. Her breath hitched at Jabir's touch, the memory of pale hands crawling over her skin sending cold lightning through her veins.

"That isn't necessary, Jabir. Release her," the gold voice said.

Jabir gave Serein a shove as he released her shirt, grunting. Serein's gaze swept across the sandaled feet, sorting through the different colors of voices and breaths. Four soldiers stood around the room, their uniforms black and red with scale armor and breastplates instead of the tan robes and leather cuirass of the Harpy's Chest guards. Jabir stood nearby, scowling.

Alive. For now, Serein thought, tasting blood as smarting pain spread from her nose. *A study. No windows. One door. The warden and Jabir. At least eight people I don't recognize.*

"I'm interested to know how an assassin who should be in prison ended up here. I'm sure the Malik would be interested to know that you're selling prisoners' life contracts without sending a portion of the profits to the crown," the golden voice went on.

"Sayyidi" Gharib began.

"I had a chance to look at your prison records while I visited Grasdan," the other man said. "Twice a month, the prisoner numbers drop by six on a specific day, which is unusual. This number keeps recurring every month for the past three years."

The blood on her clothes had dried in stiff patches. *He was at Grasdan? Why? What would a nobleman be doing at a prison?* Serein thought, trying to stay above the waves of consciousness.

Warden Gharib stood over her, his leather armor and sword hidden underneath his tan robes. "Prisoners die, and sometimes it's hard to get accurate counts. There have been a lot of new prisoners the past few years," Gharib said, rubbing the stub of his missing finger, the end a dull red color.

"You don't know who's in your prison? Or are you forging those death numbers in order to move prisoners out of Grasdan? You're not in charge to mismanage prisoners and abuse your position," the man behind the desk said, his gold voice shimmering around him. "And you, Jabir, are entrusted with overseeing trade activity here. Grasdan's prisoners are meant to serve their sentences, not to be sold in a trading den for your own profits. Yet, there seem to be a few here. Care to explain?"

Jabir stiffened. "I haven't done anything illegal, sayyidi," he said.

"Then you will not mind me looking at your records further."

The torchlight popped, the smell of burning oil strong in the air. "Of course, sayyidi." Jabir bowed, anger simmering under the steel-gray surface of his words.

Torches burned along the sandstone walls. A low desk sat at the front of the room with a dark-haired man behind it. He wore a long white qamis tunic with gold embroidery that reached his ankles and covered his loose, pale sirwal trousers. Papers rustled in delicate plum threads as he moved things on the desk. Two small gold bells hung from his earlobes, giving off peach chimes. Wavy black hair curled against the man's ears, escaping from an ivory-colored turban. The pristine clothes stood out against his dark brown skin, his presence illuminating the dim space.

The face that haunted Serein's dreams for the past fifteen years shadowed the man's younger features. His oval face was smooth, high cheekbones accentuating his aquiline nose and golden, almond-shaped eyes. A dark beard followed his jawline. Smoke and fire flashed behind Serein's eyes, broken by a sweeping black blade and a spray of crimson.

Golden eyes. A Sarddon royal. A prince. He has the same face as Sethos. What does the son of the Murderous King want with me? Serein thought, dizziness pushing behind her eyes.

The man moved around the desk, bells chiming with each light orange step. A bearded guard in black and red robes and a maroon turban with a lion crest shadowed the amir. The umber-skinned guard had a scimitar and a curved khanjar dagger at his side. Torchlight bounced off the bronze studs along the etched buckler shield on his hip. Warm brown eyes set above a hawkish nose watched her.

"This is no way to have a conversation. Uriah, help her stand," the amir said.

"Aye, Your Highness," a forest-green voice said on her right, words rumbling like storm clouds. The roughened accent was different from the Sarddonian voices.

Serein tensed as boots hit the floor in gray ripples, chainmail rattling orange-red. *Nine people. I missed him.*

Serein pivoted her gaze upward to meet the stiff jawline of the captain. Pink sunburn wrapped around his neck, a pale mark visible from the leather cord he wore that disappeared underneath his tunic. A scar ran across the man's top lip, mirroring the one on the bridge of his nose. His red hair was pulled into a short, tufted ponytail, and a scruffy beard hid his frown. His pale complexion made him stand out among his dark-skinned companions.

Uriah gripped Serein's arm and hauled her up, her head coming below his shoulder. His free hand went to the woven gold hilt of the scimitar at his left side. Embossed on the breastplate was a roaring lion between two swords with its paws atop a round shield—the symbol of Oyon's city guard. A white sash cut across his front and wrapped around his waist. Scale cuirass armor covered his shoulders. A khanjar rested on his right hip next to a round shield, the grip unworn. The smell of beeswax and aloe vera drifted around her.

Right-handed. Mid-twenties. Experienced with a sword, but not with a dagger. Military experience. A strong sense of duty and honor. Close with the prince. Friends. Wendish yet is part of Sarddon's city guard. A captain, Serein thought as the man glared down at her, eyes like chips of emeralds with shadows underneath them. *A captain that doesn't sleep well.*

"What's your name?" the amir asked Serein, the question smooth as a smile wrapped around it.

Serein looked back at him. Each blink and wheezing breath aggravated the pain in her nose. Death passed behind the men, eyes on her.

"I'm Rameses Nasr ibn Sethos al-Amirmoez, Amir of Sarddon. The man to your right is Uriah Stormheir, Captain of the Oyon Guard. Now that we have all introduced ourselves, please tell me, are you the Grinning Assassin?"

Serein remained silent. *That name doesn't matter. It's dead, as I'll probably be soon, either from the captain's sword or from listening to this prince talk and hearing those damn bells,* she thought.

But you want to know why the Murderous King's son would seek you out, the white voice said.

She bit the inside of her cheek, shaking her head to clear the scaly words.

Rameses' brow crinkled. "Do you know her name? Does she understand Sarddonian or Common Tongue?" he asked Jabir.

"I was never given one. Her papers only provide a number. 799. She's a Ravanassë, so she might only know Sarlyrian. She appears stupid, but I can see it in her eyes that she understands Common at least," Jabir said.

The golden eyes turned back to Serein. "What's your name?" Rameses repeated, switching to Common.

"His Highness asked you for your name," the captain said to her in Sarlyrian, the musical edges of the language roughened. "If you value your life, answer him."

The bells rang with soft peach chimes as Rameses approached. Serein's ragged face was distorted in the reflection on the earring's metal surface. His gaze stopped on the blue tattoo on her left arm, its inky leaves and vines woven into her tapestry of scars. He wrinkled his nose but didn't step away. Faded streaks of ink stained the sides of his fingernails, faint outlines of words still visible on the side of his right hand. A few calluses and thin scars marked his left hand. Around his right wrist was a gold Sarddonian haya bracelet with twenty-three gold bands along the strands of corded silk.

Right-handed. Twenty-three bands on the haya bracelet. The last band is newer, not as marked, so his name day must have been within the last month or so. Some fighting experience, she thought. *Muscular upper arms, calluses on his fingers, scars on the left hand. An archer. Prefers reading and writing, judging by the ink stains, and the imprint of words on his skin.*

Rameses twisted the ring on his right hand, tapping the gold lion's head with an emerald set on its forehead. "I have a proposition for you," he told her. "I want you to come with me to Oyon and be one of my guards—a wali like Ilderim here is." He gestured to the bearded guard behind him.

A woman for his guard? Sarddon doesn't let women become guards, let alone fight. The work he wants me to do is one of two things, she thought.

The prince offers you a path to the king. What better way to the heart of your enemy than through his son? The Lights smile upon you, volchitsa—*my she-wolf.*

"You could live out the rest of your life here, but I think you want to be free," Rameses said and walked back to the desk.

I may not die free, but I'll die on my terms. Serein's eyes darted to Uriah's dagger. *Let's see how badly the princeling needs me.*

Serein gathered her strength and swiped the curved dagger from Uriah's belt, lunging for Rameses from behind. Shouts rang out. The guards moved to draw their weapons as Rameses whirled around. Serein pressed the blade against his throat. Uriah's sword kissed her neck. A trickle of blood ran down her collarbone. The bearded guard behind Rameses pointed his weapon at her forehead, Death's face reflecting in the blade.

Too slow. Just like in Grasdan. Too weak and slow to escape.

"I see your victory in the pit was no coincidence," Rameses muttered, eyes wide. "You're indeed who you say you are. And a woman of all things."

The wali sheathed his weapon as Serein lowered her arms. *Men don't control the game of killing,* she thought as Rameses took a step back.

White light cracked across Serein's eyes as her head connected with the ground. The dagger flew from her hand, spinning across the floor toward Rameses' feet. The room fragmented as she blinked, a boot pressing between her shoulder blades. Pain split through her skull as her vision blurred.

"Uriah, stop," Rameses said. "There's no need for violence. Let her up."

"Your Highness," Uriah said, "if His Majesty finds out about this—"

Rameses motioned for the soldiers to step away, and the pressure on her back lifted. "He will not hear about this. Is that understood?" Rameses replied and picked up the dagger, glancing at his soldiers. They nodded wordlessly.

"Aye, Your Highness," Uriah said with a bow, sheathing his sword.

Serein peeled her face off the floor. Blood droplets hit the floor in opaque purple drips. She spat out a glob of bloody saliva, testing her front teeth with her tongue, and found nothing chipped or missing.

Uriah held Serein's shoulder with a vice-like grip. Death's shadowless form seeped into her periphery. Serein sucked in sharp breaths as she stared at Rameses.

"What do you want?" Serein asked, pale yellow words scratching the roof of her mouth like a rusty blade. *This prince needs me enough to let me live after threatening his life.*

"Ah, she speaks!" Rameses said, smiling. "I would like to know what to call you."

"Why are you *really* here?" she rasped, jaw moving with aching stiffness.

His brow creased, the smile faltering a bit. "I already told you what my intentions are. To have you as one of my guards," Rameses replied.

"Is your own guard insufficient?"

"There are some things they cannot do that you can. I have need of your specific skills."

"They don't make good bedmates? Would you prefer a prostitute?"

"How dare you talk to His Highness that way!" Uriah snapped, jerking her back. Pain shot through her arm as the forest-green words stabbed the air.

"I can assure you that I have no intentions of making you do anything against your will," Rameses told her, giving Uriah a hard stare. "You will be compensated for your services, your life contract returned to you, and your crimes forgiven. I will give you your freedom in six years."

Serein's breath caught in her throat. Uriah's right index finger twitched along the sword hilt. *The hand offering freedom always has something else hidden in the other. There's nothing to be gained from working for Sarddon. Only death. He's hiding something. His words are false gold.*

Thoughts of freedom had been ripped from her chest with serrated edges when she'd been thrown into Grasdan, fading as the years dragged on. Hope wormed its way in, a small tendril weaving around her ribcage with promises that made her heart ache.

"Do you accept?" Rameses asked.

Freedom in six years as the prince's guard. Can I start hoping again, my Sun and Stars? Or will it be taken from me again? she thought, licking her cracked lips.

"I would prefer your answer now and not delay things," Rameses added.

Death ran his thumb over the smooth piece of wood, waiting. *You don't have to fight anymore,* he said, silver words cool against her cheek as he held out his hand. *You can rest.*

Serein felt everything teetering on her next breath. *Death would be a mercy, but a chance has been offered—a chance to get my vengeance and return to you, my Sun and Stars.* "I accept," she said.

Death withdrew his hand. "I'm pleased that we have reached an agreement," Rameses said as he smiled, the corners of his eyes crinkling.

"Your Highness," Jabir's steely voice cut through the golden cloud, "her life contract belongs to me."

Rameses' gaze swept to Jabir and the warden. "Not anymore. This arrangement between you two ends today, or my father's men will be paying you a visit," he said, his gold words carrying the weight of his promise.

Jabir stopped, face twisting with rage. He bowed, trembling fingers touching his forehead. "I...understand, sayyidi. Thank you for being merciful," Jabir said, voice tight.

Rameses nodded and glanced back at Serein. He gestured to the desk as he pulled two thin scrolls from his sirwal pocket. Uriah shoved Serein forward, the eyes of the guards on her.

"These are copies of your contract. I made sure it was written in Common and Sarddonian. You will have one to keep, and the other will be for me. I have already put down my signature. All that's needed is yours," Rameses told her, pulling Jabir's inkwell over and unrolling the contracts.

She glanced over the words, her gaze becoming unfocused. *Six years' service. Attending to the prince's daily activities. Salary of ten gold a week. Failure to fulfill the terms means getting sent back to Grasdan. Seems too simple,* she thought, taking in the gold lion seal.

"I forgot to ask if you could read," Rameses said.

"I can read," she replied.

Serein grabbed the quill from the desk and bent down, joints cracking. The nib hovered over the vellum, a drop of ink pooling at the end. Her throat tightened, hand froze over the words.

"Is something wrong?" Rameses asked, his gold voice staining the contract.

Serein sucked in a breath and signed her name, gazing at the word as the ink dried. Rameses stared at the name, brow creasing as he tried to decipher the name at the bottom of the contracts. He rolled up the scrolls and held one out to her.

"I'm glad that we have reached an agreement," Rameses said. "Now, I'll have a healer tend to your wounds. They'll let you bathe and give you some food and fresh clothes. We leave in two hours."

What new horrors await me? Serein thought as Rameses' smile returned. *My life is a series of transactions.*

You don't belong to anyone but me, volchitsa. *You'll always be mine. I found you first.*

T HE FORGE FURNACE ROARED, BLASTING SEREIN WITH ITS FIERY, purple-blue breath. Her head pounded as hammers struck metal, sending out dark orange tongues of lightning. Serein's wrists were covered in tingling salves and bandages after the healer had dug his knife to lance the sores and wash out the pus and blood. A clean bandage with a poultice was wrapped around her head. The torc had been removed, leaving behind dark smudges on her sallow skin. A long tan djellaba gown draped off her, and a pair of loose sirwal trousers barely clung to her boney hips.

Despite the hurried bath, the dirt remained on Serein's skin and underneath her nails. *Keeping this food down might be harder than fighting Sa,* she thought as the meal sloshed in her stomach.

A burly blacksmith held two copper contract bangles around Serein's wrists. Sweat beaded on his bronze skin, his brown hair slicked back off his face. He clamped the bands shut, the hot ends cooling as her hands were dunked in water. Sarddon's crest, a small lion with twelve moons, was pressed into the metal with gold inlay.

Rameses stood nearby with his guards and the red-haired captain. "Make sure they're not too tight," Rameses said before glancing at

Serein. "You will have the status of an indentured servant. The bangles will be removed when your service has ended. For now, they show that you are under my protection."

Serein's arms bowed under the weight of her new shackles. *No matter what he calls it, I'm still a slave.*

Chapter Four
Little Details

VERMILLION STREAKS FROM THE HORSES' HOOVES CLOUDED Rameses' envoy. A wagon loaded with fresh supplies rolled behind the group of fifteen soldiers. Serein squinted as bright light and noisy colors slammed against her skull. The shackles Uriah placed on her wrists hit against the copper bangles with every cantering step of her silver mare. Serein bit her cheek to hold down her meal. Amethyst-colored wind rushed up her djellaba gown and trousers, weaving its fingers through her short hair underneath her tan headscarf.

Uriah rode on her left, scowling beneath his keffiyeh. A faint waxy sheen from a salve coated his face. Rameses brought his dark horse alongside Serein, a draping gray rida' covering his qamis. A bow and a quiver of arrows hung from the saddlebag.

"Are you all right? It's an eight-day journey to Oyon. Riding handcuffed cannot be comfortable," Rameses said, gold clinging to his grin.

"I'll manage," Serein muttered, the cantle digging into her lower back. *It'll be easier than listening to the prince talk all the way to Oyon.*

Rameses patted the horse's neck. "If you get too tired, you can ride with me. I don't think Jabbar would mind."

Uriah shot Rameses a look. "Absolutely not," he said, the green words sharp. "I'd sooner put her in the wagon."

Serein tried to keep herself in the saddle as the gold and green conversation floated around her. She scratched her itching scalp. *Eight days. Let's see if I can survive for that long.*

URIAH SCANNED THE ROAD AS THE ENVOY HEADED ALONG THE main trading route—the Gold Road—around Locklin Forest. The noonday sun bore down on him despite the cool waxy paste he used to keep his skin from burning and the keffiyeh covering his head. The Tamuj Plains wrapped around the edges of the forests—miles of grasslands, acacia trees, caper bushes, and rocky crags. Locklin Forest bled into the landscape, marked with crumbling towers where the Old Kingdom's original border had extended. Remnants of woodlands dotted the plains, rotting stumps of once massive trees hidden behind the rippling seas of grass.

We should arrive in Oyon by Ennaar, seven days from now, Uriah thought, spotting Rameses' black horse in the middle of the other riders. *There was rebel activity here several months back. Troops have been monitoring the Gold Road for weeks with no issues. It's too dangerous for Rameses to be traveling like this. There's still the matter of this assassin.*

Uriah glanced at the woman riding beside him as she gripped the saddle with her bound hands. Scarred, tawny skin stretched over jutting cheekbones. A pink scar split her lips, and her nose was crooked, discolored from her injury in the fighting pit. Along her neck, dark and silvery scars formed a necklace with black and blue bruises strung together by a red slash mark. Her bright blue eyes stood out against the greenery—Ravanassë eyes. A woman made of sharp edges with danger lurking beneath her emaciated form.

Is this really the Grinning Assassin? Some starved woman barely able to sit on a horse? Uriah thought.

He'd seen faces like hers in the hollow expressions of the Ravanassë while on the front in the Old Kingdom. Faces filled with fear and mouths twisted in screams as they fled.

The smell of water hit him, a ringing sound growing in his ears. *No. I'm here. That was the past,* Uriah thought, shaking his head. *Stone protect me, Fire strengthen me, Water purify me, Wind guide me.*

The stone pendant underneath Uriah's armor pressed against his chest. Its weight centered him, the quiet mantra traveling the familiar channels of his consciousness.

"What are you staring at?" Uriah asked the woman in Sarlyrian.

Her sharp eyes turned to him. "What's today's date?" she replied, the smooth Sarlyrian broken by her raspy voice.

Uriah arched an eyebrow. "Lemenyaar the 17th. The month is Ista."

"The year?"

"592."

Her expression shifted, brow creasing. Uriah caught a flash of worry and confusion, but it vanished as she stared back at him again. He laid a hand on his sword.

"I'm not foolish enough to challenge you, Captain Stormheir, so you can relax." Her words prowled around him, preparing for the moment to strike.

"I should've killed you," Uriah said.

"You're loyal to your prince. Are you an old friend of his?" she asked.

"Why are you now speaking freely?"

"The tongue's a great weapon. You're an excellent target to practice on."

"Perhaps I should cut your tongue out and leave you weaponless."

A dark grin spread across her face. "I thought you wanted me to talk more, so I'll spill my secrets. If you wanted that kind of conversation with me, you should just say so," she said.

"You're a monster, so why would I want to have a conversation with you?" Uriah asked.

"What do you know of monsters?"

SEREIN STARED AT THE BLUISH-PURPLE AND DARK ORANGE COLORS of the flames licking the cracking wood, the scar tissue along her side prickling at the sound. Her body ached from riding, the stiffness making it difficult to sit. Sparks twisted around each other before they burned out, drifting around the skinned hares cooking over the fire. Pockets of stars pierced the black velvet sky. Remnants of stone walls surrounded the camp, overtaken by vines.

Two soldiers stood behind Serein. Tents and cooking fires filled the campsite, the horses tethered by the supply wagon. Soldiers sat in small groups, voices mixing with the hum of the camp. Old birch trees with spotted, flaking bark twisted as they grew out of the ruined outpost. Crickets and nocturnal animals trilled, their cries coloring the night. Amidst the sounds of the camp, a weak opalescent song of magic whispered through the earth. The thin strands vanished into the heart of the forest miles beyond the rise the ruins sat on.

So little magic remains, Serein thought as the smell of cooking meat and smoke wrapped around her. *It's been fifteen years since the Murderous King was able to drive it away. It's only a matter of time before it vanishes completely.*

Uriah sat across from her, eyes trained on her as he ate. His sword lay across his lap while the dagger was sheathed at his side. "Why are you staring at the flames like that?" he asked, his words burning up in the fire like verdant leaves.

"I'm observing the different colors," Serein said. *It's been a while since I was near a fire without having to throw bodies into it or almost be burned alive myself,* she thought, her clothes brushing against the numbed scar tissue along her side.

"Colors?" he repeated, raising an eyebrow.

"The fire has many colors. You might notice if you used your eyes for something other than glowering. Or is that expression permanent?"

Uriah glared at her. "Flames are just flames."

She rubbed the copper bangles, jostling the chains of her handcuffs. "If you think that way, then you'll miss all the little details in the world."

"And you can see all these 'little details'?"

"You broke your right index finger. It's bent slightly. You're right handed and favor a sword over a dagger. Wendish accent, but your Sarddonian's perfect, so you've lived in Sarddon a long time. Not married, no ring or haya bracelet. Judging by the way you so gently slammed me into the ground, you're used to physical labor and combat. Probably from a farming family since you don't appear to be from money," she said, lifting her gaze.

Serein tore off a hare leg from the spit, blowing on the hot meat.

"Strong sense of loyalty, which is why you're here even though you disagree with the princeling's decision to seek me out. You have a long friendship with him since he uses your first name instead of a title. You're older than him by a few years. Being here makes you uncomfortable, and you don't get much sleep, judging by the shadows under your eyes. I'm assuming you spent some time here since you speak Sarlyrian well. Probably fought during the war. Does being here bring up bad memories?"

Logs gave way, sending up a flurry of sparks. Uriah's hand tightened on the hilt of his scimitar. "What are you exactly?" he asked.

"You've already made up your mind about what I am. I still haven't decided about you, though," Serein said, staring at the cord around Uriah's neck. *Wonder what he hangs around his neck. A keepsake from home or a religious symbol? Doubt he's a believer of the Saints like the Sarddonians are. Might be a protection charm associated with the Wendish deities.*

"I don't care about what you think about me."

"What are you and the prince not telling me?"

Uriah stiffened, index finger twitching as his hand rested on his sword. "Nothing," he grumbled.

"I'm sure there's more to it than what he told me," Serein said.

The broken finger twitches when he lies. It twitched when the princeling talked about me being his guard in the Harpy's Chest. Could be involuntary, but it twitched again just now.

Uriah crossed his arms. "You know all you need to know."

So, there is something else to this. The prince was in a hurry. Something hinges on me being his guard. Something the captain's not happy about.

Leaves crunched behind Serein, mulberry-colored rustlings swept under orange footfalls. "Discussing anything interesting?" Rameses asked, grinning as he approached with his wali. He took a seat between Serein and Uriah, his earrings catching the firelight. "What do you think about these trees? I have read that Locklin Forest is sacred to the Vale, Elves, and the Fae. The ruins here look Elven, judging by the rune marks on the stones."

"The princeling should be careful what he says in these woods,"

Serein said, licking grease off her lips. "Golden words won't keep ghosts at bay. They say the spirits of the Immortals and the Ravanassë watch over the forest."

Her pale yellow words dissipated into the fire, the echo of her mother's turquoise voice distant. The X-shaped scar across her chest ached. Serein pulled the rida' tighter around herself.

Rameses glanced at the trees. "Many have superstitions about these woods, but I think we're safe. The Immortal Kings died in the plague, although some are rumored to have fled to the Silver Shores behind the Fog that surrounds the country of Bar Elenion," he said. "I have heard tales about the giant spiders, beasts, and dragons of the Old Kingdom that are seen from time to time."

"The Immortals were the first children of Mirarnediad's Lights, formed from magic. They don't die easily. And neither do the creatures of myth." *The rebels believe that some of their kings survived, and that magic can be restored.* Serein's eyes fell on the dagger at Rameses' side. *Guess he realized that I'm dangerous after all.*

"Perhaps we will get to see some of these creatures." Glittering words danced around the flames. "You know a lot about the myths of the Old Kingdom."

"I've lived long enough, picked up a few things."

Rameses propped his arms on his knees, head tilted. "How old are you?" he asked. "I have heard that many half-bloods can live longer than most mortals."

Serein met his gaze, face blank. *It was hard to keep track of time in Grasdan. It's Ista 592, so I suppose I'm twenty-two now. I feel like I've aged decades,* she thought. *Two years in prison. Almost three months since they threw me in that cell to die. I didn't think I had lost that much time.*

Rameses sighed and threw a stick into the fire. His eyes glowed like molten gold. He twisted the ring around his finger, the lion's head catching the firelight.

"Will you give me silence when I ask questions?" Rameses asked.

"Will you keep asking pointless questions?" Serein replied. "I'm not as young as you think I am." *He twists the ring when he's worried or irritated. He did the same thing at the Harpy's Chest.*

"You appear younger than your reputation would lead people to believe," Rameses said. "I thought the Grinning Assassin would be older. Even after capture, speculation about your identity remained. The only descriptions were that you killed with a grin, were scarred, and were always seen in dark, hooded clothes. You have many nicknames. The Black Wraith. Scarred One, but I would prefer to call you by your name rather than Grinning Assassin. I have not been able to decipher what you wrote on the contract."

Serein tossed a few small bones into the fire, watching as they cracked. She held a greasy leg bone the length of her hand, and she slipped it under the folds of her clothes when no one was watching.

"Serein," she replied, placing the word between them. *Give him a small piece to make him think he's gained my trust. Use trust to manipulate this game.*

Rameses' face lit up, dimples appearing. "Do you have a last name?"

She stared at him in silence. *You don't get to own that information.*

"Well, Serein, this is much better than calling you assassin or Black Wraith," Rameses said. "Uriah, I want to speak with you a moment."

"I feel it's unwise to let her out of my sight," Uriah said as Rameses stood.

"Ilderim will watch her," Rameses said, looking at the bearded wali.

Uriah rose and followed Rameses toward the edges of the camp, casting an apprehensive glance back at Serein. Ilderim watched her with an indiscernible expression, brown eyes turning amber in the light of the flames.

How long will it take for the prince's game to unravel and stab him in the back? Serein thought. *Wonder if I'll be the one to do it?*

THE MOONLIGHT TANGLED IN THE TREE BRANCHES AS RAMESES and Uriah left the campsite. Through the thinning trunks beyond the camp lay the sprawling expanse of Locklin Forest.

Gnarled wood dug into Rameses' shoulder blades as he leaned against a tree. He glanced back at Serein by the fire. The phantom feeling of the dagger against his throat remained like a cold whisper.

The Grinning Assassin, a Ravanassë woman. Why was there so much confusion about her real identity? Rameses thought.

He looked at Uriah as his friend reached into his pocket for the smooth rock he always kept there. Exhaustion clung under Uriah's eyes, his body tense as he scanned the forest. Uriah tugged at the leather cord around his neck as he turned the rock over in his hand.

"I know this past month and a half has been difficult for you. Are you still having nightmares?" Rameses asked. *He's been tugging at his necklace since we left. I wonder how many rocks he's picked up and put in his pockets.*

Uriah's jaw tightened, and he glanced down. "I'm fine," he said.

"Please take care of yourself, sadiqi. I'm worried about you," Rameses told him, expression softening. "What do you think about her—Serein?"

"I think she should've been left to die," he replied as his thumb moved in circles across the stone. "Her silence is unnerving, but she's more aggravating when she talks."

"Interesting that she speaks freely to you. Maybe it's because you speak Sarlyrian? Did she tell you anything meaningful?"

Uriah shook his head. "No. I doubt you'll be able to get anything out of her. Don't let your guard down. She's too observant. She knows you're not being upfront with her. She somehow knew things about me that she shouldn't. She's able to take what you say and watches your movements to uncover what you're hiding. It's like she's peering into your heart."

Rameses tilted his head. "Oh? That almost sounded like a line from a romance novel," he replied, grinning. *What things she said to Uriah that rattled him so much. Her observation skills will be exactly what I need. I wonder how much she's uncovered about me just through observation.*

Uriah rolled his eyes, muttering something in Wendish. "Whatever you're implying is a delusion of your mind," he said, making a fist around the rock.

"I was not implying anything. I think it's nice that a woman is paying close attention to you," Rameses said. "By the Saints, she has the most intriguing eyes I have ever seen. They seem to glow. Is that common with all Ravanassë?"

"It's part of their mixed lineage from the Immortals. The color depends on their Immortal ancestry." Uriah met Rameses' gaze. "Serein might not even be her real name. The Ravanassë don't tell their names to just anyone."

"What do you mean?" Rameses asked.

"They believe knowing a person's full name gives access to their soul," Uriah told him. "Many people in the Old Kingdom don't give their names to people they don't know."

"I know it will take time for her to trust me. I will tell her the truth once she's settled in Oyon." Rameses pushed off the tree. *This will be a challenge, considering what Serein's gone through. Will the fact that my father started the war prevent her from trusting me? I need her to see that I'm not a threat,* he thought, feeling the cool surface of his ring.

Uriah's usual seriousness shifted to concern. "I don't think she'll agree to help you when you finally tell her. She's hiding something. She didn't hesitate to hold a blade at your throat. What's to stop her from doing it again?" he asked.

"If she wanted to kill me, she would have done so. I believe she wants to live. I need someone cunning and patient, who notices details. I need her," Rameses replied. "Would you help train her?" *He's been saying this was a mistake ever since we left Oyon. I cannot use anyone from the palace. It has to be someone with no loyalty to my father.*

Uriah's expression darkened. "Why? Shouldn't Ilderim take charge of her?"

"You're the most capable person I know to handle it since you oversee the training of the city guards. She needs to regain her strength. Plus, you will be able to keep an eye on her."

Uriah chewed on the inside of his cheek. "That doesn't mean I *want* to be around her if I can help it. Firoz is handling things until I return, but I still have a city to protect," he said.

"Please consider it. In the meantime, I will take your warning to heart, fretful Uriah," Rameses said and clapped him on the shoulder. "Try and get some rest."

"I won't rest easy until we're back in the palace, and she's in a cell," Uriah muttered as he tugged at the cord around his neck again.

.   .   .

Serein plucked a nit from her hair and tossed it into the flames. Beyond the campfires, darkness shifted through the trees. She listened to the conversations drifting through the camp, the open space leaving her exposed after two years of confinement.

Free. Limited, but I have the opportunity to figure out what to do next, Serein thought. *I could try and find out if Eneca survived the raid on the hideout…I haven't seen her since I escaped. You'd like her, my Sun and Stars.*

A pang of sadness worked its way into Serein's chest as she stared beyond the ruin walls.

I'd need a weapon and a way to remove these shackles. Her eyes darted to the soldiers nearby. *I could sharpen this bone and maybe pick the lock. Then there's the matter of these bangles. I'd be hunted again—*

An arrow struck one of the soldiers behind her through the eye with a yellow-orange streak. He collapsed with an aqua gasp before falling still. Serein rolled to the ground, limbs screaming in pain, as an arrow struck the other soldier in his throat. A volley of bolts shot from the tree line, hitting two more soldiers before they could draw their swords.

"We're under attack!" a wheat-colored voice shouted.

Figures melted out of the forest, climbing over the crumbling outpost. The horses pulled at their tethered reins, pawing at the ground. Ilderim's head snapped toward the forest. He looked at Serein before running in the direction Rameses and Uriah went.

She sifted through the colors of the soldier's voices and the unfamiliar ones. *Ten men, at least. A group from the Old Kingdom. I can't tell what tribes. Are they targeting the prince?* she thought, grabbing a dagger from the fallen soldier.

Serein yanked the arrow from the corpse, rising from her crouch. A man charged at her from the trees, his brown shout rising as he swung his weapon.

Eleven men.

Serein dodged the orange whistle and rammed the arrow into his neck. The manacle chains grew taut, digging into her bandaged wrists. The shaft broke with a carmine *snap*, and she stuck the dagger into his chest. His brown breath ran down the front of her clothes as he fell. She stared at her trembling, blood-soaked hands as she turned to the other attacker.

Death stood before her, souls nestled in his hand as he met her gaze. A shiver ran down Serein's spine. *I didn't survive Grasdan to die here.*

RAMESES FLINCHED AS URIAH'S SWORD TORE THROUGH THE leather armor of the bandit. He pressed himself against a tree, drawing the khanjar dagger from his belt. The sounds of fighting rose in the distance, swords clashing and the panicked cries of horses.

"Are you all right, Rameses?" Uriah asked him as the man crumpled.

"I'm unharmed," Rameses breathed, eyes wide as he clutched the dagger. Ilderim appeared, and relief washed through him, tamping down the rising fear. "Ilderim! What's happening?"

"Bandits. A dozen, maybe. Archers ambushed from the trees," Ilderim told him, weapon drawn and his shield strapped to his arm. "You need to get somewhere safe, Your Highness."

"What about—" A sword flashed under the moonlight. Uriah parried the attack of a second bandit emerging from the shadows.

"Stay close," Ilderim said.

Rameses glanced through the trees at the bodies strewn around the camp. Bile rose in his throat as he took in the splashes of red, the coppery smell of blood stinging his nose.

Serein moved through the chaos. She hit the ground, her shackled wrists pulled close. Dagger in hand, she sliced into the back of a bandit's legs. The man screamed and stumbled to his knees. Serein sprang to her feet and slashed the blade across his throat, opening a smiling stream of red.

A wounded man limped toward her, and Serein threw a small knife at him. The man stared at the bone handle sticking out of his chest, crumpling to the ground. She stalked over to him and pulled the knife out before driving the blade through his eye. Gore streaked her clothes, painting her face crimson. Her curved mouth made Rameses' blood run cold. The quiet woman had transformed into something dangerous.

Grinning Assassin, Rameses thought, stomach lurching.

The sounds of fighting faded as the soldiers overpowered the attackers, driving them back into the woods. Rameses exhaled and walked toward Serein, sheathing his dagger. She turned, and the grin vanished, sweat smearing the blood on her skin.

Uriah lunged between Rameses and Serein. "Drop the weapon before I cut off your hand!" he shouted, his sword pressed against her throat.

Serein stared at the blade, chest heaving as the weapon fell to the ground. "She did as you asked, Uriah. Put your sword away," Rameses said, placing his hand on Uriah's shoulder.

Uriah lowered the blade. "What happened here?" he asked.

"Men ambushed from the trees," Serein replied. Uriah stared behind her at the bodies of the two guards. "I didn't kill the guards. The wali saw it before he ran off."

"Are you hurt?" Rameses asked, taking in her blood-splattered appearance.

"No."

A soldier ran up, bowing to Rameses. "What are our casualties?" Uriah asked.

"Three dead, five injured. Sakhr, Ikraam, and Ahmed. We captured two of the bandits. The rest are dead or escaped into the woods," the soldier said.

"Question them. See if they're part of the rebel groups that have been attacking trade caravans. Make sure the wounded are tended to and gather anyone who isn't badly injured to clean up the bodies. Have three men scout the area. I want extra men guarding His Highness," Uriah told him. "We'll bury the dead bandits in the morning."

Rameses stared at the corpses with lifeless eyes and blood seeping from their wounds, nausea rising. *No one was supposed to die. This was not supposed to happen...*he thought, the iron smell of blood clinging to his nose.

"And I want someone watching *her.* Tie her to a tree." Uriah's voice broke his thoughts.

"That's excessive," Rameses said. "She's already chained."

"That didn't stop her from killing two men," Uriah said.

Rameses gave him a tired look. "Let her clean herself up and get a fresh pair of clothes. She's not to be chained to a tree."

Uriah sighed again, his jaw tight. "Fine. Take her to get cleaned," he told the soldier. "Don't take your eyes off her."

"Thank you, Serein," Rameses told her. *I was not wrong. She's the one I need.*

SEREIN PULLED THE BLANKET CLOSE AGAINST THE CHILL, THE FIRE warming her back. The gore and grime had been cleaned from her skin, the fresh clothes too big for her. The rabbit bone remained tucked in the hem of her trousers next to a sharpened rock she picked up. Dark spots of blood dried on the grass.

I wonder if the rest of the journey will be this eventful. Let the rebels attack again once I've gotten some sleep, Serein thought, body aching as exhaustion pressed down on her.

Will you become their pet now, volchitsa? the white voice asked. *I'll always find you. I always do.*

Her eyes flew open, and she sat up. A ghostly touch ran along the back of her neck, bringing a wave of sickness. The guards looked at her, hands on their weapons.

He's not here, she told herself and settled back down, welcoming the darkness rid of screams. *He can't find me.*

Chapter Five
Alqamar Palace

THE HEAT CONTINUED TO MELT SEREIN'S SKIN AS THE DAYS stretched on. Cool water streamed past her lips as she drank from the waterskin. A week of riding turned the painful stiffness in her legs into a dull ache. The two captured rebels were tied up with the bodies of the three fallen soldiers in the wagon. The smell of death lingered in the air despite the attempts to preserve the bodies and slow the decay.

"If you keep drinking all that water, you'll make yourself sick," Uriah told her, green words floating along the amethyst-colored wind. "I don't want to watch you vomit again."

"In Grasdan, water wasn't this delicious," Serein said, putting the stopper back in the skin. The roughness of her voice had faded to a faint rasp.

Uriah's frown disappeared under his beard, the scar across his nose creasing. "I could throw you in the ocean if you'd prefer. Then you'll never run out of water."

"Does the princeling keep you around for your sense of humor?"

"Don't call him princeling."

Rocky formations dotted the edges of the Tamuj Plains, casting shadows across the grasslands. Spindly acacia trees rose above the tall grasses and sparse bushes. Ribbons of golden sand twisted around the horses' legs. In the distance, the outline of a city appeared, swathed in the folds of the Albahr Alrraml Desert. Jawahrat Alsahra, a sprawling city along the Gold Road carved into the rocky formations and hedged with palm trees. It stood out like a jewel among the sandy expanse.

As the miles stretched on and Jawahrat Alsahra vanished behind, Oyon came into view. The peaks of the Three Sister Mountains sat in the east between Ginjarr and Sarddon with their cloaks of thick jungles. A winding streak of blue broke away from the ocean, curling around Oyon. Ocher walls surrounded the city like a half-buried snake.

Orchards dotted with apiaries, palmeraies, and fields of farmland grew around the city, green contrasting with the golden sands. A graveyard marked with colorfully painted headstones filled a hillside. Houses and buildings were stacked on top of each other in a sloping labyrinth within the city. Alqamar Palace, with its glistening domes, towers, and white stone sat at the top of Oyon on a hill.

Sunlight turned the ocean into a blanket of rippling azure jewels. Sailing boats and large ships dotted the harbor while the waves crashed, giving off a sparkling, opaque purple sound.

The Ocean of Sarddon, Serein thought. *You'd love the ocean, my Sun and Stars. Perhaps I'll be able to draw you a picture and get it to you somehow.*

Gulls shrieked to each other, circling overhead as they threw out burgundy cries. Serein leaned back in the saddle, watching the birds.

"Don't lean back too far, or you'll fall off your horse," Uriah told her. "It'd inconvenience His Highness if you broke your neck."

"I'd hate to inconvenience the prince by dying," Serein said, straightening.

Bleating animals and human voices clashed together as Rameses' envoy entered the city through the wide blue, white, and orange arch. Camels with tasseled reins towered over the horses. The aroma of bread wafted through the air as the envoy passed a communal oven tucked down a side street. Smells of fatty, spiced meats and cooking fish mingled with the bitter odors of dyes and salt. People leaned out the windows of their houses, and women dressed in vibrant, flowing gandora dresses and headscarves parted as the horses passed.

It's been almost eight years since I was last here. The city looks like it's grown since then, Serein thought, watching as Rameses waved to people. *Still a city of many blended cultures.*

Colored sounds dug behind Serein's eyes as they passed the looming form of a half-domed coliseum of polished sandstone. Oyon's famous House of Knowledge overshadowed the markets, scholars crowding the steps of the university. A ruddy building with three domes and towers sat among the sprawling houses, Sarddonian script etched into the stone. Green banners with a white flame in the middle of a silver twelve-pointed star hung from the balconies of the House of the Saints.

The bazaars tucked down long alleyways contained bright pottery and glittering lamps, clothes and rugs, and skeins of silks fluttering like slivers of rainbows. Colorful fruits, loaves of bread, bowls of towering spices, and salted meats were sold from sooq stalls and carts. Lanes of bright mazarine and sun-bleached houses mixed with the ocher buildings. Teahouses with latticed pavilions dotted every corner.

Storefronts had signs written in different languages. Dark skinned Ginjarrians, fair-haired sailors from Sinabrac, and Zhao merchants in bright tang suits intermingled with Sarddonians, wandering through the bazaars, running shops, and moving goods through the streets. A few people with contract bangles marking them as indentured servants passed by.

An ache stabbed through Serein's head with each jolt of the horse. *My head feels like it's going to explode,* Serein thought, closing her eyes. *So many sounds. Too many colors.*

The road to the palace inclined, and Serein opened her eyes as the horse's gait changed. Guard towers were built into the gray ramparts of Alqamar's wall, contrasting with the white stones of the palace. The roaring lion of Sarddon surrounded by twelve moons watched from the white tapestries flapping along the walls.

I stood outside these walls ten years ago and vowed I'd find a way inside to kill Sethos. Now, I'm entering through the front entrance to serve his son. The Lights have a sense of irony.

"What's wrong?" Uriah said, glancing at her. Dark freckles dotted his skin, clustering along with his nose underneath a splotchy sunburn.

"It's just a headache," Serein said, watching a white bird as it circled overhead and disappeared around one of the palace towers.

"You've been giving me a headache this whole trip," Uriah grumbled.

"You're the one who slammed my head onto the floor."

"I should've taken it off and saved us a lot of trouble."

A sharp smile slid onto Serein's face, and Uriah's shoulders squared as the main gate of Alqamar Palace's wall grew closer. The iron-studded gates swung open, and lines of glinting conical helmets ran along the battlements. Torches burned along the walls of the wide-mouthed arch they passed through. A heady scent filled Serein's nose, and a chill prickled underneath her skin.

"Don't go all quiet on me now, Captain Stormheir. I thought you wanted to talk," Serein said.

"I'm tired of talking with you," Uriah told her.

Two glistening pools sat on either side of the promenade lined with stone arches and large hanging braziers. Gold-plated towers pierced the sky on top of massive domes. Twelve towers encircled the palace. Barracks and stables clustered near the wall on either side of the palace grounds.

"You have younger siblings, don't you? You're probably the eldest of...five or six?" Serein asked. "Wendish families tend to be large."

Shock crossed Uriah's face, green eyes narrowing. "How do you know that?" he asked as the envoy stopped. "You're just guessing."

"A person's movements, mannerisms, and appearances can tell a lot about them. If you know how to read the small details, you can figure a person out." Serein climbed out of the saddle, and a wave of dizziness overtook her. "Being the eldest sibling explains your relationship with the prince. Your friendship goes deeper than your duty. You look out for him like you would a sibling."

Uriah remained silent as he dismounted, the smell of beeswax and aloe vera wafting off his skin.

Rameses walked up, smiling as he shook dust from his rida'. His dark beard had grown out from days of traveling. "You survived the journey," he said, golden words vibrant. "Uriah, you can remove Serein's shackles now."

Uriah frowned and grumbled under his breath. He grabbed the key from the saddlebag, knuckles white as he stepped toward Serein. His grip was tight around her wrists, and her flesh crawled.

"Welcome to Alqamar Palace," Rameses said as the shackles clicked open.

The den of monsters, Serein thought, the palace's shadow looming over her.

JASMINE SCENTED STEAM ROSE FROM THE WATER OF THE HALF-sunken bathing pool. Serein's skin was scrubbed raw with the gritty, orange-scented soap, removing the last traces of Grasdan. The water stung her cuts and wounds. Dark brown hair stuck to her skull, detangled, and cleaned. The indigo ink spiraled from her collarbone, vines and leaves growing across her arm and shoulders.

Serein stared at the lion's head spout on the rim of the pool. *I can't remember the last time I had a bath this nice,* she thought, gaze drifting to the glazed geometric-patterned zellij mosaics on the walls.

Rizwana's hands stopped against the gnarled red lines sprouting from the tree of scars across Serein's back. The maidservant muttered a lapis-blue prayer under her breath.

"Is this your first time seeing so many scars?" Serein asked, touching the contract bangles on her wrists. The sores had scabbed over, less red and infected looking. "Or is it the murderer's brand that scares you?"

"Forgive me! I..." Rizwana stammered, hands moving again over the whip marks. Her words sloped and dipped like waves. "Alkhaliq forgive me. I was just surprised, miss. I didn't think people could inflict such wounds on another person."

The late day sun streamed through the upper window and reflected on the rippling bathwater Serein scooped up, her fingernails jagged and old wounds sketched across her fingers. A faded scar sliced through the lines of her left palm. A handful of straight, pale marks clustered along her right shoulder. With each breath, the puckered X-shaped scar on Serein's chest shifted. Pink burns stretched along her left side and down her leg like patches of melted wax.

"How did you get all these scars?" Rizwana asked.

"The hands of men can be cruel," Serein said. "Do all the guards here get servants and rooms this nice, or am I the exception?"

Rizwana set aside the cloth and picked up a bucket of water. "You'll have to ask His Highness that. He thought you needed attending to," she replied. "This water will be a bit cooler."

Cold water cascaded over Serein's head, washing away the rest of the soap. She shivered, goosebumps breaking out along her skin. "How does the palace have running water in this climate?" she asked, wiping her mouth.

"Many of the guest rooms in the towers have their own baths. There are a few hammams in the servants' quarters, guard barracks, and in the Royal Wing. The palace uses an underground aquifer filled with ocean water. The salt's good for healing aches and pains."

"Alqamar Palace is quite ingenious." *Saltwater explains why my wounds hurt.*

Strong fingers dug into Serein's scalp, bringing relief from the itching. Rizwana's round face rippled across the water, her mousy brown hair pulled back under a white headscarf, a few strands escaping. A dark mole rested under her left eye. Water spots stained her white, long-sleeved gandora and tan apron with embroidered flowers. Keys rattled dark green in her apron pocket.

Rizwana's haya bracelet was reflected as the pool stilled. Worn iron bands looped around the brown and tan leather strands, three glass beads—two green and an amber-colored one—were strung along the knotted end.

"You have children, don't you? Three?" *Thirty-two bands. Married. Three beads—green for boys and amber for girls,* Serein thought. *Callused fingers. She's been a maidservant for many years. Good-natured but speaks her mind. Her accent isn't florid like the Oyon one. More roughened and sloping. Probably from a coastal village.*

Rizwana paused, glancing at her wrist. "I didn't realize you saw my bracelet," she said. "My sons are eleven and eight, and my daughter is six. My husband's a blacksmith in Oyon." Rizwana *tsked*, pulling out the nits with a fine-toothed comb and setting them in a small bowl of alcohol. "You have got a bad case of lice. Whoever cut your hair did a poor job, so I'll need to make it shorter."

"My hair isn't a priority," Serein said. "Cut as much as you want or shave it all off." *I have to worry about* him *finding me, working for the son of the Murderous King, and surviving the next six years.*

A razor left its sheath in a pale green flick as Rizwana pulled Serein's hair straight and began to cut it above her ears.

"A woman shouldn't have short hair like a man or be bald. Women only cut their hair short if they're in mourning," Rizwana said. The smell of tea tree and olive oil cut through the jasmine scented water. "This will kill the lice. It'll need to be reapplied until they're all dead."

Flakes of skin fell into the water as Rizwana massaged the oils into Serein's hair. "It'll be nice not to be itching all the time," Serein said.

"Your accent...Are you from the Old Kingdom?" Rizwana asked. "What part?"

Fire devoured green forests. People ran screaming as swords cut through Serein's entire world. Home was a word shattered and bloodstained. She felt the black blade slicing across her chest.

Serein inhaled the perfumed air, chasing away the smell of smoke and blood. "Now, Rizwana, we've just met. I'm sure there will be plenty of time to spill my secrets later. Tell Captain Stormheir, if he wishes to know more about me, he should ask me himself," Serein told her. "Did he order you to spy on me?"

Rizwana stopped and sighed. "His Highness instructed me to take care of you, but Captain Stormheir asked me to find out things about you. I think he should wait until you've had proper rest and food first."

She doesn't seem worried that I'm not giving her answers. Either the captain's not that intimidating or is actually considerate of others. He's foolish to think that a nice bath will loosen my tongue.

"Captain Stormheir told me that you're a Ravanassë assassin," Rizwana said.

"Are you the only one brave enough to approach me?" Serein asked.

"The Ravanassë and the Sahriminha are the same. Many fear your kind because you can use magic, but you're still human. Right now, I'm more worried about your lice than anything else," she said, and Serein chuckled.

Most people blamed the Immortals and half-bloods for the death of the previous king and his family. She doesn't seem to have any prejudice toward me though, Serein thought. *She might be useful for gaining information about this place.*

Serein gripped the rim of the pool and stepped over onto the tile floor. A mirror hung from the wall, holding her emaciated reflection. Sunken blue eyes stared back. Grasdan had gorged itself on her flesh and what came out of the crucible was wrought iron. Bone traded for steel, skin for armor, a heart for stone.

Look what you've become, my volchitsa. *How long before the prince realizes he's brought a wolf into his midst?* the white voice asked, sending shivers along her skin.

Would it be worth it to break the glass and use the shards? Or steal the razor? Rizwana has a ring of keys. I could steal that and unlock the door. I have the sharpened rabbit bone, but I'm not in any condition to try and escape. Serein grabbed a towel and wrapped it around herself. *Another time.*

Rizwana slipped the razor into her apron and reached into the brackish water, pulling out the stopper. The water rushed down the drain with a dark purple gurgle. The plump woman stood a little taller than Serein, brown eyes round.

"I'll be back later to remove more of the lice. Keep a towel wrapped around your head for a few hours. I'll get a healer to bring something for your wounds. There's a pot of tea and some food on the table. Dinner will be at the seventh bell," Rizwana said, pausing. "What's the mark on your shoulder?"

Serein stared at the water trickling along the tiles. A white snake shaped scar was branded onto her left shoulder, its diamond-shaped head pointing upward while the rest of its body coiled into a spiral.

"Just a reminder," Serein said, the presence of the mark slithering across her skin.

SEREIN ROLLED THE SHARPENED RABBIT BONE BETWEEN HER fingers. Her scalp prickled under the towel wrapped around her head. The smell of tea tree oil clung to her nose. The blue gandora dress draped off her body, barely clinging to her thin frame.

In the bedchamber, a glass-paned door led to a small balcony. The four-poster bed with a carved headboard filled most of the room, facing a low vanity decorated with intricate carvings of landscapes and a mirror. Serein ran a finger on the floral patterns on the wooden divider screen by the armoire.

She touched the exposed back of her neck, tracing the raised lines of the knife-shaped brand. *This room is too lavish for a guard,* Serein thought, opening the empty armoire. She left the pointed babouche slippers by the bed, the geometric-patterned marble floor cool beneath her feet.

Two empty bookshelves, a carved cabinet, and the low table with cushions around it were the only pieces of furniture in the other chamber. Sunlight streamed through the latticed windows, spilling over the red and gold ogee-patterned majlis sofa flush against the wall. Indigo rugs covered the floor, and colorful painted tiles with plant motifs rimmed the windows. Three glass lamps dangled from the rafters, stars and moons cut into the glass.

How nice of the captain to get rid of everything that could be used as a weapon. I guess he decided I couldn't strangle someone with the bedsheets or the curtains, she thought as she went to the door and found it locked. *Doubt the lock is for my safety. One assassin in an empty tower.*

Serein glanced back at the sparse living chamber. A sky-blue glass of tea with gold-painted lions sat on a silver tray, steam twisting up from the bronze teakettle. The amber liquid in the glass had layer of foam on the surface and a sprig of mint floating in it. Chunks of sugar were piled in a tiny gold dish next to a plate of fruit and pastries drizzled with honey and chopped figs. A bowl of golden-brown, rose-shaped cookies covered in honey and sesame seeds gave off a sweet, fried smell.

Hunger clawed at Serein's stomach as she reached for a persimmon, scooping a few pears into a cloth napkin. She stopped.

I don't have to hide food anymore. I won't starve here. Dinner will be in about four hours unless they forget about me.

Serein put the fruit back, tearing off a small piece of pastry. Flakes stuck to her lips, and she licked them away. She ate a few of the fried cookies, the sweetness shocking her tongue. The sweet tea burned her mouth as she sipped it and left a refreshing mint taste behind.

Mint tea. As good as I remember, but too sweet for me, she thought.

Serein peered out the window. Beyond the palace wall, the rippling ocean stretched toward the horizon. Ships dotted the white waves. The umber voice of a chanter in the distance called out the hourly prayer in undulating Sarddonian. Rosewood-colored trumpets rippled through the air.

Elephants? Serein thought, stepping onto the balcony.

Craning her neck, she spotted a lumbering, gray shape with mottled pink across its head. The elephant raised its trunk before dunking it in the pond, spraying water over its leathery hide. It sank into the water, swimming out of sight as other rumbling sounds echoed its call.

A small smile spread onto Serein's face as she closed the balcony door and drew the curtains. She sank to the floor, setting the empty glass down as she leaned against the wall. Serein studied the rafters overhead and the dark crevices they housed.

I'll have to begin sketching a layout of this place. I'm in the furthest point from the Royal Wing, east side of the palace. About a fifteen minute walk from the central courtyard. A guest tower. Six floors, six rooms on each. I doubt anyone would want to stay on this floor, knowing there's an assassin here, Serein thought, staring at her clean fingernails. *Rizwana managed to get all the blood out from under my nails. I can't remember the last time my hands were clean.*

Your hands have never been clean.

The white voice crept up, and her hand clenched, yellow breath shaking. She gripped the wall as she pulled herself up, legs aching. *He's not here.*

Serein set the empty glass on the armoire, finishing the last bite of pastry. She collapsed on the downy sheets of the bed, clutching the bone. No screams or rattling chains filled her ears. The taste of mint followed her into sleep.

Chapter Six
Meaning of Regret

The girl rode through the night, heavy with the years of hardship etched across her skin. Her pale yellow breath clouded the darkness as the hoofbeats left vermillion trails behind. The girl waited for her past to find her, but the morning came as another day stretched before her.

The rolling miles made the girl bolder but didn't remove the painful fear curled in her stomach. Thick trees waved at her in the distance, branches sweeping aside to usher her in. She urged the horse onward, straining to reach the green safety.

Almost there, the purple wind whispered.

The ground cracked open, oily blackness sloshing out. The horse tumbled in, throwing the girl into the thick pool. She tried to scream, but the darkness spat her into a room caked in shadows and streaks of blood. Pain split along her body, her cries falling on deaf stones. Cold horror clamped around her wrists in iron shackles.

Death stood over her. "You can't escape," he said, silver words falling like tears. "You can never escape."

"Get up."

Uriah's green voice broke through the blackness, kicking her leg.

Serein heard the orange-red *chink* of chainmail, and she flinched, eyes opening.

A moment of disorienting panic set in when she didn't recognize the room. Bright green irises burned behind Serein's eyelids, a white smile cutting into her skin. The warden's bloody fingers dug into her face. The sapphire *crack* of a whip across her back, hands holding her down as cold steel sliced her throat. The fragments of her dreams scattered, blood-streaked walls and pyre flames clashing with the pale marble room.

Serein grabbed Uriah's ankle as he went to kick her again, gripping the rabbit bone in her other hand. Uriah stumbled back and shook her off, reaching for his weapon.

The bed pressed against Serein's back, the hard floor digging into her side. *Not in Grasdan. No shackles or screams. No worrying about being killed in my sleep or eaten by rats,* Serein thought, each breath quieting the fear and chasing away the lingering nightmare.

Uriah stood dressed in a dark tunic, sirwal, and his chainmail armor. "Why were you sleeping on the floor?" he asked in Common.

"I guess I'm used to sleeping on the ground and found the bed uncomfortable," Serein muttered and sat up, the sheets slipping off her shoulders. "Do you always kick people awake? Afraid of a sleeping woman?" *How* did *I end up on the floor? I don't remember moving. Am I sleepwalking? I've been asleep for about four hours, so maybe I moved.*

"I'm not afraid of you," he told her, finger twitching as he scowled.

"You're not good at lying," she said, standing. *I had the curtains closed. He's also wearing chainmail.* "Don't you get hot wearing that armor all the time? Or is it permanently stuck to you?"

She gathered the sheet and tossed it onto the bed, slipping the rabbit bone underneath. The towel had come undone from around her head. Sweat, beeswax, and aloe vera cut through the aromatic tea tree oil. Seven deep peach-colored tolls of a bell hung in the air, followed by the umber chants of an evening prayer. Shadows crept across the chamber, tinged orange by the sinking sun. Her joints gave dingy amber cracks as she stretched.

"Did you come to see if I'd escaped?" Serein asked.

Uriah's jaw tightened as she brushed past him. Serein followed the smell of food to the other chamber, stomach clenching. Rizwana straightened as she finished arranging the food on the table. A colorful plate with honey-glazed spiced lamb and saffron rice sprinkled with rosemary sat next to a basket of warm msemen flatbread. Yogurt filled a small azure cup. Sliced cucumbers fanned around purple olives. Pieces of yogurt-coated chicken were mixed with cooked eggplant, fava beans, and tomatoes.

Seems I slept through Rizwana setting the table. It's been a while since I've been able to sleep soundly, Serein thought, mouth watering. *I'll have to be more careful next time.*

"I told Captain Stormheir to let you sleep a bit longer," Rizwana said, lapis voice pointed at Uriah, "and to let you have dinner in peace."

"Were you that impatient for answers that you had to barge in and wake me up?" Serein asked Uriah, sitting down on a cushion.

Rizwana came around with a bowl of orange-scented water and a towel. Serein washed her hands in the warm water, drying off her skin.

Uriah crossed his arms as he stood on the other side of the table. "You were avoiding answering the questions," he grumbled.

"I told Rizwana that if you wanted to know answers, you'd have to ask me yourself. You don't strike me as a man to use spies and other people to do things for you," Serein said. "You can either let me eat and get answers later, or you can settle for this instead of interrogating me in a cell."

Sighing through his nose, Uriah took a seat across from her, setting his sword on the floor beside him.

Serein scanned the table for utensils but found only wooden serving spoons. *Sarddonians don't use utensils,* she thought. *I'll have to brush up on my knowledge of Sarddonian culture and customs.*

"I'll be in the bedchamber if you need me, miss. I want to continue working on your hair after dinner," Rizwana said, inclining her head. She adjusted her white headscarf before heading to the other room.

"I was worried that I'd have to resort to eating the mice when the fruit ran out," Serein told Uriah as she grabbed pieces of lamb, revealing the bright orange and yellow pattern on the ceramic plate underneath. The hot meat pulled away from the bone, the honey glaze sticking to her tongue. "I bet they taste better than Grasdan rats since they're fattened from the royal kitchens."

"You're uncivilized," Uriah said, shadows resting under his eyes.

"Grasdan is where civility goes to die," Serein replied. "Where's the princeling? He hasn't come to check on me yet. Perhaps he's grown bored with me already." *He wouldn't stop talking the whole journey, asking so many questions. I thought my silence would make him grow bored, but that seemed to only encourage him.*

"You," Uriah snapped, voice spiked with agitation, "will address him as His Highness, sayyidi, or Amir Rameses. Not princeling. And His Highness said you're supposed to rest for a week."

Serein dipped a cucumber slice in the yogurt. *A week locked in this room? At least it has windows,* she thought, the cucumber crunching as she bit into it. *Hopefully, I can keep this meal down. It'd be a shame to throw it up.*

Uriah watched her as she ate. "You don't seem concerned with checking if your food is poisoned."

She reached for a piece of msemen bread. "Because that seems unlikely. Familiarity with poisons is one of my skills. Would you like to know what else I can do?" *I could pretend to choke and foam at the mouth, but he'd probably sit and watch.*

His green eyes narrowed. "Are you threatening me?" Uriah asked.

"What would I be able to do to you in my state? Stab you with a bone? Stuff your body under the bed or string you up on the balcony?" Serein replied.

The white words slithered through the depths again. *It wouldn't be hard. You know you could do it.*

Serein's stomach twisted. "There's no logical reason for me to kill you. I want to complete this contract and start a new life," she said, elbows resting on the table.

"You expect me to believe you?" Uriah asked. "You're an assassin. Killing's all you know how to do."

Her smile unfurled. "I know how to tell a decent joke and write my name." She poured herself a glass of water and took a sip. "Randomly killing isn't logical."

"Even with your *logical* planning, you were still captured and sent to Grasdan. If you had done something else with your life, you wouldn't have ended up in prison."

"The war didn't leave many options for children." Serein grabbed a piece of chicken. The yogurt and ras el hanout coating left a tangy taste in her mouth. "I'm sure a man of honor such as yourself has *never* done things you couldn't wash off your hands. You call me a monster, but we're not so different."

"I never said I didn't have faults," Uriah said, fingers grazing the leather cord around his neck, "but I'm nothing like you."

Serein scooped up rice with a chunk of bread. "The only difference between you and I is that I don't try to justify murder," she replied.

Shadows moved behind Uriah's eyes as something prowled in his mind. He stared at something unseen. His hands clenched into fists, knuckles whitening.

She swiped another loaf of bread and a lamb rib bone, hiding them under the folds of her gown as he blinked. "Does the princeling know all the things you've done in service of the crown?" *Some of those scars probably came from fighting in the war. He touches that necklace when he's bothered. Seems he has demons in his mind. There's a schism between his sense of duty and his conscience. His main weakness.*

"*Boed tân yn mynd â chi,*" Uriah spat, eyes refocusing with a hard glint.

"You're a long way from Wendale," Serein said. "Judging by your accent, I'd say you're from the southern region." *Wishing for fire to take me. Wonder what other lovely Wendish curses he'll say to me,* she thought. *I unnerve him, and that gives me the advantage to break him down slowly.*

Uriah's mouth curved downward. "Do you feel the need to point out useless things?" he asked.

She took another sip of water. "These useless things have given me great insight into who you are, Captain Stormheir. You're the one who wanted to have this chat. I've given you all the information I wish to give today. I want a little favor in return."

Uriah scowled. "You haven't told me anything."

"You haven't been paying attention to our conversation then," Serein said. "Now, about this favor"

His jaw clenched. "I don't make deals with *you*," Uriah said.

"I was only going to ask for some paper and a quill. Or a piece of charcoal will do," Serein replied.

"What do you need that for?"

"To pass the hours of boredom." *I'll need to draw a map of the palace. When I'm stronger, I'll try sneaking out and exploring.*

"You survived Grasdan without anything to pass the time."

"Not much time to be bored when trying to survive," Serein said, wiping her hands on a cloth napkin. *I also dreamed about killing certain individuals to pass the time.*

The umber call of the chanter rang out as another hour passed, the lyrical words floating through the open window. Uriah glanced up, frowning. He grabbed his sword as he stood, heading for the door.

"Is our conversation over already? I was hoping to discuss morality with you a bit longer," Serein said. "I hope you remember my request. If I don't get something to pass the time, I might die of boredom."

"Good," Uriah replied without looking back, slamming the door with a teal *thud*.

Rizwana poked her head out of the bedchamber. Serein grabbed another piece of bread, tearing it into chunks. *The captain's easily wound up,* she thought. *This will be interesting.*

Chapter Seven
Shadow of Doubt

RAMESES FLIPPED A PAGE OF THE BOOK PROPPED AGAINST HIS KNEE, lounging on the maroon cushions of the majlis seating area. A day of council meetings faded away as he buried himself in the story, trying to leave the week behind and forget the empty eyes of the dead soldiers for a moment. The familiar story of two lovers, twisted in a growing conflict between their two kingdoms, unfolded across the pages. Intricately woven threads of betrayal, love, and magic kept Rameses enthralled.

He sipped hot coffee spiced with cardamom and sugar, a cool evening breeze coming in through the open windows. The amber light of the lanterns kept the darkness at bay. Two sleek, cream colored dogs, Na'il and Na'im, lay on the rug in the middle of the chamber, long limbs splayed out. Two servants, Amran and Deneb, dressed in white and gold robes straightened his chambers.

I wonder if Serein's settled in. A few days' rest and decent meals will give her a chance to leave Grasdan behind, Rameses thought, leaning back against the pillows. *I will have to visit her soon to see how she's doing. Maybe she will be in a more talkative mood. She hardly spoke on the journey here.*

Warm hands brushed Rameses' neck, dark hair tickling his cheek as the scent of peppery sweetness wafted up. "Bit late for reading, Your Highness," a voice said, sliding across his skin like silk.

"It's never too late to read, Yasmine," Rameses said, staring up at the heart-shaped face hovering over him.

Yasmine's almond-colored eyes glittered in the lantern light, her bronze skin smooth. Her blue gandora draped rippled like ocean waves as she leaned closer.

"Why keep your nose buried in a book instead of spending time with me? Is what's written there better than what I can offer?" she asked, lips trailing against his.

Her fingers undid the front buttons of his blue qamis. He leaned up to her kiss, fingers tracing the hollow of her throat. Rameses smiled as she pulled away, stroking his beard.

"You make a compelling argument. Let me finish this one chapter, and I will join you," he said.

She gestured to the adjacent wall lined with three, dark-wood bookshelves. "Haven't you already read *Twisted Boughs*? Why not read something new?"

The taste of ginger of Yasmine's mouth lingered on Rameses' lips. "Yes, but this is one of my favorites."

"I'll leave you to your romance, but don't keep me waiting too long," she told him, brushing her hair over her shoulder.

Yasmine headed toward Rameses' bedchamber. Dark ringlets cascaded down her back. The dogs lifted their heads, feathery tails wagging. She scratched Na'im behind his ears. Na'il pushed against her hand, vying for attention.

A servant dressed in gold and red robes appeared outside the chamber and knocked, making Rameses glance up. "Enter," he said.

Ilderim let the servant in, and the thin man bowed, fingers touching his brow. "Sayyidi," he said, "His Majesty requests your presence in his study."

Rameses set down the book on the pewter table next to his cup of coffee. *Saints. I thought my father would be too busy to speak with me until the end of the week,* he thought, the sense of dread that had been hanging over him since he returned to Alqamar Palace growing.

Sighing, Rameses rose from the sofa, buttoning his qamis. Deneb rushed into the bedchamber and returned with a pair of sandals.

Rameses rubbed Na'il behind his pointed ears. "Tell Yasmine I will be back," he said to Deneb.

The quiet nighttime sounds filled the riad as Rameses and Ilderim went down the stairs to the ground floor, nightjars calling from the lush gardens beyond Rameses' apartments. The doorkeepers stood by the large doors, the hallways of the Royal Wing quiet.

Rameses' earlobes felt light without his earrings. The silence left in their absence made the echoes of his footsteps in the hallway louder. Torches flickered against the marble columns while soldiers stood in polished armor and black and red robes.

"You look upset, sayyidi," Ilderim said, breaking the quiet.

Rameses twisted the ring around his finger. "I was wondering about what level of disappointment my father will show when he questions me about my trip," he said with a sigh, glancing at the older man. "Will I be disgracing my ancestors or unworthy of leading Sarddon?"

Ilderim tugged at his beard, left hand resting by the scimitar at his hip. The torchlight caught the small gold lion's head pin on his maroon turban. "I'm sure His Majesty just wants to speak to you since you've been gone for almost two months."

"He will hold the deaths of the soldiers over me for a long time... No one was supposed to get hurt."

"You couldn't have predicted a rebel ambush. Those men gave their lives in service to Sarddon. You paid for their funerals. Their families won't forget that kindness."

The closer Rameses got to his father's study, the more his sinking dread grew. "But my father will add their deaths to the list of things he considers to be my failures."

They stopped outside the double doors with a roaring lion encircled by twelve moons carved into the dark wood. Rameses swallowed, back straight. The two doorkeepers bowed before opening the door. Tapestries with the Sarddon crest hung along the walls of the antechamber. Lanterns illuminated the white marble chamber in amber light, catching the golden palmette motifs on the rugs.

Rameses passed family portraits hanging from in gilded frames, marking the years—Rameses' youth, the birth of his sister, Rasima, and younger brother, Rahim. Uncles, aunts, grandparents, and cousins watched him with gold eyes. Rameses lingered by the painting done when he was five, his wide smile matching his parents'. The years stole away his father's smiles as the portraits continued leading toward the desk until all that remained was a hardened line.

Six of the Malik's Guards were stationed throughout the study. Kamau, his father's muharib, stood in the corner with a long spear strapped to his back. The Ginjarrian remained stoic in his dark red cuirass armor, ebony skin scarred like crocodile skin. Ilderim hung back in the antechamber.

Sethos stood with his back to Rameses, his sword laying near the desk. There was no smile on his bearded face as he turned, deep lines set in his brown skin. A scar cut across the left side of Sethos' jaw. Black hair with graying streaks curled around his ears where two small golden lion heads hung. His imposing figure in a black and gold qamis seemed to fill the whole room, commanding it with his presence.

"I heard you acquired what you were looking for," Sethos said, his voice deep making Rameses feel smaller.

"Yes, Father," Rameses replied, glancing at the floor. "The Grinning Assassin lives up to her name."

Sethos picked up a book from his desk, walking to the bookshelf on the opposite end of the chamber. "Was this worth all the money and time you spent traveling across Sarddon?" he asked and slid the tome in its place. "Was it worth the loss of three soldiers? You put yourself and the soldiers at risk for what? A Ravanassë criminal?"

Each word stabbed like an accusation, chipping away at Rameses. "I regret the loss of the soldiers. We did not know about the rebels, but the two that were captured might provide valuable information," Rameses replied.

"Do you think that erases the damage done? It was a reckless and unnecessary risk." Scorn laced Sethos' voice. "You are the crown prince. You do not get to chase whims and expect there to be no consequences. Lives are affected by your actions."

The words of the condolence letters he wrote to the soldiers' families weighed in the back of Rameses' mind—a weight he didn't know how to bear. *Sakhr Ayad. Ikraam al-Gaddafi. Ahmed al-Badawi.* The three names burned behind his eyelids, their blood appearing on the edges of his dreams. Sometimes, late at night, he could still smell the decay from their bodies.

Rameses glanced at the recent family portrait on the wall behind the desk, solemn expressions staring back at him except for Rahim who was too young to know the weight of the world.

Documents and maps covered Sethos' desk next to an empty cup. The smell of paper and coffee stirred Rameses' memories. Sitting on his father's lap, looking at maps of Sarddon and the rest of Cemiyon, a warm smile and strong hands that stroked his head.

Hands that didn't move troops across the war map like shatranj pieces—that hadn't signed battle or execution orders. Hands that Rameses prayed to the Saints hadn't done the things he feared they had.

"It is my choice. She is the wali I need," Rameses said, tongue sticking to the roof of his mouth.

Sethos walked toward him, standing a foot taller. The stony gaze drifted over Rameses, a sigh heavy with disappointment. "I never thought I would see the day a lion of Sarddon would rely on a woman for protection. I let you indulge with the women you entertain, and the vanity projects you pursue, but I never thought you would do something like this," he said, shaking his head. "Saints, how your ancestors grieve."

So, it's disgracing my ancestors this time. "Serein's gender does not diminish her abilities," Rameses replied, keeping his gaze from lowering. "She helped to kill the rebels that attacked us. I want her as my guard. Nothing more."

Sethos eyes narrowed, and Rameses swore he caught a flash of concern in the dark golden depths. "People like her have no loyalty. You have brought danger to Oyon—into our home. Would you have a criminal walk the same halls as your siblings and your mother? Did you stop and think about what would happen if she turns on you?"

"She has served her time, so I am giving her a chance to redeem herself. Is not showing mercy the sign of a wise leader?" Rameses asked.

"Mercy has a place, but do not mistake it for foolishness. You think people like her can change? I fear you are a poor judge of people, Rameses, and that will destroy your legacy before it begins," Sethos said, walking around his desk. "Il-Makah will look into this woman, and I will have her brought before me this Mettaar."

"No need to send the Golden Jackals after Serein. She is my responsibility, Father, so I ask you not to interfere." *Hopefully, he will not find out that she held a knife to my throat. Then he may kill her,* Rameses thought, the ring rubbing against his finger as he twisted it harder.

Sethos sat, rubbing his forehead. "I am worried that you will continue to let your feelings cloud your judgment," he said. His cold expression broke, exhaustion resting under his eyes. "There is so much for you to learn, and I worry you will not be ready when the time comes to make difficult choices in order to protect what you love, abnay."

Rameses stopped touching his ring. For a brief moment, he saw the man who taught him how to ride a horse and play shatranj, the warm smile that once existed. The man he called Baba as he was flung into the air, giggling as he was caught in strong hands.

Rameses took a half-step forward.

Sethos straightened, his softness vanishing like morning dew evaporating in the sun. "Be warned, Rameses, if this ends badly, you will bear the consequences. You carry Sarddon's future, so start acting like it."

"Yes, Father..." Rameses muttered, stepping back. *He thinks I cannot make difficult choices, but I already have.*

Chapter Eight
Buried Wounds

A TAN AND WHITE MOUSE PERCHED ON THE EDGE OF THE cushioned couch, nibbling on a breadcrumb Serein had laid out. Amber sunlight warmed her face as she lounged against the pillows, working on an embroidery square. She held the thin wooden hoop with the white cloth stretched taut across it, tugging on the green thread making up the edge of a crude-looking leaf.

Rizwana makes this look easy. Reminds me of the embroidered patches Zhao spies use to hide code within the designs, she thought as the needle poked a callused fingertip. *Maybe I should hide the needle and tell Rizwana I lost it.*

Serein's skin began to flesh out over her bones, the hollowness under her eyes receding with each day. Her scalp no longer itched, the tea tree and olive oil killing what lice remained. The cuts and scabs had crusted over, and bruises speckled her face in yellow patches.

She peered through the latticed window. A white raven flew by and wheeled out of sight. *That bird again. I saw it when I first arrived. It must live on the palace grounds. A pet maybe?*

Quick hazel-colored protests were exchanged outside the door, overlapping with peach chimes and golden tones. The mouse scurried away as the door opened. Serein tensed, a flash of Grasdan's dark cell bleeding over the bright room. She reached for the sharpened rabbit bone in the small pocket sewn into the right sleeve of her green robe.

Rameses stepped into the chamber with orange footsteps, dark hair curling around his ears. The pearl buttons of his blue qamis shone in the sunlight. His gold eyes sparkled as he closed the door, smiling.

Serein withdrew her hand from the bone. *No guards with him,* she thought, searching for a weapon but saw none. *The princeling didn't bring a knife. It's either stupidity or a sign of trust. I'm guessing it's stupidity.*

"What a week of food and rest will do," Rameses said, glancing at her face. "The bruising looks better. Your hair is so much shorter."

"It was the alternative to shaving my head," she replied.

"Ah, you speak to me. You were so silent on the journey here," Rameses said, glancing at the embroidery in her hands. "Are you doing embroidery?"

"There's not much else to do besides stare out the window." Serein set the hoop down. "Why are you here?"

"I wanted to see how you were adjusting." Rameses brushed off fine white hairs from his qamis. "Hopefully, the food and quarters are to your liking. I want you to be as comfortable as possible here. I hope the food has been to your liking. If you want Sarlyrian foods, I can ask the kitchens to make meals special for you."

"The food is fine. The room is bigger than my last accommodations, and it's nice not eating rats and moldy food," Serein replied. *Dog hairs. He has one, probably two. Medium-sized based on the hairs stuck to his legs. Pets. He's sentimental.*

Rameses' grin wavered. "Well, those days are behind you now," he said, touching her arm. "I also wanted to inform you that my father has summoned you to meet with him tonight."

Serein grabbed Rameses' wrist as acrid fear beat in time with her heart, fingers digging into his skin. Sethos' face appeared in place of Rameses', his features shadowed by smoke and fire. A turquoise scream, the colorful house once filled with warmth eaten by flames. Family, friends, neighbors crumpled like felled wheat as her mother dragged her away, red spilling across the trampled grass. Buzzing flies and crows pecking at decayed flesh.

Something that had been slumbering for years cracked open an eye. *Break his hand, twist his arm, then break his neck,* she thought, knowing what his pulse would feel like as it died underneath her fingertips.

Gray footsteps curled in the corner of her eye, and the door opened. "Step away from him!" Uriah's green voice filled the chamber, sword half-drawn.

Sethos' face melted away, leaving behind confusion and worry on Rameses' features. Serein released him and stepped back, the smell of smoke and death lingering in her nose.

What's happening to me? she thought, dragging her fear back to its confines with a deep breath.

Rameses turned as Uriah crossed the room. "I hardly think that sword's necessary, Uriah. I'm fine," he replied, rubbing his wrist.

"Where's Ilderim?" Uriah asked, stepping between Serein and Rameses.

"He's used to me slipping away by now," Rameses said. "Are you all right, Serein?" he added in a quiet voice.

"I'm fine. Just anxious to leave this cage," Serein said. *An audience with the Murderous King. I'll be close enough to drive a blade through his heart.*

Rameses arched an eyebrow. "Cage? Have you been forcing her to stay in here the whole week?"

"I thought it'd be best until everything was sorted."

"Everything's been sorted. Let her leave the room. There's no need to keep the door locked either. The guards can remain in the hallway," Rameses said. Discontentment settled on Uriah's features as he opened his mouth to protest. "I will have a kaftan sent for you to wear, Serein. The summons will be at the eighth bell. Also"—Rameses' gaze traveled around the chamber—"I will bring you some books from my collection. An empty bookcase is such a tragedy."

"I'd like a chair," Serein said.

Rameses' earrings jingled, spilling peach rivulets down the front of his blue qamis as he turned. "A chair? Not something to read?"

"I sat on a cold hard floor for so long that I'd like a bit of comfort."

"I will have one brought up," Rameses said, nodding. "You seem quite irritable today, Uriah. Let's walk and discuss what's bothering you."

Uriah opened his mouth to speak but followed Rameses out of the room in silence.

Serein's pulse tapped against her throat, Sethos' face burning in her mind. *So many years, dreaming of meeting Sethos again. I never imagined I'd be meeting him in a dress.*

URIAH AND RAMESES' FOOTSTEPS ECHOED DOWN THE STAIRWELL AS they descended the tower. *Why would Rameses risk being alone with her after the incident at the Harpy's Chest?* Uriah thought, reaching into his pocket for the rock. His fingers pressed against the smooth surface, working his frustrations into it. *All it takes is for him to let his guard down, and she'll kill him.*

"Uriah." Rameses' voice nudged him from his thoughts. "Is everything all right?"

"Have you forgotten about what happened at the Harpy's Chest? What was she trying to do to you before I arrived?" Uriah asked, giving Rameses a disapproving look.

"I think I startled her by touching her so suddenly. Serein didn't hurt me," Rameses said. "You removed anything that could be used as a weapon. I doubt she's going to kill me with the curtains."

Uriah kept seeing the shadows roaming behind Serein's eyes, her stillness masking the killer beneath her starved form. Every smile was a glinting dagger, ready to strike.

"She's trained to kill without any weapons." *Why can't Rameses see she's a danger?*

"I think you're overreacting." Rameses wrapped his arm around Uriah's neck. "Maybe you should take up a hobby and relax a bit. Serein is learning embroidery."

Uriah put his hand on the wall to steady himself, the earrings jingling in his ear. "Embroidery? How did she get a needle?!" he asked, turning around. *What's Rizwana doing, giving her needles? I warned her not to trust the assassin.*

Rameses pulled him back down the stairs. "Calm down. It's an embroidery needle. Not a knife."

They stepped out into the white marble hallway. Sunlight caught the zellij tiles along the archways. Two female servants in tan gandoras bowed to Rameses as they passed. He nodded to them, and their cheeks flushed.

"Have you gleaned anything about Serein?" Rameses asked Uriah.

Their voices bounced off the high-vaulted ceilings. "Nothing of any use," Uriah said as they passed through the palace's main entryway. *The prison records mentioned she had been interrogated by Golden Jackals, so why isn't there more information about her?*

Rameses removed his arm from Uriah's neck, stopping by a pillar. "Perhaps if you tried being gentler with her, she might tell you more."

"She's not going to open up with a few gentle words," Uriah said. "Don't forget that."

Rameses' expression darkened. "Between you and my father, I doubt I will."

He must have spoken to the Malik about what happened with the rebels. Doesn't seem like it went well.

"Did you find out anything about Serein's tattoo?" Rameses asked and fidgeted with one of his earrings.

Uriah squinted against the sunlight pouring through the windows. "What's with you and that tattoo?" he replied.

"You know how curious I get about these things. Most women around here don't have tattoos, at least none of the ones I have met. I wonder if it's a Ravanassë custom," Rameses said, looking at the motifs painted across the ceiling. "What about her scars?"

"She has numerous scars and burns along with the Bone Viper brand. Rizwana said there's a large burn on her side."

Rameses' gaze snapped to Uriah. "Burns? Do you think they burned her in prison?"

"Probably tortured her to get information. She told the Golden Jackals about the Bone Vipers, but they didn't catch them or find Xansas. She could still be working with him."

"You saw the state Serein was in. Do you think she would be working with a man who left her to die in prison?" Rameses asked.

"She gave them the location of Xansas' base, told them pretty much everything about him except what he looked like," Uriah said.

"Why wouldn't she give a physical description? It's like she's protecting him and hiding things."

"Do you distrust her because she's a Ravanassë?"

"I don't have an issue with the Ravanassë," Uriah's shoulders tensed as faces flashed in barbed fragments. "I don't trust her because she's murdered people for profit."

"What if she's trying to redeem herself?" Rameses asked.

"She told me that she doesn't have any regrets about what she's done," Uriah said as the rock dug into his palm. "She's more likely to kill you once she gets what she wants."

"I think you should give her the benefit of the doubt. Her freedom seems more valuable to her than anything else. Working for me is how she will get it, and I don't think she will risk losing that chance."

Uriah sighed. "Rameses, just get rid of her and be done with this," he whispered.

Rameses glanced at the palace guards down the hallway before gesturing to the nearby riad. They cut through the garden filled with orange bougainvillea growing along arched trellises. Sunlight burned the back of Uriah's neck as he ducked under the shade of a vine arch. A calico cat darted into the bushes with a mouse in its mouth.

"You know I want to look into what my father's done, and I cannot ask you to help me," Rameses muttered. "You have your oath."

Shadows of birds flying overhead flashed through the twisting vines. "I pray it doesn't come back to bite you," Uriah said. *His plan's too risky if it requires a person like Serein to dig up supposed secrets on the Malik. Why does he want to pursue this so badly?*

Rameses twisted the lion's head ring. "That makes two of us," he told Uriah with a wry smile. "I still want you to consider overseeing her training. Lieutenant Firoz could take on some of your workload along with the other officers."

Uriah rubbed his eyes until spots danced behind his eyelids. "Fine..." *Why am I even agreeing to this? I'd like nothing to do with her, but it's safer to keep an eye on her.*

Rameses clasped Uriah's shoulder, concern settling in his face. "How are you sleeping?" he asked. "You were tense when we were near the Old Kingdom, but it seems that you're still upset about something. You have probably worn that rock of yours down to dust. Are the nightmares still bothering you?"

"I thought they would lessen when we returned," Uriah said, squeezing the rock in his pocket. "But they're still happening." *It's already been a week, but I still have them every night.*

"I know you don't want to speak about the war, but it's been four years since you came back, and you're still having these dreams," Rameses said.

Uriah stared beyond the riad. "It's not something I want to talk about."

The thick smell of water clogged Uriah's nose. A chill ran along his arms despite the heat, his fingers going to the worn leather cord at his neck. Faces rose from murky depths in the back of his mind. Red bled through the swirling waters as bodies passed. Women and children stood on the shores as fires burned behind them.

I'm not there. That was the past, he told himself, grip tightening around his necklace to keep himself from being swept away in the current of memories. *Stone protect me, Fire strengthen me, Water purify me, Wind guide me.*

"Uriah?"

A stone broke through the depths, and Uriah looked up, blinking away a blood-soaked image of a red sword in his hands. "I've done things I'm not proud of. If I tell you, I'll have to face those memories again," he said, tasting silty water on his tongue.

Rameses squeezed Uriah's shoulders, features softening. "Uriah, I cannot begin to understand what you went through and how much loss you have suffered," he said. "You probably had to make difficult choices, but it doesn't make me think any less of you. I don't want you to carry your burden alone."

"I'm not ready to talk about it. It's not that I don't trust you...I just don't fully trust myself." *How can I tell him? I can't have another face looking at me with horror. We had orders. It was my duty to carry out those orders.*

"When you're ready to talk, I will listen," Rameses said.

"Do you think you'll be able to stay quiet for that long?" Uriah asked, swallowing the lump in his throat.

"For you, sadiqi, I will do anything. I will be so silent that you will be begging me to speak again," Rameses told him, and Uriah rolled his eyes. "Have you thought about going home to visit your family? Have you written to them recently?"

"I've taken enough time off from my job this year already," Uriah replied. "I sent a letter to my parents to thank them for the gift they sent for my name day. Afanen had her second child last month. I have a niece."

Rameses' smile broadened. "Congratulations! All the more reason to take a few months off at the end of the year. Sarddon will still be standing when you return."

The familiar ache of homesickness settled in Uriah's chest. "I'll see how things are closer to Endien when the major festivals are over," he muttered. *I haven't seen my family since last winter. I'm sure Eira and Owain have had another growth spurt, and Rhosyn will be engaged soon. Wyn's probably still a handful for Ma.*

"I'm sure Firoz is more than capable of maintaining order in your stead," Rameses said. "We should go into the city tomorrow for a drink. We have not been out in ages."

Uriah arched an eyebrow. "Didn't we just spend the past month and a half traveling? And at the beginning of Nésa for your name day when you insisted on going out for drinks *after* the diffa?"

Rameses waved his hand. "But that was then. This will be to make up for the fact that we were traveling and didn't get to celebrate your name day properly."

"I don't have time," Uriah told him as they left the riad.

"Too busy interrogating Serein, you mean," Rameses said, a knowing glint entering his eyes. "For how untrustworthy you think she is, you have spent a lot of time asking her questions. If you're *that* charmed by her, all you had to do was say so."

Uriah stiffened, his jaw tight. "Don't give me that look. I'm not *charmed* with her! There's *nothing* charming about her." *I feel like I'm going to go gray before my next name day.*

SEREIN STARED AT THE OCEAN BEYOND THE PALACE WALL. THE umber voice of the chanter called out the hourly prayer of the afternoon—the prayer of Saint Esmail. Each word rang like a musical note, rising and falling on metered lines.

"I think I've got the clothes altered to fit now," Rizwana said from the other room, lapis voice filling the room. "I'll leave your kaftan and headscarf on the bed while I draw your bath. I'll check your hair again and make sure there are no more lice."

Rizwana passed Serein with hazel footfalls with the dress and white trousers folded over her arm. *Not very practical,* Serein thought, glancing at the azure silk kaftan embroidered with silver vines and leaves. *I suppose I could hide a knife in the folds.*

Sethos' face appeared as she blinked, the memory of his black steel sword engraved on her flesh. The X-shaped scar ached, vengeance tattooed in her bones.

A reckoning is coming for you, Murderous King. I hope you're prepared.

Chapter Nine
Before the Crown

THE EIGHTH BELL TOLLED, EACH RING FOREBODING. URIAH'S HAND tightened around the pommel of his sword as the guards unlocked the door. He tensed as Serein stood in the chamber while Rizwana adjusted the layers her kaftan and checked the buttons along the front.

Rizwana turned and frowned. "Captain, you should knock before entering a lady's room," she told him through the silver pin held between her teeth. "She could've been changing."

"She's no lady," Uriah replied. *Putting her in a dress doesn't change what she is,* he thought.

Serein grinned at him, eyes mocking as they caught the amber light of the lanterns. "I doubt Captain Stormheir has any interest in seeing me naked," she said.

Rizwana *tsked* as she wrapped an indigo headscarf around Serein's head, fastening the draping folds with the pin. Silver leaves outlined the hem and cuffs of the blue kaftan. Black kohl rimmed Serein's eyes, making her bright blue irises stand out. A layer of makeup covered up the faded bruises along her face, smoothing her edges. The curved neckline exposed pale scars along her neck.

Danger dressed in silk.

Rizwana adjusted the ends of the scarf to cover Serein's back.

"Do you think I'm underdressed?" Serein asked, inspecting her pointed slippers. "The bangles are too plain."

"I'd be more than happy to put you in chains," Uriah said through his teeth.

The grin held its secrets in the shadows of her face. "If you're going to talk like that, there'd better be dinner," Serein said.

"His Majesty won't tolerate your sharp tongue." *She's probably going to end up getting herself killed because she can't keep her mouth shut.*

Uriah kept his hand near his weapon as he escorted her out of the tower, two guards following them. Serein's gaze traveled over the paintings hanging throughout the palace, the gold eyes of past royals watching them. The last rays of the sunlight hit the colored panes of glass from the arched windows, throwing shards of red, yellow, and blue along the corridor.

They crossed through an open riad courtyard filled with lemon trees, white bougainvillea, and a lion statue to an atrium with different arteries branching off it. Golden lantern light illuminated their path. Uriah and Serein approached a set of staircases winding upward to the second floor, splitting like two hands. The audience hall doors on the lower level were shut, decorated with a silver mandala.

Uriah watched Serein out of the corner of his eye as she climbed the stairs, her breathing labored. *Rameses thinks just because she's weak that she's not dangerous,* he thought. *But that didn't stop her from killing that man at the Harpy's Chest, or the rebels in the woods. She must harbor some resentment against the Malik and doesn't seem like the kind of woman to forgive.*

Soldiers stood by the massive doors of the throne room on the second floor. Swirls of gold spread across the mahogany panels, mixing with the white Sarddonian calligraphy. Above the doors, gold script was etched into the marble with two small lions on either side with the al-Amirmoez House motto:

> *We are the lions that do not fall.*
> *We are the pride that endures.*
> *We are the ones who roar in victory.*

"You'll bow to the Malik when you enter," Uriah told Serein. "You can stand only if he gives you permission."

"Is that because I'm special?" she asked.

Uriah's hand clamped around her upper arm. "Don't make quips like that in front of His Majesty, or you'll lose your head," he said.

Something dark flashed in her eyes for a moment. "And risk getting blood on my dress?" she said through her grin.

Jaw clenching, Uriah dropped his hand, biting back a response. The doorkeepers pushed open the doors, and they stepped into the throne room.

SEREIN'S GAZE LANDED ON SETHOS ZULFIQUR IBN ABLAH AL-Amirmoez through the opening doors. The Malik sat on his low throne of carved, white wood, dressed in black, gold, and white robes. Her light blue footsteps resounded off the polished stone floor, matching her thundering pulse. The black beast inside her raised its lupine head, lips peeling back over sharp fangs.

Not yet, Serein thought, biting the inside of her cheek. *The "backbone who honors others." He doesn't live up to the name he bears. More like "the one who cleaves spines."*

Flowering designs made of colored stones curled across the dais while blue agate veins curved along the supporting pillars. Four raised mezzanines with two guards were on the edges of the throne room. A mosaic depicting battles, lions, Saints, and monsters covered the massive domed ceiling where dozens of lanterns hung. Tapestries with Sarddon's crest hung along the walls, the gold lions and silver moons bright against the white fabric. Night bled through the arched windows behind the thrones.

Men in embroidered qamis and richly colored robes stood on the left side of the dodecagonal-shaped room, their whispered voices catching in the corners. The Malik's Guard stood along the walls. Rameses sat on his father's right, wearing a smaller crown with six gold leaves and twisting the ring around his finger. Ilderim and another shorter wali with a goatee remained behind him, wearing black and red robes and crimson turbans.

Near Sethos' throne, a tall man with brown hair and a thick, graying beard watched her. His gold and wine-colored robes and white turban matched the attire of three other men standing near him, marking them as viziers. Behind the thrones, a bald man in pale gray and white robes stood next to a dark-skinned Ginjarrian in red armor.

Six shahrbans—city governors—four viziers, eight members of his court. Two royals. Twenty of the Malik's Guard. The prince's two wali, the man in red armor, and the bald one, Serein thought as she drew closer to the throne.

Armor shifted in orange-red ringlets behind her as Uriah and the soldiers bowed, fingers touching their foreheads. Sethos' golden eyes swept over her without a hint of recognition. The years had sculpted his face to resemble a statue, marred by the deep scar along his cheek. A crown of twelve golden olive leaves with opals affixed to them rested on his head. Graying black hair brushed against his gold lion's head earrings. His white and gold corded haya bracelet had fifty-two thin gold bands around it and three stone beads—two emeralds and one amber tiger's eye—for each of his children.

Serein kneeled, staring at her reflection on the polished floor. *It's been fifteen years since I last saw him,* she thought, her legs burning under the strain. *Right-handed, skilled with a sword. Fifty-two. Calculating and cruel. Age hasn't made him any less formidable.*

"Rise," Malik Sethos said, voice rumbling like red thunder.

Words dipped in blood spilled across the floor as she stood. The familiar longsword in its plain black sheath hung at Sethos' side. The people of the Old Kingdom knew the black-bladed sword as Vastator the Destroyer.

She glanced at the tall, dark-skinned Ginjarrian with a shaved head and a red spear strapped to his back. A jagged line ran down his face and throat, and scaled scars marked his arms like crocodile skin. A thick cord around his neck disappeared under the plates of red cuirass armor.

That man's not a regular Malik's Guard, judging by his appearance. A Ginjarrian mercenary or something else? Right-handed, mid-thirties, skilled with a spear. The scarring looks like that the jungle tribes of the south have.

"The Grinning Assassin is a woman. And a Ravanassë," Sethos said as he leaned forward, and the whispering of shahrbans increased. His words stilled Serein's pulse. "I find it hard to believe that you are a notorious assassin. You do not look strong enough to lift a sword."

Serein looked up. *Hand me yours, and I'll show you,* she thought, imagining the flash of the sword across his throat as she kept her hands folded in front of her.

Sethos leaned back in his throne. "I would like to see a demonstration of your skills to see why my son wasted two months searching for you," the Malik said. "Since you were able to win in the fighting pit, surely you can hold your own against Captain Stormheir? Or perhaps I should just kill you here."

Serein's heart stopped. *Does he know about me holding a dagger to his son's throat at the Harpy's Chest? But if he knew, I would be dead already. Or he's waiting to make an example of me.*

Rameses sat up, face paling. "Father, that is unnecessary—"

"I want to see what this woman is capable of. Are you not confident in her skills after praising them?" Sethos asked, red silencing the trembling gold. Rameses shut his mouth, sinking into his throne. "Give her a sword and let us see if she is as skilled as you claim she is."

A guard walked over and handed Serein a scimitar. Uriah stood between her and Sethos, drawing his weapon. *Sethos will probably let the captain kill me,* she thought, gripping the heavy sword.

"Proceed," Sethos said, the red word falling like a blade.

Uriah lunged, gray steps hitting the marble floor. Serein parried his thrust, pushing in as steel screeched orange. Her arms trembled, breath ragged as she tried to keep her footing. The heaviness of the kaftan's layers hindered her movements.

He'll win the longer this drags out. I don't have the stamina or strength for a prolonged fight. Break through his defense and end this quickly. This dress is making things more difficult, Serein thought as Uriah pushed her back.

Darting to his right, Serein hooked her foot around Uriah's ankle and slammed her elbow into his stomach. He stumbled and countered her next strike, scimitar sweeping down. Serein heard it pass as she disengaged, the blade slicing the back of the kaftan and leaving a whisper of pain along her skin. She put her blade up to deflect his next quick strike as she twisted around. He advanced and kept his blade close, his green breathing steady. Serein's grip slipped as sweat coated her fingers, her free hand pressing against the dull back of the scimitar.

Teeth gritted, Serein tried to pivot to attack Uriah's left, but he parried. The headscarf came loose, the ends fluttering around her. She pulled back to avoid the curved blade slashing near her chest. Serein ducked, rolling forward, and twisted around in time to see Uriah bring the sword down before she could block.

"Enough!" Rameses' golden shout echoed through the throne room. Uriah froze, the blade hovering in midair above Serein's head. "Father, stop this. Making her fight like this is unfair." He kept his voice steady as he stood, but Serein saw his hands trembling.

Sethos met his son's gaze, eyes narrowed. "You may stand down, Captain Stormheir," he said. "It appears you may have some small amount of skill, assassin."

Uriah lowered his sword, yanking the weapon from Serein's hands. He handed it back to the guard as he sheathed his blade. Rameses' shoulders slumped, watching Serein as she crouched on the floor. Her lungs ached, chest tightening.

"You may leave," the Malik told her.

Serein managed a bow, skin crawling under Sethos' gaze. The split fabric tore further down to her shoulder blades. *I survived, but just barely. I'm not strong enough yet to kill Sethos,* she thought, swallowing the bitterness as she walked away. *That will change.*

The doors shut with teal groans behind her as Serein left the throne room. Uriah her followed down the stairs, his scowl burning into the back of her head. Serein glanced at the taut lines of his face.

"Are you upset that I had a sword in the throne room or that I was able to hold my own against you?" Serein asked. *Or is he upset that he only wounded me instead of killing me?*

"You would have lost that fight if Rameses hadn't stopped it," Uriah told her. "You're lucky the Malik didn't kill you immediately."

"Yes. I'm most grateful for the king letting me keep my head," she muttered.

Peach-colored jingling bounced down the steps. Uriah turned as Rameses walked toward them with his wali. "Serein, I apologize about what happened. I didn't think my father would do something like that," Rameses said, brow creased. "It should not have happened. Both of you could have been hurt. Are hurt?"

Uriah rolled his eyes. "No. It was barely a scratch, although Rizwana will be upset that the dress is damaged." *I'm sure if the king had ordered him to kill me, he would have*, Serein thought.

"Let her check to make sure you aren't wounded." Rameses sighed, arms dropping to his sides. "Still, I thought the meeting went better than expected," he said. "You lived, so that's a good sign."

"Next time, I'd like something more suitable for fighting. A tunic and trousers. Maybe some light armor," Serein said.

"You managed to fight decently in a kaftan. I would think that there would be plenty of room to hide knives underneath the skirts or in the sleeves."

Serein began fixing her headscarf. "Do you expect me to make for an intimidating wali while wearing a dress?"

"You make a valid point. My mother would faint if she saw you without a headscarf and dressed in men's clothing in the palace..." Rameses trailed off, glancing behind her.

Serein turned to see Malika Lujayn Fadila bint Afzal al-Amirmoez walking down the hall with a group of guards, servants, and court women in bright kaftans. Her hair was swept under a silver headscarf with curling Sarddonian holy texts stitched across the fabric. Her green and silver pleated abaya flowed around her.

"Umm," Rameses said, smiling as he kissed her cheek. Uriah and the soldiers bowed. Serein's back ached as she did the same.

"I was taking Rahim and Rasima to evening prayers before dinner. Rasima has been helping me plan my name day diffa," Lujayn replied in a pinched mauve voice, dark brown eyes regarding Serein with disdain.

Lujayn smoothed unseen wrinkles across the front of Rameses' qamis. Around her wrist was a gold and white corded haya bracelet with forty silver bands and three stone beads strung along it. Amir Rahim Ridwan ibn Sethos al-Amirmoez looked up at Serein with eyes that matched his mother's. The Malika stroked his hair, smooth fingers getting lost in the dark curls. She fixed the collar of his green qamis, gaze softening.

Forty, soon to be forty-one. Right-handed. Religiously devout, according to Rizwana and the words of Saint Rahat she wears on her headscarf. Not Oyon-born. Probably from one of the larger cities in the eastern part of Sarddon, judging by her stilted accent. Dotes on her youngest son. Likes to control things. Rizwana mentioned the queen is prone to headaches and gets anxious often, Serein thought, rising from her bow.

Amirah Rasima Amal bint Sethos al-Amirmoez toyed with her purple haya bracelet, her finger tracing the thirteen silver bands. She wore a violet abaya, face hidden behind her matching headscarf, leaving only her wide golden eyes visible. Rameses smiled at Rasima as he squeezed her hand.

The prince's younger siblings. He's closer with the sister, who has a similar habit of fidgeting when she's nervous. Instead of a ring, she touches her haya bracelet, Serein thought. *Right-handed. Thirteen, almost fourteen, but hasn't started bleeding yet, judging by the full veil she wears. Nobles usually keep that tradition more strictly than commoners. The younger brother is close with his mother. Right-handed. Eight. Seems spoiled.*

"Akhun, can I go with you? Will you take me to see the horses?" Rahim asked, pulling on Rameses' arm. His ice-blue voice bounced like a toy ball, the eight gold bands of his green haya bracelet like small scales.

"Not tonight. I have something I need to do," Rameses replied, his smile never wavering as the boy's full lips twisted into a pout.

The Malika pulled Rahim closer as she continued to smooth out his brown hair. "Who is this?" Her mauve question hit Serein's chest as it was flung at her.

"This is Serein, my new wali," Rameses told his mother.

"When your father told me, I thought it was a joke. A woman wali is unheard of, Rameses. And a *Ravanassë* at that," Lujayn said, spitting the word before she continued down the hall. Rameses' smile thinned.

Rahim whispered something to his mother, pointing at Serein as they passed. "Umm, what's wrong with her back?" Rahim asked.

Lujayn turned and let out a mauve gasp as her eyes locked on the edges of the scars on Serein's back, exposed by the askew headscarf and rip in the dress. Her face paled as she pulled her children along, her wali, servants, and the court women trailing behind.

Serein tilted her chin higher. *Stare. Sethos' atrocities are engraved on my skin.*

Rameses' gaze went to the scars, eyes widening as he sucked in a quick golden breath. "Well, you have now met my family. I apologize for my mother's behavior. She means well, but she has strong opinions," he told Serein as they walked to the East Wing. "My mother believes women should be scholars and fight with quills and words rather than swords. She almost fainted when I told her you were going to be my wali."

She smirked. *I would've loved to see the queen faint.*

"Looks like I said something amusing," Rameses said.

"I've had a shortage of amusing things since arriving here," Serein told him.

"How about I take you on a tour of the palace?" Rameses asked. "It will be more exciting than being in your chambers or being challenged to fight in the throne room. Tomorrow at the ninth morning bell, I will come by to retrieve you."

I'll be able to create a better map than the one I've started. Rizwana's information about the palace and the people here has been insightful, but I need to explore on my own.

Serein's legs burned as the stairs continued to twist upward. Her pale yellow breaths were ragged clouds as she reached the top of the winding stairs.

If Sethos really wanted to torture me, he should've made me climb stairs, she thought, sweat sticking to her back. *The stairs may kill me before he does. Why does this dress feel heavier than before?*

"Do you need to rest, Serein?" Rameses asked as he slowed his pace.

"I'm fine," Serein said as she tried to catch her breath. "Who were the three men near your father's throne?" *The man in the robes and the Ginjarrian near Sethos don't appear to be ordinary soldiers or viziers.*

"The older, bald man was Il-Makah, spymaster of the Golden Jackals," Rameses told her. "Umar el-Hassan is the Grand Vizier, and the men in purple robes are the other viziers. The rest of the men were members of my father's court. The Ginjarrian was Kamau Artoli, one of my father's three muharib. He won the last Aikhtiar five years ago."

"Where are his other two *muharib*?" *The Sarddonian kings often have those elite fighters in addition to their guards.*

"Admiral Ezio commands a fleet of ships in the Dark Sea and the Strait of Teeth between Sarddon and Sinabrac. General Hisein is in the Old Kingdom with his battalion, the Scourge."

"I've heard the Aikhtiar's quite the competition," she said as they reached the top floor.

"Yes. It happens every five years and lasts a whole month," Rameses said as they walked down the hall. "People from all across Cemiyon attend. It's one of the biggest events besides the Sister Moons Festival. The year Ezio won was the first Aikhtiar I remember. That was fifteen years ago. The next one will happen at the end of this year."

Who will Sethos use next in this war? Serein thought. *Ezio gave Sethos the naval advantage to invade from the north. Hisein's Scourge helped him cut into the country. Kamau seems to offer personal protection. These men will be dangerous obstacles.*

Rameses' earrings chimed as he glanced back at Ilderim. "I don't believe you had a chance to really talk to Ilderim, my senior wali. And Sayid," he said and nodded to the shorter man with hazel eyes following on his left, "is one of my other guards."

Sayid straightened. Ilderim regarded her with a nod, his brown eyes deep and thoughtful. A dark beard climbed up his high cheekbones.

"Pleased to speak with you finally," Ilderim said with an ocher voice that rolled like shifting sands.

"At least now we're not meeting with weapons drawn," Serein said. *Right-handed. High cheekbones of the desert peoples. Military training. Not easily thrown off guard. Has served the prince for many years,* she thought, remembering the blade he pointed at her in the Harpy's Chest.

Wrinkles creased near the corners of his eyes. "I've no qualms about you or previous occupation," Ilderim told her. "I look forward to working with you."

"It's always nice to meet a person who isn't eager to kill me," she replied.

"I'm sure there's no shortage of people who want you dead,"

Uriah muttered under his breath, the green words crinkling on the floor. Rameses turned to him with raised brows.

The list is long and will probably grow. Serein caught a whiff of cooked meat and cumin. *What delicious things Rizwana has brought for dinner tonight?*

"Well, I will let you get some rest," Rameses said, stopping in front of her chambers. The guards bowed to him. "Have a good night, Serein."

Uriah shot her a narrowed look as Rameses wrapped an arm around his neck, wheeling him around. Ilderim nodded to Serein before he followed them.

Amber light wrapped around Serein as she stepped into the chamber, shutting the door. She tore the scarf from her head and flung it down, freeing the pins and hiding them in her sleeves. The lump of ice in Serein's chest remained. Vastator's phantom teeth gnawed at her flesh.

"Everything all right, miss?" Rizwana asked, her lapis voice spilling over the terracotta tagine she placed on the table. "What happened to your kaftan?"

"It ripped," she muttered. *I was so close I could've gouged out Sethos' eyes. I'll be patient and bring you a storm, Murderous King.*

"Run! Keep Running!" the mother shouted, turquoise leaving her bleeding lips.

Her feet tripped over the uneven ground. Crystals caught the firelight as they hung from her veil. People screamed before steel silenced them. Horses whinnied, and magic screeched as it spilled onto the ground. Flames trampled over the earth, growing with each thing they consumed. The seven-year-old girl looked back as her cousins crumpled in the fields like broken dolls, aunts, uncles, and friends swallowed by smoke.

All the king's horses and all of his men rode with fire in their eyes. Golden eyes spotted them, blood red words staining the lion's mouth. The forest tried to usher the runaways into its green arms, but it withdrew from the orange tongues, revealing the woman and her child.

The sword sliced the girl's chest open, carving an X on her skin. Her mother screamed and tried calling upon the magic in the ancient tongue of the earth, but it didn't answer. The sword turned to the woman and feasted on her heart. The girl watched the world burn, pinned under her mother's body. Crystal shards lay broken and bloodied as the king faded into the smoke.

The girl crawled out from under her mother, passing between consciousness and unconsciousness. Ants and flies took away tiny bits of her mother. Blue buzzing darted around as black flies landed on her face.

Life and Death sat nearby. Death perched on a crumbling rock and turned a piece of silver wood over in his hand. Life dangled in the branches of a tree, tossing and catching three gold rocks in his palm.

Death smiled, black eyes deep. "Come with me," he said, holding out a papery hand as his ancient and silvery voice fell like leaves.

"His country is nothing but bones and ghosts. A shadow," Life snapped, his bright yellow words warm as sunshine, white eyes narrowed.

"Life is hard, child. It's fickle and favors no one," Death said.

"My brother doesn't lie, but my country has other things besides bitterness and sorrow. There's joy and sweetness. You're strong, girl," Life told her. "My country is for the strong."

"Strength brings pain and exhaustion. You will bear the weight of your sorrows on your body, and despair will be your crown. Rest, child. Come with me where no one will hurt you, and you can be with your mother again," Death told her.

"She wants to live. Let the Sarddon king fill your country," Life spat.

"Everything comes to me eventually. I'm patient," Death said. "I will watch over her since you are too busy."

The sun lumbered away. Each breath urged the girl to listen to Death as her mother's corpse stiffened, the stench of decay filling her lungs. Wriggling white clustered in the dark wounds, spilling out onto the grass. Crows gathered to feast, their sharp claws digging into the girl's arms. The lavender caws mocked her as they echoed Death's urgings.

Dawn's light came over the horizon. People moved through the fields of the dead. A man carved out of the moon with pale green eyes stood over the girl.

He held a pale hand out to her. "Do you want to live?" he asked, white words cold on her feverish skin.

Chapter Ten
Stones & Ghosts

"...This section of the West Wing's the recent part constructed after the fire. My grandfather, Ablah, spent almost a decade repairing it. It killed him to see the original stones destroyed since the palace is over three hundred years old," Rameses said, his gold voice sparkling with excitement. "They say you can hear the ghosts of those who died here. There's a rumor about the singing ghost that wanders the halls. Supposedly it's one of the servants who died in the fire."

Serein followed behind him as they walked through the large open riad, Ilderim and Uriah keeping pace nearby. She caught glimpses of armor behind bushes and columns, and the soldiers along the wall's ramparts. Uriah's stare burned the back of her neck.

That scowl's going to be stuck to his face if he keeps doing it for the next six years, Serein thought, the aches from the morning's exercise pulsing through her body.

Rameses ran a hand along the bright marble wall. The white turban contrasted with his green qamis with gold embroidery. Water gurgled from the mouths of three marble lions, rising out of the fountain in the middle of the large riad, leaving opaque purple streams across the stone. A pair of white cats lay sprawled in the sunlight. Vibrant tail feathers of a peacock fanned out as it strutted around, shaking the iridescent eyes as a gray-feathered female pecked at the ground.

Gardens stretched toward the wall, dotted with various trees and vegetation, paths leading to the pink marble building—the Royal House of the Saints—pressed against the back of the palace grounds. White dome apiaries sat like mini palaces in a grove of orange trees and wildflower patches. Yellow and black-striped butterflies and honey bees landed among the vibrant blossoms. Rows of tea bushes sparkled with the last bits of morning dew.

Serein looked at the gulls overhead, their sharp burgundy cries splattering the blue sky like dark bruises. She held up her hand to shield her face as the heat burned her skin.

It's not even summer yet, and it's already this hot, she thought, sweat making the djellaba robe stick to her back. The white raven flew by, heading for one of the towers. *That raven again.*

Rameses stopped. "Are you listening, Serein?" he asked, his voice drawing her back.

"Fire. Grandfather. Ghosts," she said, stepping into the shade of the overhang encircling the edge of the riad.

White calligraphy of holy texts covered the ceiling like pale veins, the phrase *"The one who bows under the lessons of humility will rise like a cedar"* curling next to an etching of an olive tree.

"Is architecture that boring? I find it fascinating," Rameses said, sunlight catching the curvature of his earrings. "I always admired the different architectural styles of the Old Kingdom and the distinct styles each of the Immortal races have. When I was five, my father took me to visit ruins in the Old Kingdom. He told me that it was once a temple built by Elven priests thousands of years ago. It had these massive arches and statues."

A faraway look entered his eyes, sadness muddying the golden depths.

Sethos destroyed hundreds of ruins just like that, trying to wipe out any traces of magic's history, she thought.

"Since then, I became enamored with how buildings are constructed. I discovered some old maps here on the palace grounds a few years ago and the detailed records of Alqamar's dome—which took about a hundred years to design—and I was intrigued."

Rameses pointed to the palace's middle dome. "The stones came from a quarry near the Three Sister Mountains. Saint Alath was the only one who discovered the solution for the dome. She figured out that by using a double layer of—"

"You almost had me at the ghost stories." *If he's studied the palace extensively, he must have more detailed maps. The one I've been making will work for now, but I'll need a complete one.*

"Maybe the West Wing of the palace isn't the most interesting thing. Most people like it when I tell ghost stories. I can make it especially gruesome if you would like," Rameses said.

"What other exciting things do you have planned for today, princeling?" Serein asked.

"Serein," Uriah warned, hurling the green name at her.

The edge of the blue robe wrapped around Serein's legs as the wind picked up. "What else do you have planned, *Your Highness?*"

Rameses gestured to the expansive gardens beyond. "There are the Elephant Gardens near your tower. The pleasure gardens are the finest in the kingdom. A malika a few generations back had imported a lot of trees and flowering bushes from Ginjarr, the Black Isles, and Zhao. Toward the center, there's a large pond with fish of almost every color. There's also the mews where the hunting falcons and birds are kept."

"The number of gardens here seems unnecessary. One could get lost in them." *Or hide a body.*

"A result of many generations of wealth and creativity," Rameses told her and paused, stroking his beard. "I think I know a place that might pique your interest."

"The suspense is killing me," Serein said.

Rameses smiled as he continued down the worn walkway that wound around the Royal Wing toward the barracks. Serein left the shade after him. "We would not want that."

"I would," Uriah muttered as he trailed behind them.

Two pistachio-green barks broke through the air as a pair of slight, cream-colored dogs bounded through the sea of flowers and greenery, startling birds hidden in the branches. They quivered with excitement, tongues lolling as they bounded up to Serein. Feathery tails wagging as they barked, sniffing her sleeves and licking her fingers.

The dogs panted as they stared up with round, brown eyes. "They like you," Rameses said.

"Looks like you don't give them enough attention," Serein replied, running her hands across their heads. *So, he does own dogs. Archery. Architecture. Animals. Is he really Sethos' son?*

His mouth tilted into a smile as he approached the dogs. They turned to him as he crouched down to rub their muzzles. The dogs rolled over, tails wagging. "I would prefer to spend time with Na'im and Na'il rather than attending my other duties. *Yes, I would,*" Rameses said, his voice rising a few octaves.

Na'im and Na'il whined as Rameses stood. They licked his hands and followed him through the gardens. As Serein turned away, the edges of a white scarf and a green abaya disappeared around a column.

It seems someone else is following me beside the captain's men.

Torches burned along the gray walls of the kennels. Beams of sunlight came through the round windows, illuminating the hexagonal antechamber. Eight sections branched off from the main room. The smell of animals and hay permeated the air. Dogs barked from the kennel chambers in the back, the sharp, pistachio-green sounds exploding off the walls.

Na'il and Na'im darted around Rameses. "Behave," Rameses muttered to the dogs as his hand brushed across their backs.

Na'im and Na'il sniffed the air, ears going back as they trotted back out of the kennels. Na'il stopped to lick Uriah's hand before following Na'im.

Larger beasts filled the cages in the chambers to the left. Sleek, spotted Idris leopards and Ygris tigers with gold, black, and white pelts from the Old Kingdom paced behind bars, glowing eyes peering out. The multicolored growls of large cats swarmed in jagged blue and purple tendrils. Tawny lions lounged against the walls of their enclosures.

"My father likes big cats," Rameses said as he walked past the cages, stopping to pet a few of the dogs through the kennel bars. "The others are kept in the coliseum, but that will have to wait until another day. Then I can show you the renowned saifrakasas, the coliseum fighters."

Are they indentured and have to fight for their freedom, or did they choose it willingly? she thought, remembering every blow, wound, and hard-won victory in Grasdan.

A man crouched by one of the cages, speaking in a low voice. A Ygris tiger prowled behind the bars, its gold-ringed tail swishing and a low peacock-blue rumble building in its throat. The tigress swiped at the man, and he jumped back, cursing.

Rameses glanced at the tiger prowling around in the cage. "What's wrong with the tiger, Salatis?" he asked.

Salatis looked up and stood, bowing. The loose-fitting brown robes hung like a second skin, his dark hair pulled back with a blue string. "Marhaba, sayyidi, I wasn't aware you'd be visiting today," he said, his powder-blue voice flowing down his bearded chin and carrying a faint Lóng Shé accent. "She was brought here three months ago and has been hostile toward the males. Her eating habits have also changed. I can't get near her either."

"Is that not normal?" Rameses asked.

Salatis scratched his receding hairline as he squinted at the cages. His long nose seemed out of place on his round face, wrinkles creasing his dark skin. The worn brown haya bracelet on his right wrist was marked with forty-seven bronze bands. Two lotus flower tattoos with Lóng Shé characters inside the petals bloomed on the inside of each wrist.

"I haven't dealt with tigers much before," Salatis replied.

Forty-seven, unmarried. Has worked in the kennels a long time. Failing eyesight, Serein thought, reading the inked names. *He has Zhao remembrance tattoos. "Aizere" and "Akmal." Perhaps his parents' names. A Lóng Shé accent and perfect Sarddonian. Probably born in Zhao to Sarddonian and Zhao parents.*

Serein crouched by the cage, blue eyes meeting large amber ones. Black stripes ringed the tiger's eyes, a thick one running down the beast's spine. The growling subsided as the cat moved toward her.

The gentle predators of the Ygris region of the Old Kingdom. They get big enough to ride. The Immortal royals and several tribes in the Ygris region used them as mounts. Some still do along with the massive elk.

Serein reached through the bars, palm up. The tiger approached, sniffing her hand. The black nose nudged the copper bangle. Serein stroked the white fur as the tiger's growl faded, feeling a bulge along the stomach.

So, that's what it is. No wonder she's stressed.

"Saints! What in Alkhaliq's name are you doing?!" Salatis' voice was sharp in her ears.

"Serein!" Rameses shouted, trying to pull her back.

The tiger growled at the sharp gold and powder blue sounds, fangs bared. Serein shrugged off Rameses' hand, shooting him a glare.

"There's no need to shout," Serein said.

"Let her lose a hand if she's so insistent," Uriah said as he stood next to Ilderim. "One less to worry about."

"You're not being helpful, Uriah," Rameses muttered, eyes darting to Serein as he twisted the ring on his finger. "Serein, please take your hand out of there."

The tiger lay down, body pressed against the bars as Serein's hand trailed up to its ears. "If you think they're vicious and treat them as such, that's what they'll become," Serein told them as she stood, limbs aching. "Ygris tigers are docile unless frightened. Keep her separate from the males. She's pregnant. That's why she's irritable."

Salatis stepped closer to the cage. The tigress rose, stalking to the corner. "How do you know that?" he asked.

"Careful observation," she replied. *Years in this dark have taken their toll on his eyes. I wonder what six years in this place will do to me,* she thought, glancing back at the tiger with a pang of sadness.

TENDRILS OF STEAM ROSE FROM THE TEAKETTLE, MELTING INTO the fading sunlight through the open window. Serein rested her head on the table, tapping one of the inked leaves on her arm. Aches burrowed into her bones, the soft fabric of her blue gandora brushing against her skin. Her half-finished embroidery project was thrown on the chair in the corner of the room.

I'll have to ask Rizwana for some aloe salve when she brings dinner. My face feels like it's burned, Serein thought, touching her warm cheek.

Gray and orange footsteps outside the door made Serein sit up. A dark blue knock resounded through the wood.

Guess I still have to entertain the princeling. Is this going to be a tour of his childhood or maybe his consciousness?

Uriah stepped in, still dressed in his armor, eyes green slits as they landed on her. He held a dark bottle of wine in his hand, the other resting on his weapon.

"Uriah, you really should not walk into a woman's room without permission," Rameses said, carrying a stack of books. Two servants followed behind with platters and tagines. Ilderim stood by the door.

"I knocked," Uriah replied, the green words monotone.

Seems he wasn't joking when he said he would lend me some books, Serein thought.

Rameses sat on the cushion across from her, setting the books down beside him. Uriah put the wine bottle on the table. "Hopefully, you're hungry," he said. "Consider this the final part of the tour. A culinary exploration."

A bowl of rose-scented water was passed around, and Serein washed her hands. "Will this meal be filled with gold flakes? Wine from the royal cellars?" she asked, drying her fingers.

"Nothing that fancy tonight. Next time I would suggest trying Oyon's famous golden cake made with oranges, honey and has a cream-filled center. It's also covered in gold leaf you can eat," Rameses told her, smiling.

"Sounds too sweet."

"I did take one of my father's vintage bottles from the cellar. Spiced wine if you're interested." Rameses held up the dusty bottle with a red wax seal over its mouth with the year "580" on it.

A whole roasted pheasant rested on top of tiny yellow tomatoes and dark green leaves. Baskets of msemen bread were placed next to a plate of kebabs and a dish of hummus. A blue tureen had chunks of lamb floating in a thick, dark soup. Saffron rice sprinkled with roasted almonds filled a wide bowl like a captured sun. Small dishes of smen, olives, and diced carrots with cinnamon-orange dressing brightened the spread. A servant set out three spoons on napkins near empty serving bowls.

"Uriah, come sit with us," Rameses said.

"I ate already," Uriah said as he stood a few feet away. She saw his index finger twitch along the hilt of his sword.

"You can still sit down and relax for a bit," Rameses said, uncorking the bottle. Uriah sighed through his nose and sat down next to the Amir. "Care for a drink, Serein?"

Dark, red wine spilled into the goblets with pale purple ripples, and Rameses passed Serein a cup. The smell of alcohol stung her nose as she took the cup. Her face became distorted in the depths of the liquid.

One drink won't hurt, volchitsa. Her stomach twisted, and she set the cup down.

Rameses took a sip of wine, staring at her. "What kind of foods do you eat in the Old Kingdom?"

Serein popped an olive in her mouth, covering the cooked vegetables in yogurt and wrapping it all in bread. "Meats, breads, soups. Lots of corn, bean, potato, and chicken dishes. It depends on what region you go to," she replied.

"Do you have a favorite dish?" Rameses asked.

"Milcaos and cazuela were my favorites growing up."

"What's that?"

"Milcaos are potato cakes with meat," Serein told him, swallowing a bite of bread. "Cazuela is similar to tagine dishes. It's usually some type of stew, but everyone makes cazuela differently."

The smell of cumin and pepper wrapped around Serein, pulling her back to her mother's side as she cut up orange pumpkins. Silky corn hairs shone like strands of gold on the table, the large clay pot bubbling as it was stirred. Other voices mingled in the kitchen with the smell of spices. Serein tasted bitter ash on the edges of the memory.

"I'm sure the cooks here can find a recipe and make those foods for you if you're feeling homesick," Rameses told her.

I have no home anymore. My only home is with you, my Sun and Stars, she thought.

Rameses wiped his hands on a napkin. "I have something to help ease your boredom. I would have brought them by sooner, but I didn't know what you might like."

He picked up one of the worn, leather-bound books. Rameses studied the title with a faint smile. *Twisted Boughs* was written along the spine in faded silver ink.

"I hope you like to read. These are a few of my favorites. *Twisted Boughs* is written in an older Sarddonian dialect, so if you need help translating it, let me know."

"I'll manage," Serein replied as he set the book down. *The embroidery might be more exciting than reading.*

Rameses dug into the food, taking portions from each dish. Uriah reached for a kebab, eating in small bites as his gaze shifted to Serein.

"Seems like you changed your mind, sadiqi," Rameses said as he glanced over.

"You're not going to eat all of this. I don't like seeing food go to waste," Uriah muttered.

Chuckling, Rameses scooped up rice with a chunk of msemen. His gaze darted to the tattoo around Serein's bare arm. "Tell me about that tattoo of yours," Rameses said to her.

"It's just a tattoo. Nothing special. It's common for people in the Old Kingdom to have tattoos," Serein said, wrapping strips of pheasant and rice in pieces of flatbread. The nutmeg, ginger, and mace on the crispy skin mixed with the salty smen.

"I find it hard to believe that you would mark yourself with something that has no meaning."

Serein felt the presence of the snake brand on her shoulder. Bright, green eyes burned in her memory. A pale hand rested on her shoulder, fingers brushing her neck. She shivered and blinked the image away.

"I wanted a mark I chose, not one inflicted by someone else," she said.

Rameses' elbow rested on the table. "What do you mean?" he asked.

Serein filled a cup of water. "I didn't get most of these scars by accident. Failure comes with a price."

Rameses shifted on his cushion. "Why did you become an assassin?"

You became what you are because you desire vengeance, the white voice answered.

The taste of chicken soured on Serein's tongue. She could almost hear Rameses' anticipation as he waited for an answer. The hourly umber prayer rang out and elephants from the nearby garden let out rosewood-colored trumpets.

"I understand you have your secrets, but I would like to get to know you better," Rameses said as he selected a few olives from the dish. "I want us to get along."

The glittering gold hung between them as she chewed on a piece of seasoned lamb from the soup. "You put bangles on me and brought me here. I haven't been told when I'll be starting my duties or been allowed to leave this room except by your permission," Serein told him, heat flaring in her veins. "Don't insult me by bringing books and suggesting outings like I'm one of your dogs!"

A quiet moment passed as her pale yellow words settled, the heat still resting in her chest. Rameses' eyes widened, and he dropped his gaze to his plate, twisting the ring around his finger.

Uriah's hand rested near his weapon as he swallowed a mouthful of rice, scowling at her. "How dare you speak to him like that!" he snapped, his forest-green voice rumbling like thunder.

Serein pushed the anger back into the dark corners. *I let myself get carried away,* she thought. *He wants to find out information he can use to manipulate me with. He's shown that he's not above using blackmail to get what he wants.*

Rameses placed a hand on Uriah's shoulder. "I thought I was giving you time to rest before I pushed anything on you," he said, the emerald on the golden lion's head twinkling.

"And you thought I'd be happy in a locked room with guards?" Serein shot. "You might as well have put me back in a cell."

Rameses' lips pursed. "That was not my intention. You're free to go where you please in the palace. I will have Rizwana bring you your own key for your chambers."

Uriah straightened. "Rameses—" he said.

"There are guards in the hall. Is that not enough?" Rameses asked, squeezing Uriah's shoulder.

"She's yet to prove that she can be trusted, Your Highness," Uriah said.

Rameses poured himself more wine. "Serein will prove herself. She cannot begin to do that from here and without being allowed out," he said, smiling, but worry flickered in his eyes like a dancing flame.

Uriah's mouth twisted, fingers digging into his arms as he crossed them. A green Wendish curse writhed around him.

Serein picked up a kebab, the metal stick warm as she pulled off the pieces of chicken with her teeth. *I'll still be watched, but at least I can leave. Time to investigate the palace and see what information I can gather,* she thought.

Rameses looked back at Serein. "Is there nothing I can do to get you to trust me?" he asked. "What if, for every question you answer, I will give you anything you desire."

"You think bribery will work on me?" Serein replied. *I wonder how much "anything I desire" covers. Probably not an early release. His resources could be useful.*

"It's more of an incentive. I'd rather not order you to answer," Rameses said, smile thin.

"Order me? You really are like your father," she told him. "You only know how to get what you want through force."

Uriah's frown disappeared underneath his beard, his glare cutting into her. Rameses fell silent as he took another sip of wine. "I'm not like my father," he muttered, twisting his ring again.

The way he talks about Sethos is detached. Every word his father said in the throne room set him on edge. Rameses spoke about Sethos taking him to the ruins, yet that memory made him sad, she thought. *A division between father and son could be exploited. Maybe he's hired me to kill him.*

Rameses drained his cup. Serein put the kebab stick down to scoop rice up with more thin msemen.

"One personal question a day," she said, and Rameses looked at her. *He likes a challenge, needs to feel like I'm starting to trust him. Sacrifice what I can afford to lose, so I can get what I need. No attachments, no tangled threads.*

"One?" Rameses repeated. "How will I learn anything with one question a day?"

"You'll just have to find the right question to ask," she replied.

"You're overstepping your bounds. You're not in a position to make demands," Uriah said, forest-green barbs striking her plate.

Rameses gave Uriah a reassuring pat on the back. "What if I decide you're no longer worth the effort and send you back to Grasdan?" he asked.

"That'd make Captain Stormheir very happy, but you won't do that. You put a lot of effort into finding me. Your father already disapproves. If you sent me back, you'd only be proving him right."

Rameses shook his head, shoulders rippling with quiet laughter. "One question a day...I have so many to ask. In the meantime, you can start training if you feel rested enough."

"Will I be allowed weapons to train with, or will I just be relying on my sharp wit?" Serein asked, eyes shifting to Uriah.

"You will get weapons. I asked Uriah to oversee your training. I trust you both will try *not* to kill each other," Rameses said.

Uriah stiffened as he ripped another piece of bread in half, right index finger twitching. He wiped crumbs from his beard as he chewed stiffly.

"He's normally not like this," Rameses told her while Uriah sat in tense silence.

Angry. Moody. Irritable. I'm sure he's usually a cheerful ray of sunshine, Serein thought.

"Would you like to start training tomorrow?" Rameses asked. "I want to make sure your injuries have healed and that you feel well enough."

"Yes," she said, wiping the grease off her hands with a cloth napkin.

Serein's gaze darted to the metal kebab stick lying on the table. She grabbed it when Rameses and Uriah weren't looking and slipped it underneath the cushion. *This will work better than the bones,* she thought. *Pins, needles, bones, and a metal stick. A formidable array of weapons.*

"I think I have a question," Rameses went on. "When you kill, why do you grin?"

Serein tilted her head. "You want to know whether I mask my emotions behind a smile or whether I enjoy killing," she said, running her finger along the edge of her untouched wine.

"It's a part of your title."

"Xansas told me I needed to smile more. So, I did. Grinning while I killed. It made it easier to spread fear," Serein told him.

Smile, volchitsa. *Show them your fangs.*

The blackness inside stirred, and Serein's scars twisted with old pain. Xansas' cruel grin and vicious hands, the feeling of his knife carving into her skin, helpless as he held her down. Serein's nails dug into her palm as the memories tried to claw their way out.

Uriah shot her a glance. "And what else has Xansas told you to do?" he asked.

Serein unclenched her hands. "Do you also want to play the question game?" she asked. "What will you give me in exchange for my answer, Captain Stormheir? I don't need scowls and contempt."

Rameses poured the last of the wine in his cup, raising it to his lips. "That story was less climactic than I thought it would be," he said.

"If you wanted a thrilling story, you should've found a minstrel," Serein told him, taking a few olives from the dish. "I'm not a storyteller."

"I don't believe that. I think you're an intelligent woman who knows more than she lets on." Wine softened the golden words. "How do I know you're telling the truth?"

"Either I'm who I say I am, or a madwoman driven insane by Grasdan," she replied.

"'One man's insanity is another's brilliance,'" he said, his gaze going to the scars on her neck.

"Staring is rude, princeling," Serein shot. "'If a man stares too long at the sun, he'll go blind from his desire to see its beauty.'"

Clearing his throat, Rameses sat up straighter, gaze dropping to the remnants of the meal. "Quoting Saint Rahat? I didn't think you knew about the Saints," he told her.

"I've picked up many things in my travels." The door opened, and servants came to clear away the dishes in noisy ruby *clacks*. "Since I answered your one question, I'd like more paper and ink," Serein said.

"What for?" Rameses asked.

"So I can write out the elaborate murders I have planned in the future," she said as Uriah's scowl deepened. "The grisly details can only truly be captured on paper."

Rameses tilted his head. "Only paper and ink? Nothing else for your amusement?"

"I'm sure I'll think of something in the future."

"Well, I will let you get some rest," Rameses said, standing. He picked up the books and set them on the table. "I hope you enjoy reading these. I'm interested to hear what you think of them."

"I'm sure I'll have some thoughts on them," Serein told him, scanning the titles. *Some of them look like romance novels. Odd choice.*

Uriah got up, eyeing Serein as his hand returned to the hilt of his weapon. "Good evening, Serein," Rameses said, inclining his head to her as he and Uriah left. Silence settled over the room, the gray and orange footsteps fading.

Serein rose, legs aching. She shut the window and headed to the bedchamber. Stripping off her djellaba, Serein threw on a robe and wrapped herself in the sheets as she settled into the bed.

The prince thinks he can win my trust with gifts. He's mistaken.

Chapter Eleven
Blood & Sweat

SEREIN'S KNEES HIT THE SAND, HER BROWN TUNIC STICKING TO
her back. Her throat burned as she vomited onto the beach.
Breakfast lay splattered on the sands, stomach clenching. The
opaque purple crashing of waves hit the shore with each churning
crest. Gulls let out burgundy shrieks as they landed nearby.

She wiped saliva off her lips with the back of her hand. *A shame.
That was a good breakfast,* she thought, the hot sands sliding over her
bare feet.

Hooves thumped across the sand in vermillion ripples. "Get up."
Uriah's verdant voice cut through Serein's roaring pulse.

He sat on his sorrel mare, the shadows of the noonday sun adding
to the familiar gloom on his face. His white keffiyeh flapped in the
purple sea breeze, red hair pulled back in a tufted ponytail. The waxy
sheen of the salve shone on his cheeks. Sunlight reflected off his
armor, the red sleeves of his uniform trailing down his arms.

"Let me finish throwing up my breakfast," Serein breathed. *How
the captain can wear long sleeves in this heat is beyond me. For him, it's either
sweat or burn.*

"I don't want to hear any complaining," he said.

Serein unhooked the waterskin from her belt next to where her sandals hung at her side. The cool water washed down her throat, and she splashed her face.

"I think I've only vomited twice today. Quite an improvement from the past few days."

Serein heaved herself up, the bile burning her throat. The wind cooled her damp skin. Sarddonian dhows and larger three-sail baghlahs bobbed along the horizon. Sinabrac man-of-wars and streamline merchant ships were visible in the distance, the blue gryphon rippling along their sails.

"Keep running," Uriah grumbled.

"As you wish, milord," Serein said with a smile, reattaching the waterskin to her belt.

She took off down the beach as Uriah's horse trotted beside her. With each passing day, she felt her strength returning as muscle began fleshing out over her bones. The stairs became manageable, her lungs aching less.

Serein stopped at the stone steps leading to the docks, the city wall rising above the rocky crags of the hillside. Sailors and merchants unloaded cargo from anchored vessels. Palm trees and scraggly bushes lined the sloped cliffs spilling down to the beach. The waterfront houses stood out in bright colors against the backdrop of Oyon's ocher wall, piled on top of each other as they overlooked the water.

The horse moved in front of her, Uriah gripping the reins with tight fists. "Run back to the guard's courtyard for weapons training," he told her.

"I can hardly wait," she replied, following the footprints she had left behind.

THE GUARDS' COURTYARD, A FLAT TRAINING AREA FILLED WITH pale dirt, lay adjacent to the sand-colored barracks surrounded by loquat trees with clumps of yellow fruit on the southwestern part of the palace grounds. A large, rounded annex constructed of pale stone housed the officers' quarters, extending from the palace.

The armory was a large, squat building in the middle of the barracks. Red and black tapestries for the city and palace guards hung from the walls. Racks of training weapons filled the room. Sunlight streamed through high windows.

Four guardsmen looked up from polishing their breastplates on low benches, saluting to Uriah. "At ease," he told them with a nod as he walked by. Their gazes flicked to Serein.

Uriah picked up a pair of wooden swords from a rack in the corner. Serein looked around at the rows of swords, lances, bows, daggers, slender-headed tabarzin axes, and pieces of armor lining the walls. She moved toward a set of daggers hanging from the wall.

"If I find anything missing, it won't end well for you," Uriah said, tossing a leather set of training armor to her.

Serein caught the padded breastplate and the vambraces, the smell of oil and stale sweat hitting her nose. "Such a terrifying threat," she said.

Grumbling, Uriah jerked his chin for her to follow. She flashed a grin to the guards still staring at her, talking in low voices. Stares followed her, whispers cutting the air.

Serein put on the armor, tightening the straps. "Your men look surprised. Is it because they've never seen you with a woman before?" *Or is it because they know who I am? It will be harder to blend in if people know,* she thought.

"Sarddonian women aren't allowed to fight. You also look like a man with those clothes and short hair," Uriah said, his white keffiyeh fluttering as he threw the wooden training scimitar at her.

"The fact that I'm here as a guard must be causing quite a stir," Serein said, catching it.

Uriah twirled his weapon, blue whistles streaming off it. "If you're going to be a wali, you'll need to learn how to use a sword properly. You're used to using the element of surprise and planning to win your fights, but you'll face threats without those advantages. You got lucky in the pit."

Serein gripped the wooden sword in her left hand. "I hear the skepticism in your voice. Do you think that man just happened to fall onto the sword? I do know my way around weapons, as you saw in the throne room."

"You were going to lose that fight."

They circled each other. *He'll have the upper hand with a sword. It gives him a sense of control,* Serein thought, following his fluid movements. *He has height and length. Go for his legs and try to land a blow along his torso. The curvature of the scimitar makes it easier to maneuver inside defenses for slashing, less effective for stabbing.*

The wooden swords clacked against each other. Serein lunged, and Uriah parried with one hand. Serein swung at his wrist, but he stepped aside and aimed the sword at her right side. She put up her weapon to parry, the jarring force causing her hand to slip. Pain shot through her wrist as Uriah maneuvered past her guard, pressing the end of the blade against her throat.

"Dead," Uriah said, a few loose strands of red hair sticking to his forehead.

Favors his right side. The left is weaker, but it's a matter of speed to break through his defenses. Any weak spots will be well guarded.

The scent of beeswax and aloe rolled off Uriah's skin. He lowered the sword and took two steps back. "Again. Your grip is weak. The scimitar needs to be kept moving to protect your guard. Its fluidity allows it to change directions quickly, so keep moving."

She grabbed the stick by the worn leather grip. "As you wish, milord."

His mouth twisted into a hard line. "Don't call me that."

They circled again, weapons raised. A few soldiers gathered around, watching. "Did I hit a nerve?" Serein asked. "I thought you were a noble, *Captain Stormheir.*"

Uriah darted forward, the blade sweeping up in a backhand strike. Serein skirted backward, deflecting his sword as it changed directions. Serein's body settled into the familiar movements as she watched Uriah's footwork and the angling of his wrists. Parrying and striking, dodging and weaving, darting and slashing. The ground met the balls of her feet, torso turned sideways, and body centered.

He's trained in Sarddon's traditional style with the curved attacks and low sweeps, she thought, blinking sweat out of her eyes, *and the long sword style of Wendale that favors heavy overhead strikes and Z-motion attacks. He can combine the two flawlessly.*

Over and over, Uriah disarmed her, maneuvering around her defenses. The group of spectators grew. Serein's palms stung from gripping the sword for so long, and her arms trembled, breathing labored. Cuts bloomed along her knuckles where Uriah's weapon struck.

The sun shifted in the sky, shadows lengthening. "Again," Uriah said, breathing steadily.

A dull pang of hunger rumbled in her stomach. *Two hours, fifty-six tries. He's just showing off,* Serein thought as she took up her stance again.

Uriah swung his sword upward as she brought the stick toward his right side. With a swift parry, he forced her back, moving in a blur. Serein ducked and rolled behind him. As she stood, she raised her sword a split second too late as Uriah twisted around. The wooden blade hit her side, and pain shot through her ribs, causing her to stagger back.

A grin spread across her face. *That'll bruise. I was too slow again.*

Uriah's hair stuck to his temples with sweat. "Why are you smiling?" he asked.

"Your sword skills are impressive. Give me a dagger or two, and you won't have the advantage," Serein said, holding her throbbing side. *Not at full strength yet. It'll take some time. He can bruise me now. Soon, that won't be the case.*

"No. You're going to become decent at fighting with a sword first," Uriah replied. "We'll start again tomorrow. Once you have the stances down, you'll learn how to fight with a shield. Then hand-to-hand after that."

He snatched the wooden sword from Serein, staring at the blood on her knuckles and blistered fingers. For a moment, the scowl loosened its hold on his face.

"Go get those checked out by a healer," he said, throwing the green words over his shoulder.

If I didn't know any better, I'd say he almost cared.

CHARCOAL STAINED SEREIN'S FINGERTIPS AS AN OCEAN SPILLED across the page, waves shifting under the flickering candlelight. Letters lay around her, the ink drying on the parchment. Serein flexed her fingers, blisters stiff and smelling of salve. Her whole body ached, arms and wrists sore. Cool aloe vera ointment soothed the pink sunburns along her face and arms.

To write again is a dream. My Sun and Stars, I have so much to tell you, she thought.

Under the silvery shafts of moonlight, a bird alighted on the balcony. Rune symbols shimmered across its form, feathers blending in with the night. The bird morphed into a shadow and snaked across the ground. Black tendrils climbed up the desk and collected by the candle, spitting out a small scroll and a vial the length of her finger.

Serein unrolled the message. The words grabbed her, dragging out emotions she kept hidden away. Faint opalescent traces of magic trickled out of the morphling, lacing themselves around her fingers in fluttering notes.

Titus and Abelia found me, Serein thought, tears blurring the words. *They have a little bottled magic left to send a morphling. I thought something had happened when I didn't receive any messages during those last months in Grasdan.*

Folding the message up, Serein grabbed a quill and a new sheet of paper. The nib left behind an inky amber-orange trail as she piled on word after word until no more space remained. Serein slipped the letter under the drawing of an ocean before pulling out another sheet.

Finishing the letter, she reached for a bundle or papers in the drawer, the sheets rustling in light, plum-colored whispers. The black shape morphed back into a bird as she whistled. It opened its mouth and swallowed the papers. Serein uncorked the vial, sprinkling a few drops of its contents onto the bird.

"*Wil.*" She whispered the spell, and opalescent veins spread through the morphling. It flapped its wings as the song thrummed. The magic wove itself together, flickering before it seeped into the blackness.

Putting the stopper back in the vial, the morphling swallowed it before launching itself into the night. It darted across the moon like a flash of shadow.

Serein's eyelids closed, warmth unfurling in her chest. A tear slipped down her cheek. *After all this time, I can let you know that I'm alive. I never stopped thinking of you, my Sun and Stars.*

"Hello?"

Serein's eyes opened. She sat up, wiping the tears away as the soft violet voice floated into the bedchamber. Rasima appeared dressed in a green gandora nightgown with silver trim. She pushed off her black veil, gold eyes round. Her dark hair hung in ringlets around her heart-shaped face.

"Coming to an assassin's room is dangerous for a princess to do. I didn't think your parents would allow such a thing," Serein said, her body shrieking in protest as she stood. *Why is she here? Did she see the morphling? If anyone knows that I'm in contact with someone or that magic can get into the palace, my life will be at risk. And yours, my Sun and Stars.*

"They don't know I'm here," Rasima replied, head held high. "I told the guards not to say anything."

"The guards in the hall won't stay silent no matter how prettily you batted your eyelashes. Your parents will soon find out," Serein told her. "I thought girls, especially nobles, weren't allowed to show their faces to members outside their family until they come of age." *Her being here's a risk for me. She was probably followed by Sethos' spies. Too curious for her own good. Takes after her brother.*

"We are in private, so I don't see the need to wear my veil. I don't remove it because I dislike it, but because I wish to look at you face-to-face," Rasima said.

Serein stepped toward the girl. "I didn't realize that we were on such familiar terms."

Rasima held her ground, shoulders straightening. "Your name's Serein, correct?" she asked, keeping her violet words steady.

"I go by many names. Grinning Assassin, Black Wraith, criminal," Serein said. "What do you want at this hour?"

"I have heard rumors about you. I wanted to meet you." Rasima stared at Serein's vine tattoo. "I have never met a Ravanassë before."

"There are better times to meet than in the middle of the night. That day in the riad would've been ideal."

Rasima's eyes widened. "You knew I was there? I-I didn't want anyone to know. Mother would have forbidden it. She thinks you're unsavory because you wear men's clothing and have scars. But Rameses thinks you're a good person."

"I've done more unsavory things than wearing tunic and trousers." *Rameses didn't tell her that I held a knife to his throat. She's stubborn and optimistic like he is. Lights help me,* Serein thought. *She's intuitive. Still, I don't think she saw the morphling.*

Rasima gripped the front of her nightgown. "Why did my brother bring you here?" she asked.

"To be his guard," Serein replied.

"You must think I'm a silly child who believes everything she's told. I know you're a criminal, so why would he bring you here?"

Serein took another step toward her. Rasima sucked in a breath but didn't move. "You're braver than most, but don't mistake stupidity for bravery. You *are* a silly child if you think that you can come in here without considering the risks." *There's steel behind that soft face. I was her age when I learned the true cruelty of the world.*

A link to the brother. She could be a useful piece, volchitsa, the white voice said. *So soft. So eager. You had the same look in your eyes when you were her age.*

"Rameses comes here without his guard, and you haven't hurt him," Rasima told her, swallowing the slight tremble in her voice. "He says you're a logical person and would not do something reckless to endanger your own life."

"You haven't seen what happens to people who irritate me. Many have lost their lives that way," Serein said. "It's late. I'm tired."

Rasima pursed her lips. "Are there scars all over your body?" she asked, looking at the marks along Serein's arms. "How did you get all of them?"

"In Grasdan, I was known as *Oraque Unum*, the Scarred One. Sword, knife, arrow, whip, I'm familiar with many forms of cruelty." Serein watched the flicker of fear in Rasima's eyes. "If you've heard rumors about me, then you should stay away because most of them are true."

URIAH STOOD UNDER A STARLESS SKY, THE MOON A WHITE EYE AGAINST the indigo expanse. Dark trees swayed and unseen whispers swirled in the air.

Fog rolled off the black lake as cold wind crawled up his back, raising the hairs on his neck. He whirled around, reaching for the sword, but found the sheath empty.

"Show yourself!" Uriah shouted.

Warm breath caressed his face. Uriah whipped his head around and met a pair of bright blue eyes. White teeth appeared as Serein's face broke into a smile. Every scar shown like silver veins on her dark skin.

"Stay back!" he spat and jerked away.

She vanished, her cool hand touching his cheek a moment later. Uriah shoved her back, heart pounding. Serein flitted away and laughed, wrapping the darkness around herself until only a pair of blue irises remained.

"What scares you? Battle? Death? The faces of those you've killed?" she sang.

Her glowing eyes appeared again. Uriah swung a fist at her, grabbing only mist.

"Or perhaps you are afraid of me?"

Hands appeared and grabbed his face. Uriah stood frozen. Ice poured out of Serein's fingers into his veins. Her gaze stripped away flesh and bone until everything was laid bare. The dark, wraith-like smile drew closer.

"Come, Captain Stormheir," she whispered. "Let me show you death."

The ground fell away, and the dark waters wrapped around Uriah's legs. White marble hands reached up and pulled him down. A silent scream ripped loose as liquid rushed into Uriah's lungs, crushing and heavy—

Morning's light assaulted Uriah's eyes as he bolted upright in his bed, sweat running across his chest. Serein's malicious smile burned behind his eyelids. The taste of murky water coated his tongue. He grasped the cool, black tourmaline around his neck, the leather cord brushing his knuckles.

Stone protect me, Fire strengthen me, Water purify me, Wind guide me, Uriah thought as he grabbed his clothes from the edge of the bed.

Chapter Twelve
The Fine Line

Serein gripped the thin marble lip above her head, finding a foothold on some of the uneven stones of the wall. She ignored the lingering soreness from the days of training, the aches in her wrists and tender blisters. Inch by inch, she climbed, the roughness digging into her palms and the soles of her feet.

Halfway up, her feet slipped, dangling by a few fingers. Serein dropped to the ground, rolling to her side as she landed. Thin cuts nicked her palms, and she wiped her sweaty hands on her trousers as she stood.

Not yet, she thought, arms shaking. *I'll try tomorrow and see if I can reach the rafters from the bookshelf.*

Serein picked up the wooden chair spindle lying across the majlis, balancing it in her hands. The air whistled in blue tones as she twirled the stick around as it cut the air. The white voice overlapped with Uriah's rough green instructions.

I haven't seen the prince in a few days. Perhaps his pride is wounded from the other night. Maybe he's writing a list of questions to ask me, Serein thought.

Serein finished the last cycle of the stances as the sunlight stretched across the floor. She put the spindle back in the chair and sat at the table to finish the last bites of breakfast. Hurried green footsteps approached the door.

A soldier stepped into the room without knocking, his pinched face supporting a hooked nose perched over a thin mustache. His left hand rested on his scimitar. A khanjar with an ornate sheath hung from the right side of his belt, bearing the sigil of an ox. His thin haya bracelet had thirty-three metal bands adorning the leather cords.

Someone new. Not one of the usual guards, Serein thought. *Right-handed, thirty-three, uses a sword. Some noble's son with a minor title from the looks of the fancy dagger. I don't recognize the sigil. He seems frustrated that he has to come and summon me.*

"The Malik commands you to meet with him," the man said in a gruff, gray voice that seemed to catch in his throat.

"Did his Majesty say why he'd like to meet with me?" Serein asked, taking a sip of coffee.

"He didn't," he told her.

"Will I be allowed to change into something more suitable?" she asked as she set the cup down. *Sethos wanting to speak with me so suddenly can't be good.*

The soldier's lips curled. "Be quick."

Grabbing a green kaftan from the armoire, Serein headed for the bathing chamber, shutting the door behind her. She stripped down, wiping away the sweat with a damp rag before drying herself with a towel. The kaftan felt tight over her muscles as she moved.

Rizwana will have to alter my clothes again. It's nice not being able to see my ribs anymore.

Smoothing out her hair, Serein wound a pale olive-colored scarf around her head and slipped on the babouche slippers. Serein tucked the two sharpened bones and pins into the small open seams of her sleeves.

Stepping back into the bedchamber, she found the soldier bent over her desk. "Hasn't anyone told you it's rude to poke around a person's things without permission?" Serein asked, and he whirled around. *He won't find anything interesting. I hid anything that might be incriminating.*

The man scowled at her, jaw clenched. He jerked his chin to the door before stomping out of the room without a word.

I wonder if this will be the last time I see these halls, Serein thought, following him. *Let's see what the king has in store for me.*

The door to the palace prison was located in the West Wing, near the tower of the Golden Jackals. Serein and the soldier descended a twisting staircase to a maze of cells underneath the palace, their green and blue footfalls fleeing into the dim. Each step pulled at the unsettling inkling in her gut. Black scorch marks rose along the dark stone arches. Firelight glowed against the soldier's armor. Muted cries and moans smeared the walls in bleeding colors.

Sethos faced a cell at the end of the row, dressed in an indigo qamis. He spared Serein a glance, his golden eyes igniting the fiery memories of her nightmares. The sword, Vastator, hung at his side. Kamau remained close by with two members of the Malik's Guard.

The soldier lowered himself to the ground, a fist over his heart and fingers touching his brow. Serein's body screamed as her knees touched the cold stone. Fear squeezed her throat, holding her pulse hostage in its grip.

"Leave us." Crimson words painted the bars. The gray-voiced soldier turned away, his mouth turned downward. "Rise."

The dark beast inside Serein stirred, growling as she rose. She imagined wrapping her fingers around Sethos' throat and watching his blood run along the mortar of the stones.

"Come," Sethos said.

Dejected faces sat behind bars, ratty clothes hanging off bent bodies. *Underground. Heavily guarded. One exit. Trapped,* she thought, the word echoing around in her head like a yellow warning bell. *This is where Sethos must keep special prisoners. This place isn't big enough to house all his enemies.*

Sethos passed the cells, footfalls crushing the moans. Serein walked behind him, putting a large gap between them. "A noble found conspiring with rebels from the Old Kingdom," he said. The Malik held the torch up to illuminate a shriveled man cowering in the corner, knuckles bloody stubs where fingers used to be. "A rebel caught smuggling goods." A woman with a shaved head sat shackled to the wall in the next cell. "This woman tried to escape her life contract."

Sethos moved to another row. A man huddled behind the bars in the corner, head turned away. Blood stained his clothes, dark marks etched onto his dirty skin.

"This is one of the rebels that attacked my son a few weeks ago."

There were two prisoners brought back, Serein thought. *They must not have needed the other one...*

Sethos led her deeper into the prison. Kamau and four Malik's Guard followed. The stones darkened, and a chill seeped through the stained walls. A scream tore through the air, smearing the shadowy tunnel with milky blue streaks. The whip marks tightened along Serein's back.

If Sethos' brought me here to throw me in a cell, I'll kill him before he can give a single command, she thought, feeling the bones hidden in her sleeves. *He's so close. It could all end here. Choke him. Tear out his eyes. Smash his head against the bars until his skull breaks.*

The guards pushed open a large iron door, dark teal screeches grating against Serein's ears. The stench of excrement and putrid wounds brought her back to Grasdan. Sunken eyes reflected under the light, and skeletons dressed in skin peered out of the shadows.

Sethos continued down the rows until he came to a stop. A man in the cell hung from the ceiling, arms suspended by chains. His head snapped up, teeth pointed and face angular. Light reflected in his sunken eyes, slitted and green like a cat's. His skin was red and torn where the shackles touched his body, three fingers missing on each hand. Blue hieroglyphic tattoos ran across his cheeks and wrapped around his arms, circling the image of an eagle inked on his chest. Greasy brown hair clung to his skull, ears sharp points.

Burns from iron. The power mark tattoos. He's a Fae, Serein thought. *I haven't seen an Immortal in years. He's not able to transform here with the iron and lack of magic.*

"A Fae caught in possession of illegal bottled magic, attempting to perform magic," Sethos said.

The Fae's green eyes blazed as he thrashed against his restraints, face twisting. "You'll meet death soon, Golden King!" he shouted in heather-colored Common.

His features shifted, becoming hawk-like as feathers appeared through his skin before his face contorted with pain. Goosebumps ran along Serein's skin as the breath of the prison closed in.

May the Lights take you quickly and give you rest, she thought.

"There are whispers about you. I do not like what I am hearing," Sethos said, stopping.

Torchlight spilled into an empty cell. Nail marks scoured the walls, and empty shackles lay like iron snakes. Serein's heartbeat quickened, the rancid breath of the prison clogging her lungs.

I could knock the torch from his hands then slam his head into the wall. Kill him with his sword. Ten seconds before Kamau runs me through or the other guards make a move. If I'm to die here, then I'll be taking you with me, she thought.

Sethos whirled around, hand at Serein's throat as he slammed her against the bars of the cell. She thrashed, gasping as his fingers pressed under her jaw. Spots danced across Serein's vision, the lion heads hanging from Sethos' earlobes snarling at her.

Blackness seeped around him, a buzzing white whisper armed with teeth. Darkness flashed in his eyes, eclipsing the golden irises. "Rameses thinks he needs you. I will put up with his whims for now," Sethos said, his words spreading in a red pool across the ground. "But if you do anything to endanger my family, what you endured in Grasdan will pale in comparison to what I will do to you here before I kill you."

Sethos released Serein, and she sank to her knees, sucking in gulps of stagnant air. The blackness vanished as she blinked.

"You walk a fine line, assassin. I suggest you watch where you step."

URIAH'S SWING CAME WITH A BLUE WHISTLE, AND SEREIN parried at the last moment, raising the small round shield strapped to her left arm. She shifted back across the sparring circle, sweeping Uriah's wooden sword away with the buckler. She stumbled through the movements, feeling the sting of Uriah's blows against her exposed arms. Dirt and sand clung to her sweaty skin.

Each time Serein swallowed, she felt the dull ache of Sethos' hand around her throat. *There's a cell waiting for me, and I won't be able to escape it a second time. Sethos will torture me and kill me, not because I have any information he needs, but because he can. He can't be allowed to find you, my Sun and Stars,* she thought. *Were those moving shadows I saw real or a trick of the light?*

"You're not focused," Uriah said, his green words snapping through her thoughts.

"I was thinking about how these sparring sessions would be much better if we were using steel," she replied, bringing her shield up in time to deflect a blow aimed at her left side.

Serein knocked aside Uriah's sword and lunged for his torso. He sidestepped out of her reach and countered. As her movements quickened, she started pushing him back.

"How about we make a wager? If I can steal your hair tie, can I finally use daggers?" Serein asked as the wooden blades clashed.

"You think you can handle steel if you're struggling with these wooden sticks? You've been trying to beat me for days, and you haven't come close."

"Then you have nothing to worry about, do you? Or are you afraid of your men finding out how unskilled with a dagger you are?"

"Saints, you're annoying," he said, his keffiyeh fluttering in the breeze. "*If* you can pull out the string from my hair...we'll use daggers."

"That's the spirit, Captain Stormheir," she said, smiling.

Legs coiling, Serein rushed at Uriah, swinging at his legs. Uriah moved out of the range of the sword. Serein grabbed a handful of sandy dirt and threw it at his face. He recoiled, cursing. She slipped behind him and reached up underneath his keffiyeh. Uriah whirled around as his hair came loose, swinging at Serein as she sprang back. Serein dodged the attack, their swords clashing in navy-blue bursts.

"Looks like I win," she said, holding the woven string between her fingers.

Uriah lowered his weapon. "That was dirty!" he snapped, rubbing his eyes.

"Aw, poor lamb. Chivalrous swordplay may be how you do things, but one must use anything and everything to get the upper hand," Serein told him.

His scowl returned. "Do you want me to congratulate you?" he asked, wiping his sweaty brow with the back of his hand.

"I want you to switch out these wooden toys for real steel."

Uriah stalked over to the water basin, peeling away the leather armor, and removed his tunic. A black rock hung from a cord around his neck. Seven scars ran along his red-haired chest. Water ran down the planes of muscles as Uriah splashed his face, rubbing his eyes. Dark freckles covered his skin, shoulders sun-tanned. A dark red gash cut across his right side and curved up to his shoulder, standing out against the threads of scars along his back.

How many of those scars did he get in the war? The gash across his side looks like someone tried to kill him. Doesn't seem to affect his fighting abilities, Serein thought, staring the woven ropes of black ink interlinked into a fourfold symbol between Uriah's shoulder blades. *A Wendish protection symbol linked with the earth deities given to children when they turn six. He also wears a rock pendant around his neck. Probably a protection charm. What's he trying to protect himself from?*

Uriah dunked his shirt in the water and wrung out the excess water. The fabric stuck to him as he put his tunic back on. "Tomorrow, you can use daggers. Now give it back," he said as he turned around, holding his hand out.

He cares a lot about this hair tie. A keepsake from home? she thought, inspecting the frayed orange and brown string.

Serein pushed the sword against his chest. She dropped the string in his open hand before walking away toward the barracks.

"Where are you going?" Uriah asked.

"I'm going for a walk along the beach," Serein replied.

"No, you're not," he told her and gripped the wooden sticks. "Too late. I'm already walking away."

THE WAVES NUDGED AGAINST SEREIN'S ANKLES AS SHE WADED INTO the water, rolling up the trousers to her knees. Her boots were tucked underneath her arm. The opaque purple chorus of the sea swathed the horizon. Alqamar Palace sat behind them, its alabaster body bright upon the hill.

You'd love the ocean, my Sun and Stars. It's bigger than the lakes we swam in back home, Serein thought, broken shells and smooth rocks brushing against the bottom of her feet. *Someday I'll have to show you the ocean...if I make it out of here alive.*

Uriah stood on the shore, arms crossed as he scowled beneath his keffiyeh. Gulls hovered overhead, painting the skies with burgundy shrieks.

"Do you get homesick, Captain Stormheir? Being surrounded by sand and separated from your family?" Serein asked, sand shifting between her toes.

Silent moments dropped into the sand before they were swallowed by the waves. "My Da and I came to the palace seventeen years ago for work when we weren't busy on the farm. I see my family when I can," Uriah said, green words catching in the surf. A hint of longing deepened his voice.

Serein looked back at him, ocean spray hitting her. "Why fight for a crown you owe no loyalty to? Wendale is a neutral country that keeps to itself, their soldiers existing only for defensive measures," she said. "Strange that you would support a man who has deemed magic illegal since Wendish deities are elementals linked with magic."

He tensed, shifting. "Magic isn't evil, but it's been used by enough bad people that it's a threat. The Immortal Kings killed the previous Malik and his family and tried to kill His Majesty after the two countries had been allies for years."

"Killing thousands justifies the death of a few?"

Anger flashed across Uriah's face, color creeping under his skin. "I fought for Sarddon because I believed it was the right thing to do," he snapped, reaching for his necklace.

Is that the lie he tells himself rather than admit that he's done things in the name of the crown he can't justify, so he can sleep at night? Or is he that blinded by his sense of duty? Serein thought as she waded out further into the water. *What makes someone like him serve a man like Sethos?*

"Don't go any further!" Uriah yelled.

"Are you going to stop me?" Serein said, facing him as the currents pulled at her legs. "Or are you afraid of the water?"

He uncrossed his arms. "No."

"Oh? Tense shoulders and the distance between you and the surf says otherwise."

Uriah stepped closer to the water, swallowing. Roiling waves hit his boots, and he stepped back as his footprints filled with saltwater.

Serein grinned. "You *are* afraid of water," she said.

The scar along Uriah's nose wrinkled as he glowered, green eyes narrowed. "It's none of your damn business!" he snapped.

"Always so touchy," she said, sloshing back to the shore.

Chapter Thirteen
The Tower of Secrets

SEREIN PAUSED AROUND THE CORNER, THE SOFT LIGHT OF THE lanterns melting across the hallway floor. The white gandora, a few sizes too big for her, brushed her ankles. A basket of rumpled sheets rested against her hip, the bones tucked into the sash around her waist, and the kebab skewer strapped around her leg. The long sleeves cinched at the wrists covered the bangles.

This will only work a few more times before the guards begin to wonder why Rizwana's been coming for the laundry so much, Serein thought, adjusting the headscarf.

She moved between the colonnades, the pale red whirring calls of nightjars speckling the air. Moths clustered around the glowing lanterns. Every riad, staircase, door, and corridor filled in the rough map of the palace she began sketching.

Umber footsteps hit the marble floors, the color darkening as they drew closer. Serein tucked herself into a corner of the riad as a guard passed by. She waited until the footsteps vanished before leaving her hiding spot and tucking the basket behind some bushes.

Glancing up, Serein spotted alcoves carved into the tops of the arched entryways. She gripped the stone reliefs of a column and climbed upward. Her arms trembled, sweat beading on her skin. Serein tucked herself into the alcove at the top, giving her a vantage point between the intersecting hallways and the small riad. Sounds collected in the space—amethyst-colored wind, aqua chirping of crickets, whispered voices, footfalls on stone.

She settled back against the corner to catch her breath. *This will be useful. Let's see what things I'll hear tonight.*

STARS POKED OUT FROM THE DARK BLANKET OF THE SKY AS THE night darkened. Hours passed, marked by hushed conversations of passing servants and guards about their lovers, griefs about work, and the things they heard behind closed doors.

Best head back before Rizwana wonders where I've gone, Serein thought as she stretched her limbs.

Serein climbed down the column and readjusted her headscarf before retrieving the basket of laundry from the bushes. A figure dressed in black appeared at the end of the hall. A woman's face, pale as bone and hair like platinum, glowed under her hood. Tendrils of opalescent threads surrounded her with a low cadence.

She blinked, and the woman was gone. *I keep seeing things. Maybe that's the ghost the prince mentioned.*

"You must be Serein," came a smooth onyx voice in Sarlyrian.

Serein stiffened, turning around. A slight man with light brown skin smiled at her. Lantern light hit his bald head. The black edges of an owl's head and wing were tattooed along his collarbone. Thin, faded scratches lined his hands, and ink stained his fingertips. His wrists were bare. A worn, bone knife hilt was visible under the folds of his gray robes.

Il-Makah, she thought. *He was behind Sethos in the throne room. Right-handed. Late fifties, but hard to tell since he doesn't have many wrinkles or a haya bracelet. Paler complexion suggests he spends time inside. A lilting accent from the eastern towns closer to Ginjarr. Speaks Sarlyrian fluently. Most likely knows other languages. Stains on his teeth and the aromatic smell on his clothes. A heavy tea drinker, and not just of mint tea.*

"I'm Il-Makah," he said as he approached, squinting.

"Spymaster of the Golden Jackals," Serein said. *Was he following me? I thought I was careful. No guards, so I'm not going to be dragged away.*

He squints, so he must be unable to see things far away without spectacles. He might not have seen me.

Il-Makah chuckled. "I'm flattered that my name has reached your ears. I've been wanting to talk with you. It's the usual information gathering done for everyone in the palace. Then you can return to your laundry."

His gaze dropped to the basket at her hip, sharpness glinting in his hazel eyes. "Where are we having this talk?" she asked. *His demure features lulls people into thinking he's harmless before he extracts their secrets. Highly intelligent. Very perceptive. Probably the most dangerous person here.*

"I prefer not to have discussions in hallways. I like to chat in more comfortable places over tea," he said, his feathery black voice collecting at Serein's feet. "You've created quite a stir. Even Captain Stormheir has been asking about you."

So, the captain also asked the spymaster for information because he didn't get enough from Rizwana. What else is he trying to uncover?

Il-Makah motioned for Serein to follow him through the quiet hallways toward the West Wing. Nervousness slithered in her stomach as they approached the prisons with the familiar dark door guarded by two soldiers. Grasdan swirled in her mind, dark flashes of pain, fire, and cracking whips.

Breathe. Breathe. Each pale yellow breath fell in time with her footsteps.

Il-Makah passed the door and turned down a corridor on the left. An olive tree with a woman beneath it was carved into the wall. Six names were etched around it—water, earth, fire, air, light, and shadows. Flames danced in the brazier mounted over the carving.

"Is something wrong?" Il-Makah asked, glancing over at Serein. "Did you think I was taking you to the prisons? The dungeons are no place to chat. Too damp and cold."

The wall changed, curving outward to form the base of a tower. A pair of guards with spears, wearing golden jackal masks, didn't move as Il-Makah and Serein approached.

"I'm sure you've heard about the masks the Golden Jackals wear. The previous spymaster thought it'd be more intimidating to have such attire for us, and the name has stuck," Il-Makah said. "I think the nameless threat instills more fear. People fear what they can't see."

"Good rumors are hard to kill," Serein said.

The spymaster nodded. "Xansas was smart to keep the identities of his assassins secret to spread fear. He and the other Bone Vipers have been evading us since we tried to capture him almost two years ago. Seems the information we got from you in Grasdan wasn't enough to catch him or dismantle his network."

Serein's gut twisted as cold realization settled her stomach. Xansas' smile carved through her mind. *He's still alive. Does he know I betrayed him? Will he try and punish me for it? Eneca might have gotten away if he didn't kill her for helping me escape.*

Il-Makah inclined his head to the stairwell. "The Tower of Secrets isn't as foreboding as the name suggests. The stairs are probably the most intimidating part of it," he said with a laugh.

Convenient to have the tower so close to the dungeons. I wonder if the screams from below can be heard at the top, Serein thought as their footsteps echoed in hushed tan and pale blue tones through the stairwell.

Lavender squawking and bright coral chirps sparked the air as they entered a large room filled with cages and roosts. Bird droppings splattered the stone ledges, and feathers littered the floor. Ravens perched in the rafters, heads tucked under their wings. Men and women untied slips of paper from the birds' legs, moving about like shadows.

Il-Makah stopped. "This," he said, gesturing around the rookery, "is my favorite place in the palace."

"You seem fond of birds," Serein told him. *How many letters does he receive in a day? How many rooms are overflowing with secrets?*

He looked at her. "Oh? What makes you say that?"

"Claw marks on your hands, ones much smaller than the messenger birds used. Possibly songbirds. The larger ones along your wrists are from a bigger bird, most likely a raven or a falcon. Your tattoo also appears to be part of an owl."

Il-Makah's thick eyebrows rose. "I'd love to have your eyes working for me. Perhaps I can persuade His Highness to lend some of your time to me."

"I have to decline your offer." *I'd gain more information with the Jackals, but being closer to this man would put me in a riskier position. I don't need more eyes watching me.*

Il-Makah let out an obsidian sigh. "A shame," he said, stroking the head of one of the ravens.

The raven clacked its beak at him as he pulled away. A tall woman in brown robes approached him, holding out a scroll. Il-Makah slipped it into his pocket as he and Serein continued to the top of the tower.

Il-Makah ushered her into a room filled with bookshelves, ornate tapestries, and various items from across Cemiyon. Feathers of different sizes and colors were mounted in glass frames on the walls. Thick rugs quieted their footsteps. Gilded cages hung on hooks from the ceiling next to lanterns with intricate lattice patterns. Red and black birds let out darting coral-colored chirps. Cool night air swept in from the open window.

A pale girl with blonde hair appeared from behind a curtain, carrying a tray of tea in her arms. The glasses clacked against the hammered metal as she set it on the low table in the middle of the room. Faded cuts lined her fingers and callused fingertips. She glanced at Serein, sea-blue eyes round and inquisitive.

Il-Makah sank into a cushion as the girl set the glasses on the table. "Come," he told Serein, beckoning her over to sit.

Serein set the basket down and sat on a blue cushion. Fragrant stream carried the scents of cloves, pepper, and ginger as the girl poured dark tea into the glasses. *Eleven or twelve. Edolasian. Right-handed. Probably an orphan. Being trained with a knife, either for cooking or as a weapon,* Serein thought. *Being a Jackal is probably the only way a woman can learn how to fight.*

Il-Makah lifted his glass, inhaling. The girl returned with a small bowl of brown sugar, and a plate of maamoul cookies and rose-shaped chebakia covered in honey and sesame seeds.

"Thank you, Inga," he said, switching to Edola, and the girl darted out of sight, slipper-covered feet silent on the rugs. "She's a smart girl. Found her a few years ago, abandoned at the docks. She tried to pick my pockets, so I offered her the chance to work for me." Sarlyrian slipped off his tongue with ease, carrying only a faint accent.

A spy in training. Few pay attention to children, making them effective spies. No doubt he has more in the palace and throughout the city. He seems to treat this one more as a protege.

"When I went to Zhao, I fell in love with this tea. It warms the soul." Il-Makah lifted his glass, inhaling before he took a sip. "Although I still favor Sarddonian tea."

Serein's gaze drifted to an elk figurine carved out of silver-painted wood on one of the shelves. Its twelve-pointed antlers curved upward. *A gwae elk, like from the stories,* she thought. *Probably from a market in the Old Kingdom.*

"I got that on one of my trips to Sava many years ago. I was fascinated by the tales of giant elk protecting the forests on the Silver Shores. I enjoyed visiting the Old Kingdom when I served under Malik Ablah," Il-Makah said. "Your accent's from the northern region, correct? I've always found the Sarlyrian language quite beautiful."

Serein watched the steam brush against the rim of her cup. *He served Sethos' father, watching Sarddon change over the decades and collecting so many secrets. Does he know the truth behind Sethos' rise to power? If he does, did he play a part?*

"I remember when there were Immortals all across Sarddon. I once saw a Fae transform into a wolf when I was a child," the spymaster said, the corners of his eyes crinkling. "I wanted to change into a bird, but sadly I learned that I was only human, so that dream could never happen. The Sahriminha and the Ravanassë are the only mortals blessed with such abilities."

"You sound like you miss the old days," she replied, meeting his gaze.

Il-Makah shrugged. "The world has changed. Old ways crumble, and new ones arise in their place. I'm simply an observer." He folded his hands together on the table. "The Ravanassë are known for their songs and melodies, using music to resonate with magic's vibrations. Were your parents magic users?"

Her mother's smiling face remained preserved in Serein's memory as she sang to the earth, shaping it to her will as she called the opalescent magic. Melodies had hummed in Serein's throat when her mother tried to teach her, but the sound stirred nothing. A man's face appeared in the distance, his features blurred in a silvery outline.

"My parents died when I was young," Serein told him. "I don't remember much. The plague struck and killed those who could use magic. I never was able to use it." *I can hear it and see it, but I can't call it.*

The emerald-green flapping of wings brushed against stone. A white raven landed on the windowsill, letting out a raucous lavender caw before flying across the room.

That's the bird I've seen around the palace. One of Il-Makah's pets. Has it been watching me? she thought.

The spymaster's face broke into a smile as the raven landed on his shoulder. Il-Makah ran a finger along its feathery chest. The bird nipped at his ear until he held up a date cookie. In its claws, it clutched a silver dijil with an elephant head and pomegranates embossed on it. The bird dropped the coin into Il-Makah's hand.

"Bal is always stealing things," Il-Makah told her, setting the coin on the table. "You should drink your tea before it cools. It's not poisoned. That would be a waste of good tea."

The hot tea left a trail of fire down Serein's throat. "Does His Majesty want you to interrogate me about the Bone Vipers? I told your spies everything I knew in prison," she said, peppery sweetness and ginger lingering on her tongue.

Il-Makah's eyes landed on the scar across her throat. "Nizar interrogated you, correct?" he asked, and Serein's scars along her abdomen ached. "Did you know he died suddenly not too long after the raid of the Tenebris Mountains? Tragic. What's even more interesting is that he was unable to give us a physical description of Xansas. He was a capable agent, so I find it strange that he didn't get that information from you."

Serein set her cup down, thoughts racing behind her impassive features. *Nizar made sure he got all he could from me, and I was happy to expose the Bone Vipers. What happened to the rest of the information about Xansas? Did he find out about the raid beforehand and kill Nizar? Something's not right.* A seed of dread burgeoned, digging thorny vines into her chest.

"While I'm interested in this discrepancy of information, I'm more interested in who you are and why you suddenly decided to leave the Bone Vipers and then get caught by Sarddonian soldiers in a town in Sava. You could have fled anywhere. Yet you stayed in the Old Kingdom."

"Why do I need to give answers when you already seem to know them?" Serein asked. *Saying nothing will give him silence to interpret. Saying something would give him just as much. This won't be the last time he'll want to chat about my past.*

"I merely want to fill in the gaps," Il-Makah said. "So much isn't known about who you really are. Even the sentencing report was incorrect. Everyone thought the Grinning Assassin was a man until your true identity was discovered in Grasdan, mostly by chance. We only got parts of Nizar's reports after he died. Then there are claims that you died in prison, yet here you are."

Serein's gaze traveled around the room. "Guess the Lights decided they weren't done with me yet. Life is as greedy as Death is patient. Seems it's easy for prisoners to go missing in Grasdan. The warden is prone to making mistakes."

Il-Makah's fingers tapped against the smooth tabletop, each blue rap leaping like tiny frogs. The white raven cocked his head and hopped over to the sweets.

"So it seems. It's the time before your capture that interests me more. One of your last kills didn't go as planned, correct? A Lord Abarca. He was injured and took several days to die from his wounds. You never left a job unfinished or done sloppily with lots of witnesses, so it's curious that you made a mistake like that."

Heat seeped through the glass, warming Serein's palms as she stared at a chunk of amethyst on the shelf. *These questions are meant to corral me toward the main one. Since he's not writing anything down, his memory is excellent. How vast is that library in his head?*

Il-Makah's lips pursed together in thought. "I've studied your kills. A slash to the throat or a single stab to major organs and arteries. Wounds that kill quickly and effectively. Very methodical and efficient compared to what you did in Grasdan. Those kills were more brutal, desperate. Vengeful I'd say."

He stroked the raven's head as the bird gulped down a cookie, feathers puffing up.

"Was there someone or something important to you in the Old Kingdom? Is that why you fought so hard in Grasdan and tried to escape—why you're here now?"

Serein kept her face impassive as she glanced back at him, pulse tapping against her throat like a worried finger. "You invited me to chat and have some tea," she said. *I'm outmatched here. If I can get him to think that he can see through me, I can use that to gain the advantage,* she thought. *I won't let him find out about you, my Sun and Stars.*

A polished black chuckle rolled into his tea as he refilled his glass. Bal picked apart the cookies, scattering crumbs. "I know you're skilled, but an assassin as a royal guard is a strange choice."

"It seemed better than dying in chains. The prince thought my skills would be useful. If His Majesty believes otherwise, then he should talk with his son."

Il-Makah's hazel gaze continued to strip away the layers of Serein's armor, dissecting and inspecting her words. "The questions I ask aren't always for the benefit of the royal family. I'm loyal to the truth," he said.

Bal flapped his wings, grabbing another sweet. A dark, glassy eye turned to Serein, the thin membrane eyelid sliding over it for a second. "The truth is often subjective and easily twisted. It's never pure," Serein replied.

"An interesting perspective. You look like you'd be good at shatranj. Bal likes to cheat when I play." Il-Makah whistled a single onyx note, and Bal took to the air, circling the room. "I've kept you long enough. Would you like some more tea before you leave?"

Serein uncrossed her stiff legs. "No, but thank you," she told him, picking up the basket and readjusted her headscarf. *It's been a long time since I've had someone more skilled than me at finding the truth. I'll be better prepared next time. Best keep my distance from him for now.*

"A pity. Next time then," he said, sipping his tea.

Chapter Fourteen
Cracked Armor

Sunlight came in through the armory's high windows, catching the dustmotes floating in the air. Serein picked through the rows of daggers, ignoring Uriah's glowering stare. The smells of oil, leather, and steel permeated through the lingering odor of sweat.

"How long are you going to take to pick out a weapon?" Uriah asked, his forest-green voice serrated with irritation. "They're training daggers. Just pick one."

Serein inspected a pair of curved blades under the light, testing their weight in her hands. The worn hilts fit into her scarred palms. "A good weapon makes all the difference. They've helped me win against you before," she said, twirling the knives around. *Decent balance. Perhaps I can convince the prince to give me a real set. Remind him what a woman really wants a good pair of weapons and revenge.*

"You haven't beaten me as many times as you think," Uriah said, adjusting the straps of his padded armor.

"Forty-two to thirty-six, not to mention the five draws," Serein replied.

"It's forty-*four* to thirty-six."

"You *have* been keeping score. Are you counting the fight in the throne room? That was a draw."

Uriah shook his head. "We're not going to talk about this. You're wasting time," he grumbled.

Peach chimes tapped on Serein's shoulder. "One dagger just isn't enough for you, Serein?" Rameses asked.

He stepped into the armory with Ilderim, his gold voice encircling his face. His dark blue qamis and a white turban were out of place among the rows of weapons and armor. The smell of cardamom and coffee wafted off his clothes.

"What are you doing here, Your Highness?" Uriah asked, bowing.

Rameses turned to a suit of chainmail and cuirass armor next to him. "Taking a break from council meetings and helping my mother finalize everything for her name day diffa and the trade negotiation meetings."

"Why don't you jump into the sparring ring instead of standing on the sidelines?" Serein told Rameses.

"Absolutely not!" Uriah snapped at her.

"I will watch this time," Rameses said, his gaze landing on the black and blue splotches along her arms. "Seems Uriah's not been going easy on you."

Serein twirled one of the daggers in the air. "Compared to whips and knives, bruising's a tickle."

Rameses' eyes shifted to her. "Why do you use daggers instead of a sword?"

"Why do you drink out of a cup instead of using your hands?" Serein asked, walking out toward the courtyard.

The hot sunlight and sweat made the beeswax salve shine along Serein's tawny skin. Her tunic stuck to her underneath the padded armor before she reached the sparring ring. Men moved between the brick barracks, bowing to Rameses before saluting to Uriah. After a week of training, many of the faces had become familiar, along with their mannerisms, weaknesses, and fighting styles.

"I thought we were past this whole answering questions with another question thing," Rameses said, a peach chime trickling down his arm as he fumbled with one of his earrings.

"If you can't figure out the question, then you have no answer," Serein said.

He sighed. "Because it's absurd to use your hands to drink."

"It's more practical," she replied and stepped into the ring, sand shifting beneath her sandals. "A sword is hard to conceal and not good for quick kills compared to a dagger. Both work, but one is more suitable."

"That analogy isn't very exciting."

"You seem to think my life is constantly exciting," Serein said.

Rameses sat on a wooden crate on the edge of the ring next to a straw bale. Ilderim squinted against the bright sunlight, his shadow falling across the Amir. "I think you're packed with stories. With all the rumors surrounding you, I think that some of them are true."

Uriah stepped into the sparring circle. His large hand clenched around the dagger hilt. The sunlight turned the hairs along his knuckles into copper strands.

"You're going to use one dagger?" Serein asked.

"I'll be fine," Uriah replied.

"Want to make another wager?" She dipped the words in her grin.

Uriah frowned. "You ended up in Grasdan. I'd say your luck's awful."

"Talk all you want now because it will be hard to do when your face is in the dirt."

As Uriah opened his mouth to speak, Serein rushed at him, orange arcing behind the weapon as she slashed up. Uriah brought his arm up too fast as the blades scraped against each other. She aimed the other dagger at his side. Uriah twisted away and swung down to block Serein's other weapon. The dull metal hit the surface of his vambrace.

Uriah shifted to steady himself, and she came at him again, the weapons glinting. Each blow she landed on his padded side sent him skirting backward. Wagers were tossed around, the amounts and bets changing with each strike. Uriah shoved Serein and curved the dagger toward her midsection. She smiled as she feinted left before parrying. Serein slipped past his guard and rammed her elbow into Uriah's ribs. She knocked his feet out from under him, pushing him to the ground.

Grunting, Uriah rolled as Serein brought the daggers down. She leapt back as he kicked at her, dancing on the balls of her feet as he stood. Uriah grabbed her right wrist as she aimed a punch, giving it a hard twist as he curved the weapon toward her chest. His grip dug into her bruises, the dull pain intensifying. Flashes of white hands and blood made her tense. Serein shifted and brought the pommel of her dagger down on the inside of his wrist.

A green curse crackled in Serein's ear as Uriah released her. Serein hooked her foot around Uriah's ankle as he moved to turn, ramming the pommel into the side of his knee. Uriah lost his footing, and Serein slammed him into the dirt with a dark blue *thud*. The smell of sweat and beeswax rolled off his skin. A rock rolled out of his pocket, stopping in an indent in the sand.

"Don't look so upset, Captain Stormheir," Serein said, pressing a dagger against his neck. "You can't be good at everything." *He keeps a rock in his pocket too. How many does he have on him?*

Uriah's glare became withering, jaw muscles twitching. Strands of sweaty hair clung to his skin, and dirt streaked his cheek. Several guards passed coins around, their voices low while a few beamed at their newly won profits.

Uriah grabbed the rock as he retrieved the dagger. *Four minutes. A little too slow for me, but I'll soon be back to my old self,* Serein thought, aches running through her arms.

Bright blue clapping filled the air, making her turn. "I definitely will *not* be jumping into a ring with you now," Rameses said.

Serein studied the nicked steel of her left dagger, tracing the blade's curvature with a scarred finger. "Insecure about your fighting abilities?" she asked. *Underestimating a woman is an easy way to end up dead.*

"Uriah and I spar occasionally, so I can hold my own. Against you, it would be embarrassing for me," he replied.

Uriah turned and stalked off toward the armory, knuckles white around the hilt of the dagger. *Embarrassment is a bitter taste for him. Small cracks grow larger. Find the weak points until it's time to strike.*

"At this rate, you two might become friends," Rameses said as he walked up to her.

"Such great friends that we'd want to slit each other's throats every chance we got," Serein said. "I want paints and canvases."

Rameses raised an eyebrow. "You paint?" he asked.

"Only one question a day, princeling."

The smile tilted on Rameses' face. "Any particular colors?"

"Any color will do."

"Very well. I will have them sent to your chambers tonight," Rameses told her. "I never would have guessed you were a painter. I would love to see some of your work."

Serein brushed the sand off her arms. "I met Il-Makah yesterday. I've been offered a job with the Golden Jackals."

Rameses' eyebrows rose, and his smile slackened. "You talked with the spymaster? Don't tell me that you accepted his offer and that I have to find a new wali?"

"Seeing as I've yet to become a wali, I may take him up on the job."

"What did you two talk about?" Rameses asked.

"Tea and birds. He wanted to know why you brought me here," Serein replied.

"I thought I made that fairly obvious," Rameses said.

"Some people would find it easier to believe that I'm your lover." *The prince wouldn't be the first man to lie and betray me, and he won't be the last.*

He laughed, the gold sound rippling through the air. "I'm sure *those* rumors have made it halfway through Sarddon by now." Four loud bells rang out, dark peach-colored tolls spreading over the tops of the barracks. "I need to get back before my mother throws a fit. No doubt she has found some other detail that's not right for the diffa. Guests have been arriving all week, which has been adding to her stress."

The guards parted and bowed as Rameses walked by. Serein left the sparring circle for the armory. A few guards smiled at her as she passed, the rest watching and talking in low voices.

Uriah stood by the training weapons, shoulders tense. He had stripped off his armor, shirt streaked with dirt. His right hand clenched around the black stone pendant around his neck. A few guards passed by as they grabbed scimitars from the back. Hazel and dark lavender voices faded, mixing with the sharp orange sounds of sharpening blades from another room.

"Don't sulk too much, Captain Stormheir," Serein said as she approached. "Otherwise, you won't be able to smile again, if you ever knew how to do that before."

Uriah's head snapped up. "Where's His Highness?" he asked.

Serein set the daggers back in their place. "Oh, I slit his throat and buried him behind the barracks," she replied.

Molten anger burned in his eyes. "You've been pretending to struggle during training, haven't you?" Uriah crossed his arms.

Serein removed her padded armor and tossed it onto the bench. "Isn't the point for me to get good enough to beat you?"

"I don't know what your game is, but I'll find out what you're hiding."

Serein leaned against a barrel of wooden staves. "Oh? Are you going to hurt me to find answers? Is that all Sethos' men know how to do?" she shot. "You think we're different because you wear the sigil of the king, and I'm a criminal." *So many cracks. So many weak points to start chipping away at.*

Uriah stepped toward her, shoulders tense. "You think you look at people and know everything about them. Don't act like you know me." He stalked past her, hands clenched at his sides.

Serein selected a crack, aiming a pale yellow blade at the weak point. "Stormheir doesn't fit you."

His gray footsteps stopped.

"Stormheir's a noble's name," Serein said, "yet you're not one. So, what are *you* really hiding? You pretend that you're here to serve some great cause, but you've done things in the name of duty you're ashamed of. Do you dream of the people you've killed?"

"Shut up!" Uriah shouted as he whirled around, knocking over a bucket of wooden poles. They clattered against the floor in navy blue *clacks.* The guards in the armory fell silent. Uriah sucked in a breath, glancing down at the mess.

"I might wear my crimes on my skin"—Serein tapped the back of her neck—"but your hands are as bloody as mine. You can keep digging for my secrets, but I will rip yours out from where they're hiding."

Chapter Fifteen
The Weight of Words

Serein climbed the tower stairs, the coolness of the marble a relief from the stifling heat outside. The four guards by the stairs spared her a glance as she headed for her chambers. Uriah's irritation from the previous day's sparring match seeped through every strike, his quick and forceful movements giving her little time to counter.

Serein began unbuttoning her damp shirt to release the heat trapped against her sweaty skin. She went to put the key in the door but found it unlocked. *Rizwana is probably gathering laundry. The guards didn't seem any different,* Serein thought, feeling the kebab near her leg before stepping into the chamber.

She met Rameses' surprised expression as he moved away from the bookshelf. Brown robes replaced his usual qamis, and a tan keffiyeh covered his head. Copper rings hung from his ears where the bells usually were. His gaze landed on the open front of her shirt, taking in the jagged lines of the X-shaped scar across her chest. Shock cracked his features, eyes wide.

I didn't know he was here. I've gotten too comfortable with these chambers, she thought.

"I—Saints..." Golden sputtering collected in Rameses' throat. "I'm sorry, Serein. I was not—"

"What are you doing here?" Serein asked, closing the front of her

124

tunic. *He saw the scar. If he knew that it was a gift from his father, how would he react?*

"I was dropping off some more books for you and wanted to take you into Oyon..." he told her, averting his gaze. "My mother's diffa is the day after tomorrow, and she's in one of her moods. Too many aunts and cousins trying to help and providing opinions she doesn't like. I want to get out of this place for a while until she calms herself."

She dropped her boots on the ground. "You'll have to excuse me if I'm not in a hurry to go out. I just finished training, and I want a bath." *Venturing into the city will give me a chance to see how much it's changed. He's dressed like a commoner. No wali, ring, or earrings. He wants to go in disguise.*

His hand rested on the back of the wooden chair as he lifted his head. "Of course. I will wait."

Serein grabbed a pair of sirwal and gray robes from a drawer, and the belt pouch from the armoire. "Do you usually show up in a woman's bedchamber unannounced?"

"No. Usually I'm invited in," Rameses said with a thin grin as she shut the door behind her.

RAMESES GLANCED OUT THE WINDOW, TOUCHING THE SPOT WHERE his ring usually was. The scars across Serein's chest circled through his mind. *How did she survive a wound like that? Was it from Grasdan?* he thought.

He looked to the bathing chamber door before stepping into her bedchamber. Papers lay stacked by an inkwell, colored pastels and charcoal sticks sitting on the left side. A cloth with an embroidered black and white tiger was folded next to a needle and colored threads. Everything was organized and straightened.

Embroidery. It's so...womanly, Rameses thought, opening the drawers.

He flipped through the blank sheets of paper. Dark lines underneath the pile caught his eye. Moving the crumpled wads aside, he found pages filled with drawings. A churning blue ocean. Colorful birds. Dapple light through verdant forests. Detailed faces of people.

Surrounding them were extra colors that didn't fit the scenes. Rameses held a picture of a woman wearing a veil with crystals hanging from the ends.

She does draw. And she's good at it, he thought, remembering the walls in Serein's cell covered in charcoal faces and blood. *Some of these were on the walls of her cell. Are they people she killed?*

"Hoping to find anything interesting in my things?"

He whirled around, the papers clutched in his hand. Serein's blue gaze was frigid. "Curiosity got the better of me," Rameses said, setting the drawings down.

She gathered the papers and put them back in the drawer. Blue leaves peeked out along her collarbone. The short ends of her damp hair stuck to the back of her neck, the red knife brand standing out against her skin.

"Are your drawings something to hide? They're incredible. Where did you learn to draw?" he asked.

"Nowhere," Serein said and grabbed a pair of sandals.

"I saw some of these faces inside your cell in Grasdan. Who are these people?"

Her face remained unreadable, secrets hidden underneath the scars. "Just faces."

A BREEZE DANCED THROUGH THE GARDENS, AMETHYST-COLORED whorls playing with the bushes. Serein stared at the back of Rameses' head, trying to push away the flashes of Grasdan that materialized in her mind. The rabbit and lamb bone were tucked through her sash, the metal kebab skewer in the secret pocket of her sirwal trousers.

Why would he visit my prison cell? Serein thought. *Too much was exposed on those walls. Things that would've been smeared away when I died. I'll have to hide my drawings in the rafters too.*

Rameses led Serein past a star-shaped fountain covered in zellij tiles through an archway of magenta bougainvilleas. Little white eyes peered out from the wrappings of petals, swaying above her head. She sucked in a breath full of the smell of honey and pomegranate blossoms.

Even in this pit of monsters, beauty still exists, she thought, glancing over her shoulder to scan the riad.

As the bougainvillea tunnel curved, Rameses stopped, pushing aside the plants to expose a worn door covered in vines and iron filigree. "This is one of the ways I get out of the palace unseen," he told her.

"Seems foolish to have an unguarded door along the palace walls," Serein said. *A secret door out. Must mean there's also a secret way in.*

"It only opens from the inside." Rameses undid the rusted locks. Teal groaning crumbled from the ancient hinges as he pushed it open. "I found this when I was about ten, playing hide and seek with Uriah, and I followed it into the city. It took him and the guards hours to find me. Uriah said I cheated, so I showed him the door and swore him to secrecy. I have more stories about when we were children. Most are about us getting into trouble."

"I can't picture the astute Captain Stormheir as someone who gets into trouble."

The corners of Rameses' mouth turned up as they slipped out the door. "We have had our fair share of misadventures. I was usually the one getting us into trouble, though."

White, blue, and orange houses cast shadows over them as they walked toward Oyon's Gold District. Dust rolled off the sloping streets, and gulls wheeled overhead. Small domed koubbas with offerings and depictions of saints painted on their interiors sat on each block of the wealthier district. Lush gardens were hidden behind stone walls, palm trees casting shade on nearby houses.

The city's grown since the last time I was here. I wonder how many of Xansas' contacts are still active. Maybe the ones I've used in the past are still around, Serein thought.

"The Gold and Silver Districts are where most of Oyon's nobles and upper class live," Rameses told her. "The districts circle the palace walls. Some of the buildings here are older than the palace and have existed since Oyon's beginning five hundred years ago. You can see how the earlier building styles have shaped the city's current architecture."

The streets meandered downward into a city square lined with shops. Colors rose and fell like tides as people called out their wares.

City guards roamed the streets in red and gray uniforms, the lion and shield embossed on their armor.

"The Copper District is filled with most of the city's shops, markets, and warehouses. Many foreign merchants live here because it's close to the docks. The Bronze District on the southeast side of the city by the Amber District is where most of the metalworkers and farmers are. It's also where the coliseum and the garrison are," he went on, gesturing to the ocher and white buildings. "There's a bazaar in the Copper District not too far from here—one of the largest in Oyon. The largest in Sarddon is in Jawahrat Alsahra."

The prince must come here often since he has no problem navigating these streets, Serein thought. *It wouldn't be hard to kill him in an alley. Without the bells and his fine clothes, he looks like an ordinary man. Except for the gold eyes, but in the right lighting, they could pass for amber.*

Rameses dodged a man pulling a donkey with glass orbs strapped to its saddle. They turned down a bazaar crowded with noonday shoppers. Smells of fresh-cut wood and smoke drifted up. Loud colors darted through the street, mixing with the throngs of people. Amidst the Sarddonian voices, Serein caught bits of rippling Lóng Shé and the various Ginjarrian dialects. A dark-skinned Ginjarrian man called out ruby-red prices for vases.

The first half the street contained shops selling rugs, cloths, and household wares while further down there were stalls with foods and mounds of spices. Rameses stopped by a shop with stacks of books on display where a portly Zhao man sat in the shade, smiling as he fanned himself.

Sweat curled the ends of Serein's short hair as the sunlight broke through the thatched covering over the street. "How did you meet the captain?" she asked, squinting as the sun blazed down.

Rameses looked up and turned. "I was six, and Uriah was ten. He worked in the stables when he and his father, Tobias, would work at the palace during the winter months when they were not managing their farm in Wendale. I thought Uriah was much more interesting than my cousins and the children of noblemen. We practiced sword fighting together. Sometimes Uriah would lose on purpose to make me feel better even though he was more skilled than me."

A white cat darted out in front of them, tail swishing as it vanished down a narrow side street. "Was he as grumpy as he is now?" Serein asked.

Rameses approached a cart with baskets of bright fruits, selecting two oranges. He dropped a few copper dijils into the fruit vendor's hand. The breeze tugged on Rameses' dark curls as he held an orange out to her. Serein took the fruit as they passed through a section of the market with foods and goods from Ginjarr and the Black Isles.

"Uriah actually smiled a lot and knew how to laugh back then," Rameses said, chuckling. His gold laughter faded, and somber shadows encroached on his face. "That was before my Uncle Salman and his family were killed, and my father became Malik...I was nine when the war began, and the plague appeared. Tobias wanted to return home before Wendale closed its borders, but Uriah wanted to stay and learn how to fight. I convinced my father to let Uriah live here while Tobias returned home."

Seems the captain wanted something more exciting than farming. Perhaps he's served Sethos for so long because he feels that he owes the king, Serein thought as her reflection passed over a pewter serving tray hanging outside a shop.

A pair of green eyes passed behind her on the tray's surface, and she whirled around, heartbeat quickening. The man's brown skin was flecked with dirt as he led a camel behind him, the bronze contract bangles around his wrists catching the sunlight.

Not Xansas. She clutched the orange tighter in her hand, the smell of citrus spurting from the fruit as she dug her nail into its skin. *He doesn't know where I am. He can't. Not yet.*

She caught Rameses staring, questions poised on his lips.

"I know you two don't get along. Uriah can be a difficult person to understand, but he's not a bad person," Rameses told her, picking at the orange peel.

"He made it clear how he felt when he slammed me into the ground and threatened to throw me in a cell," she said as she peeled the orange. Tangy sweetness hit Serein's tongue as she ate a slice, spitting out the seeds.

"Uriah's loyal to a fault. He doesn't dislike you because you're a Ravanassë, but because he still sees you as a criminal. He will come around. I think he's afraid of making another mistake." The jovial tone dipped, the gold words dimming.

"What mistake did he make?"

"Uriah went to the front at seventeen," Rameses said, popping a slice of fruit into his mouth. "Two years later, he became a lieutenant. There was an ambush while his group was crossing a river. Rebels released the dam. A lot of soldiers drowned. Uriah was badly injured. He blames himself for what happened. Uriah's...quieter now and has these nightmares he doesn't talk about. I worry for him."

Serein dropped the orange peel on the ground. *So, he did fight in the Old Kingdom. Almost drowning explains his fear of water and why being so close to the Old Kingdom put him on edge. I wonder if those scars were from that attack.*

Rameses sighed. "I think he worries that he's unworthy of his station, that he still has to earn it. Even if he's not a noble, Uriah deserves his position more than anyone I know," he said. "His men respect him and would say the same."

"He's only a noble in title," Serein replied. "Where did you get the last name Stormheir from?"

"I convinced my father to have a noble title drafted to satisfy the laws so Uriah could have an officer's position. Stormheir was a lesser known noble house in Wendale. Uriah didn't like the idea of using a different surname, but he gradually began using it," Rameses told her.

Seems I was right about the captain hiding his real surname. It seems to cause him discomfort, another reminder that he's not everything he appears to be.

"I don't think someone's birth should prevent them from being able to achieve things. Nor should their gender," Rameses went on. "I wanted to do what I could to help Uriah since I don't have the power yet to change the laws."

Serein weighed his words, rolling them around in her palm. *He's not like his father in that regard. How might he be able to reshape Sarddon with that kind of thinking? Putting those words into action is a very different matter.*

The bazaar took up almost six blocks. A woman in the stall across from them arranged bowls of green and amber-colored beads for haya bracelets made of different materials on the table facing the street. Thin bands of metal, bone, shell, and painted wood. Leather cords of various colors, woven strands of fabric, and thin ropes hung from a rod over her head, twisting in the slight breeze. Light caught in the hanging colored lamps, throwing blue, red, and green shards across the ground. Glittering jewelry and ceramic wind chimes hung from stalls. Bolts of rich fabric were dyed a variety of colors, from royal blues to saffron yellows.

"See anything you like?" Rameses asked, brushing against her.

Serein moved away from him. "There's nothing I need, save for one of those weapons over there," she replied, jerking her chin to the short knives, curved blades, and polished swords lay across a piece of dark green cloth on the ground in front of the stall.

"I don't think Uriah would be happy if you came back with a dagger. How about a necklace?" Rameses asked.

"I don't need fancy adornments when I have such lovely scars and bangles," Serein replied, stooping down to inspect the weapons.

A sharp shafrah with a carved handle and a koummya with silver inlaid in the hilt and hooked sheath caught her eye. Ripples ran through the steel blade like currents of water, a bluish hue catching the sunlight.

Sarlyrian steel. Sharp enough to cut through bone and never dulls. A piece of art, she thought. *Sarddon has its own variation, but it lacks the blue sheen that real Sarlyrian steel has. Very little of the real stuff remains in the Old Kingdom anymore.*

Serein picked up a pair of matching khanjars made of Sarlyrian steel, the mahogany hilts engraved with half a moon. Their scabbards were black with silver filigree flowers weaving around crescent moons.

"The Sister Moons," the man in the stall said, his ash-colored voice scraping his teeth like gravel. "Real Sarlyrian steel. An excellent set of daggers."

She studied her reflection in the blade. *The Sister Moons. Based on the Sarddonian myth of the two sides of the moon the Light sister and the Dark sister. The Festival of the Sister Moons celebrates the first harvest moon of the year and lasts for a month.*

"Ninety gold and ten silver dijils," he said, stroking his beard.

A hefty sum for a set of blades. But if they're real Sarlyrian steel, then the price is reasonable...I was sold for less than these daggers, Serein thought, swallowing the bitterness.

"Sorry, we were only looking," Rameses said, giving the shopkeeper an apologetic smile.

She set the weapons down and stood. The shopkeeper frowned, eyes narrowed. He looked her over, eyes dropping to the bangles around her wrists. The metal bands were turned to hide the royal crest.

"You should teach your servant better," the man said and turned to another potential customer.

"It's customary that you don't pick an item up if you're not going to purchase it. Otherwise, people think you're going to steal," Rameses told her as they continued through the bazaar. "I could teach you about Sarddonian culture if you like."

"I visited a few times, but it wasn't for socializing," Serein replied.

A tan and white dog tied next to a shop lifted its narrow muzzle, tongue lolling out. Rameses stopped and bent down, scratching behind its floppy ears. He grinned as he spoke to it. The dog let out a pistachio-green whine as Rameses left.

A large fountain stood in the center of the next open square. Women doing laundry crowded the area, some selling folded colored cloths from small benches. A group of nomadic Azraq traders in bright indigo robes and turbans brought their camels to the fountain. Their skin was leathery brown from years under the desert sun.

"Are you aware that gambling is part of Sarddon customs?" Rameses asked.

"I've heard that a Sarddonian's two favorite loves are tea and gambling," Serein replied.

Rameses smiled. "Also drinking and feasting. And a well-timed joke."

Rameses stopped by another food stall between two houses, catching the attention of one of the women stoking the fire. She grabbed the steaming rounds of pastry and wrapped them in thin pieces of cloth. Round bread baked inside a large stone oven in the back while spits of meat cooked over an open fire. Dried herbs hung over a long workbench where dough was rolled out and flattened. The smell of sumac, za'atar, and cumin from the meat made Serein's mouth water. Fresh mutabbaq was cut into squares, steam rising from the flaky meat-filled pancakes.

A dull ache hit Serein's stomach. "This is some of the best goat in the city," Rameses said, handing her one of the pastries. "Not even the palace cooks make food as good as this."

She took a bite, cumin and chili flakes hitting her tongue. Grease ran down her fingers. "Do you often come into the city in disguise?" she asked.

Rameses took a couple more bites, wiping crumbs from his beard. "Sometimes. I like to see the city when nobody can recognize me. Exploring alone gives me a chance to think and escape palace life for a bit. My father said the only way to learn is through experience. How can I know about my citizens if I cannot move among them, experience their lives?"

"Must be nice not having those bells ringing in your ears." *No doubt the Golden Jackals follow at a distance to make sure nothing happens to him,* she thought, scanning the streets.

Rameses touched his earlobes where the holes were. "I hardly notice they're there anymore."

Serein finished eating the mutabbaq, licking grease off her fingers as they left the square and headed down an alleyway. The smell of salt and ocean water became stronger. White and gray feathers littered the ground. Voices grew louder as the alley opened into a wide street. People gathered around a raised platform in the center where a row of men stood with wrists bound and wooden signs with numbers on them hanging around their necks. An auctioneer in yellow robes called out prices of life contracts with booming steel-blue shouts while people in the crowd raised their hands.

Serein was pulled back to Grasdan and the Harpy's Chest. Chains rattled in speckled green hisses. Dead eyes stared back. Jabir's tobacco-stained smile hung over her. Serein bit the inside of her cheek, tugging on the bangles.

"Everything all right, Serein?" Rameses asked, the gold voice breaking through the roar of blood in her ears. "Saints! I apologize. We can go another way."

"Does the selling of people's lives mean so little to you that you'd rather turn away from it?" Serein asked, stopping.

"Selling a person's life contract is for those unable to pay debts and to keep prisons from overflowing. The indentured person has to work to pay off their debts," Rameses told her, brow creasing. "But the system's become corrupt, and auctions like this have grown since the war. I don't like that people are being sold without any way to be free."

Serein pinned him with a stare. "Yet you still own people."

His mouth pursed. "I don't own you."

"You have my life contract, and I wear bangles with *your* insignia on them. You keep trying to convince me that you're different when your arrogance and apathy toward the sins of your country say something very different."

Irritation formed in the corners of Rameses' mouth. "What would you have me do?" he asked. "Demand those people be set free? Tear places like the Harpy's Chest down? I would, but it's not that simple. I cannot fix everything on my own."

"It sounds like cheap excuses, prince," Serein said.

Rameses' hand went to his finger where the ring usually was.

One of the guards near the crowd approached, sunlight hitting his breastplate and helmet. "Is there a problem here?" he asked, his dark purple words bruising the air.

"No. We're just talking," Rameses told him, keeping his voice calm.

The guard's eyes darted to Serein, taking in the scars before noticing the bangles. Serein crossed her arms, hiding her hands in the folds of her robes. "Better mind yourself, boy, when speaking to your betters. Otherwise, you might end up here," the guard told her, gesturing to the square behind him.

"She's done nothing wrong, so refrain from speaking to her like that," Rameses said beside her.

Frowning, the guard stepped closer to stare at her face. His brown eyes narrowed. "A woman? And a *Ravanassë*! With all those scars, I doubt you'd even be worth being sold to a brothel in the

Tafall District." Serein turned away, the sounds of the auction clustering in the narrow alley. "I'm talking to you!" the guard snapped, and his hand clamped on her shoulder.

Skin prickling, Serein whirled around, grabbing his arm and twisting it. Anger cracked open inside her chest, the weight of the bangles growing heavy. The guard let out a painful, purple cry as Serein shoved him against the wall.

"Don't touch me, or I'll give you scars to match mine," she hissed, giving his arm another hard twist before he could grab his weapon.

"Serein, stop," Rameses said, worry creasing his brow. A few other guards near the auction platform looked in their direction.

Surprise crossed the guard's features as she released him. "Control your servant!" the guard shouted at Rameses. "Have her punished!"

"*You* were out of line, sidi," Rameses snapped, anger hardening his usually soft features. "She's done nothing deserving of punishment."

Serein stalked off, breathing in salty air to cool the rage simmering in her throat.

"Serein, wait!" Rameses called as the guard shouted curses behind them.

The prince talks of making things better, but he has no resolve to take action, she thought. *It's all just empty, golden words.*

Chapter Sixteen
Trust on a Knife

Mazarine-blue painted the walls of the houses they passed, magenta bougainvillea climbing up the sides. The honey-like smell of the small paper lantern-shaped blossoms mixed with the salty air. Cats lounged on the sunlit steps. A dog barked in the distance, the bright pistachio-green sound bouncing against the houses as the street became a steep incline. Serein looked around for the red and gray uniforms of the city guard but saw none nearby.

"Serein, I'm sorry. I will speak to Uriah about that guard," Rameses told Serein, golden words hovering beside her like nervous, chirping birds. "He should not have spoken to you like that."

Serein glanced at him from underneath her rida's hood. "What good will that do? I'm an indentured servant, a Ravanassë, and a woman," she said, irritation simmering beneath her scars. In his eyes, there's no reason for him to see me as being worthy of respect. This is how the world is."

Rameses sighed through his nose, jaw set in a tight line. "That doesn't make it right."

"Life isn't fair. You've spent so long looking over the world from a gilded palace that you don't know what goes on below."

Rameses remained silent and turned up a set of worn steps curving around the side of a house. A mottled gray lizard scrambled along the stone wall, beady eyes watching them. White splotches of gull poop stained the bricks.

"I want to show you one of my favorite spots in the city," Rameses said, gesturing to the flat roof. "It provides one of the best views of the city."

The burgundy cries of gulls hit Serein's ears as they perched on the thatched covering shading half of the roof. The birds took flight as Rameses and Serein approached. Fig, lemon, orange, and moringa trees grew in large painted clay pots on the rooftop alongside herbs in colored containers.

From the elevated rooftop, most of Oyon was visible. Geometric and floral patterned rugs hung over the sides of houses to dry. Pools of dyes spotted a section between stacked tenements like honeycomb cells while workers soaked fabrics in the vats. Small rooftop gardens brightened the earth-toned buildings. A woman hung up laundry on her roof across the way, a small child resting on her hip. Beyond the city wall, the docks and the ocean cut across the horizon.

"Do you often trespass onto people's houses?" Serein asked, tracing the lines of the streets in her mind.

"The couple who owns this house, Rajiya and Baqir, don't mind. They're not home right now, which is a shame because Rajiya makes a delicious chicken and lemon tagine."

"Do they know that a prince has been sitting on their roof?"

"I think they do, but they don't say anything or treat me differently," Rameses said with a smile. "When Uriah and I were teenagers, I once dared him to break a rule, so he came up here to try and steal some fruit. Rajiya caught us. She almost called the city guards, so Uriah told her we would clean their roof if they let us go. I didn't think that would get us out of trouble, but Uriah was quite persuasive."

"I'm sure Sarddonian royalty getting arrested for stealing fruit would've been great gossip," Serein said. "Did the captain go through with the dare?"

Rameses shook his head. "No. We ended up arguing about it, which is how we got caught. We did a decent enough job cleaning to keep us from getting arrested. Afterward, she gave us some tea and fruit. Uriah and I still come here, and Rajiya makes food for us. They like us because they usually can get us to fix and clean stuff."

The coliseum rose beyond the markets in the distance, its large half-dome plated in bronze. Beyond it, a large green dome of the medersa stood in the southern part of the city, towers reaching skyward. Rameses pointed to the expanse of Oyon to the south.

"Adjacent to the Copper District is the coliseum. I studied at the Oyon House of Knowledge in the Amber District a few years ago," he said. "Most of the medersis are there, along with the largest House of the Saints in the city. It's where all of Oyon's royals have been crowned and consecrated." Rameses moved his hand to the east where houses stacked on each other and cascaded down to the city walls and the main gate. "Past the ports and the docks is the Tafall District where most of the slums are," he went on.

The golden words formed an outline of the city, traveling over the sprawling rooftops. *A current city map will be useful. When I'm not under observation, I'll need to see which contacts are still active. Maybe get some supplies,* Serein thought.

Rameses sat on the edge of the roof, legs hanging over the ledge. Serein remained standing, staring at the shards of light hitting the ocean's surface.

"You're not wrong about what you said earlier. I have been able to stand on top of things and look down. That's why I like this house so much. It gives me a better vantage point of the city," Rameses said. "But I want to know what goes on in Oyon because I want to do better. I realize how little I know about the world, but please don't mistake my ignorance for apathy."

Clouds passing overhead cast shadows over them. "No matter how many times you say something, it means nothing without actions," Serein said.

Rameses stared up at her. "You look troubled."

"Why do you think that?" she replied.

"You tend to stare off when you're thinking about something that bothers you," he said, hands folded in his lap. "Are you upset about what happened with the guard?"

"I'm bothered by a multitude of things that I don't wish to discuss with you," Serein told him.

He followed her gaze to the horizon. "Why did you become an assassin?"

The amethyst-colored wind blew against her. "Children of war don't have many options. I had three. Kill to survive or join the world's oldest profession."

"What was the third?"

A white hand flooded her mind, outstretched with the offer of false hope. "Death." *When I realized the price of living, it was too late to escape...*

The heel of Rameses' sandal tapped against the wall of the house with crumbling indigo *thuds*. "You have a choice now," he said.

"Making a selection from a limited list isn't a choice. It's only a matter of time before I'm asked to kill again. Either by you or your father."

"I will not ask you to kill anyone. I didn't bring you here for that purpose."

Serein glanced at Rameses, robes billowing out around her. "Don't make promises like that unless you can see the future." *What is an assassin that doesn't kill? What am I now, my Sun and Stars? If I'm not here to kill anyone, what does he intend to use me for?*

"That's the thing about promises. We make them, trusting that despite what comes, we can hold true to them," Rameses said and stood, brushing dust off himself. "There's this nice teashop in the Amber District I think you will like. The Ginjarrian woman who runs it makes excellent tea and pastries that are to die for."

Serein remained on the roof as Rameses headed for the stairs, peering over the edge at the street below. *I wish today was the day when I could return to you, my Sun and Stars,* she thought before following Rameses. *For now, read my words and know that I love you.*

"Rameses! You don't show up for months, and then you try sneaking off without saying hello?" a bright orange voice exclaimed, and Rameses turned.

A tall woman in a saffron-colored gandora stood in front of the house with a basket of vegetables on her hip, the bright colors complimenting her dark brown skin. A yellow and red haya bracelet flashed its copper bands as she moved. Long graying hair escaped from her white headscarf. Wrinkles creased along the corners of her mouth as she smiled. Beside her was a short man with light brown hair in a gray qamis. His bushy beard parted as he flashed a gap-toothed grin.

They look to be in their mid-fifties. Oyon natives, judging by the woman's accent. The cords of their bracelets are worn, so they've probably been married a long time, Serein thought, crossing her arms to hide the bangles.

"You were not home, and I didn't know when you would be back, Rajiya," Rameses said as the woman came up and kissed his cheeks.

The man, Baqir, moved his leathery hands, forming words and letters with his fingers. He waved his hand at his head. His red and yellow haya bracelet moved too quickly for Serein to count all the bands.

Signing. He's deaf, she thought as his right fingers pinched together, moving in an arc in front of his face.

"I was showing Serein the city and told her that your house has the best views." Rameses smiled and signed as he spoke.

Rameses knows sign language. Serein followed most of the conversation between Baqir and Rameses. *Did he learn it for this man, or did he already know it?*

"Are you eating enough? You look like you've lost weight," Rajiya said, glancing from Rameses to Serein with sharp brown eyes. "Come, I'll make you and your friend some food. Where's Uriah? We miss him. Perhaps he could fix the sidewall. It's starting to show cracks."

"Uriah's working, unfortunately," Rameses told her with a laugh. Baqir turned to Serein, hands moving through the air. His amber eyes were watery and full of warmth. "Baqir says that your eyes are very pretty."

"Thank you," Serein replied, signing back. Rameses arched an eyebrow at her.

"We just got food from the market," Rajiya went on. "I'll make you some tea."

"Forgive my rudeness, Rajiya. I wish we could stay, but we have to get going. We will have dinner with you both soon. I was telling Serein about your amazing chicken tagine."

The woman's face fell. "You're breaking my heart, Rameses. You know I always make too much food, and Baqir doesn't need to eat anymore." Rajiya patted her husband's stomach, and Baqir swatted her hand with a topaz laugh.

A curious prince that he'd form such a strong relationship with these people.

"On the lives of the Saints, I promise that Uriah and I will be by soon." Rameses placed his hand over his heart. "Believe me, I hate to miss your cooking."

Rajiya sighed and shook her head. "Fine. I suppose we'll see you in another few months," she said, signing to Baqir. "How long will it be before we see him again? Two silvers that it'll be four months." Baqir stroked his beard before holding up a finger. "One month? You're optimistic, habibi."

Rameses chuckled. "It will not be that long," he said, squeezing Rajiya's hand. "It was good to see you both. I'm glad to see you both are well."

The woman rolled her eyes. "We'll be here," Rajiya told him.

Baqir pulled Rameses into a hug, patting his back. Rameses signed something Serein couldn't decipher, and the man laughed as they walked away.

"I didn't know you knew Sarddonian sign language," Rameses said as he and Serein left.

"I dealt with informants who couldn't speak and a few who were deaf," Serein replied.

"Uriah taught me after we learned that Baqir was deaf. The soldiers and the city guards use a bit of it in their hand signals. Firoz, Uriah's lieutenant, lost his tongue after being tortured by rebels, so Uriah learned it from him."

"You don't use a different name with them."

Rameses gave a small smile. "My name isn't that uncommon. It certainly gained popularity after I was born, but the name 'Rameses' has been around for a while. At the time, I forgot to use a fake name, and then it was too late to lie."

"You can pass off your name, but your eye color identifies you as a royal."

He blinked. "That's harder to hide, but so far, I've almost been recognized only a few times. Most people are too busy to pay too close attention."

People moved through the narrow alleys as the smell of cooking fires rose. A woman with a basket of covered bread passed them, scents of butter and cumin wafting behind her.

"Rajiya and Baqir are proof that the world isn't a truly dark place. They don't care who you are, so long as you know how to clean and enjoy a good meal," Rameses told Serein.

I know light exists in the darkness. You are proof of that, my Sun and Stars, she thought, touching the faded scar along her left palm. *But some days it's hard to see any good in the bad.*

LONG SHADOWS MOVED THROUGH OYON'S STREETS AS RAMESES and Serein headed back to the palace. Orange and pink spilled across the sky, the clouds soaking up the colors as dusk poised to swallow the dregs of the day. The hourly prayer from a nearby House of the Saints rose in orange-red tones. Merchants in the sooq began to close their stalls while food sellers continued to call out evening prices.

"...Afterward, Ummi was so furious about the kaftan I ruined that she threatened to take away all my meals for a week," Rameses said, the golden words of his story floating between them. "It lasted a day because she felt bad about starving her only son. I learned that day that I have no skills at mending clothing and not to use her clothes as a pretend maiden to save."

Serein stifled a yawn. Rameses took a right down a narrow backstreet, and she slowed her pace. "Why're you going that way?" she asked.

"This is a quicker way back to the palace," he told her.

It's a quicker way to get attacked, she thought.

Dark shadows obscured the twisting alleyway, a quiet stillness hanging in the air around them. Shadows moved across the rooftop, vanishing before she could make them out. The alley lay empty as the path wound downhill and curved. Rameses' outline darkened as the light faded.

A tile slid off the roof and landed with a mahogany *crash*. Rameses stopped and jumped back. A man in dark robes dropped from the rooftop in front of them with a knife in his hand.

"I was wrong. This way *is* dangerous. We should run," Rameses said, backing up.

Serein turned, and another man in a tan rida' appeared behind them, blocking their way. He unsheathed a short sword. A second of silence snapped as the first attacker lunged for Rameses, the blade slicing through the air. Serein pushed Rameses against the wall. His golden curse crashed against the alleyway.

"Stay down," she hissed and lunged for the man.

The man's dark eyes widened, and his attack faltered. She grabbed his right wrist and rammed her fist into his throat. He crumpled to his knees, gasping.

Perfectly safe, he says. Serein shook her hand as sharp pain radiated from her knuckles. *Right-handed. Early thirties. Decent with a knife, but not good with hand-to-hand fighting. He seems thrown off that he's fighting a woman.*

She wrenched the man's arm behind his back until she felt his shoulder pop with a dingy amber sound. His olive cry filled the alley, and he dropped the knife. Serein punched him in the jaw. He went limp and slumped forward, unconscious. Serein turned to the second man charging toward them. Grabbing the fallen knife, she blocked the attacker's swing, metal clashing orange in the dark. She dodged the short sword slicing through the air.

Right-handed. Late twenties. Decent with a sword. Uses a Tahtib martial arts form. Like what the soldiers of Sarddon use, she thought, blocking his fist with her hand.

Serein sprang past his guard and seized the corner of his robes, pulling him back into the ground. Fearful eyes stared up at her as she spun around and kicked the weapon out of his hand before he could move.

"Don't move," she said, pressing her foot against his neck. *Their movements feel restrained.*

Rameses stood, dusting himself off. "Best not to kill anyone, Serein," he told her, gold words sparkling in the dark. "Satisfied, Uriah?"

Serein turned around as gray footsteps approached, lantern light chasing away the darkness. The familiar red hair appeared, eyes narrowed into emerald slivers. "She injured my men. That wasn't part of the plan," Uriah said, his green voice clipped.

"I apologize. I should have foreseen that. Serein's too good at what she does," Rameses replied.

"Let Giaffar go," Uriah told Serein, hand resting on his weapon.

She removed her foot from the man's throat. *A test to see if I'll be a decent wali? Good thing I didn't kill anyone. That would've made things awkward,* she thought.

Giaffar scrambled to his feet, sucking in quick breaths as he eyed Serein. "Are you all right?" Uriah asked him.

"I am, Captain," he replied, shaky, marigold-colored words collecting at his feet.

Serein approached the unconscious man. She propped him against the wall and pulled aside his robes, exposing the bony socket protruding against the skin. "A bit of light over here if you don't mind, Captain Stormheir," she said.

"What're you doing to Harith?" Giaffar asked, watching her.

She didn't respond and rotated the man's arm in slow movements. Harith moaned, eyes fluttering. Lifting the arm above his head, she pushed the joint back in place with a dull amber *crunch.* Harith woke with an olive scream, jerking away. Serein picked up the dagger.

"If I'd known these men were yours, I would've been gentler," Serein told Uriah. "Next time, try to put more effort into your ambush. A few more men would have made it more convincing."

"I thought it was believable," Rameses said, smiling. "Excellent acting if I do say so myself."

Giaffar helped Harith to his feet as Uriah looked over their injuries. "Do all wali get tested this way, or am I special?" Serein asked Rameses.

"Uriah still had apprehensions, so I thought this would help prove your trustworthiness," Rameses replied. "It was to see if you would protect me or not."

She fixed her robes. "And if I had decided to leave you to fend for yourself?"

Rameses grinned. "I trusted that you would not leave me, and this proved I was right. You're officially a wali now. I'll have your robes and weapons brought to you tomorrow morning so you can begin your duties."

"How about you drop the knife in your hand?" Uriah said to her as he approached, eyes on the dagger.

Twirling the weapon around, Serein handed it to him, handle first. He took it, leaving behind a thin line along her thumb. Blood bloomed across the cut.

The captain isn't fully convinced I can be trusted. Still, one step closer, Serein thought, looking up at the outline of the palace shadowed by the encroaching night.

Chapter Seventeen
Red & Black

Darkness wrapped around Uriah as he walked through Oyon, *the lidless moon giving off no light against the inky shroud of night. Buildings loomed around him, tall towers with empty eyes. Blue pupils glittered in the dark, a smile hanging like a scythe as Serein stood over a body. She held a curved knife painted red. Rameses' lifeless eyes stared up, blood spreading across the ground.*

Uriah reached for his sword. "What did you do?!" he shouted.

"Looking for a heart. His was too soft," she said. "But yours is just black enough for me."

Serein sprang at Uriah, her blade plunging into his chest. She dragged the knife through his ribs and opened his chest. His beating heart lay exposed, blood racing out in dark ribbons.

Her fingers clenched around the heart, ripping it out. "This will do."

Pulling aside her robes, Serein exposed an abyss inside her ribcage. Uriah tried to speak, but nothing came out as his veins filled with burning ice.

Serein leaned in, her lips near his ear. "Don't worry. You can sleep now. Forever. Just like the others."

Indigo sky pressed against the windows of Uriah's chambers. Bloodstained waters, faces swallowed by murky depths, and suffocating pain sparked under his skin. Uriah sat up, old aches cutting along his side. He sucked in a breath, touching the old scars running down from his shoulder.

Uriah rubbed his eyes with the heels of his palms until spots danced behind his eyelids. He massaged the scar on his side, trying to erase the memory of the blade.

Is this how the next six years will be, haunted by nightmares of her? he thought. *Is this my punishment?*

BLUE POUNDING JOLTED SEREIN AWAKE. SHE TENSED, HAND GOING to the kebab skewer under the pillow. "Get up!" Uriah barked, muffled verdant irritation growing behind the door.

Serein cracked open an eye and rolled on her back, blinking against the dim light. *Again, he comes between me and my sleep. Wanting to kill someone for such a reason seems petty, but I can see why someone would,* she thought, getting out of bed.

"Don't make me break down the door," Uriah snapped.

She shuffled to the living chamber, jaw popping as she yawned and unlocked the door. "Aren't you a cheerful sight to wake up to," Serein muttered, meeting Uriah's scowl. "Did you come to bring me breakfast?"

Uriah's armor was polished and nicked, his red and gray uniform contrasting with the white sash. He held a dagger and a scimitar in his hands, fingers tight around them.

"Get dressed. You need to be up before His Highness. Today you're going to learn his routine," he said.

"My excitement is written on my face."

His mouth pursed in a hard line. "Change quickly," Uriah said, arms crossed.

Serein spun on her heel and headed back to the bedchamber. "As you wish, milord." *How long will his paranoia last? He's stubborn, which could pose a problem,* she thought. *His loyalty to Sethos and Rameses will make it hard to get close enough to the king to kill him. He'll probably be another obstacle.*

Rizwana had left the red and black clothes on the armoire, the buckler catching the sunlight. Serein put on a fresh pair of undergarments before donning the robes and the loose sirwal. The flowing sleeves fell past her hands, and she slipped on a pair of black gloves with brass studs across the knuckles. Serein strapped on the leather vambraces, and the thin breastplate conformed to her body. The buckler rested against her hip, a lion embossed on the studded metal surface.

It'll be strange, wearing a headscarf all day. It's not a requirement for most Sarddonians to wear, more of a choice for modesty or to show religious devotion, but everything is stricter in the palace, she thought, wrapping the dark red scarf around her head.

Uriah stood next to the low table laid out with a plate of batbout bread, beghrir pancakes, and dates. Steam curled from a teapot with an empty glass beside it. He frowned as she stepped into the living chamber.

Her outstretched hand filled the space between them, eyes on the dagger and scimitar in his hands. "Now, will you hand me the weapons, or are they ornamental?" Serein asked.

A moment of hesitation passed before he released the weapons.

Serein removed the khanjar from its scabbard, inspecting the curved blade under the light. *Decent metal. I half expected it to be made of wood.*

Sheathing the weapon, Serein tied the sword belt around her waist. She hung the sword on her left next to a pouch, the dagger on the right next to the buckler.

"Can't let my new position change our relationship," Serein replied with a grin.

"We don't have a *relationship*," Uriah snapped, jaw twitching.

"It's the kind where we both are holding blades at each other's throats," she told him.

He rolled his eyes, grumbling. "Eat quickly. We need to leave soon."

Serein slipped a piece of batbout and some dried dates into her pouch, slathering some cream on a beghrir. The spongy pancake was still warm as she devoured it. "Get dressed quickly. Eat quickly. Is your whole life a rush?" Serein asked, washing the food down with the mint tea. *Tea's not too sweet. I'd recommend Rizwana for sainthood.*

"I don't have time to be slow. I'm in charge of protecting the whole city," Uriah told her.

"Must be a boring job if you had time to spend the past month with me."

Uriah's green eyes flashed under the sunlight, a few bloodshot veins visible in the whites of his eyes. "I only helped train you because His Highness asked me to."

The bad dreams must be keeping him up at night. Let him fight his demons. It'll make things easier for me, she thought.

Uriah stalked out of the room. Serein stuffed another piece of bread and a few dates into her mouth before following Uriah through the tower.

"His Highness is usually up around dawn and eats breakfast for an hour," Uriah said.

He rises early. Interesting. I expected him to be one to sleep in late, she thought, swallowing the food.

The palace stirred with early morning activity, the sound of the dawn prayer twisting through the misty morning. Servants moved through the halls with quiet footsteps, pale specters that kept the palace operating. Lavender and pink light fell across the marble columns through the stained-glass windows. Shards of blue, green, and yellow fell across Serein's arms, and the gold leaf paint on the script along the domed ceilings glowed.

They turned down a corridor, leaving behind the hall of colored refractions. "How's Harith?" Serein asked.

Uriah shot her a sideways glance. The guards in the hallway saluted him. "He's fine," he said, green words trickling across the front of his breastplate.

Four guards stood around an ornate set of double doors with words of Saint Rahat, *"Lead with honor and justice, and see the world changed."* The doors opened into a large blue and white riad with a fountain and trellises covered in flowering vines. An apricot tree twisted upward, its branches reaching the second-story balcony. Two doorkeepers stood by an arched doorway leading to the palace gardens. Four sets of staircases led up to the second floor, six doors lining the walls.

Uriah and Serein climbed a set of stairs on the left. The smell of coffee wafted from the open windows of the nearest room, mixing with the scents from the garden. Gossamer curtains fluttered in the amethyst breeze. Rameses' face appeared in the window, smiling as Uriah stood in the doorway.

"You don't need to stand there, Uriah. You can enter," Rameses said, golden words tinged with mirth.

Rameses lounged against the cushions of the majlis, wearing a blue and gold robe with a pair of white sirwal. A plate of flatbreads, orange slices, and half-finished beghrir drizzled with honey and cream were laid out on a pewter table.

Rameses set his cup down, hair curling against his brow. "Good morning. I was finishing breakfast. Coffee?" he asked Uriah as they entered.

The dogs perked up, rushing over to greet him. "Were you up all night again?" Uriah asked, glancing around at the scrolls and dusty volumes on the table. He stroked the dogs' heads as they jumped around him, licking his hands.

"I got caught up in some reading," Rameses replied, grabbing a blue qamis off one of the cushions and an orange slice.

The breeze rustled the vellum scrolls. Palace outlines were drawn on the yellowed surfaces, along with sketches of the riads and dimensions of the walls. A map of Oyon spilled across the paper, streets and buildings mapped out like veins. Books poured from the shelves and cooled puddles of melted candles formed on the edges of Rameses' desk. A black and gold bow hung on the wall next to paintings of the palace and other buildings. Ilderim watched Serein from the other side of the room.

A bit of luck that these maps are out where I can see them. Serein scanned the room, glancing at the map out of the corner of her eye. *This room's more disorganized than I thought it'd be. Must drive the servants mad that there's always a mess.*

The dogs turned their attention to Serein. Their tongues lolled, feathery tails wagging as they sniffed her sleeves and licked her fingers. Serein scratched Na'im under his chin while Na'il yawned.

She caught Rameses smiling at her. "Ilderim will go over today's schedule," he said as two servants followed him into his bedchamber.

The dogs padded after Rameses, claws clicking pink against the smooth floor.

Ilderim faced Serein, hands clasped in front of him. "After breakfast, His Highness has a meeting with an ambassador from Sinabrac," he said, his ocher voice warm. "He usually takes lunch around noon if he isn't needed anywhere. There are four of us who guard His Highness. I'timad, Nasir, Sayid, and myself. Two wali usually accompany the Amir outside the palace or to large gatherings. Within the palace, he prefers to have one wali."

Serein looked at the woven strands of Ilderim's dark leather bracelet with three amber beads and thirty-nine bands. "You're from one of the desert tribes, correct?" she asked.

Ilderim's eyebrows rose. "Did you guess or gather whispers?"

"Your accent's like that of the nomadic traders. Rolls off the tongue unlike the Oyon dialect. I met a few nomads during my travels. Your features are similar—sharp nose and round face. I'm guessing one of your parents was from a desert tribe."

The corners of Ilderim's mouth turned upward. "My father left his tribe to come to Oyon many years ago to become a weaver and met my mother. I'm impressed you surmised that."

"I was taught to be observant."

"That'll be a useful skill. I can see why His Highness chose you to be his guard," Ilderim told her.

"I have good taste," Rameses said, dressed in his qamis and a silver-gray turban. "For the next few weeks, you will be paired with my other wali until you learn the routine. Then you will be able to guard on your own from time to time."

"I hear and obey," she replied.

Light poured from the latticed skylight, casting midday shadows of the scriptures of Saint Alath onto the table in the middle of the meeting chamber. The shadowy words *"The stars may guide, but a man must take the first step"* curved over the papers and tea glasses. Serein followed the merchant's hurried pale orange Sinabian as the discussion dragged on. Rameses and the Sinabrac merchant shook hands over the low table before rising from the cushioned majlis.

Rameses let out a golden sigh as the merchant and his companions left the chamber. "That meeting seemed to go on forever," he muttered, glancing at Serein as she and Ilderim walked behind him. "Despite Ernesto's poor communication skills, he's an adept trader. He oversees a vast network, mostly dealing with textiles and dyes."

"Seems you deal a lot with Sarddon's trade," Serein said.

"Yes. Trade and economics have always interested me, along with architecture. Since I never showed an interest in military tactics or the governing policies courses my father made me take, he put me in charge of overseeing most of the negotiations with the different trade ministers from across Cemiyon," Rameses said.

He must keep a close eye on Oyon's economy. Another reason he probably spends time in the city in disguise, Serein thought.

Rameses stopped as two young noblemen in orange qamis approached. He clapped them on the shoulders, speaking with excited tones. The taller man with darker skin tugged on the small hoop earring dangling from his earlobe, while the man with light brown skin and sandy blond hair waved his hand through the air. Gold, bright green, and light blue laughter mixed in the hallway.

"Those men are cousins of the al-Ghamdi household," Ilderim told Serein, his ocher voice quiet. "Their fathers oversee the construction of most of Sarddon's ships. They attended courses with His Highness years ago."

"The taller one seems to spend more time outside judging by his tanned skin, so he must handle more of the shipbuilding aspects," Serein said. "I'm guessing the other one oversees more of the bookkeeping aspects indoors. The paler complexion, blue eyes, and hair make me think he has Sinabrac blood."

"That's Isaff. His mother's from one of the northern islands along the Strait of Teeth. Hamid frequents the shipyards near Rigasan while his brother handles contracts and manifests," Ilderim said.

Not surprised that Rameses knows a lot of people, especially with all the trade he handles. He's charming enough to get along with most people. I suppose I'll learn more about who he keeps company with. See if any of them could be useful in the future.

Hamid and Isaff bowed to Rameses as they continued walking in the opposite direction.

"When you look around at others, what details help you to determine what kind of person they are?" Ilderim asked.

Serein gaze flicked to him. "It depends," she replied. "Different smells can tell me where they've been. Clothes can show wealth or lack of, and what kind of work they do. Speech patterns can reveal background and character. Gestures can tell me if a person is relaxed, nervous, angry. Not everything is important, but it can be useful."

"And are your observations always right?"

"It depends on how easy a person is to read and how much I know about a particular thing. Human behavior can often be predicted, but it's about studying a person long enough to know what they might do. It's helped me stay alive and be good at killing, so I'd say I've decent accuracy. A well-placed question or bit of information can be as lethal as any dagger."

Ilderim nodded. "Do you contemplate killing a lot?"

"Only when I'm bored."

Rameses turned back to Serein and Ilderim. "There's nothing else I need to do until this evening. How about we go for a ride?" he asked, cutting through the riad leading back to his apartments.

"Serein!" a violet voice called.

She turned to see Rasima hurrying toward her, sandals slapping the floor in bright green splashes. Rasima's gold eyes peered out from the opening of her white veil as her sky-blue abaya fluttered behind her. Ilderim and Uriah bowed as she approached. Rasima's wali and her handmaiden, Laia, mirrored the movements to Rameses.

"Rasi, I thought you would be with Umm," Rameses said as he walked over.

Rasima looked up at him. "She's having one of her headaches again and told me to practice my weaving in my chambers, but I don't want to do that. Can I come with you?" she asked. "You look like you're going somewhere interesting, and I don't want to help Umm plan the diffa anymore."

"Not today, Rasi," he said, taking her hand as he smiled. "But I will have tea with you tonight after I have dinner with the princess that's here from Sinabrac."

The corners of Rasima's eyes crinkled as she frowned beneath her veil. "You're always so busy now," she muttered, disappointment heavy in the violet words. "Can Serein have tea with me later when she's not busy?"

Sethos' bloodied words echoed in Serein's head, and she felt the weight of uneasy gazes resting on her. She heard the sound of her heartbeat, the cell door swinging open behind her as chains rattled.

She doesn't know how dangerous her request is. Telling her no is best, Serein thought.

"Perhaps when Serein's not busy," Rameses replied, placing his hand on his sister's head.

A smile glowed in Rasima's eyes as she hugged him. "Thank you, akhun! I will call on you when you have time, Serein," she said.

"I'd be honored," Serein told her, the words carving the roof of her mouth. *Too fine a line to walk. It'd be better if she just forgot about people like me.*

"Hopefully, I will see you tomorrow at the diffa, Serein," Rasima said, waving to Serein before heading down another hallway with her wali.

"Rasima's quite taken with you. My parents may disapprove, but I see no problem with her visiting you," he said. "My mother has become more protective over the years since Rahim was born and with everything that happened with my uncle."

She and Rameses seem to be expecting something more from me, Serein thought. *I hid my heart away long ago. Isn't that right, my Sun and Stars? There's nothing left to give.*

Chapter Eighteen
Snake & Dagger

THE HEAT OF THE DAY PRESSED DOWN ON THE GARDENS, disturbed by a wayward amethyst breeze. Sweat formed under Serein's armor as she followed Rameses toward the royal stables with Ilderim and Uriah. Bal glided near the Royal House of the Saints, a pale ghost against the blue.

I wonder how much spying that raven does for Il-Makah. It must bring back things other than coins, Serein thought.

"Confident with your riding skills, Serein? The Aljawhral Alkhadra is almost an hour's ride from the city," Rameses said, wearing plain robes, a tan rida', and gray sirwal.

"I survived eight days of riding. I'll be fine," Serein replied. "Will you be hunting today?" *The Royal Hunting Grounds northeast of here. A place where Sethos' eyes probably won't be.*

Rameses shook his head, peach chimes spilling down. "Not today. I requested the kitchens to prepare lunches for us to take instead," he said as golden words trailed behind him. "I like to get away from the city for a bit. Helps one to get a fresh perspective."

Hammers pounded against metal, resounding through the stables in bright orange clangs as a farrier shaped a pair of shoes on an anvil. Thirty stalls lined the royal stables, filled with horses of various colors. The light blue buzzing of flies trailed through the clamor of colors. The scent of hay, leather, and wood mixed together in the air.

Ilderim and Uriah went to retrieve their horses as stablehands moved past the stalls. Rameses' black stallion was led out, the horse shaking its head. Uriah held the reins of his sorrel mare that nibbled on his shoulder, and he stroked her white blaze. Ilderim muttered to a stocky gray gelding he selected.

A stablehand walked up to Serein with a bay mare with a white whorl between her eyes. The horse shook its head, ears flicking. A black and silver saddle with a high-backed cantle was tied across its midsection and chest with tasseled straps.

"Rala's easy to handle. Rasima learned to ride on this horse," Rameses told Serein, patting Jabbar's side.

"What about the one I rode here on?" Serein asked. She moved down the stalls until she arrived at the end where a silver mare was. Dark dappled pattern ran along the horse's back to its hindquarters. "This one."

Rameses turned to the stable boy and gestured to the horse. "Please saddle the Salvian mare." Bowing, the boy hurried to unsaddle the bay. "I'm surprised you remembered what horse you rode."

Serein held out her hand, and the horse nuzzled her palm. The horse didn't move as the dark blanket and saddle were slung across her back.

"You can keep the horse if you want," Rameses said.

Serein ran her fingers through the silver strands of the horse's mane as she grabbed the reins. *He keeps giving me gifts to gain my trust. The last man who did that was a monster.*

HOOVES STRUCK THE GROUND, LEAVING VERMILLION CLOUDS behind. Swirls of sandstone ran along the escarpments around the hunting grounds, a lush and rocky cradle nestled against the desert. Curved-horned ibexes darted across the steep cliffsides and navigated the narrow ledges of the Aljawhral Alkhadra.

Serein rode on Rameses' left, dappled sunlight falling across the path. Ilderim kept to the right, relaxed in the saddle. Uriah's gaze burned the back of Serein's neck as he brought up the rear, red hair covered by his white keffiyeh. Mulberry-colored rustling from the leaves caught in the amethyst streams of wind.

If only I could keep riding keep going until I'm far from this place, Serein thought, imagining the burning sands and the shadows fading behind her.

Rameses' black stallion gave a goldenrod snort. "I think the horses deserve to rest," he said, patting Jabbar's neck. "We should take lunch too. There's a lake a little way off that's a good spot to rest."

Sunlight played with the surface of the small lake nestled in the opening of the wadi. The trees cupped the turquoise waters in their green hands. Rameses dismounted and crouched by the lake, splashing water on his face. The opaque purple sound spread across his skin before dripping back down into the lake in delicate ripples. Mashed-up footprints rimmed the banks. Wide prints of camels, flat hooves of antelopes and oryxes, clawed paw prints of hyenas and jackals. Ash, dry pine, and ironwood trees groaned. Shadows brushed against the worn rock faces surrounding the wadi.

Rameses brushed back his wavy hair, drying his face with the collar of his rida'. He rummaged through his saddlebag and pulled out a tin of food wrapped in a red cloth. "Walk with me. I have something to discuss with you," he said.

Serein grabbed the container from her saddle, catching the smell of chicken and aged butter. *Is he finally going to tell me why I'm really here?*

Uriah and Ilderim dismounted, leading their horses to the water. The silver mare waded into the water, opaque purple splashes spreading around her. Uriah gave Serein a narrowed look as she followed Rameses to the other side of the lake.

Rameses sat down on the grass by the sandy banks. Balancing the tin on his knee, he lifted the lid, pulling out two pieces of msemen bread covering rice, grilled yogurt-coated chicken, roasted chickpeas, and olives. "I know you have been wondering why I wanted you to be my wali," Rameses said.

Serein leaned against a weathered boulder, nibbling on a piece of chicken. "It wasn't for my looks," she said, scooping up rice and chicken with the bread.

Rameses tore apart the bread, a golden inhale teetering over the pause. "I want you to monitor what goes on in the palace." He paused. "I want you to spy on my father."

Inside Serein's chest, the beast cracked open an eye. "Why do you want to spy on Sethos? You couldn't find one of the Jackals to work for you?" she asked.

Rameses glanced across the lake at Uriah and Ilderim. "I cannot use anyone in the palace because everyone is loyal to my father," he said, the sunlight glinting off his ring as he turned it. "I cannot ask Uriah to do this. You..."

"There's nothing too traitorous for an assassin to do," Serein said, biting on the sharp yellow words.

Rameses picked up a rock and ran his thumb over its rugged surface. Heavy words settled across the lake's surface, sinking into the depths.

"I have heard things about my father." Rameses reached for an olive. "The official story is that a Vale assassin sent by the Immortal Kings murdered my uncle and his family and tried to kill my father. The assailant was killed after wounding him. Some whisper that my father killed the Malik to take the throne and staged his injuries. He was not always this...cold. Uncle's death broke him. I had never seen my father cry before. He refused to eat for months, staying locked away in his study while my mother was inconsolable after losing the baby she was carrying."

What Sethos has done is written in the bones and blood of those he's slaughtered, Serein thought, watching Rameses. *He can't be that blind to what's been happening. What made him decide that he couldn't trust his father?*

Rameses popped the olive in his mouth, chewing on the seconds of silence. "Two years ago, my father asked me to attend one of his war councils. Rebels had dug themselves into one of the key cities in Idris. My father's troops were breaking through the siege, and there had been petitions from the rebels to let the citizens leave without harm." He paused, mouth twisting. "He gave the order to burn the city with everyone inside it. I tried to reason with him, but he said, 'war requires sacrifice.' I could not believe that he would give such an order.

"I keep digging deeper on my own. I don't believe all the rumors, but I have doubts," he told her, brow furrowed. "You have a way of gleaning the truth. I'm sure you will be able to see what I cannot."

"You seem to think I can approach your father whenever I wish," Serein said, setting the tin of food down on top of the stone.

"There are other ways of moving through the palace unseen," Rameses replied. "If I happen to *accidentally* leave maps of the palace out, then you might find the network of corridors and old secret passages. My chambers get disorderly, and I may not always notice if manuscripts go missing."

He had those old maps out on purpose. The prince of architecture may be useful after all. His plan is still flawed. Serein crossed her arms, touching the bangles. *Still, this whole thing could be a trap.*

The Lights smile upon you, volchitsa. *He's giving you an invitation to look for secrets, access to Sethos' underbelly, so you can strike when the time is right.*

Serein shuddered as the white voice settled on her skin. "This is a fine line to walk. A traitorous one. You can't guarantee my safety." *His trust in me is based on the assumption that I'll choose his version of good and morality. It's a blindfold of his own making.*

The amethyst-colored wind stirred ripples on the lake. He tossed the rock in the air, watching it flip and land in his hand. "I will do everything I can to make sure you're protected."

"Why are you so insistent you need me to do this?" Serein asked.

"I didn't choose you because you're a criminal. It's because you will not be swayed by my father. I don't know who else to entrust this to."

"You didn't even know who the Grinning Assassin really was until you came to the Harpy's Chest."

"I read about an assassin that could slip into places no one else could. The Grinning Assassin who had this ability to find and kill difficult targets, and gain hard to come by information," he said. "I told Uriah about what I wanted to do, and he thought it was a terrible idea. It took a while to search for you. It seemed as though most information about you was incorrect. I didn't know that they had listed you as deceased until I got to Grasdan."

Serein rolled her eyes. "You chased after a ghost for a flawed and dangerous plan," she said.

Worry crept across his face. "Will you help me with this?" Rameses asked, holding onto the question, afraid to let it go. "I apologize for not being truthful with you, but I'm being honest with you now. No one else can know why you're really here."

Sparse clouds rolled across the sky, casting thin shadows. *Death waits at the end of this path. There are too many moving pieces and uncertainties,* she thought.

You've been given an opportunity to stalk your enemy. The prince won't ask questions if you vanish. He's someone you can manipulate, Xansas said. *You'll be able to uncover all the bloody truths and present them to the prince so that by the end, he'll beg you to kill his father.*

Serein shuddered at how much the voice sounded like her own. "For six years, I'm to serve as your eyes and ears, figuring out what your father's been doing and bring you the proof?" she asked, staring out at the water. *Six years on the edge of a knife, awaiting death if I misstep.*

Rameses threw the rock into the water with an opaque purple *plop*. "If it turns out that I'm overreacting, you will still get your freedom, serving as my guard. I will not ask you to do more than that."

The dark cell loomed again in Serein's mind, Sethos' words like bloodstains on the walls. Orange and blue voices danced at the end of the dark tunnel, twisting her heart.

"For the sake of my freedom, I'll help you," Serein said. *If this is how I'm to survive this place, so be it.*

Rameses' face broke into a smile. "Thank you," he said, reaching for a chunk of chicken.

Uriah's red hair blazed underneath his keffiyeh, contrasting with the green trees and grassy slopes behind him. He kept glancing over as he paced around his horse. "Do I need to worry about Captain Stormheir?" *He's already suspicious of me. If he knows the extent of what I'm doing, he may decide that I'm too much of a threat to be left alone.*

"No. Uriah knows I don't fully trust my father, but he would not help me because of his oath as a member of the city guard. He serves my father first even though we are friends, which I don't begrudge him for. Still, he will not say anything about this."

"What of Ilderim or your other guards? Who else knows about this?"

"Only you, Ilderim, and Uriah know, although Uriah doesn't know the specifics," Rameses told her. "Ilderim left the Malik's Guard to be my wali when I was eleven. He has been with me most of my life, so I trust him completely. I think he also senses things are wrong."

"Have you told me everything?" Serein asked, fixing Rameses with a stare.

He met her gaze. "Yes."

Serein examined his every blink and inhale. The familiar features of Sethos on Rameses' face made her stomach twist. "What will you do with what you learn?"

Rameses sighed, shoulders slumping. "I don't know yet..." he muttered. "I'm not looking to hurt my father, just look into what's really going on with the war."

"When do you want me to start?" *The prince hasn't fully considered what will happen as a result of his actions. The captain may side with Rameses if he decides to take the throne, but he may be forced to turn against his friend if something happens before that. If Rameses does nothing, then I will,* she thought.

"Always so quick to the point," Rameses said with a breathy chuckle as he finished off the remaining rice with his last piece of bread. "A few weeks as my guard should make you a familiar presence. Observe my father in meetings whenever you can. Then you can start looking for information on your own. The diffa tomorrow night will be a good chance for you to listen to gossip and see many of the familiar faces of my father's court."

Serein's mouth settled in a hard line. *He lied about his true intentions before. There has to be a larger endgame to this plan.*

"How did you end up in Grasdan?" Rameses asked.

The bitterness bloomed, reaching toward the hatred bubbling over. Dead soldiers littered the ground. Cold chains and painful blows. Yellow screaming and stinging tears as everything was wrenched away, her heart tearing as she was hauled away.

Serein blinked as the churning waters of her memories calmed, settling back in the dark depths. "I made a mistake," she replied in a quiet voice.

Rameses sat up straighter. "What mistake?"

"One question."

He sighed. "I guess the mistake proves that you're human and not a monster."

"If stories have taught us anything, it's that even monsters make mistakes," Serein told him. *And that they can be killed.*

A band of white the length of Serein's forearm slithered from underneath a pile of stones near Rameses, and her blood ran cold. Two ruby eyes sat in its diamond-shaped head, tongue flicking out.

A bone viper.

She imagined the fangs sinking into Rameses' skin and his body writhing in pain. Blood oozing out from the orifices, his screams drowning as he choked. No one survived longer than an hour.

Serein grabbed Rameses by his collar and yanked him back, food scattering from his container as it fell from his grip. She drove her dagger through the serpent's skull as it coiled its slender body. It thrashed as she twisted the knife, red seeping over the bone-white scales.

"What the hell?!" Rameses shouted, gold arrows stabbing into Serein's back.

"What's going on?" Green thunder rumbled across Serein's vision as Uriah and Ilderim ran up.

"Are you all right, Your Highness?" Ilderim asked, his ocher question wrapping around Rameses as he helped him stand.

"Yes. Saints, Serein! What was that for?" Rameses breathed, eyes wide.

The snake's blood flecked her hand, dangling from the end of the blade. "Doing my duty, Your Highness," Serein replied, the scent of coppery blood hitting her nose.

"A bone viper. That's a rare sight," Ilderim said, staring at the serpent. "They tend to dwell in the Old Kingdom's southern region."

The corpse slid off into the lake as she angled the weapon

downward. *It's a bad sign. Is* he *on the move?* Serein thought, the dead eyes of the snake boring into her as it sank beneath the surface.

THE NIGHT AIR KISSED SEREIN'S SWEATY SKIN, WRAPPING HER UP in velvet quiet. She spun on the balls of her feet, daggers slashing with whistling orange streaks. *It was only a snake,* she thought and finished the stances. *I'm too on edge about this "plan" Rameses has and with Sethos watching me. This will be very different from the missions I've done before, where I could complete them and be done. Now, I won't be able to escape into the shadows.*

Boots crunched against the sandy ground in gray crests, rolling up to her ankles. Serein turned, daggers raised. Uriah's usual armor was replaced by a dark tunic and sirwal, his scimitar hanging at his side. The stone pendant rested against his chest. Firelight from the torch he held pooled around his boots.

"What are you doing out here?" Uriah asked. The verdant brusqueness didn't carry its usual edge.

"Training. Rameses' dinner with the princess ran longer than expected," she said. *Not wearing his usual armor. His guard's down a bit,* she thought, wiping the sweat off her upper lip.

"Rameses told you about his plan," he said, and the outline of a scowl shadowed his face. "Are you helping Rameses because you despise the Malik?"

"I agreed because I get my freedom when this is over. That's what I care about." Serein held his stare. "This must be difficult for you. Caught between helping your friend and upholding your loyalty to your king."

"It's my duty to serve His Majesty. Even if Rameses is my friend...I can't betray the Malik's trust in me." Uriah lowered his voice as his shoulders tensed.

"Best leave traitorous deeds to those of us with black hearts, right?" The dagger spun through the air. "While I'd love to go into detail about your life, I'd like to finish training."

Uriah shifted, jaw muscles tight. "Wait," he said, and she stopped, looking back at him. "I...I wanted to apologize. You saved Rameses' life."

Serein arched an eyebrow. "You seem to be struggling with the words 'thank you' and 'I'm sorry,'" she said.

Purple-blue sparks popped as the flames guttered. Uriah glared at her, color creeping into his face. He turned and left, the light following him.

She returned to the stances as darkness pressed around her. *The less hostile the captain is, the less likely he is to get in my way. Slow steps. Move the pieces carefully. I'll uncover what the king is hiding. I'll use every last one of his sins as a knife to bring him down.*

Chapter Nineteen
Masquerades & Lies

SEREIN LOUNGED ON THE MAJLIS, THE LIGHT OF THE LAMPS spilling over the book in her hand. Sunset coated the sky orange and pink, throwing shadows across the tea glass on the table. Rizwana straightened things in the bedchamber, humming a lapis-colored song under her breath.

It's almost been a month since Grasdan. Only seventy-two more until I'm free, she thought as she turned a yellowed page, working through the Sarddonian script as the dry sentences ran together. *The prince has interesting tastes in literature. A romantic. This book has too much flowery prose. An odd choice to pair with the philosophy of Abdullah al-Halabi, the tragedy of Fingrad, and the sagas of Khalid.*

The mouse scurried along the edge of the majlis, pausing to clean itself. Its pointed nose twitched and long whiskers moved. Serein reached out and touched the mouse, running a finger along its soft back.

"You must live well in this palace. Best not let Rizwana see you," Serein whispered. "I used to eat your cousins in Grasdan. They'd try to gnaw off my fingers and toes while I slept. It was nothing personal. I was starving."

Orange footsteps appeared underneath the door crack, and a

dark blue knock sent the mouse scurrying. "Serein?" Rameses' golden voice asked. "Are you awake?"

"Yes," she replied with a sigh.

Rameses stepped in, wearing a white and gold qamis. An indigo mantle flowed over his shoulders, his hair swept back under a navy-colored turban. Ilderim and another other wali, I'timad, waited in the hallway, wearing shiny bronze lion masks.

Rizwana peered into the living chamber, straightening. "Your Highness!" she said, bowing. "Let me get you some tea."

He turned to her, smiling. "Thank you, Rizwana. I will not be staying long," he told her. "You look comfortable," Rameses added to Serein.

Serein saw a shadow move in the doorway where Rameses left the door ajar. "You look like you're being strangled," she replied.

The peach chimes from the bell earrings spilled over Rameses' shoulders. "I enjoy parties, but my mother's name day tends to be a stifling affair. She gets stressed about small details not being right that she forgets to enjoy herself."

Pulling a cushion over, Rameses sat across from Serein. He turned a black and gold mask shaped like a pointy-eared hound over in his hand. He held a second mask shaped like an owl's head, the gold filigree glittering against the blue and white paint.

"So why are you sitting alone in your chambers rather than being at the feast?" Rameses asked, looking at the books on the shelf to the one in her hand. "I'm all for an evening of reading, but I thought giving you the night off would encourage you to attend the party. I even had Rizwana prepare a kaftan for you."

"My idea of fun is very different from yours," Serein said. *I planned to sneak around while everyone was distracted by the feast. Parties are too noisy and colorful. I'll probably get a headache.*

Rizwana set out another glass and held the tea kettle high over the glass as she filled it. Mint leaves floated beneath the foamy top. Rameses nodded to her and took the glass, sipping it.

"It's a masquerade party," he went on. "Everyone will be wearing masks. Why pass up an opportunity to observe and gather information without being recognized? Before you glare at me, I already have a kaftan for you. It's only for a night, Serein."

She rolled her eyes. "I assume you won't be taking no for an answer?" *This book is heavy enough to stun him if I hit him in the head just right. Might knock some sense into him,* Serein thought, closing the book.

He smiled. "I have been known to be persistent. A royal diffa isn't something to miss. If nothing else, the food's always good."

Serein uncrossed her legs and sat up. "With that convincing argument, how can I say no?"

"Don't make it sound like I'm twisting your arm. You might even enjoy yourself a bit tonight," Rameses said, his beard crinkling as he smiled.

Hard to enjoy myself when spies will be watching and that one wrong step could land me in a cell, she thought. *This party may be a good way to gather information.*

"Rizwana," Rameses said, looking at the maidservant, "would you please show Serein the kaftan?"

Rizwana straightened. "Yes, Your Highness," she said, ducking back into the bedchamber.

As Serein stood, she caught a glimpse of Rasima's face behind the open door before the girl ducked out of sight. "Do you want to invite your sister in, or is she going to lurk in the hallway?" Serein asked, setting the book aside.

"My sister?" Rameses repeated, blinking.

Serein headed for the bedchamber. "Yes, the one who's been eavesdropping outside the door."

RAMESES STOOD, BROW CREASED. *WHY WOULD RASIMA BE HERE? SHE should already be in the audience hall with our parents,* he thought and crossed the chamber in long strides.

Rasima jumped away from the door as he opened it, eyes wide behind her silver antelope half-mask. Her dark purple headscarf matched her white and lilac-colored abaya. Henna covered her hands in dark floral patterns. The thin circlet with four tiny bells on her head jingled as she moved. Her wali, Karam, and handmaiden, Laia, stood nearby with lion masks on.

"Rasima? You should be with Umm at the party already," Rameses said, staring at his sister. *Umm might start panicking if she cannot find Rasima. She would have a fit if she knew Rasi was visiting Serein. She's already stressed enough.*

"I told her I would be arriving with you, akhun," Rasima replied. "I-uh I wanted to see her—Serein."

Rameses leaned his arm against the doorframe. "Why?"

Rasima crossed her arms. He could almost see her frown hidden under the scarf covering her face. "You get to see her, so why am I not allowed to?" she protested.

Sighing, Rameses smiled. "I have no problem with it, but our parents would not be happy that you're here. They're not fond of Serein," Rameses said. His fingers brushed the bells of Rasima's circlet as he patted her head, sending ribbons of delicate peach streaming down her headscarf.

"Then I will have to be better about making sure they don't find out," Rasima said and swatted his hand away, peering past him.

Following Rasima's gaze, Rameses stared at Serein dressed in the kaftan and wearing a pair of satin slippers. Sapphires were sewn into the blue material, sparkling as she moved. The white headscarf made her tawny skin stand out. Her kohl-rimmed eyes were sharp, the scars across her face worn like jewelry.

Intimidating and refined, Rameses thought, clearing his throat. *She would give me a death glare if I voiced that thought aloud.*

"Not much for words tonight, prince?" Serein asked, pulling at the sleeves over the bangles.

He held out the owl-shaped half mask to her. She took it, turning it over in her hand. "What can I say? Sometimes even I'm left speechless. Shall we get going?" Rameses asked, offering his arm to her.

"Are you asking me to break your arm?" Serein asked as Rizwana gave a nervous cough.

"I would prefer that my arm remains in one piece," Rameses said, tying the mask around his face. *This will be harder than I thought. Seems we still have a long way to go.*

Serein glanced at Rasima as she stepped into the hallway. The ground beneath her feet groaned, faint cracks appearing. Her bangles grew heavier under the kaftan's cuffs. The sharpened pieces of bone were tucked into a broken seam along the inside of her sleeves.

"You look pretty, Serein," Rasima said, violet words blooming around her.

"Thank you. I prefer a tunic and trousers to a dress," Serein replied, keeping her words stiff.

The wali followed behind them as they left the tower. "My mother would never let me wear clothing like that," Rasima said, her green footfalls light as bird wings on the steps. "Have you been to a diffa before?"

Their voices mixed in the hallway, the polished floors reflecting the melted lantern light. "Not one this large, but I've been to parties before," Serein told her. *But they always ended in death.*

The corridor opened to the entryway with the two split staircases winding upward to a second floor. Music floated around the corner in threads of fiery red, thrumming chartreuse, and luminous yellow. The larger doors on the first floor stood open as partygoers entered the audience hall, voices bouncing off the high ceiling. Guards wore matching lion masks, faces hidden behind the gilded muzzles.

Peals of laughter filtered through the audience hall amidst the colorful notes of the thin-necked ouds, ney flutes, and small kamanchehs. Tombaks hung at the musicians' sides, hands drawing out lively emerald beats from the small drums. Santurs sang marigold tones from their stringed bodies. The music spun together with living colors. People danced and wandered the edges of the hall, their fine clothing resembling bright plumage. Grinning mouths hung under masks.

The polished floor reflected the decorated ceiling like a still pool. Columns grew upward, reliefs of plants and animals inlaid with pink marble. Twenty large windows with tiled ogee-shaped arches lined the walls, geometric-patterned screens letting the night air in. Light glittered from the hanging lanterns.

The smooth wood pressed against Serein's skin as she attached the mask to her face. "Tonight, you can be whoever you want," Rameses said as he stood beside her. "When you wear a mask, the world's yours."

. . .

RAMESES HAD BEEN SWEPT AWAY BY A GROUP OF NOBLEMEN WHILE Rasima was flocked by several court women ready to escort her back to her mother. Serein disappeared into the crowds, observing the different people moving around the edge of the room—men in turbans and qamis, women in flowing kaftans and abayas, and guests from across Cemiyon mingling together.

Your first mission was at a party like this. Do you remember it? You wore a dress then. The white words broke through the mass of colors.

A chill ran through Serein as Xansas Regor's voice crept in, growing louder. She headed for the food table. Three golden cakes rested on silver trays, light reflecting on the gold leaf. *These must be the golden cakes. Tempting, but they'll be too sweet for me,* Serein thought, drifting to the savory dishes.

Sethos moved about the hall, wearing a golden lion mask. She stopped, stomach twisting.

A shard of glass to the throat. Right across the jugular. Or I could break his neck, she thought as the black beast stirred. *My little bones would only maim him.*

Lujayn hovered at Sethos' side with a silver filigree lioness mask on her face. On her head was a silver crown made of twelve leaves with a large green stone resting in the center sat on her head, six white teardrop gems on delicate chains hanging from the sides. Rahim held her henna-covered hand as he stared out from behind his blue elephant mask. Rasima had broken away to speak with a group of girls and a few court ladies in a far corner of the room. Some of the girls' faces were hidden behind colored veils.

Serein turned away, keeping to the edge of the crowds. *Perhaps I'll become someone different tonight,* she thought. *A noblewoman who's never contemplated killing. One who enjoys food and secrets. Find those with loose lips and listen.*

Uriah came into view, scanning the hall. The roaring lion on the back of his cape rippled. A simple, wooden bear-shaped half mask was pushed off his face as he spoke with a man next to him. The man wore a matching cape, his short hair sandy blond and skin a soft brown color. He gestured with his hands, fingers moving quickly. Uriah nodded as he spoke.

That must be Lieutenant Firoz, Serein thought. *Best avoid them. The captain will draw too much attention to me if he spots me.*

A heavyset man in an emerald qamis with white trim approached her. Small gold disks around his turban swayed as he moved. A silver horse mask with delicate green leaves painted across it covered the upper half of his face.

"Good evening, sayyida," he said in a coffee-brown voice, squinting at her. "May I ask your husband or brother for permission for you to dance?"

"My apologies, sayyidi," she replied, covering her mouth with her hand as she raised the cadence of her voice. "I have no husband here. And my brother-in-law went off with some...female company. Should I go find him?"

"It's normally customary, but tonight it can be our secret," the man said. "Your accent is from the Old Kingdom, but your Sarddonian is excellent. I'm Hasim Jafar al-Ziadeh."

The gold ring shaped like a horse's head with two ruby eyes around his finger winked at her. A pale green and cream-colored haya bracelet wrapped around his right wrist, marked with a black bead next to three green stone beads and an amber-colored one.

"Yes, you're correct. I hear that you breed the finest horses in Sarddon." *Head of the al-Ziadeh family. Fifty-seven. Supplies horses to the king's armies, which has made him very wealthy. A widower since his haya has a black bead. Three sons and a daughter. The shakrban of the city of Alwadi a few miles outside of Oyon. I remember his second cousin's life was worth a lot nine years ago.*

"You praise me too much," Hasim said with a laugh. "May I have this dance, sayyida...?"

"Lady Accalia Lycaon," Serein said, batting her eyelashes. *Let's see if this noble has any interesting information to share. Time to make up a story since I doubt he'd want to dance with me if I said I've killed people.*

He held out his hand to Serein. "Lady Accalia."

Serein took his hand, skin prickling. She didn't pull away as she let him guide her into the group of dancers. People raised their wrists, barely touching as they waited for the next dance to start.

Flitting, fiery red notes of the kamanchehs' strings came in, and the couples moved in slow circles around their partners.

"Are you and your husband friends of the Malika's?" Hasim asked as he moved in time with Serein.

"I have no husband, sayyidi. I'm a widow, you see," Serein said, letting hesitation creep into her voice as it tapered off. *Saying I'm a widow will cause him to let his guard down. He might be more willing to talk if he thinks he can sympathize with me.*

From behind the mask, Hasim's dark eyes softened. "My deepest apologies. Who was your husband?"

"Renatus Lycaon."

He squinted. "Forgive me, but I haven't heard of that name before."

"A great lord like you wouldn't have heard of us. The Lycaon household is a small noble family in the Denathon region in the eastern part of the Old Kingdom," she said, keeping her voice light. "My husband had a few mines that produced a special type of ore only found in the Old Kingdom. Aithril. It makes the sharpest blades next to Sarlyrian steel."

"How did Lord Renatus depart from you?" Hasim asked.

Serein slowed, hand trembling as she fell out of time with the dance. "It was three years ago. We were riding to the edge of the Zhire Forest when a pack of wolves attacked. When Ren tried to rescue me, his horse threw him. The beasts fell upon him. I can still hear his screams..." Her voice caught in her throat, and she bit her lip. *This story might be too gruesome for him. Still, tragedy makes for good storytelling.*

"If it's too painful, sayyida, you don't need to finish," Hasim told her.

The partners moved closer, arms twined, and hands clasped. "No, I'm fine," she sniffed. Hasim's arm bumped the bangle, and his gaze went to her wrist. "They're prayer bangles for the Lights." Serein's fingers wrapped around it. *Thankfully, he's farsighted and can't see things up close well.*

"Your faith keeps you strong," Hasim said, head bobbing.

Serein gathered her breath to continue. "I tried to fend off the wolves and escape into the woods. My horse ran for hours until it expired, and I was tangled in the saddle. I managed to cut myself free but was hopelessly lost and injured. I don't remember much before some merchants found me and took me to a temple. The acolytes said I was unconscious for days. It wasn't until I was well enough that they told me...told me what happened to Renatus," she whispered. "I knew, but I needed to hear it."

"Sometimes, the truth does more to help us than the bliss of lies. I am saddened that you had to suffer so much at such a young age," Hasim said, patting her hand.

She caught a glimpse of Uriah's red hair as Hasim spun her around. Rameses stood beside him, laughing. Uriah cracked a smile underneath his mask. *So, he* does *know how to smile. I wonder if it's painful for him,* she thought.

"Is something the matter, Lady Accalia?" Hasim asked.

"My apologies. My brother-in-law says I'm easily distracted," Serein replied and looked back at Hasim. "I can't seem to stay focused anymore..."

Hasim gave a small smile. "After my Marwa passed away, I had a hard time focusing on anything. I still find myself staring into the spaces where she once was," he said, his coffee-colored voice smooth. "How did you survive such an ordeal?"

Serein looked down as Uriah glanced at the crowd. "To be honest, sayyidi, I didn't want to come tonight. I haven't been in a festive mood for a long time. My brother-in-law insisted I stop wearing mourning clothes. The Malik invited him, so they could discuss opening a new mine here in Sarddon."

"They say time assuages grief, but it tends to only bury it for a while. It's been almost twelve years, and I still feel the loss of my Marwa keenly," he said, touching his bracelet. "Thirty years felt like no time at all with her."

"I'm sure your sons will continue to carry on your legacy and aid in the war efforts," Serein said. "Sarddon wouldn't be achieving such victories without your excellent horses."

Hasim coughed as his smile stiffened. "Hopefully, this war will end soon," he said. "We've had some of our horses stolen from different estates over the past few months by rebels. It's not enough to ruin us, but it's worrisome."

"Oh, I'm sorry to hear that. I wasn't aware the rebels had made it that far into Sarddon." *Stealing horses. Interesting. That's a risky operation for just a few mounts. Then again, the al-Ziadeh family owns over three thousand horses, and he governs a key city near the Gold Road. There might be more going on,* Serein thought.

"Some days I pray for things to return to how they were before the war," Hasim added, his voice quiet.

"Do you think things were better before?" Serein asked quietly, watching his expression.

His gaze darted past her, hesitating. "The loss of magic and the former Malik has shifted things out of balance. I worry what will happen if magic disappears forever," he muttered. "You're from the Old Kingdom, so you must mourn the loss of your people's culture."

Serein lowered her eyes, keeping her voice a whisper. "Yes, it's a tragedy. So many innocent lives were lost to that terrible plague. Still, wasn't the war justified after the assassination of Malik Salman and the attempts to kill Malik Sethos?" *He doesn't seem to be in favor of the war even though it has increased his wealth. Does he sympathize with the rebels?*

"The loss of Malik Salman was saddening. Thank the Saints that Sethos survived. However, when you get to be my age, it's best to not reminisce on what once was and just enjoy the present moment."

"You hardly look a day over twenty, sayyidi," Serein told him with a pale-yellow chuckle.

"You're too kind, sayyida," Hasim said, smiling. "I have lived a full life. You're young, so you have your whole life ahead of you. You shouldn't waste it in widow's clothes."

"I would say the same thing about you. 'A man only stops living when he gives up pursuing joy.' My husband told me used to tell me that," she said through a painted smile.

The corners of Hasim's eyes crinkled. "Your husband was a very wise man. I hope you don't find this too forward, but I'm glad you're here. It's been a while since I've had someone to talk to like this. Especially someone so pretty."

"You can't mean that. I'm scarred...and most would call me ugly or recoil in horror."

"There is so much more to a woman than having flawless skin.

Your scars tell of the struggles you have overcome," Hasim told her. "There is beauty in that strength."

If you only saw the others, you wouldn't smile. "Thank you," Serein said, bringing tears to her eyes. "I'm afraid I'm not very good company, sayyidi."

"Nonsense. I have enjoyed talking to you. No one seems to have time for an old man like me besides my daughter. I haven't been able to talk about my wife in such a long time."

The music wound down, and the dancers slowed. Uriah moved around the room, looking over the faces. "I'd love to hear more about her, sayyidi, but I'm afraid this dance has exhausted me," Serein told him, the last fiery red and marigold notes wiggling inside her mask.

Hasim let go of her hand and walked with her toward a long table with food and cushions. "My apologies. Please, sit down. I'll get you something to drink," he told her, trying to find a servant.

A man dressed in dark brown and gray robes approached Hasim, mouth set in a grim line underneath a metallic fox mask.

"Excuse me, sayyida," Hasim said. "It seems I have some business to attend to. I'll be back as soon as I can."

Serein's smile vanished as Hasim walked away, vanishing into the crowd. *The stranger bearing unfavorable news. Intriguing. I'll have to see what else I can get from him,* she thought, snatching a warm mutabbaq from a platter on the table before following after Hasim.

Chapter Twenty
Dancing with Danger

Drunken gossip drifted from the women lounging on maroon cushions as Serein tucked herself into a small alcove, eating and listening. Hasim and the masked man stood in the far corner, voices low and postures huddled.

The idle chatter of the nobles. So many affairs, midnight rendezvous, and dangerous dealings. Sounds like one of the princeling's novels, Serein thought, taking a bite of the flaky mutabbaq, the smell of garlic and lemony sumac wafting up from the lamb filling. *I'll have to get closer if I want to hear what they're saying, but it's risky with so many people around. Perhaps I can convince the shahrban to go to someplace quieter, see what else he's willing to talk about.*

Hasim's mouth was pressed in a worried line, the other man's face turned away. She caught a few of the shahrban's coffee-brown words. *Too risky. New plans. Need to know more.*

A guard walked by, and Serein lowered her head. Servants wearing white lion masks darted around with silver trays of fragrant wines in colorfully painted ceramic cups, others refilling the empty patters on the food table with sizzling meats and spiced rice dishes. Sethos and Lujayn passed around the edge of the room, greeting people as masked guards followed them. Rasima trailed behind her parents with Rahim beside her, Rameses nowhere to be seen. Serein thought she spotted a golden jackal mask, but it vanished in the crowds.

I haven't seen Il-Makah around. No doubt he's here. Wonder if his little spy is watching.

Peach-tinged ringing slipped around the column, and she sighed through her nose. "This is a party," Rameses said, appearing around the corner, "so why are you by yourself, Serein?"

The women turned at the sound of his voice, moths drawn to a golden light. They blushed and hid behind their hands as they bowed. Rameses waved, smiling. Ilderim and I'timad waited a few feet away. Their polished lion masks reflected the swirling colors of the room.

"You must have mistaken me for someone else, sayyidi," Serein said with a bow. "I'm Lady Accalia Lycaon." *I was hoping to avoid him for at least another hour,* she thought, eyes darting back to Hasim. *I'll have to find Hasim later.*

"Seems you decided to take my advice," Rameses said, smirking. "Very well, *Lady Accalia.* Would you care to dance?"

"I'm afraid I don't dance, Your Highness," she told him, finishing her food.

"Really? I thought I saw you dancing earlier with a nobleman, or was I hallucinating?"

"It seemed rude to tell him no. I'd hardly call it dancing. Just a distraction to keep me from getting bored," Serein said.

"I see. Would you join me for choreographed movements set to music to kill our boredom then?" Rameses asked, holding out his hand to her.

"Aren't you clever? How can I say no to the prince?" *It would've been better to have come as a guard. At least then I wouldn't have to dance.*

"You have done it plenty of times with less civility."

I'll have to track Hasim down later once the prince is gone, she thought, eyes darting to the corner where the two men had been.

They moved to the dance floor. Rameses placed a hand on her waist and took her left hand, holding it up at eye level. "This dance is from Edolas, with some Sarddonian movements thrown in, so it's livelier than the traditional dances. My mother prefers it over some of the classical ones," he said. "Do you know any Ravanassë dances?"

"I didn't have much time for dancing. I learned only what I needed for missions," Serein said as her skin crawled under Rameses touch, the heat from his palm seeping through the kaftan's fabric.

"I see." He inclined his head. "So, how did you make up a name like Accalia Lycaon?"

"The Lycaon house *is* from the Old Kingdom." *Although I doubt anyone with that name is still alive.*

The music changed, sweeping up the dancers in a slow melody. The swirls of gold in Rameses' mask glittered under the lantern light. "I would love to hear more about this amicable Lady Accalia," he said. "How are you enjoying my mother's diffa?"

"There are a lot of colors, and I haven't had the chance to sample everything on the food tables," Serein replied, the ache behind her eyes growing.

The world rushed by as Rameses spun her around, pale-yellow and gold words twisting like fluttering ribbons. She caught sight of the jackal mask again from across the room.

Serein's stomach tightened. *Will Sethos decide to lock me up for dancing with his son?* she thought. *At least three Golden Jackals. How many others are watching me?*

"Is something on your mind?"

Serein met Rameses' gaze, the figure disappearing into the crowds, but the unease of their presence lingered. "I was thinking how easy it would be to kill everyone in this room," she told him. "Does that make you uncomfortable?"

The muscles in Rameses' shoulder stiffened under her fingers. "A bit, but I'm interested about how you would go about doing that without being caught," he said.

She leaned in. "Did you ever hear about the unfortunate shahrban Khalil al-Ajlani of Thanab?" Serein asked. "Fifteen noblemen suddenly dropped dead."

"I heard about that. It happened almost ten years ago," Rameses said under his breath. "They called it the Black Dance. The survivors said the shahrban and his guests were coughing up black. Was that your doing? How did you manage to kill almost half of the partygoers?"

"A single touch was all it took. And a bit of Shuyì on some gloves."

"I'm not familiar with what Shuyì is."

"It's a nasty one. Quick absorption through the skin and takes about two hours to thicken the blood and turn it black, causing a person to suffocate." Rameses glanced at her hands, thumb twitching. "There are too many people here, so Shuyì wouldn't be effective."

"As fascinating as this conversation is, I think we should discuss something else. It *is* a party after all," Rameses said with a chuckle.

"Here I thought my topics of discussion would excite you," Serein said. "You said my stories are too boring."

A crescendo hit, luminous yellow and marigold chords vibrating against her skin. Rameses took a step back and spun her around. "Another time," he said as he pulled her back toward him. "I noticed you were reading some of the books I lent you. How are they?"

"Where did you find such *thrilling* reads?" Serein asked.

"Judging by your sarcasm, you don't seem to have enjoyed them. I first found *Twelve Moons at Dusk* and *The Twisted Boughs* in the back of the library when I was a child and took them. I had never read anything like that before and have loved them ever since. The others I discovered over the years," he told her with a grin.

"You're a prince *and* a thief," Serein said.

"I could not help it. And I didn't steal most of my books. Did you enjoy any of the ones I lent you?"

"Not particularly. The one on the philosophy of war was only a pompous author spouting his opinions. I'm finding it hard to get into *The Twisted Boughs*. You must think I'm secretly a romantic if you suggested that and *Twelve Moons at Dusk*."

His eyes widened. "I thought you would be dying to get your hands on some literature. You struck me as one who reads," Rameses said. "*Twisted Boughs* is one of my favorites."

"I don't enjoy reading fiction for pleasure. Historical texts are very important. Fiction's less practical in my line of work."

Rameses spun Serein around in time with the music. "You didn't enjoy the other book then? I thought Quasim wrote *Twelve Moons at Dusk* very well."

"He may have written it, but his wife gave him the idea and told him how it should be written." Rameses' movements slowed. "The women are written with great insight into female behavior, not to mention that the main character is female," Serein told him.

The skirts of the kaftan brushed against the floor as Serein and Rameses mirrored took two steps back. She scanned the couples around them, feeling unseen eyes.

"A woman pining for a nobleman, but because of the class difference, she can't approach him, so she tricks him into thinking she's nobility," Serein continued. "I'll admit that there was some depth to it. Quasim mentions his wife in great length in the dedication."

"I will need to reread it and pay closer attention," Rameses said. "Do you secretly desire a lover of a higher class? Or perhaps you have already seduced some lord?"

"Is that your question?" she asked.

Rameses let go of her hand as the music slowed, a faint sheen of sweat accumulating on the hollow of his throat. "No. I have a few other questions lined up," he replied as she turned to leave. "What? Exhausted already?"

"Spinning around in circles is tedious. No wonder the upper class is prone to affairs and dark games. I wouldn't trade my bare head for your shackled crown."

"Expectations of perfection are more stressful than mundane. Sometimes it makes one want to do something scandalous to remind people that you're only human. Heavy is the crown," Rameses said, following her as she left the dance floor.

A servant passed by with a tray of chilled wine, and Rameses grabbed two cups. Serein stared at the drink offered to her, shaking her head. *I need to see if I can find Hasim again. Or at least find someone else with interesting secrets,* she thought.

A woman sauntered over in a red abaya and a white headscarf. She slipped her arm around Rameses' as he turned. "I've been looking everywhere for you, Your Highness," she said, her ginger-colored voice warm.

"Yasmine," Rameses said with a smile, voice dropping low as he kissed her cheek. His fingers brushed the inside of her wrist.

"Father's hinting that we should meet with you about his newest trading venture. The black peppercorn and saffron crops from the Three Sister Mountains have been bountiful this year, and there's been an increasing demand for them from Sinabrac and Edolas," Yasmine told Rameses as she ran a finger down his wrist. "We may even be able to expand our cacao trade."

Delicate gold chains draped around the woman's head, a single opal hanging against her forehead. Her cinnamon-brown eyes were rimmed with kohl, appearing through the eyeholes of her carved gazelle mask. The woman's turmeric-colored haya bracelet had twenty-four copper bands along it. Her fingertips were stained a dark color, and the strong smell of cardamon and pepper wafted off her.

This must be one of the women Rameses has been sleeping with, Serein thought. *Right-handed. Twenty-four. Confident. Spends a lot of time with spices due to the stains on her fingers. Spice merchant. A woman who knows how to run a business and get what she wants.*

Rameses gave Yasmine a knowing look. "Are you sure the meeting is his idea, or are you wanting to put forth more of *your* trade ideas?"

Yasmine smiled. "He has the vision, and I have the insight to make it a reality. Our last venture to open up the Bronze Route to the western coast of Ginjarr has benefited both Sarddon and my father's company. He's received several offers from prominent merchants in Zhao to expand and set up permanent markets there."

"I will be sure to speak with him before the night's over." Rameses gestured to Serein. "This is Serein, my new wali."

Yasmine's gaze flicked to Serein, staring at the scars along Serein's face. "The woman guard. You're shorter than I thought you'd be," Yasmine said.

"I'm not what a lot of people were expecting," Serein replied.

Yasmine took the second glass of wine from Rameses. "Many don't expect a woman to defy expectations. People are always surprised when we do."

Rameses leaned in closer to Yasmine, touching her arm. "Give me a moment. I will join you in a little bit. I promise," he whispered.

"Don't keep me waiting too long again, or I might share my ideas with someone else," Yasmine said, the crowds of shifting partygoers swallowing her up in a sea of bright clothes and glittering jewels.

Rameses' gaze followed Yasmine as he sipped his wine. "Is she one of the scandalous things you engage with to stave off boredom?" Serein asked.

"That was Yasmine al-Bashar," he replied. "We attended the House of Knowledge together. Her family has built a spice empire over the past few decades. She's working to take the business over when her father retires."

"Which lover is she?" Serein asked. *He's not hiding their relationship well, so it must be common knowledge. Or Sethos must keep it quiet since I haven't heard any of the servants whispering about it,* she thought.

"Why do you assume I have more than one?" Rameses replied, and Serein arched an eyebrow. "I don't have *that* many."

"Did you seek her out because of her beauty and wit?"

Rameses gestured for Serein to follow him to a plush seating area by the nearby windows. "Yasmine's the one who approached *me*," Rameses told her as Ilderim and I'timad walked behind them. "My family might consider it scandalous, but her parents think differently. They come from the desert tribes who have more openminded views on relationships and sexuality than most Sarddonians."

"So, you have no feelings for her beyond physical attraction?"

"Not romantically, but we enjoy each other's company. Yasmine made it clear that she only wanted a physical relationship. She has her eyes set on aspirations beyond me." Rameses sat down against the green cushions. "The women I have engaged with over the years have their own aspirations. I try to learn about their dreams, likes, and dislikes because I enjoy learning about their lives."

Serein remained standing, ignoring passing stares. Rameses' wali stationed themselves at the nearby columns. "Yasmine isn't using you for her own gain?"

"She probably is, but she doesn't need me to be successful. Her successes have been accomplished through her own hard work and ingenuity. I don't doubt that she will expand the trade empire her father has built."

"I thought you were a romantic considering the books you read," Serein said. "Your views on relationships seem to be the opposite."

"Oh. I am. I believe in love and deep emotional connections. Someday I hope to have a love like what my parents have, but I don't think the relationships I have now are meaningless. I know it's only a matter of time before a marriage is arranged," Rameses said, the golden humor in his voice dimming. "I suspect my mother will decide a match whether I say yes to it or not. Political marriages are about creating the best match to bring prosperity and unity. They tend to leave little room for feelings."

Serein spotted Sethos and Lujayn across the room, side by side. The man who had stood over corpses clashed with the one who walked white halls, smiling at his wife. Sethos' curving mouth barely broke his stony features, but the faint creases of dimples were visible. His hand rested on Rahim's small shoulder as the boy showed him a toy lion.

The taste of fruit soured on Serein's tongue. *Smiling? That monster can smile?* she thought. *Hard to imagine that he's capable of love.*

"So, what do you want to do with your life, Serein?" Rameses asked.

"Maybe take up farming or something quiet in the woods. A simple life," Serein replied, watching people moving through the audience hall.

Rameses cocked his head to the side. "Farming? Really? Not a painter?" he said with a laugh. "I cannot tell if you're being serious. Perhaps Uriah can offer you some advice."

"He'd tell me to dig a very deep hole in a field and to bury myself in it," she said.

"Surely you might want something more exciting?" Rameses asked. "You have traveled and seen so much, so I'm sure you must want to see more of the world."

"I've had enough excitement for one lifetime." *Escaping from here and going someplace where I won't be hunted where we won't be hunted, my Sun and Stars.* The image of a quiet house in the woods bathed in sunset-orange and sky-blue laughter appeared before it vanished.

"You sound like an old man. I cannot imagine you farming or doing anything like that. My guess is that you will become a famous painter or a traveling storyteller."

Another golden jackal mask melted into the crowd in a gilded flash and swirl of shadowy robes. *The king's spies have their eyes on everyone. Probably more than three here,* Serein thought. *Standing next to the prince draws too much attention. I won't be able to listen in on anyone without looking suspicious.*

Rameses took a sip of wine, and Serein's gaze went to him. "Why are you staring at me like that? Is it my handsome features?" he asked as he stroked his beard.

"Handsomeness doesn't protect against poison," Serein said, pointing at his drink.

His smile withered, eyes darting to the cup and back to her. "What do you mean?" Rameses said as he sat up.

"You're awfully trusting to drink something without having it taste tested first, especially while at a party with an assassin."

"Serein, you're joking, right? You didn't—"

"You'll find out in an hour. You'll feel a scratch in your throat first and then trembling in your hands. When your vision starts to blur, and you feel lightheaded, it'll be too late."

Bowing, Serein sauntered off, swiping a piece of flatbread from the food table. "Serein!"

Rameses' voice was lost in the sounds of the banquet hall as Serein melted into the crowds. Colors sparked through the room, and pain shot behind her eyes. She found a green wolf mask on the edge of a table, discarding the owl one. The smell of wine and sweat clung to the lacquered wood as she tightened the strings around her head.

An open balcony door welcomed her with soothing darkness, a quiet respite amidst the sea of noisy color. The masked soldiers by the door paid her no mind as she slipped crossed the veranda. Muffled sounds from the party inside drifted through the latticed windows. Stars appeared behind the thin veil of clouds like scattered diamonds from a broken necklace. Tall palm and fruit trees turned the expanse of gardens into a jungle, echoing with nighttime creatures.

She tore off a chunk of the butter-slathered msemen bread, following the stairs to a garden with orange trees and stone animal statues. *I could sneak through the gardens to the secret door and escape.*

Stealing a guard uniform would buy me some time, she thought, swallowing. *Then I'd have to find a way to remove these bangles.*

An opalescent ripple disturbed the air like a stone being dropped in a pond. Serein turned as a man in a gray qamis and black rida' appeared through the trees. Bright blue eyes cut through the dark before they faded to hazel behind the silver fox mask. A shot of platinum cut through his brown hair, vanishing as tendrils of magic hummed around him.

He's using magic! That shouldn't be possible here, Serein thought, dropping the flatbread.

"*Lacaraite,*" the man whispered in a thistle-colored voice.

The ancient language tickled her memory. *Elpahta. An Immortal. He was talking with Hasim. Is he a rebel? A spy? Is he going to kill me because I saw him using magic? What does he mean by impossible? Does he recognize me?* Serein thought, touching the sharpened bones in her sleeves. *Throat, ears, eyes, soft tissue of his hand.*

The man looked over his shoulder before approaching. "Be at ease. I will not hurt you."

"What's an Immortal doing in Sarddon?" Serein asked. *He's not an assassin. Otherwise, someone would be dead. He seems familiar with the grounds, so he's most likely been here before.*

"I could ask the same of a Ravanassë," he said, clinging to the shadows of the orange trees. "There is evil in this place. The king is using a power he does not know how to wield."

Her eyes narrowed. "What do you mean? Sethos is human. He can't use magic."

"We do not know what he is doing or how, but there is a dark presence around him. The plague he unleashed was not caused by natural means."

She blinked, remembering the flash of black in his eyes when he pinned her against the cell. "How are you using magic here?" she asked. *Was that darkness around him real? If Sethos is using magic, what is he?*

"The ley lines here are mostly dried up, but there are still a few veins of magic alive. Whatever the king is doing, he is not finished yet. Soon it will not be just this continent that suers but all of Cemiyon," the man replied.

His skin darkened, and a thick beard sprouted. Magic flowed across his skin opalescent streams.

Serein lowered her arms, eyes widening. *The platinum hair, blue eyes, the ability to change his face...He's a Vale,* she thought. *A Vale in the heart of Sarddon, in Sethos' very palace, using magic.*

"*Galu.* May Yestarë's light guide your path," the man said, tossing something at her.

Serein caught the object—a smooth, brown rock. She ran a finger over the crude tree with twelve branches carved into its surface. When she glanced up, the man had vanished.

A rebel symbol. It's similar to the sigil of the royal Vale house.

Questions flooded her mind, and the headache burrowed deeper behind her eyes. She stepped back into the audience hall, clinging to the edges of the room. A hand grabbed her arm, yanking her to the side. Serein tensed, reaching for the lamb bone.

"What are you doing? Why aren't you in uniform?" Uriah hissed through gritted teeth, the sharp green words bristling as he lifted his bear mask. His hair was brushed back, and his smooth jaw clenched.

A pale-yellow sigh collected inside Serein's mask as she released the bone. *I was hoping he wouldn't see me.* "Whatever do you mean, sidi?" she asked, eyes wide . "The prince invited me as a guest."

"I don't know what game you're playing," Uriah said, squeezing her bicep, "but this—"

"There you are, Serein," Rameses said, walking up with a cup in hand. Red flushed his cheeks, the smell of wine thick on his golden breath. "That's not the mask I gave you."

"I found a different one," she replied. *I guess his solution to possibly being poisoned is drinking more wine.*

"Abandoning your post already, Uriah?" Rameses asked with a smile, lifting his hound mask. "If you're still worried about it being safe, apart from her conversation about death and a thousand and one ways to kill a person, she's not hurt anyone."

Grumbling, Uriah released her. The guests left the dance floor as a group of performers moved to the center. Sethos and Lujayn sat on the raised dais at the front of the hall with Rahim and Rasima. Four female dancers wearing anklets with small bells and tiny cymbals on their fingers were draped in bright, fluttering kaftans with metal disks woven into the fabric. The women rippled with living light as a slow beat rose. Yellow and orange scarves twisted through the air like flying serpents.

"So, Serein," Rameses said, the gold voice stoking her headache, "I believe you *are* bluffing about the poison in my cup."

"Poison?" Uriah's head jerked toward Serein. "What do you mean?"

Serein's gaze followed the twirling bodies of the dancers. "Poison is a substance used to kill people or cause bodily harm. I thought that was obvious," she told Uriah.

"Did you poison someone?" Uriah asked, voice rumbling like a green storm. "Did you poison *Rameses*?!"

Rameses downed the rest of his wine, handing the cup to a passing servant. "She was joking. I feel fine. A little drunk, but nothing more," he said, patting Uriah's shoulder.

Serein tugged at Uriah's cloak. A silver medallion with an embossed bear surrounded by storm clouds was pinned to the front of his white sash. "If you keep scowling, your face is going to be permanently stuck like that," she told him. "That's quite the regal outfit you're dressed in. You even shaved." *So, he even has a sigil for his "noble house." I wonder if it's the actual sigil of the Stormheir family or if he and Rameses came up with it.*

Uriah yanked the cape away from her, glowering. "So," Rameses began, "Shahrban Hasim approached me after you left. He asked about you, calling you Lady Accalia Lycaon, a widowed woman. Survived a wolf attack. Soft-spoken and kind. Seems it was not a hallucination, and I *did* see you dancing before."

"And what did you tell him?" Serein asked, leaning against a carved pillar.

"I went along with it but told him I had no idea where you went," Rameses replied. "What did you think of him?"

"The Horse Lord prefers the company of his gardens and horses over politics and court life. He's lonely and needed someone to talk to," Serein said.

"Seems like you made an impression on him. Are you trying to seduce him?"

The encroaching headache tapped harder against Serein's skull.

"Maybe he'll be so enamored with me that he'll ask for my hand in marriage." *Hasim may be problematic if he starts inquiring about Lady Accalia,* she thought, the stone tucked into her sash. *Still, I should try and learn what he was doing with the Vale. If he's working with the rebels, are there others in Sethos' court plotting against him? I can't think with this headache.*

"Those bangles will shatter your false persona, *Lady Accalia,*" Uriah sneered. "Once he sees what you really are, he'll be repulsed."

"You found my weakness, Captain Stormheir. Cutting words and vicious mockery," Serein said, putting a hand to her forehead.

Rameses jostled Uriah. "Oh, Uriah. Serein said she wants to become a farmer. Do you believe that?" he said, laughing.

Uriah shot her a furrowed look. "A farmer? Of what? You've probably never planted anything in your life. You'll just kill anything you try to plant," he scoffed.

"Well, I guess I won't know unless I try," Serein said.

Rameses leaned against the column. "Do you have any friends, Serein?" he asked.

"There weren't many instances to make friends in a world where you kill or get killed. I had one once, but she's gone." *Hopefully, alive and free,* she thought, remembering the yellow and rose-colored secrets shared in the dark.

"What happened?"

You have too many openings, volchitsa. *You're afraid that if he knew what you're planning to do, that he'll despise you that they'll hunt you down.*

"You've asked a second question," she said, another wave of pain cracking through her head. "I want to ride and go beyond the city." Serein brushed past Rameses.

"Where are you going?" he asked.

"To bed."

"What if Hasim inquires about you?"

"You'll make something up because you don't have the heart to tell him that the truth about Lady Accalia," Serein replied as she slipped through the giant doors.

. . .

MOONLIGHT DRIPPED DOWN SEREIN AS SHE CLIMBED THE WALL and hauled herself up into the dark rafters. The thick wooden beams were clean of dust. Lantern light illuminated the corners where she tucked away bundles of letters and drawings wrapped in oilskins. Serein looked over the collection of sharpened bones, the metal kebab skewer, makeshift lock picks made from the dress pins, two black stone elephant figurines, a bag of coins, and a training dagger from the armory.

Throbbing pain moved from her eyes to the front of her skull. *I'll have to steal some rope, so it'll be easier to get up here,* she thought.

She set the small pouch of jewels she removed from the kaftan and the rock with the twelve-pointed tree next to the figurines and the green wolf mask. Reaching for the stack of letters, Serein settled against the wall. Each word was engraved on her heart, woven through her bones. A sad smile rested on her face.

Sethos using magic seems impossible, but how else would he have caused such devastation? Serein thought. *Is he a Sahriminha and has been hiding it? I didn't think anyone in the royal family was a half-blood. Bottled magic could be sold in the Tafall District's black market. But what kind of magic could create a plague that kills those with magic and makes it disappear?*

A shiver coursed along Serein's spine at the thought of Sethos manipulating the opalescent strands, turning them black with his touch. The stench of death and dying magic became real again. Blood flowed and screams bled out. Strong hands grabbed her, and cold blades cut her open.

Serein's eyes flew open, the scars tight, hands clenched around the letters. *What was done can never be forgiven. What blood was spilled can never be forgotten.* Inside, the beast stirred, catching the scent of rage. *I'll sheath my claws until the time is right. I'll survive, my Sun and Stars, and do whatever it takes to protect you.*

PART II

THE STIRRING BEAST

Chapter Twenty-One
Pieces of War

S EREIN STOOD AGAINST TAPESTRY-COVERED WALL BEHIND R AMESES with members of the Malik's Guard and Kamau, memorizing the faces of the twelve men of the war council—generals, commanders, captains, local governors. All men with powerful names and connections. She noted every gesture and movement they made, dissecting every word they exchanged.

Sethos sat at the end of the long map table with Rameses on his left and Grand Vizier Umar on his right. Raised mountain ranges, clusters of forests, and rivers were painted across the map. Red flags marked the conquered areas while black ones stood next to cities and spots of rebel activities in the Old Kingdom. Golden soldier figurines were spread across the landscape, each one representing a thousand men. Wendale lay tucked between the two large counties in the south, bordered by the Baltha Gorge and the Dullah Sea.

The black sword lay close to Sethos, his shadow unmoving. Lantern light turned the gold embroidery of the Malik's dark qamis into molten lines and made the white jewels affixed to his pale turban sparkle. He seemed to absorb the light of the room while remaining a cold, resplendent center.

How has he managed to hide his atrocities for so long? Serein thought.

How many of the men in this room are involved? He couldn't have killed his brother and started this war on his own.

"With contingents of soldiers stretching from Savas to Sava, the Silver and Gold Roads, and the surrounding forests are well guarded. The Scourge has been keeping the resistance fighters from the borders. Rebels have been coming from the Vinguis Mountains, Marnediad's Seat near Ygris, and the jungles near the Olsen Desert, totaling roughly three thousand troops," Captain Mansaka said, his deep saffron-yellow voice seeping over the mountain ranges split by the Olsen Desert in the west. A jagged scar ran across his head, cutting through his dark curls.

"Calling them troops is a stretch. More likely, they are regular civilians conscripted to fight. The remnants of the Immortal Kings' armies have been wiped out, and we've had no reports of ships coming from Bar Elenion," another captain, Jorham, said with a dry blue-gray laugh. His leathery hands rested on the table, brown eyes taking in the map.

"Those *civilians* have been a thorn in our side for the past decade," Mansaka snapped. "More Immortals have been sighted in their ranks, and it's unclear if they are leading these pockets of rebellion. Even without magic, Immortals are stronger and faster than ordinary men. The Ravanassë know the land and use that to their advantage."

"Only small platoons have been attacking the trade routes. They've been using Locklin Forest to hide and move through," General Afzal told them as bits of cobalt-colored words snagged in his gray beard. He pointed his stick to the green mass between the Old Kingdom and the Albahr Alrraml Desert.

"It's taken years to carve into the forest. The trees are unnatural," the Grand Vizier said, mouth set in a hard line. A breath of hesitation lingered in his dark orange voice.

Sethos glanced at him, and Umar held his gaze, unflinching. "You are not one to be superstitious. They are just trees, and they can be burned," the Malik replied, blood-red words stilling the air.

You think those superstitions are dead and gone. Magic may be dying, but it'll come back to haunt you, Sethos. You'll burn when this forest does, Serein thought as Sethos' gaze rested on Locklin.

"I don't fear the forests, but they're still dangerous even with our forts there. There are creatures in there, ancient ones. The trade routes allow us to move into the country from the north and in the south by Wendale, but that also makes us vulnerable. The attack on the Amir has shown that," Umar went on.

Rameses shifted on the cushion, hands tightening on his knees underneath the table. *The attack still bothers him. Probably the first time he's seen people die,* Serein thought. *It probably won't be the last.*

"The rebels might launch an assault on Oyon using those routes," a shahrban, Kosai, said with a raspy, teal-colored voice.

"But nothing suggests that they're organized enough to launch such an attack," Jorham interjected, waving his hand.

"Not yet, but the rebels keep gaining numbers," Afzal replied, brow creased. "Several caids are reporting raiding parties near their towns, even as close as Mamari Alsakra'."

The different voices continued to fly over the map, rising and falling as they clashed. Rameses remained silent, staring at the gold line near the Tamuj Plains.

Sethos tapped his stick in the middle of Locklin. "It is time then to revisit the idea of constructing the Steel Road," he said. "Having a route from Oyon that cuts straight through the desert to forests will allow our troops to move into the very heart of the country. A garrison could be built along the route to supply more troops to the surrounding areas and protect the other routes."

Serein's hands tightened behind her back, nails digging into her skin. *Sethos won't be satisfied until all of the Old Kingdom burns. Is this all really to avenge his brother? Men have gone to war for less, but there has to be another reason behind all this.*

"Magic is gone. Whatever dwells in the forest's center can be dealt with," Sethos went on. "Even the Immortals fall. So will the forest."

BEES FLEW BETWEEN THE BUDDING FLOWERS ALONG THE WALKWAY. Their soft blue buzzing sprinkled the petals like pollen. The ruddy stones of the Royal House of the Saints stood out against the pale walls of the palace. Green banners with the flame and stars flapped in the breeze. Four towers rose, the bronze-plated tops catching the late afternoon sun. A fenced garden overflowed with fruit trees, herbs, and flowering vines. Two acolytes in green robes moved among the vegetation, laughing as they collected baskets of herbs.

Rameses' sandals crunched on the gravel path in orange ripples, overlapping with Serein's quiet blue steps. *Cutting a path through Locklin,* Serein thought, the map burning behind her eyelids. *The forest will fight Sethos, but if he's able to do what he did at the beginning of the war, you might not be able to stay hidden for long, my Sun and Stars.*

The shadow of the House of the Saints fell over them. "This kanisa was built at least a hundred years before the palace was erected," Rameses told her, waving to the carved archways. His gold voice spun in the air like birds. "It used to be only a small building, but more chambers were built onto it as the Sarddonian rulers began to use it for worship and interning their dead in the catacombs beneath. Rumor has it that there are passageways that connect to the old city beneath Oyon."

I wonder how extensive the catacombs are. There must be tunnels leading beyond the wall. Maybe that's how that Vale got in.

Warm light from hanging lanterns spilled over them as they entered the kanisa into an antechamber with a bowl of water in the middle of a recessed dais. Mosaic patterns reached the domed ceiling, forming a sun with a large yellow lantern suspended in the middle. Rameses removed his sandals and scooped up water with a cup hanging from the side of the metal bowl. He poured water over his feet and took a towel to scrub his skin as the water ran down through small holes in the floor in opaque purple streams.

"Before entering the inner sanctum, you have to remove your shoes and clean your feet," he told Serein, his hushed voice echoing off the walls. "Here, everyone's equal before Alkhaliq and the Saints."

Serein removed her boots, the water smelling of orange blossoms as she cleaned her toes and dried her feet. An acolyte came to collect the towels, her head wrapped in a green headscarf. The marble floor was cool beneath Serein's feet as she followed Rameses into the inner sanctum. The cloying smell of frankincense and sandalwood wafted through the air.

Colorful fractals of light poured through the stained glass dome overhead across the rug-covered floor of the dodecagonal chamber. Twelve columns lined the room, each one held up by a statue of a Divine Saints. Twenty people, a mixture of men and women, sat on cushions, eyes closed in prayer or reading from books in their laps. Murmuring sounds hummed around the worshipers like hovering glows.

"Saint Alath of Heavenly Knowledge, grant me wisdom from above."

"Hear my plea, Zaman. Heal my son."

"Luminary Rahat and resplendent Alkhaliq, show me the way."

The mingling voices caught in the olive tree with a twisted trunk growing upward from a circular patch of earth in the middle of the sanctum. Ripe olives hung from its sweeping branches.

Lujayn sat opposite to the statue of a woman with Rahim and Rasima beside her, her honey-colored abaya flowing around her. Three pairs of shoes lay behind them. Five court women were spread out nearby, heads bowed in prayer. Their guards stood against the wall, barefooted.

The peach chimes of Rameses' earrings cracked the peaceful quiet. "I didn't think my mother would be here. Usually, she's having lunch with her court ladies at this time," he muttered. "Something must be bothering her."

Rasima lifted her head from the prayer book in her hands. Faded henna designs still clung to her fingers. Her eyes lit up as she moved to stand. Lujayn's hazel eyes snapped to Rasima with a disapproving look. The Amirah stopped, sinking back down on the cushion in a sigh of mauve fabric.

"Rameses," Lujayn said as he approached. Serein bowed, feeling the Malika's gaze on her. "Are you joining us for prayer, abnay?" The mauve voice softened in her son's direction.

"Not today," Rameses replied and kissed her cheeks. "I was going to pay my respects to Uncle."

"You should not neglect your prayers," Lujayn said, standing. "I wish to discuss something with you"—Serein moved to follow—"without your wali."

Rameses' eyes went to Serein as she stopped, a faint crease appearing. "Serein, stay with Rasima and Rahim."

Lujayn's mouth turned down as she took Rameses' arm and led him to a side chamber. Two of the guards peeled away from the wall after them.

Even after two weeks of being his wali, the queen still views me with contempt, Serein thought.

Rahim's wide-eyed stare darted away from Serein as he pretended to be interested in the paintings on the walls, fidgeting with the hem of his blue qamis.

"Come sit with us, Serein," Rasima said as she closed the maroon prayer book. Her violet words fluttered through the sanctum as she patted the space next to her, moving aside her mauve abaya.

"I'm on duty, Your Highness," Serein told her. "I don't want to interrupt your worship."

Rasima rolled her eyes. The veil rippled as she moved. "I've been reading the same passage for the past hour. I think the Saints will understand if I take a break." She paused, glancing in the direction her mother and Rameses went. "I know Umm doesn't like you, but she's not here, so it doesn't matter what she wants."

Serein looked around at the acolytes in green robes and veils moving about on hushed footfalls. *Unfortunately, that won't work with your father. He'll know about this conversation before the sun sets.*

A few worshipers rose from their cushions and left the inner sanctum with the echoes of prayers trailing behind them. A man shuffled to a circular apse on the far end of the room. A female acolyte handed him a bundle of herbs and a small bowl before he stepped into the room with a pool in the floor.

How many rooms does this place have? There might be a door that connects through the palace walls, unmarked tunnels and exits, forgotten maps. Maps Rameses might have.

"Is this your first time in a House of the Saints?" Rasima asked.

"I didn't have a need to visit a church when I was here. I wasn't expecting there to be an olive tree inside," Serein replied.

The Amirah glanced at the tree illuminated in golden light. "It's said that the first trees that grew on the earth were olive trees and that Saint Rahat—the first Saint—heard from Alkhaliq under one almost two thousand years ago. When service is held, the qaris stands under it and reads the scriptures, just like Saint Rahat did."

Twelve Divine Saints, like the twelve Lights of Mirarnediad. Serein looked at the statue of a woman with golden orbs resting in her outstretched hands. Faces of men and women carved out of white marble stared down at them.

"Do you know about Alkhaliq and the Saints?" Rasima asked.

"A little. I've heard of Rahat, and the others I've learned the names of from the hourly prayers," Serein said. *Saint Rahat, Zaman, Arwa, Zubaida, Hafiz, Faysal, Aziz, Basira, Raz Nura, Alath, Shukri, and Esmail.*

"These twelve were blessed with the ability to use magic, which was only reserved for the Immortals, the Alkhaliq's elemental children—the Spirits of water, fire, air, earth, light, and shadow," Rasima told Serein. "With Alkhaliq's guidance, they created the Immortal beings, the creatures of the world, and humans."

Rahim flopped back on the floor, his exasperated sigh like a pull of ice-blue smoke. Dark locks of hair fell back off his face, his small nose wrinkled. He pulled a blue stone lion from his sirwal pocket.

"What's the religion of the Old Kingdom?" Rasima asked.

"There are many people groups in the Old Kingdom, so there are many different faiths. Most believe in Mirarnediad and the twelve Lights."

Rahim turned his head, the lion held in the air. "What are the Lights? What's a M-Mir...arne...diad?" he asked, his voice rising as he stumbled over the word. A few of the court ladies raised their heads, eyes darting to Serein.

"Sshh!" Rasima hissed at her brother, sharp violet cutting the air.

The familiar turquoise voice wrapped around Serein in flashes of painted forests and blankets with woven stars. "Mirarnediad created thirteen Lights in Ië, the starlit heavens, and the world," Serein told them.

A crinkle formed between Rasima's brow. "I thought there were twelve."

"There were originally thirteen, but one betrayed the other Lights and became the Dark One."

"Dark One? Who's that? What did it do?" Rahim asked and sat up.

Serein opened her mouth, but hushed mauve and gold whispers

appeared in the corner of her eye. Rameses and his mother crossed the chamber, and Rahim pocketed the lion. Lujayn brushed past Serein and fixed Rahim's mussed hair.

"Consider what I said," the Malika said to Rameses.

"Yes, Umm," he replied with a strained smile.

"I want to stay with Rameses," Rahim said, his ice-blue voice pitching upward.

The court ladies rose, gathering their shoes. "Not today, habibi," his mother replied, and he huffed, feet dragging. Rasima waved to Serein as they left the sanctum with the guards.

"Did you have a good talk with your mother?" Serein asked Rameses.

He twisted his ring. "She reminded me that a woman wali isn't a suitable choice," Rameses replied with a sigh.

"Does this mean I should be searching for different employment?" *Or will the queen press Sethos to forcibly remove me?*

Rameses followed a hallway with a gilded archway and carved sunbursts. As the carpet ended and the geometric-patterned floor began, he slipped his sandals back on. "You don't need to worry about that," Rameses said. "My mother will just continue to bring it up for the next six years. Her true talent is holding onto things and never letting them go. Possibly forever."

Serein put on her boots. "Thinking about setting up a fake mugging I can save her from?" she asked.

"I doubt even I could get my mother to go into the city," Rameses said with a laugh. "She also wanted to inform me that she didn't find Alessandra to be a suitable match and that the princess will be returning to Sinabrac this week."

"She seemed like a nice woman who knew how to laugh at your jokes," Serein said.

"Alessandra provided good conversation, but ultimately, she didn't have enough influence for my mother's liking."

Amber light turned the ruddy walls orange, shimmering across the bronze death plaques of past qaris along the hall. A few female names drew Serein's attention.

"Women can be priests?" Serein asked.

Rameses glanced at the plaques. "Yes," he said. "Women are

encouraged to be educated. Many female theological scholars go on to be readers for alkanayis. Being a qaris is an esteemed position. Mother wants Rasima to pursue theological courses when she's old enough to go to the House of Knowledge."

"But they aren't allowed to fight."

"There used to be female guards for the malikas and amirahs. But about two hundred years ago, one of the malikas killed her husband and raised an army to take the throne. She even gathered most of the female servants to help her kill those loyal to her husband. Eventually, she was overthrown by one of her sons and killed herself rather than being taken. They called her mad. Ever since then, women were forbidden from fighting or being guards."

"Is that ancestor of yours buried in the catacombs?" *Most fear a woman with a weapon because it means she stands on equal ground with a man. Mad. Dangerous. A threat. For men, it's commonplace. For a woman, it's condemnation.*

Rameses shook his head. "No. Her body was cut into pieces and burned. For Sarddonians, dismembering is a punishment to ensure that a person never receives eternal rest. It's reserved for traitors and criminals with serious crimes," he said.

In the Old Kingdom, burning a body is the only way to release a soul to rest in the stars, Serein thought. *The Sarddonians have similar beliefs about reaching the afterlife as Zhao and many of the island nations who believe a person can't enter heaven unless their body is intact.*

The corridor opened to a vestibule decorated with stone olive branches and braziers on either side. Rameses approached a worn door, the iron hinges letting out grating teal groans as it swung open. Musty air swept out, a faint chill nipping at its heels.

"Watch your step," Rameses said, grabbing a lit lantern off one of the hooks on the wall.

Orange and blue footsteps descended the stairs, bouncing into the dim. The scents of stone, incense, and old decay rushed at them as they entered the catacombs. White marble coffins lined the walls of the cavernous space, the names of past rulers carved onto the lids. Reliefs of twelve moons and blooming plants lined the sides while two sitting lions decorated the front. Discoloration marked the older tombs where the carvings had been chipped or worn smooth. A few lids were cracked with chunks missing. Small censers of burning olive leaves hung on hooks in the middle of thick pillars, threads of pale smoke weaving around the crypts.

One day the king will lie here, sliced open by your hand, volchitsa, Xansas' voice whispered. *How many royal bodies will you fill this place with when this is all over?*

Rameses stopped by a coffin bearing the name "Salman" across it. He touched the pale stone, a clouded look pushing down his brow. "My uncle was a warm man who gave me my love of reading. He grew distant when my cousin, Nasr, died," he said, golden syllables chipping off his lips. "I remember he had a private library he would let me visit. When he died, I got many of his books, but the ones he had on magic and the Old Kingdom were removed."

Serein surveyed the crypt, searching for sounds beyond the opaque purple dripping of water and muted footsteps overhead. Faint, pink clicks, and light coral-colored squeaking raced along the edges of the chamber from unseen rodents. No other shadows moved between the tombs.

Rameses sighed and turned to her, shadows caressing his face in the flickering light. "What did you think of the war meeting?" he asked.

"It's not wise to talk about such things without being sure you're alone," Serein murmured.

"Do you think anyone's here?" he whispered, eyes darting around.

"The Golden Jackals have eyes and ears everywhere. The dead won't necessarily keep secrets"—she faced him—"but it appears we're alone."

Rameses leaned against the tomb. "Were you able to observe anything from the people at the meeting?"

"The Grand Vizier doesn't show worry when he has an opposing viewpoint. Either he hides his fear well, or he genuinely respects your father. If he was involved in a plot to kill your uncle, he must have gotten something out of it worth keeping quiet for," Serein told him. "Anyone who might have known something was probably dealt with already. Only a few of the current captains and generals were in command when the war began. Whoever helped Sethos most likely wasn't in the war room."

"Can you think of anyone else who might be involved?" Rameses asked as he looked at the two coffins next to Salman's with the name "Nasr" etched on one and "Muminah" and "Zaid" on the other.

"Obvious suspects would be the spymaster, personal guards, the Grand Vizier, people of Sethos' court," Serein replied. "The older generals and captains might know something, but right now, I don't know enough about them to narrow down suspects. I didn't meet enough people at the diffa to get more names either." *Besides Hasim and the Vale. The Vale seemed to know more than Hasim did, but it might be impossible to track him down.*

A heavy golden breath spilled across the air like withering vines. Rameses paced between the tombs, his orange footsteps laden with worry.

"How much do you know about Hasim al-Ziadeh?" Serein asked.

Rameses stopped. "The shahrban? He's looked after most of the palace horses for many years and has several estates across Sarddon, where he keeps his herds. I have spoken with him many times, but he tends to keep to himself ever since his wife died."

Hasim mentioned that his wife died almost twelve years ago. Could her death have played a part in his tension with the war? Or is he simply an old man tired of fighting? Serein thought.

"Why are you asking about Hasim-effendi? Are you showing an interest in him?" Rameses asked with a hint of amusement in his voice. "I didn't think older men were your type."

"Simply learning what I can," she said, shrugging. "He didn't seem to be in favor of the war. He said something at the feast that made me think that he knows more than he's saying." *If he's working with rebels, he may know more about Sethos. Especially if he has a Vale spy within the walls.*

Rameses blinked as smoke drifted toward him, waving a hand through the gossamer tendrils. "Do you plan to look into him more?" Serein crossed her arms. "Holding a lengthy conversation with a prominent shahrban isn't an easy matter. Building a correspondence where he might divulge such things to me would take time. Then there's the possibility of meeting him face-to-face." *Finding the Vale will be difficult since he can change his appearance to become anyone. Giving me the rock suggests that the Vale wanted to give me a chance to reach out to him. Not sure how I'll do that. The rock appears normal, not a morphing or a magical item.*

"I'm sure he will find your face charming. Would I help if I inquired on your behalf?"

"You forget that I'm known as your guard, and he's only met me under false pretenses. Letters would be the easiest way to communicate, but it has risks. It would still be difficult to make sure those correspondences don't fall into the wrong hands."

"That does make things difficult..." Rameses stroked his beard. "Hasim-effendi comes to Sarddon every couple of weeks or so to check on the horses. I can always invite him to talk more if you think that will be helpful."

Serein walked among the coffins. Mold gathered in the etched lines of Salman's name. Underneath the cloying incense and musky olive leaves, the odor of death remained entombed in the crypt.

They say Salman and his family were killed with magic. Slashed. Torn apart. Done with extreme malice. There'll be records about his death and his family's. After almost sixteen years, I doubt this body will tell me anything, Serein thought.

Rameses tapped his ring. "What are your thoughts on my father's new plan for the war?" he asked.

"Dragging the war out doesn't seem to appeal to most of the officers present at the meeting," Serein said, looking up from the tomb. "Establishing another trading route for soldiers to use would give Sethos an advantage, but it'll be costly. It also means that he intends to keep a large military presence in the Old Kingdom. Sethos doesn't intend to let the Old Kingdom remain autonomous. He means to take it over completely. That will make Edolas nervous, possibly even Ginjarr and Zhao."

Rameses adjusted his haya bracelet. "My father has always talked about growing Sarddon's prosperity through trade and influence. I didn't think he meant expanding into other countries," he said.

"If that was his intention, it might have been harder to invade the Old Kingdom without the support of the people. Avenging his brother is a powerful motivator and justification for invasion if the people were already enraged enough to fight."

"You think my father used my uncle's death as a way to start a war? That he planned it all?" Rameses asked, the furrow across his brow deepening.

Murdering to expand isn't an impossible theory, but there must be something else going on. If Sethos did kill his brother and regretted it, that could explain why he was so distraught. Unless it was all an act. Those injuries were real, but it's possible it's a part of the plot—

"Saints!" Rameses jumped back as a dark shape slunk past his feet on pink skittering.

The khanjar cut through the air with an orange streak as Serein threw it. It sunk into the rat as it gave a twisted coral-colored squeal before lying still.

"Seems the palace cats aren't doing their job," she said.

"Was that necessary?" Rameses asked, steadying his nervous gold breaths.

Serein retrieved her weapon, wiping the blood off on her dark trousers. "I'm just doing my job to protect you, Your Highness, even if it's from rats."

Rameses frowned at the trickle of blood oozing from the rat. "This is the second animal you have killed near me. I'm beginning to wonder if you have something against them."

"Only rats and snakes. I don't have a problem with animals."

"Why those two in particular?" Rameses asked.

"I've been bitten by enough snakes not to be fond of them," Serein said, feeling the phantom fang holes in her arm. "It was part of my training to build up a tolerance to venoms and poisons."

"And the rats?"

"Grasdan had hundreds of them that liked to try and eat the prisoners. There were nights I didn't sleep because they'd be crawling through the cell, biting me."

Rameses paled as he picked up the lantern again. "Xansas forced you to be bitten by snakes?"

"He's called the White Snake for a reason." *A snake that will be more difficult to kill than a lion. I'm surrounded by dangerous creatures,* she thought, sheathing the khanjar. *But I've become an equally dangerous creature.*

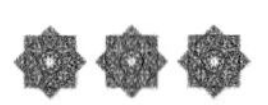

Chapter Twenty-Two
The Game of Secrets

THE BREATH OF THE LIBRARY SETTLED AMONG THE SHELVES FILLED with books and scrolls. Serein's exhale scattered the dust motes spinning in the shafts of sunlight from the latticed windows above. Muted colors seeped through the bookcases around the giant dodecagonal room as scribes wrote in alcoves.

Rameses lounged against a plush majlis tucked into the corner, a book propped on his knees. "I have always wanted to build a library with books from all over the world so everyone would have access to knowledge," he told Serein, golden words sparkling in the quiet. "I want to emulate Saint Faysal's ancient Library of Mala that burned down two centuries ago, but I cannot capture his free-flowing arches well. Do you think you could draw something if I gave you my designs and notes?"

Serein looked down at him, the edges of her red headscarf shifting along her shoulders. "Designing libraries wasn't part of my job description," she said. *The son of Sethos, building libraries. An odd thought.*

He chuckled. "In your free time, of course," Rameses said. "My father never liked me taking architecture courses at the House of Knowledge. He wanted me to focus on more practical things like economics and military tactics. Perhaps when I'm Malik, I can build it."

Serein looked across the library at the scribes and bookkeepers moving about. *Rameses might become king soon if he's gathering evidence against his father.*

He'll become king sooner if you kill Sethos. White words dripped down the back of her neck, making her shiver.

"When were you born, Serein?" Rameses asked, glancing up.

"Yelwa," she replied, hands clasped behind her back, running a fingertip over one of the bangles. *There are probably at least two Jackals here in disguise.*

Rameses turned back to his book, a light plum-colored crinkle whispering from the thin page he turned. "The last month of the year. Winter. People born in that month are strong, resourceful, and resilient," he said. "I would say that's an accurate statement. I was born in Nésa if you were wondering. Same month as Uriah."

"That explains why you're so optimistic and confident. Seems the captain didn't get those same traits," Serein said. *The second month, and the beginning of spring in Sarddon.*

"He has more of those qualities than you might realize," Rameses told her. "How old are you? You have been my wali for three weeks now, and I still know so little about you."

"As I told you before, I'm not as young as you think I am nor as old are your imagination would like me to be."

Rameses sighed. Serein spotted a man in gray robes hunched over his writing desk in an alcove, quill scribbling across the parchment in front of him. His hand stopped moving as her voice faded.

That one. Right-handed. Thirties. Good at reading lips judging by the way he keeps glancing this way and writing something, Serein thought. *He's set up in an alcove that catches sounds. Obvious, but he's meant to draw attention. Now, to find the other Jackal.*

Rameses pointed to the book lying next to him. "Would you like another book to read besides ones on Sarddon's history and culture?" he asked. "There's an adventure tale I think you might like. It's more of a tragedy."

"Why do you assume I'm more drawn to tragedies?" Serein asked.

"You don't seem to like romances, and I have not given you a comedy or poetry yet," Rameses said as he studied her face. "Have you ever been in love?"

Love has no place in a world of blood and steel, volchitsa. *You kill everything your hands touch.*

Serein rubbed the scar across her left palm. "You've already had your chance to ask your question." *Love has a cost I'll only bear for you, my Sun and Stars.*

He straightened out his leg. "One question a day yields very little."

"You'll have to be smarter with your questions," Serein told him.

Rameses placed his hand over his heart. "Oh, how you wound me. What do you want in return?" he asked.

"A set of daggers," she said.

"What about the weapons you already have?"

"Best to have more than one." *Keep them hidden in various places if the need arises.*

Soft brown footsteps entered the library. "Sayyidi," I'timad said with a bow, his fist over his chest and fingers touching his brow, "I'm here to relieve Serein." His indigo voice was soft and smooth, dusting his short beard.

"Is it that time already? Here, Serein, you may find this book interesting," Rameses said as he sat up, grabbing a book off the stack nearby and holding it out to her. "Rasima said that you wanted to learn about the Saints. There's a wonderful collection of tapestries on the second floor near the library. You should find the one of Saint Rahat. It's quite stunning."

Serein took the book, its edges worn. *Let's see if the Jackals follow.*

THE EMPTY HALLWAY STRETCHED BEFORE SEREIN, SUNLIGHT refracting off the colored glass windows. She opened the book and found a stained map of the palace inside the cover. Veins of passages between the walls had been marked in Rameses' neat script. He'd left a note on the map to show where the passageway started, drawing a line from the tapestries to Sethos' study on the west side of the Royal Wing.

The Tower of Secrets is adjacent to the library, Serein thought. *Sethos' study is on the second floor of the Royal Wing, not near his chambers. Having the room so far from his personal chambers might mean he's working on things he doesn't want his family to find out about.*

Serein followed the map to the corridor of tapestries a few minutes' walk from the library. Rich fabrics bore images of the Saints performing their miracles. Aziz, the Saint of Wind, with his hands raised to redirect a monsoon. Hafiz, the Saint of Illusions, creating an army of illusionary soldiers to frighten a horde of monstrous creatures. Esmail, the Saint of Earth, raising the wall around Oyon from the earth.

Woven eyes watched as Serein followed the stairs up to the second level of the palace where the tapestries continued. The lighter stones of the walls became darker under the corner of a large arras with a woman ringed in golden light, holding up her hands to stop a horde of shadowy red ifrit.

Rahat. The Saint of Light, Serein thought, glancing back down the hallway.

She pushed aside the heavy tapestry. A narrow gap in the wall stared at her, the unfinished stonework like a mouth with missing teeth. Scents of old dust and musty air spilled out.

Not a big space. Old servant's passages or for the builders when the palace was constructed. Guess someone decided it wasn't worth sealing up and just put a tapestry over it. Or someone removed these stones recently, she thought, tucking the book in her sash.

She slipped through the narrow opening, the tapestry covering the entrance behind her. Bits of light seeped through the thick threading. Tiny bones crunched under her boots in amber crinkles, cobwebs sticking to her fingers as she ran her hands along the walls. The darkness thickened as the muffled heartbeat of the palace permeated the stones.

Serein felt along the dusty walls as the passageway turned left, the edge of her headscarf pulled up over her nose. *Should be a hundred feet across and then another curve, assuming this passageway is clear,* she thought, shoulders brushing against the walls as she counted every step.

The uneven ground turned right, continuing to stretch on in the darkness. Dark orange and red tones seeped through the wall, sharpening the deeper she delved. A purple sliver cut through the stale air like a dancing ribbon. Serein followed it to a small crack of dim light between the stonework a few feet up. Serein whittled out the old mortar in the gaps with her dagger. Dust tickled her nose as the silver-white scraping stretched around her like vines. Opaque light broke through as she moved half of the stone over a few inches.

She peered through the crack, blinking dust from her eyes. Worn threads obscured her view with muted red light. *The "X" the prince marked on the map. Sethos' study.*

The stone was smooth against Serein's ear as she pressed it to the crack. Her heartbeat. Movement of people above. The deep red voice of Sethos, close enough to strangle.

Serein's body tensed, the scars tightening. *There you are,* she thought.

"...Have the leaders brought here. Send the others to Grasdan. Il-Makah and his men will extract the information we need and find out who is heading their resistance," Sethos said. "Hisein's army will return from Ygris to Sava's border. One of his captains can manage the Scourge in his stead. They will remind the Ravanassë of their place."

The Scourge. Sethos means to burn the towns and slaughter more in hopes that the Old Kingdom's resistance dwindles. But why's the General returning to Sarddon? Serein thought.

Her heart twisted, fields of corpses and destroyed villages flashed in her mind. Rumors of the Scourge's brutality had struck fear into the people of the Old Kingdom, a second plague of steel and carnage.

"I'll send word to the General, Your Majesty," the familiar deep orange voice of Grand Vizier Umar replied.

Papers rustled, pale plum-colored ripples fluttering like insect wings. "Il-Makah's men will be watching the palace closely. I smell rats, and I want to know how they are getting in," Sethos said.

Serein swallowed the thread of fear tickling her throat. *Does he mean the Vale spy from the feast? Or me?*

"The emissary from Ginjarr should be here soon, Your Majesty," the Grand Vizier said.

"Hopefully, this one will bring better news than the last report I received about General Suhail losing ships in the Black Ocean before reaching Bar Elenion," the Malik said. "Contact Ezio and have his fleet divert from the Strait of Teeth to sail northeast to Faldore."

"Yes, Your Majesty."

Quiet yellow footsteps receded, and a door shut with a muted teal creak. *Faldore? Why's he sending ships to Bar Elenion?* Serein thought. *Is Sethos trying to find a way through the Fog and invade Bar Elenion? The Grand Vizier knows about the ships being sent to Bar Elenion, so perhaps he's a part of a larger plan. If Sethos brings another plague and wipes out magic there, then no one will be able to stop him...*

"Any news from the parties searching the Moors?" Sethos asked.

"They are still looking for the Black Fells," a female voice replied, the curves of her accent lacing the pale amber words. "The wards were set up by the Calamor and will not be easy to destroy."

"You will find a way, Murdag. Only three tombs have been uncovered. The others must be found. Otherwise, all of this will have been for nothing." A flare of anger rose in Sethos' voice, crimson sparking the air like stoked flames.

A woman? Does Sethos have a mistress? Does Rameses know? I haven't seen that voice color around the palace before. Not a guard since he seems to have disdain for women guards, Serein thought, pulse thrumming against the stones. *Murdag...that name sounds like it's from the northern continent. Is she a spy for Sethos?*

"Patience. The thirteen will be brought together," the woman said.

Shadows moved by the tapestry, dark-purple footsteps receding. *The Calamor were the ancient mages that fought alongside the Lights against the Dark One in the stories. Thirteen what? What are the Black Fells?*

Serein withdrew from the crack, hurrying back through the tunnel. Her hands brushed along the walls, questions becoming messy heaps. She tried to pair them with answers to decipher a clear picture, but they spiraled out of reach.

How is this connected to the disappearance of magic? Is all this related to what the Vale said about there being an evil presence here? Was the whole war started because Sethos was searching for something? The Vale said the

King is meddling with a power he can't fully control. If Sethos is using magic somehow, why is he using it to look for tombs?

Serein brushed cobwebs and dirt from her clothes and boots, dusting off the headscarf. Pausing by the gap, she listened to the silence beyond. The bright light from the windows assaulted her eyes as she slipped out and descended the stairs back toward the library.

As Serein stepped into the hallway, Sethos and Kamau left the Royal Wing, flanked by the Malik's Guard. The tall Ginjarrian glanced at her, dark eyes hard to read. Serein bowed, staring at the floor. Dark purple and sienna footsteps passed, overlapped by colors of sea blue, cobalt, crimson, and tan. They disappeared around a corner, and she raised her head.

Kamau's someone I have to watch out for. I didn't hear him in the room, but he has to know what's going on, Serein thought, brushing off a missed cobweb from her knee. *No sign of that woman. I didn't see any other footsteps leaving the study besides Sethos'. Did she stay behind or go somewhere else?*

"It's good to see you again, Serein," a familiar onyx voice came from behind.

A shiver ran down Serein's spine as she turned to see Il-Makah shuffling toward her with light brown footfalls. Bal perched on his shoulder, and Inga followed beside him.

This is the second time he's snuck up on me, Serein thought. *A man who has spent so long in the shadows that he moves like one. Even the girl moves like him. I don't know what color her voice or her footsteps are.*

The wrinkles around Il-Makah's eyes shifted as he smiled. "Are you enjoying being the Amir's wali?" he asked, sunlight glistening off his bald head.

"It's been uneventful so far," Serein replied, keeping her body relaxed.

Inga watched her with round blue eyes, holding a box of writing instruments in her arms. A loose green headscarf covered her blonde hair. "It'd be poor palace security if threats made their way within the walls." Il-Makah chuckled. "What brings you here?"

"I was leaving the library after my shift. His Highness suggested I look at the tapestry corridor since I'm still learning about the Saints and Sarddon's history," she replied. *I need to leave before he starts trying to interrogate me again.*

"The palace has many wonderful pieces of art. Many of the tapestries are over two hundred years old. Which one was your favorite?"

"The one of Saint Aziz commanding the monsoon. The contrast of colors was nice."

Bal cawed at Serein, the sharp lavender sound cutting the quiet. "Aziz, the Saint of Wind. He was deaf yet could sense storms. My favorite has always been Saint Basira fighting a falak. I've always admired her courage against such a monster," Il-Makah said. "Would you like to join me for another cup of tea? Inga and I were going to finish her Sarlyrian language lessons. Perhaps you could lend your expertise?"

"Unfortunately, I'm a bit tired today. The heat takes a lot out of me," Serein told him, inclining her head. *The girl knows multiple languages. Useful for overhearing conversations and deciphering messages. A proper little spy. Another one I have to keep my eye on.*

"The heat does tend to melt you if you're not careful," he said as Bal nipped at his earlobe. "Do take care of yourself, Serein. And tell me how that book is." His eyes went to the tome tucked into the sash. "It looks like an interesting read."

Il-Makah continued down the corridor, muttering to the white raven. Inga padded after him like a shadow.

Too close. I need to be better prepared for the next steps in this game, Serein thought. *The line I walk has gotten thinner.*

Chapter Twenty-Three
Fractured Steel

The girl wiped sweat from her upper lip as the hot sun melted the air. Her skin softened like wax underneath her rida', the heat making the ocher and white buildings shimmer. Every flash of armor with the roaring lion made her freeze. The language of rolling sands stirred up memories of glinting swords and burning carnage, fear worming its way in. Her mother's empty eyes. The shadows of Life and Death. Maggots swimming in flesh. White-hot pain across her chest.

"You are a Bone Viper. Fear should be afraid of us," the White Snake had told her when he first placed a dagger in her hand three years ago.

The girl crossed the street, the amethyst-colored wind pushing her along through the winding alleyways. Each step reminded her of her goal of the mission. She came to bring death.

A cat ran by, and she spotted a ladder leaning against a wall. She scurried up to the roof. The great city in the sands stretched on, the blue ocean splitting the horizon. A gleaming white palace with glittering domes and towers sat like a crouched beast on the hill. The X-shaped scar across the girl's chest ached with fire and cold steel.

A shadow moved in the corner of her eye, and her hands went to the daggers at her side. A man climbed onto the roof, covered head to toe in long tan robes and a brown headscarf that obscured everything but his green eyes. The girl relaxed.

"Admiring Sarddon's heart?" the White Snake asked, his pale words melting like snowflakes in the heat.

"I wanted to see where the Murderous King lived," she replied.

"Alqamar Palace isn't an easy place to enter and kill the King," he told her, squinting underneath the thick folds of his cowl. "Perhaps someday you'll be able to, but right now, we have work to do."

He turned and leapt to the next roof. The girl hesitated, taking one last look at the palace before following. She vowed to return and bring the Great Lion down, the promise signed across her chest.

The guard hit the ground, lying on his back, stunned. Serein grinned down at him, dusk shadowing her face. She twirled the dagger around. "Pay up, dead man," Serein said, toes digging into the warm sand beneath her feet.

Grumbling, the man propped dug into his sirwal pocket. He tossed a silver dijil onto the sand of the sparring circle, the side with pomegranates facing up. A cluster of guards stood around the courtyard while some sat on the hay bales and crates around the edges of the ring, nursing injuries and bruised pride. Every night at sundown, they gathered to place bets on who could beat Serein. One hundred and five silver dijils later, no one had.

"How can you be so strong? You're a woman," the guard said, his leafy green words mixing with the blood running down his nose.

"Gender has little to do with strength. Just ask the Edolasians," Serein replied and picked up the coin, putting it in the pouch by her boots.

"Must be that Ravanassë strength you half-bloods are rumored to have," the man muttered as he stood.

"Or it's the fact that you leave your left side open and favor offense over defense." The dijils gave satisfying blue *clinks* as they hit against each other, the falcon and palm tree-sided coppers mixing with the silvers. *Almost twenty silver dijils tonight and a few coppers. I should have two gold by now,* Serein thought.

Serein brushed short, damp hair behind her ear. The night air cooled her sweaty arms as the sun vanished behind the palace walls.

Torches burned around the barracks, casting flickering orange over the sparring circle.

"What are you doing?"

The green question cut through the courtyard. The guards straightened as Uriah approached, their conversations dying.

He looked at the men passing coins to each other, frowning. "Are you betting on matches?" Uriah asked Serein. "His Highness pays you for your services, so why do this?"

"I was bored and wanted to earn a bit more coin. I thought I'd get creative and find new ways to keep my skills sharp," Serein replied, sheathing her weapon. "Would you like to join in, Captain Stormheir?" *These sparring matches will at least throw off Il-Makah and his Jackals so that they don't find out what I'm doing...*

Serein stared past Uriah as Kamau morphed out of the shadows of the barracks on Sienna footsteps, his spear strapped to his back.

"Kamau," Uriah said, inclining his head.

I didn't think the king's muharib ever left his side. This can't be a good sign, she thought. *Does he suspect that I was listening?*

Kamau stopped in front of Serein, staring down at her. The ivory muharib pendant carved into the shape of a lion hung from Kamau's neck next to an elephant-shaped ebony wood disk. His red cuirass armor conformed to him like a thick second skin.

A totem pendant. The elephant deity, Tembo. Represents power, loyalty, and protection.

Kamau unstrapped the spear. The scaled scars along his arms rippled as he moved. "His Majesty wants me to test your skills," he said to Serein. His throaty navy-blue voice was impassive.

"My fight in the throne room wasn't enough?" Serein asked. *Controlled features, unchanging tonal inflections. He's difficult to read. This is the first time I've heard him speak.*

Serein's feet sank into the sand as she grabbed a nearby training sword and walked back to the center of the sparring circle. The torches around the sandy circle filled the area with flickering orange. Her fingers flexed around the dagger, the scimitar raised.

I'm at a disadvantage. He has speed and distance. If I can get in close and disarm him, I stand a better chance. He won't be able to do close combat while holding the spear, she thought.

Kamau spun the spear around before he lunged forward with a two-handed thrust. The long spearhead whistled through the air in orange and orange streaks as Serein sidestepped to the left, sword raised as she deflected the attack. Kamau slashed downward as he moved, kicking up sand.

Serein darted for Kamau's side as he flipped the weapon around. She listened for the hiss of the shaft cutting through the air, parrying and defecting as she tried to close the distance. Pivoting, the muharib thrust the weapon downward, the spearhead striking the ground close to Serein's feet. Grabbing the wooden shaft of the spear, she sliced the dagger across Kamau's leg. A thin line of blood seeped through his trousers.

As Kamau yanked the spear away from her grip, Serein got in close and rammed the pommel of the dagger under his armpit between his armor. He grunted, right arm wavering for a moment.

Disarming him will be hard unless I can drive him to the ground. This may be a test, but if he wanted to, he could actually kill me.

Serein swung the back of her sword at his legs as his spear switched hands. Kamau turned his body away as he thrust forward, forcing her to deflect the blow. Kamau kicked at her side. She caught his leg between her left arm, clearing it to the right as she swept his other leg out from under him. He hit the ground and freed himself from her grasp, twisting to avoid her sword.

As Kamau rolled to his feet, his left palm shot out and slammed against her nose. Cartilage gave a wet, blue *crunch*, and spots danced across her vision. Blood ran down her face, tears escaping her eyes as the pain took her breath away. Kamau jumped into a crouch and swung the full force of the shaft against her right side.

You were too eager, volchitsa. You left yourself open. You should have slit his throat and ended it.

Serein's eyes widened, moving a second too late. *Shit*, she thought as the blow connected.

She cried out and hit the sands, breaths stabbing into her ribs. Her hands tightened around her weapons as Kamau got to his feet, preparing to thrust the spearhead at her.

"Enough!" The gold word tore through the fire. Kamau stopped and lowered the spear in one fluid movement.

Serein inhaled sharply and staggered to her feet, blood dripping onto the sands. Serein held her side. She touched her nose, light fingers testing the damage. Each pale-yellow breath jabbed underneath her eyes.

Nothing broken. Cracked or bruised ribs, she thought, spitting out a bloody gob of saliva. *I don't think my nose could take being broken again. It's already crooked. Wouldn't want to ruin my beautiful face.*

The guards turned and lowered into bows, fingers to their foreheads. "Your Highness," Kamau said, bowing.

"What's going on here?" Rameses asked as he cut through the courtyard with Ilderim.

"Orders from your father, Your Highness," the muharib said, sweat shining on his head.

Anger burned on his face. "He ordered you to attack Serein?"

"No. Only test."

"My father doesn't need to *test* any of my guards," Rameses told him. Kamau didn't answer as he straightened and walked away, the darkness swallowing him up. Whispers traveled among the soldiers. The tension left Rameses' face, and he turned to Serein.

"Are you all right?" he asked, trying to keep his voice steady.

"I've had worse," Serein muttered, blinking away the tears.

"What were you thinking, fighting Kamau?" Rameses asked.

"He wanted to spar," she replied. "One of the more interesting opponents I've fought."

"Interesting? That's what you say after he tried to kill you?" Serein bent to retrieve her boots and the pouch of money, the pain from her side almost bringing her to her knees. She stumbled, drops of blood hitting the sandy ground.

"Uriah, help Serein to the infirmary," Rameses said.

Uriah offered Serein his arm, and she scowled, wincing. "The prince should warn you what happens to people who offer their arms to me. I threaten to break them," she told him.

SEREIN LAID AGAINST THE PILLOWS WITH A COOL COMPRESS ON her nose. The deft hands of the healer applied the sharp-smelling poultice to her ribs, wrapping tight bandages around her torso. The bitter taste of willow bark, turmeric, and cloves clung to her mouth. Lantern light brightened the small infirmary room, the air thick with the scent of herbs. An earthen pitcher sat on the nightstand filled with water.

She closed the robe, sucking in a breath. *Twice today I've been outmatched,* Serein thought, each breath simultaneously jabbing into her nose and side. *First time trying to glean secrets, and I get cracked ribs and a bruised nose.*

The healer blinked her rheumy eyes. "I'll leave some poppy milk to help with the pain," she said with a papery green voice, setting a vial of milky liquid next to the pitcher. "I'll come by again tomorrow to change the poultice. The damage isn't bad, but you shouldn't be moving around for at least three weeks. I'd recommend five weeks for your ribs to be fully healed."

"A month?" Rameses said from the other side of the door, worry tarnishing the edges of his gold voice.

The healer brushed loose strands of sandy-blonde hair under her goldenrod-colored headscarf. "Cracked ribs take time to heal, sayyidi," she said, her blue gandora rippling as she stood and left.

A month. I haven't been on bedrest that long since... The lumpy lines of the scars across Serein's chest tightened.

"Any chance the rumors about the Ravanassë healing faster are true?" Rameses asked Serein, watching her from the doorway.

"I don't seem to heal any faster than other people do," Serein replied.

"Ilderim, would you excuse us for a moment?" Rameses said as he straightened his shoulders, arms at his sides.

"As you wish, sayyidi," Ilderim replied, following the healer out of the room.

The door shut, leaving heavy silence in the room. Rameses tapped the emerald in the center of the lion's head ring. "Saints!" he seethed through his teeth as he paced. "Why would he send Kamau to fight you?"

"I saw them in the hallway after I left the secret passageway," Serein said in a quiet voice. "Il-Makah was there too." *Not knowing the full extent of Il-Makah's knowledge worries me. If there are things he's withholding from Sethos, he must have another plan for that information.*

Rameses stopped pacing. "Do you think my father suspects something?" he whispered.

"Not of eavesdropping. Kamau coming to fight with me was probably another warning from your father," Serein said.

Rameses' brow creased, shadows shrouding his face. "A warning? For what?"

"Your sister keeps trying to visit me. Sethos told me the week of the diffa that he'd throw me in a cell if I continue to interact with your family. He sees me as a threat."

"You should have told me. My father cannot interfere with my wali." Rameses hesitated, rolling words around in his mouth until he found the right ones. "You're strong, Serein, but not invincible. Kamau's not someone to be taken lightly."

"You shouldn't worry about your guards, princeling. It'll ruin your face." *Still, I made a mark on the king's muharib. Spying on him will be a difficult task. He knows things that could be useful.*

"Are you saying my face is attractive?" Rameses asked, smirking.

Serein sighed. "I didn't say that," she said.

"But you implied them," Rameses told her and sat on the edge of the bed, hands in his lap. "So, what did you hear today?" he added in a whisper.

The candle by the bedside flickered, wax collecting in the brass dish it sat in. "Your father's been meeting with ambassadors from Ginjarr and Zhao. He's bringing General Hisein back to Oyon."

His eyes widened. "Hisein? Is the Scourge moving with him?"

"The Scourge will remain at the border in Sava to make an example to those who rebel. Sethos has ships going to Bar Elenion too. Some ships were lost, so Admiral Ezio is sending a fleet from the Strait of Teeth." *Could Sethos also be using the Scourge to search for those tombs in the Old Kingdom?* she thought.

Rameses shifted, worry sketching lines across his face. "He didn't mention that at the council meeting last week. Why would he be sending ships that far north?" he asked.

"The ships are possibly looking for a way through the Fog barrier since the trading city, Illamatras, is closed off to Sarddon, and it's the only safe way to get into Bar Elenion currently," Serein told him. "They haven't been successful. Sethos might be looking to Zhao for help, which may be why so many emissaries have been visiting. Grand Vizier Umar was there. I don't know if Kamau or any of the other Malik's Guard were in the room too."

"Invading Bar Elenion...I didn't think my father would ever consider something like that," Rameses said. "Hisein's return could have something to do with the ships and the construction of the Steel Road. It's too early for the Aikhtiar and I doubt he would be returning for the Sister Moons Festival happening in a few months."

"I also heard a woman in your father's study," Serein went on, the words growing heavy on her tongue. "I don't know what she looks like, but Sethos seems to be keeping her a secret." *There are so many moving pieces. Did that Vale uncover any of this?*

Rameses gave her a confused look. "A woman?" Worry swam in his eyes. "I don't know why my father would be speaking to a woman in his study. Was it a servant?"

"I don't think so. She was talking to Sethos about searching for something in Bar Elenion. Tombs. He's found three, but he's looking for more. I'm not sure why," Serein told him. "It seems to be connected to what he's doing in the Old Kingdom."

"I have never known him to have anyone besides my mother. There was strain after my uncle died. And the past few years, they have seemed distant from each other..." Rameses gave his ring another twist, leaving a red mark on his finger. "This doesn't make sense. Why's my father looking for tombs? And why would he have a secret woman?"

The exhaustion pressed against Serein's eyelids as the questions continued to grow. She winced as she stifled a yawn, the pain loosening its hold as the medicine did its work. "Sethos also suspects rebels are sneaking into the palace and is looking for them. Those secret passageways might not be hidden for much longer. There may be more guards and Jackals moving about than before."

"I'm confident they will not be able to find all of them. We will have to be extra cautious," Rameses said, his shoulders slumping as he stood. "I left you another book in your chambers when I stopped by earlier. I will bring it by tomorrow. I think you will enjoy it. Lots of surprising secrets within the pages."

"I'm sure I'll have plenty of time to read since I won't be going anywhere," Serein told him.

Concern shadowed the edges of his strained smile. "The rest will do you good. I would hate to see your face injured further." Rameses said.

Serein closed her eyes. "I'm not concerned with how my face looks."

"Your scars are marks of strength, but that doesn't mean you should continue to get injured," Rameses said. "I didn't want you to get hurt because of this. For that, I'm sorry." The bells offered their peach-colored goodbyes as he left.

Serein sank into the heavy shroud of sleep. *My face isn't meant for you. You don't know the meaning of my scars.*

Chapter Twenty-Four
Paintings & Tigers

CHARCOAL COATED SEREIN'S FINGERS AS SHE SKETCHED AN
elephant, balancing the paper on the serving tray in her lap. Light
from the window above the bed illuminated the mosaic of Saint
Zaman. Waxy sticks of various colors rolled across the bedsheet as
she shifted, the ache in her side persistent. Other drawings were
scattered across the bed. Seagulls formed in an azure sky, shrouded
in burgundy spikes. Buildings and blooming bougainvilleas. Colorful
zellij mosaics in a riad.

A dark blue knock split Serein's concentration. "Come in," she
said, pain radiating through her nose. The teal creak of the door fell
over the gray footsteps. "What brings you here, Captain Stormheir?
Did you come to admire my face?"

"The bruising's not that bad," Uriah said, his green voice filling
her peripheral vision.

Serein glanced up. Healers moved about the infirmary behind
Uriah, carrying fresh linens and medical supplies. "Is that sarcasm?"
she said. "Last time I checked, my nose is puffy, and I look like you
when you haven't slept."

Uriah crossed his arms over his armored chest as he scowled.
Shadows clung underneath his eyes with whispers of sleepless nights.
Serein picked up a gray stick, shading in the elephant.

"You still haven't told me what you're doing here." *What nightmares plague him this time?* Serein thought. *Perhaps he's losing sleep over thoughts of me.*

His bent finger twitched. "His Highness asked me to see how you're doing," Uriah said.

"Liar," she said. "Are you that concerned for my wellbeing?"

He cleared his throat as his hands tightened around his biceps. "Your recuperation inconveniences His Highness."

"'It inconveniences His Highness.' This feels familiar. Are you embarrassed because you don't want to admit that you're concerned about me? Perhaps it's guilt. Maybe you've developed feelings for me and want to proclaim your undying love."

The scowl etched deep lines across Uriah's forehead. "In what life would that be possible?" he snapped, his jaw tight. "Kamau must have hit you harder than the healer thought."

"I wanted to see the look on your face when I said it," Serein said as she straightened, ribs crying out in protest. *Brusque as usual, but there's something else. His attitude has shifted ever since I saved the prince's life. He's starting to trust me.*

What if it's concern? You can play to his sense of morality and manipulate those feelings. He can be a powerful piece if you capture his emotions and loyalty.

Serein blinked, trying to dislodge the white cloud from her mind. "When you deny it, then it makes it seem like you're lying," she told Uriah, and pink crept up his neck.

Uriah's gaze went to the other sketches on the bed. "I don't know why I bothered coming here," he said. "Since when do you draw?"

"Since you wouldn't give me any farming advice, I decided to focus on drawing. I wanted to paint, but the healers didn't want me ruining the sheets."

Uriah sighed through his nose. "Your sketches are...good."

Serein blended the white and gray colors with her finger. "Such a profound compliment. I'll treasure it always."

"Why is there red around the seagulls?" Uriah asked, picking up the drawing of the seagulls.

"Burgundy. It goes with the gulls," Serein replied. "It's called artistic interpretation."

Uriah frowned as he set the paper down. "You have strange eyes," he told her.

"To me, it's the rest of the world that has strange eyes."

"You should get another cool compress on the bruising. It'll help the swelling go down," Uriah muttered and left.

Serein stared at the space where the green sound still hung. *Still won't admit when he's wrong. I wonder how long before whatever guilt he has eats him alive.*

Turquoise laughter rang through the air like fragments of crystal. Sunlight tinged the world in golden light as it streamed through the trees, shimmering over nearby houses. The woman held her daughter on her lap. Robes of spring-green and earthy-brown wrapped around her, the three crystals dangling from her veil throwing tiny prisms into the girl's hands.

The woman stroked the child's dark hair as she told stories of ancient kingdoms on silver shores across the sea. Stories of heroes, the immortal Lights, and white elk guarding massive silver forests. The stories took on color, fleshed out with paper and paint as the girl drew the characters, brush clasped in her small hand.

"Tell me about Yestarë and her forest," the girl said.

"Very well, my little rain," her mother said. "Thousands of years ago when the world was new, Yestarë and the twelve Lights came down from Ië with the blessings of Mirarnediad. The new land lacked the lovely lights of Ië, so Yestarë poured out some of the stars to create a silver tree, Thavnath. It sprouted and raised its limbs to the heavens. She and her sister, Mulinulda, tended to it, guiding it with songs. The white gwae elk, Herutaur, left his perch in the celestial lights with his herd to aid her."

The girl drew a herd of elk with tall trees. Colors smudged her hands, paint smeared across her skin.

"From Thavnath grew four sparkling fruits. Yestarë plucked the fruit, and out of them came four beings with hair like starlight and eyes of precious stones. She called them the Vale, the first beings born on the earth from the Lights. Yestarë breathed magic into the Vale. She taught them the songs to use magic. From Thavnath came many more trees."

"The Forests of Eldataur!" the girl exclaimed.

The mother pulled her close, their noses touching. She tickled the girl, who burst into bright giggles. "That's right, carissima. *The Vale tended to the forest with the gwae elk, along with the Elves."*

"Have you seen the Starlight trees, Mama?" the girl asked, looking at her painting.

The mother gazed at the horizon. "I haven't," she replied and ran her fingers through her daughter's hair, braiding the dark locks. "Your father will take us to see them one day. Picture them in your mind—towering trees of silver that glow like the stars. Think of all the beautiful colors you'll see with all the different sounds there."

The girl finished the forest filled with elk and glittering stars. She laid the paper next to a painting of two men—one draped in black with a piece of wood and one with clothes like sunlight. Images of silver trees and Yestarë dressed in starlight danced in the girl's head, she and her mother standing on shores filled with magic.

A FRESH CANVAS SAT IN FRONT OF SEREIN, CHARCOAL LINES following her fingers as pent-up designs spilled out. Open jars of ocher, vermillion, yellow, white, and cobalt paints sat on the chair beside her with a cup of muddy paint water. Smears of mixed colors marked the flat piece of wood on her knee. The ache in Serein's side continued to gnaw at her ribs.

Steam curled from the copper kettle on the table in the living chamber. "Your embroidery has gotten better, miss," Rizwana said, a smile in her lapis voice. Flowers with bright red and blue petals and leaves grew along the white cloth square on the table.

"I've had experience with a needle, but it was stitching up wounds. Not embroidery," Serein replied.

"I'll bring you some more fabric and thread and show you how to do more complex designs if you want," Rizwana said, throwing the clothes in a basket. "Fariha's tried her hand at it, but her stitchwork looks like it was done by a blind woman. She seems to have blacksmiths' hands like her father. She shows promise, which thrills him since our oldest prefers spending time at the docks and wants to be a sailor."

Dark blue rapping on the door spread through the chamber over Rizwana's lapis words. "Enter." *So many visitors,* Serein thought.

The door swung open, and Rasima stepped in with Laia and Karam. Rizwana bowed to the Amirah. "Your Highness. I'll pour you some tea!" she said as Laia set a basket of food on the table.

"Good afternoon, Serein," Rasima said, violet voice fluttering like petals. "How are you feeling?"

Serein looked up. "I'm alive. What brings you here?" she asked.

"I thought you could use some company. The healers told me you were here. I thought you were going to be in the infirmary, resting," Rasima replied.

"I convinced them to let me recuperate here. Rizwana makes sure I don't overdo things." *The stairs were excruciating, but I'd rather recuperate in private,* Serein thought. *Rizwana's gossip this past week is the only thing keeping me informed on things happening.*

"I brought some sweets and thought we could have some tea." Rasima glanced at the painting. "This is pretty. How long have you been painting?"

Serein smeared a dab of red paint with her fingers, leaving behind fingerprints in the wet colors. "A few hours," she replied.

Rasima pulled a cushion beside Serein, lifting her white veil back off her face. Laia helped Rizwana prepare the tea as Karam stood by the door.

"You'll want to add sugar. This tea's not sweetened," Serein said.

"Why? Mint tea is supposed to be sweet," Rasima said.

"Sweet things don't sit well with me," Serein replied. "Rizwana was kind enough to make it less sweet."

"Oh, I don't think I've met anyone who didn't like sweets," the Amirah said, adjusting the skirts of her green abaya.

Laia came over with a tray with a kettle, glasses, and a plate with puffy sfenj drizzled with honey and a sugar-dusted maamoul on it. She set the tray down on a stool and poured high above the glasses, drops running down the sides of the cup. "I added more sugar to this pot. Would you like anything else, Your Highness?" she asked, red currant-colored voice soft.

"No. Thank you, Laia," Rasima replied.

The maidservant nodded and went over to Karam, giving him one of the cookies and a glass of tea. Karam's stern face broke into a faint smile, and a light blush rose in Laia's cheeks.

There's something between those two. I wonder if they're lovers, Serein thought as Laia's hand lingered against Karam's before she returned to Rasima's side.

"Do your injuries hurt?" Rasima asked, taking a date-filled cookie.

Rizwana set a glass down on the chair beside Serein. "Not as much as they did. Pain and I are quite familiar with each other. The cracked ribs are more of an inconvenience," Serein replied.

Rasima's gold eyes went to Serein's scarred throat. "Rameses says you have lots of stories that you don't share," she said, powdered sugar dusting her lips before she licked it away.

"Most of the stories I have aren't suitable for your ears, princess."

Sunlight shifted, throwing small rainbows against the wall as the light hit the glasses. "I'm not a child." Rasima held her head high.

Serein took a sip of tea. *She doesn't need to know all the horrors of the world or the cruelty of men yet.*

"Do you have any stories about the Lights? Or maybe one about the Ravanassë and magic?" Rasima asked.

Serein dabbed the brush in a glob of paint, adding a streak of green across the canvas. "You know that your father doesn't approve of you being here," she said.

"My parents are overprotective. I told my mother that I wanted to teach you about the Saints and Alkhaliq, to show you the right path." A smile crossed Rasima's face, dimples appearing. "She cannot stop me from doing my 'sacred duty of saving lost souls.' Her words. But I still want to hear about the Lights. What are they?"

"The Lights are starlit beings made by Mirarnediad. The Immortals say that they used to walk the earth with the first beings. Yestarë was the first who poured out stars to create the silver tree, Thavnath. Its fruit turned into the Vale, the first beings to have magic. The Elves were made by Yestarë's sister, Malinalda, from the seeds of Thavnath's fruit. The Vale and the Elves were tasked with tending the silver forest that grew from the great tree—the Forests of Eldataur."

Rasima's eyes widened. "I heard from Rameses that there are silver trees on the Silver Shores. Is that true? Have you seen them?" she asked.

"I haven't been to the Silver Shores. My mother told me about them," Serein muttered.

Rasima reached for another cookie. "What did the other Lights do?"

"Lalaith made the animals and all living creatures. Gwaihir, her husband, created the Fae who could take on any creature's shape. Nolmë, the husband of Malinalda, filled his library with knowledge and all the events of the world. Belegurth controlled the earth and formed the continents. Rannath, Belegurth's sister, controlled the water and created the oceans, rivers, and lakes. Egnor created the sun and fire. Lámina was the sounds present, past, and future. Laiquassë was responsible for the spirits of the dead. Rauta cherished metal and fashioned them into objects of great beauty and power. Vanya was dark as shadows and created the moon. Her husband, Dúath the thirteenth and last Light was pale as starlight. He created shadows and the night. He and Vanya created humans."

"Why did the Lights create the things in the world instead of the god who created them?" Rasima asked, pulling apart a puffy sfenj.

Serein shifted, wincing as pain jabbed into her side. "Mirarnediad created the Lights as an extension of himself. He gave them the power to create and watch over Cemiyon. But then Dúath betrayed the other Lights and plunged the world into chaos," she replied.

"What happened?"

Another blue knock rapped on the door. Rasima glanced up as Karam opened the door. Rameses stood in the doorway, his brow creasing as his gaze landed on Serein and Rasima.

Peach chimes trickled down Rameses' gray qamis as he entered, holding a small bundle in his arms. "Rasi, I was not expecting you to be here," he said, his gold words tipping upward with surprise. "Serein, I know you insisted on recovering in your room, but you really should be in bed. It's only been a week."

"We're having tea," Rasima told him. "Would you like to join us?"

"I came by because I have a gift for Serein," Rameses said as he grabbed another cushion, sitting next to them. Rizwana moved to fill a glass for him. "Do you need more poppy milk? That"—he gestured to Serein's face—"looks painful."

Serein stopped, examining her painted lines. "It hurts, but I'm not desperate for oblivion," she said. Xansas' white laugh crept up, trying to dredge up the memories attached to it.

The bundle in Rameses' arms wriggled. Peacock-blue mewling came from under the blanket. "Well, maybe this will take your mind off your discomfort for a bit."

"I'm not fond of surprises." *They turn out to be prying spymasters, threats from the king, or cracked ribs*, she thought. *There was also you, my Sun and Stars, so I suppose there are a few surprises that aren't bad.*

"I think you will like this one."

A furry white head appeared as he pulled back a corner of the covering. A small Ygris tiger cub lay curled in his lap. Rivers of gold and onyx stripes cut through the white fur, and the ears were dipped in black. The cub squeaked, eyes a milky blue. Rasima stroked its fur, smiling.

"The tigress gave birth two weeks ago. This one was blind. I thought you might like to have it to keep you company while you recover," Rameses said.

The dried paint cracked along Serein's fingers. "These gifts make me wonder what your intentions are," she said, putting the brush in the cup of water.

"What if I simply like giving gifts?" Rameses asked, scratching the tiger cub behind her ear.

The cub twisted, pink tongue curling against milky white teeth. "It's hard to believe that you possess no other motives." *He uses kind words and gifts to gain trust, but I know better.*

Serein touched the cub's nose, staring into its cloudy eyes. The tiger took Serein's finger in her mouth, the tongue rough against her skin.

"Do you want her?" Rameses asked. Rizwana handed him his tea with a bow. "Thank you."

"The cub still needs her mother," Serein told him.

"Will the mother take the cub back?" Rasima asked, her violet voice brushing Serein's arm.

"Maybe, but this one will have a difficult time fighting for milk. One of the hounds that has a litter might take care of the cub," Serein said.

Rameses gave her a puzzled look as he took a sip of tea. "You think a dog will take care of a tiger?"

Serein pulled her hand away from the cub's mouth. "I've seen dogs take care of abandoned kittens before. If nothing works, I'll feed her by hand." *Goat milk should be a decent substitute,* she thought. *I could ask Rizwana to get some from the kitchens.*

Rameses chuckled, lifting the wriggling animal back into his lap. "The Grinning Assassin feeding a tiger cub. I would love to see that," he said. "What are you painting?"

Black clung to the bristles as Serein dipped the brush into the paint. "Whatever I want," she replied, flexing her toes as tingling numbness spread through them.

"I will have to see it when it's finished." Serein felt Rameses' gaze burning into her collarbone, his voice sticking to the canvas in golden sunbursts. "Tell me, why did you get a vine tattooed on yourself?" Rameses asked her.

"Voronwa. It's a vine that grows everywhere in the Old Kingdom. Cold, rain, heat, drought," Serein answered, mixing a pale gray color on the wood piece.

He tilted his head. "So, you got a common plant for what reason?"

"It has nice flowers. They're ash-gray on the outside with fire-colored centers."

Rameses wrapped the cub in the blanket as he stood. Rizwana took his empty glass. "I see. I will let you get back to your painting then."

"You're not staying?" Rasima asked, lower lip extending in a pout.

"I have to return the cub to the kennels and get to a meeting. We can have dinner tonight, Rasi. I promise," Rameses said. Smiling, he patted Rasima's head as he left.

Serein dipped her fingers into the paint, smearing and dabbing lines across the canvas. *My Sun and Stars, it seems that I'll be caring for another baby,* she thought.

SEREIN STARED AT THE CRESCENT MOON HANGING LIKE A LOPSIDED grin. Moonlight bounced off the pool in the riad as long whiskered fish with black and white scales drifted beneath the water's surface. She muttered the names of the constellations. Venator, the Hunter. Equus Aquilonem, the Stallion of the North. Flens Unum, the Weeping One.

The seats of Ië. The homes the Lights fled to when the Dark One ravaged Cemiyon, she thought, remembering the words her mother spoke long ago.

Serein tugged on the bangles, metal meeting flesh. She stood, wincing as she slowly wandered the palace. The smell of jasmine and rose wafted from the gardens. Throaty daffodil-yellow croaks from frogs jumped through the night, bursting like bloated fireflies in the dark.

It's been a few weeks, and Rameses still hasn't found anything about the ships going to Bar Elenion or that mysterious woman. He hasn't heard anything suspicious at the meetings either, Serein thought. *I won't be able to do much until my ribs heal. I'll have to watch Kamau more closely. He doesn't seem to leave the king's side, so he must know who Sethos has been secretly meeting with.*

Serein made her way to the kennels. The tigress lifted her head as she passed, two cubs nestled against her side. Serein eventually found a kennel with a wiry dog with sandy fur. Around her were five puppies and one white cub. The cub had doubled in size over the course of a few weeks.

"I can't guarantee that you'll have an easy life," Serein whispered.

The tiger nestled against her littermates. A pale-yellow melody vibrated on Serein's lips as she hummed.

"'Run, child, run.
Catch the Lights before dawn comes.
Twelve in hand for a necklace of stars.
Catch the Lights before they get too far.
Run, child, run.
Meet Life and Death under the sun
Before the end comes.'"

Chapter Twenty-Five
The Hidden Things

THE CORRIDOR TO THE OFFICERS' QUARTERS WAS QUIET AS RAMESES walked down the hallway with Ilderim. He brushed the white fletching of the arrow he held, the bow slung across his back. Arrows clacked in the quiver hanging from his shoulder as Rameses pushed open the door to Uriah's chambers.

Uriah sat hunched over his desk, rubbing a knuckle against his temple. "You seem deep in thought tonight, sadiqi," Rameses said as he stepped into the room.

Uriah's head jerked up. "What are you doing here, Rameses?" he asked.

"I wanted to see if you would like to join me for some archery practice," Rameses said, picking up a blue stone from the neat line of rocks on Uriah's desk. *Did he get more rocks? One day a bunch of them are going to roll out of his pockets,* he thought, glancing at the shelves on the wall filled with stones of different hues and shapes.

"Now? Isn't it a bit late?"

Rameses glanced out the window as the edges of dusk stretched across the sky, bringing purple and blue shadows with it. "There's still some light left. I have been so busy as of late that I have not been able to practice much. And I need a distraction to take my mind off of things."

Uriah ran his fingers through his hair. "I'm finalizing the guard schedules at the moment."

"Maybe a break will help take your mind off whatever problem you're wrestling with. You seem more grim than usual."

"What are you talking about? This is just my face," Uriah muttered, brow creased.

Rameses twirled the arrow in his hand as he set the rock down. "You just look more perturbed than usual," he said, taking in the faint dark smudges under his friend's eyes. *I wonder if his nightmares are bothering him again.*

Uriah opened his mouth to protest but let out a heavy exhale instead. He collected the papers and shoved them in a drawer, straightening the stone Rameses had moved.

"No need to look like I'm pulling your arm, Uriah. You need to relax a bit more," Rameses said, flashing a grin.

Uriah grabbed his boots and scimitar as they left his room. "I'd prefer to get my work done before I do any 'relaxing'," he replied, following Rameses down the dim hallway.

The cooler air played with Rameses' curls as they crossed through the riads to the gardens. "Have you gone to check on Serein lately?" he asked.

Uriah shot him a look. "Why would I check on her?"

"You seemed to want to keep an eye on her and question her more," Rameses said.

The corner of Uriah's mouth twitched, his silence brewing like storm clouds.

Six wooden targets were set up in a circular garden on the west side of the palace. Torches on high posts surrounded the area, illuminating the sandy ground with flickering light. Trellises covered in creeping jasmine rose several feet in the air behind the targets, gnarled olive trees swaying around them.

Rameses unstrapped his recurve bow from his back. Gold inlay curled along its smooth wood, small falcons flying across the bow. The breeze brushed his arms, his long gray tunic shifting as he moved.

Rameses nocked an arrow, pulling back on the bowstring. "You still don't trust Serein, do you? Even after she saved me from the snake?" he asked as the arrow struck the first target in its center.

"She's still an assassin," Uriah told him, staring at the arrow. "I get a bad feeling from her."

Rameses grinned as he drew another arrow, the fletching brushing against his fingertips. It hit the next target's center. "Are you sure it's a bad feeling and not something else?"

"I don't have feelings *for* her." Irritation crept into Uriah's voice. "She has to resent Sarddon and the Malik for the war. I can't fully trust her, knowing she harbors those feelings."

"Toward my father, most likely. Toward me and other Sarddonians, I don't think so. I think she finds me irritating at most," Rameses replied. "And doesn't she have cause not to trust us because of this war?"

"What makes you say that?" Uriah asked.

Gravel crunched under Rameses' sandals as he moved down the line to the third target. His steady breaths expanded in his chest as he held the bowstring taut. The breeze shifted, and he released. The arrowhead gave a satisfying *thunk* against the wood as it found its mark in the small center dot.

"Serein's not the only one who can notice things. Her anger's more...focused. I have seen how she is with Rasima, and it's not the actions of someone who hates an entire group of people." *It's been a few months since I have practiced, but I have not lost my touch*, Rameses thought with a faint grin.

"Do you feel it's safe to have Serein around her? If she wanted to kill you or anyone else here, she's in the perfect position to do so," Uriah said. "It might not be now, but she'll eventually do something."

Another arrow found its mark. "Serein may be an assassin, but I think she cares more about her freedom than revenge. She paints and has tea with Rasi. There's more to her than violence and killing." Rameses chewed on Uriah's silence as he lowered his bow. "I know you have your concerns and always have our safety in mind, but what's really bothering you?"

Uriah reached for his necklace, clutching the black stone. "Sometimes I have these dreams about her...Disturbing ones." His voice dropped low, his brow creasing.

"Dreaming about her? Well, now I'm very intrigued," Rameses said, grinning. "You will have to define what you mean by 'disturbing'."

Uriah scowled at him. "Rameses..." he muttered.

"I hear your disapproval, sadiqi. I merely want you to find a nice woman and be happy," Rameses told him.

"And you think Serein's a *nice* woman?" Uriah shot, raising an eyebrow.

"Maybe not in the traditional sense, but she's not that bad. Sometimes she can even be charming. You're the one having dreams about her."

The muscles in Uriah's jaw clenched. "They aren't those kinds of dreams!"

"Then what kind of dreams are they?" Rameses asked.

Uriah sighed, shoulders slumping as he released the stone pendant. "I've seen her kill me, kill you. Those dreams always end with death when she appears," he said.

"I can see why those dreams might put you on edge, but I think you should give her the benefit of the doubt," Rameses told him, gripping the bow. "You and Serein are alike in some ways."

"She and I are *not* alike," Uriah grumbled, shooting Rameses a narrowed look.

Rameses inspected the six arrows stuck in the center rings and handed the bow and quiver to Uriah. "Maybe if you spend more time with her, you will see that you have a lot more in common than you think," he said. Uriah muttered something in Wendish. "Still, I didn't think you could dream about another woman besides Safiya."

Shadows rimmed Uriah's eyes as the torchlight flickered. "That was a long time ago," he muttered.

"I apologize. I didn't mean to bring up unpleasant memories," Rameses said. *Seems he still thinks about her,* he thought, swallowing a twinge of guilt.

Uriah nocked an arrow, arms swelling inside his tunic sleeves as he pulled the bowstring back. "It's not your fault." The arrow carved its way through the air, striking a few inches to the left from Rameses'.

Rameses whistled. "Well, look at that. You have gotten better. Years ago, you were just hitting the edge of the target."

Uriah frowned. "Archery isn't my strong suit. And it's also nighttime."

"There's plenty of light from the torches. Next time, we will do sword practice. No hand-to-hand combat, though. I'm not keen on being punched in the face since you almost broke my jaw that one time."

The arrows clacked against each other as Uriah drew a second one. "How was that my fault? I already apologized. You dropped your guard at the last moment. And I didn't hit you that hard," he said as he released the bowstring, striking below the center ring.

Rameses gestured to his face. "Still, I was bleeding, and I had a bruise for a week," he replied.

"There was no permanent damage done to your face," Uriah told him.

"Some of us don't wear scars and bruises as well as you do."

"I don't know what that's supposed to mean."

Uriah went down the line, shooting and missing the center. The torchlight crackled. Sparks burned in the sky as they tried to reach the stars before turning to ash. The quiet was broken by the trilling calls of the nightjars hidden in the nearby trees.

Uriah loosened the last arrow. The night darkened into an indigo shroud, firelight dotting the tops of the palace walls in the distance. From the towers of the Royal House of the Saints, the prayer of Alkhaliq rang out after the ninth bell.

"Why do you want to be friends with Serein?" Uriah asked as he handed the bow and arrows back to Rameses.

Rameses lifted the bow and stared down the shaft of the arrow. "Fret not, Uriah. I'm not replacing you. Who else would I drag out at night for archery practice?" he replied. "Do you know why I like having you as a friend?"

The arrow struck next to the one in the target's center. "Because no one else will put up with you?"

Rameses laughed. "Because you're honest with me. Even when we were children, you went along with my antics, but you always told me if they were a bad idea. You and Serein are the few people in my life who are honest with me and don't simply tell me what I want to hear."

"I think you'll have better luck being friends with a lion than her."

"See? This is why I like you. The brutal honesty."

"You often do the thing I suggested you not do," Uriah told him.

"Well, that's an entirely different thing. I always appreciate your advice and input," Rameses replied as his arrow scraped against the one already embedded in the wooden circle. *I was trying to split the arrow down the center. I've done it before, but it seems my aim still needs work.*

"When will Serein resume her duties?" Uriah asked, scratching his chin.

"The healer said another week or so. Her face looks better, and she's well enough to play shatranj and beat me at it," Rameses told him. "She's probably working on another painting right now instead of resting."

THE ROYAL ARCHIVES BREATHED HEAVY SILENCE AROUND SEREIN. Motifs of plants and stars painted the walls as rows of darkened shelves and stone niches filled the two-level library. Night after night, the winding labyrinth became familiar as she dug through the seas of words and dust.

The amber light of the small lantern beside Serein illuminated the pages in her hands. She shifted, the dull pain tapping her ribs. Two weeks had turned her bruises into mottled yellow patches, leaving faded shadows around her nose. Brittle sheafs released musty plum-colored sighs as she flipped through the curling Sarddonian script.

In the year prior to Amir Nasr's death, His Majesty continued to seek the aid of Sarddon's best healers. Many Elves and Sahriminha attended to the sickly Amir, seeing improved effects for a few days before the sickness would return. Even with the knowledge of the Immortals and the royal healers, no disease could be identified.

Before the child turned five years old and while the Malika was four months into her pregnancy with her second child, Amir Nasr succumbed to his disease. In his grief, His Majesty sank into a deep depression while Amir Sethos acted as regent in his place.

This record by Archivist Rami says pretty much what all the accounts from seventeen years ago say, Serein thought. *Was the disease a magical curse, or was someone poisoning the child until he died? Magic should have cured him. Perhaps the records of the illness are in the infirmary.*

No sounds colored the darkness as Serein picked up the lantern. She put the bound sheath back in the dusty niche, scanning the cracked spines of tomes and the handwritten tags on bound scrolls. Her black robes rustled with magenta whispers as she climbed the spiral staircase to the second floor.

Most texts about magic were confiscated or destroyed, but Sethos might have saved some to learn how to defeat his enemies. Most likely they'd be in his chambers, the Tower of Secrets, or his study. I should take Il-Makah up on his offer for tea soon, so I can be in the Tower of Secrets with cause.

The light pooled around Serein as she stopped by a shelf overflowing with camel hidebound books. She made out the faded title on the embossed front and continued to the next shelf. The worn pages and leather edges of the tomes brushed against her fingertips. A title buried behind the leaning volumes caught Serein's eye. Old sloping Sarlyrian letters stood out of place among the other titles with curving Sarddonian script.

The book gave off a musty smell as Serein grabbed it, studying the ancient language under the light. Delicate leaves were pressed along the cover, the edges of its pages curling with age.

"The Illumination of Sarlyria" by Aintzane Ibarra, Serein thought, brushing dust off the thin book. *The Archivists missed this one. Ancient Sarlyria isn't used anymore. Must be a much older book. Written by a woman too.*

A dingy silver-white scraping sound cracked the silence. Serein whirled around as the wall behind her swung open, a beam of yellow light spilling out.

Someone's here? Serein clutched the book close and extinguished her lantern. *They must've been here long before I arrived because I didn't hear anyone else come in.*

She darted to a nearby alcove, pressing into the shadows. The wall shut, and quiet yellow footsteps moved past her as an archivist in brown and white robes shuffled by. His spectacles caught the dim light of his lantern as he descended the staircase.

Minutes crawled by before Serein left the alcove, glancing around. *That hidden room wasn't on the map. A new addition?* she thought, staring at the wall between the alcove and another shelf. *I'll have to let Rameses know that his maps don't show everything in the palace.*

Serein felt along the edges of the stone, finding a gap between the mortar. Unsheathing her dagger, she left a small horizontal cut on the side of the bookshelf next to the hidden entrance.

I'll have to investigate this later. No doubt there are important things hidden in that room.

Serein's pale blue footsteps bounced against the marble stairs as she followed the shelves to the secret passageway behind a statue of Saint Faysal—the Saint of Earthly Knowledge. He smiled down at her, holding a book in his right hand while his left remained open. Serein squeezed behind the statue, pressing on one of the worn stones. A section of the wall swung inward into blackness.

Let's see if this book has anything interesting to offer, Serein thought, stepping into the tunnel.

Chapter Twenty-Six
Revelations & Intentions

SEREIN BLINKED AS THE SWORD CUT THROUGH THE MAN'S SIDE, spilling blood onto the hard-packed arena sands. The saifrakasa fell to his knees as his opponent slashed his throat, letting loose a stream of crimson as the match bell sent dark peach tolls through the air. The winner, Saddam, raised his weapon with a carmine shout as he strutted over the corpse. A pair of guards rushed out to carry the body away. Death scooped up the blue soul in his arms while the crowds cheered in the packed stands. Wealthier spectators watched from covered viewing boxes closer to the arena wall.

The sun blazed down through the open half-dome roof of the coliseum. Heat gathered underneath Serein's headscarf as she and I'timad stood in the royal viewing box on the first level. I'timad scratched his short beard, brown eyes drifting to the faces of the men and women in the crowds. Rameses lounged on the plush couch, wearing a strained look as he sipped chilled wine.

I thought Airen was a hot month, but Súru is even worse, Serein thought, catching the stray breeze from the woven fans the servants moved.

Her gaze darted to Sethos. His shadow remained still, and there were no signs of the opalescent strands of magic around him. Kamau stood with three of the Malik's Guard, his red cuirass armor matching the blood on the sands. Seven weeks had passed since their fight, but Serein's ribs still carried the dull ache of the encounter.

Sethos has been meeting with ambassadors from Ginjarr and Zhao since last month. Nothing new about the ships going to Bar Elenion, that mysterious woman, or what he's searching for. Only plans to begin construction of the Steel Road and the rebel attacks at the border.

"You seem uninterested in the fights," Rameses said, gold voice quiet.

Serein's gaze slid over to him. "I don't find them entertaining," she replied, hands clasped behind her back.

"Most of the fights are not this bloody. I prefer the other events like the camel and horse races," he told her, shoulders slumping. "Saddam's especially brutal. Most of the saifrakasas don't kill their opponents."

The shouts of the crowds grew louder as the next event began. An olive-skinned man with silvery hair and black tattoos across his body was prodded out one of the side gates. Behind him were two lanky figures, a boy and a girl, with the same features. They clutched his arm as they were shoved toward the center. The gate behind them shut with a teal slam. The energy shifted throughout the crowd. The waves of sounds lessened, and an eerie subdued blanket hung over the spectators as pockets of shouts broke through.

Children?! He's using prisoners in the fights? Serein thought, eyes locked on the dirty faces of the children. Her heartbeat wrapped around her throat, tightening with each breath. *Silver hair, tan skin, tattoos. Part of the Accipiter tribes near Idris. The children don't look much older than thirteen.*

Rameses stood, horror written on his face. "Why are children in the arena?!" he asked.

The Malik didn't respond.

The Accipiter held a spear in his hand, facing Saddam. Red whip marks stood out against his back. The saifrakasa charged with a battle cry, sun glinting off metal.

"*Abite!*" the Accipiter shouted to the children, his cream-colored voice lost in the sea of roaring colors.

The children fled to the walls, clinging to each other in the shadows. The man aimed the spear at Saddam, cutting into the fighter's side. Saddam shoved his opponent back and knocked him off balance, his scimitar slicing across the Accipiter's chest. With a carmine yell, Saddam ran his sword into the man's stomach, and the Accipiter crumpled to the ground.

"For all their resistance, the Ravanassë do not fight with half the spirit I was expecting," Sethos said.

This isn't a fight. It's an execution, Serein thought, the roaring colors of the crowds slamming against her head. She looked out at the faces shouting for death. Some glanced around or looked away. *Is this nation so eager for blood that they would cheer for the deaths of children?*

Saddam advanced toward the children. A white ringing sound crept in the edges of Serein's vision. The Accipiter hauled himself to his feet. He roared, and Saddam whirled around as the spear struck his chest. Saddam screamed at the man thrust the weapon in deeper, red staining the ground.

"*Sanguis enim sanguinem!*" the Accipiter shouted, hands slipping from the weapon.

The two fighters collapsed on the sands. Screaming, the children huddled against the wall. Death looked at them with sadness as he collected the two souls. Sethos frowned and raised his hand to the arena masters below, and they nodded, shouting to the coliseum guards.

This is how people of the Old Kingdom fight, cursing you with dying breath, Serein thought.

The bodies of the two men were dragged away, and the children were shoved to the center. Tawny lions lunged out of the dark gates of the arena, growling as they were prodded with long poles. The boy picked up the fallen saifrakasa's scimitar, struggling to lift it.

"Father, please. Do not do this," Rameses said, the golden words cracking.

"An example has to be set. These rebels cannot be allowed to threaten Sarddon any longer," Sethos replied. "Their tribe was responsible for attacking our soldiers. They used children to sneak into the camps and poison the horses and drinking water, killing dozens of our men. Do not forget what has been done. The attack on our city, the lives that have been lost because of these people."

"They are children and have done nothing to deserve this!"

The girl clung to her brother as the lions moved in. The boy swung the blade, slicing one of the lion's muzzles. The lion snarled, shying away from his sharp purple shouts.

Rameses sucked in a breath, his face paling. "Father, stop this. Please. I beg you!"

The crackling white ringing grew louder, blanketing Serein's vision like swirling snow. *May the Lights take you quickly and give you rest,* she thought, fingernails breaking the skin of her palms.

"Stop this! Please, Father!" Rameses shouted, his voice muffled.

"Enough, Rameses!" Sethos' sharp red voice silenced him, anger flaring in his golden eyes. "Your weakness has no place here. This is what must be done to remind us that our enemies do not cease to destroy us and take those we love."

Sweat stung the cuts on Serein's hands. *Drive the knife through his eye. Let Sethos writhe in agony before slitting his throat.*

Let the Murderous King know fear, Xansas told her.

The purple and orange screams, the dark peacock-blue snarling of lions, and the voices of the crowds rushed at Serein, stabbing behind her eyes. A lion lunged, teeth ripping through the boy's throat. His sister was pinned down by two more before the killing blow silenced the screams, the echoes boring in her bones.

Rameses sank back into his seat, hands trembling as he held them to his mouth. The torn bodies were dragged away from the lions. He muttered a prayer that crumpled at his feet in gold, broken shards.

Death bent by the trembling souls of the children, cradling them in his arms. He glanced up at Serein, ageless face solemn. *What other proof does Rameses need that his father's a monster?* Serein thought. *Has he truly been unaware of this kind of brutality happening within his own kingdom?*

The soiled sand was raked away, and horse-drawn carts dumped fresh sand across the ground. When the arena was cleared, Sethos approached the edge of the viewing booth. Sunlight fell across the golden adornments on his turban, creating a ring of fire on his head. He lifted his hands, and silence fell over the crowd.

"Citizens of Oyon," his voice thundered, "the time has come

again for the Malik's Aikhtiar. In two months, during the Sister Moons Festival, warriors from around the world will gather to fight. The best fighter will be rewarded with riches and the glory of becoming my muharib. While we give thanks for the harvest Alkhaliq has blessed upon us and remember the Sister Moons, we will celebrate this new age of prosperity. Sarddon's strength shall endure!"

The crowds erupted into cheers, washing away the layer of tension remained with the waves of colors. Rameses stood and hurried toward the stairs leading out of the viewing box.

HEAT ROLLED OFF THE STREETS IN SHIMMERING WAVES AS THE LATE afternoon sun dipped low. Serein and I'timad followed Rameses, the city guards shadowing them through the crowds.

You can't do anything, the purple and orange voices whispered. *You can only watch while Sethos destroys.*

Phantom screams followed her. The faces of dead children stared back every time she blinked, hollow eyes filled with judgment. The raised flesh of Serein's X-shaped scar tightened.

He'll be brought down. I'll find a way, she thought.

Rameses remained quiet, staring off with an unfocused gaze. "I didn't think he would do something like that," he said, the gold words almost lost in the sounds of the city as he turned to look at Serein. "This has to be bothering you. I don't think I can sleep with those images in my head."

Her hand rested on the handle of her dagger. "I've seen your father's cruelty up close. This doesn't surprise me," Serein replied, anger simmering in her throat. *What Sethos did in the coliseum is nothing new. He's just found a way to call murder justice. Only a knife through his heart will stop the bloodshed,* she thought.

Over Rameses' shoulder, Serein saw movement in the shadows and the glint of a blade. A man morphed out of the alley, shoving past people as he advanced toward Rameses with angry purple steps. He shouted, his sapphire voice ringing out as he raised his knife.

Serein lunged, latching onto the man's thin wrist. Bystanders cried out, dispersing as she shoved the man to the ground with a dark blue *thud*, twisting his arm until he dropped the dagger. Dark green eyes and light brown hair appeared under the tattered hood. His angular face twisted in pain. The stale smell of alcohol clung to him. White flecks crept into his disheveled beard. The guards closed in around Rameses, and I'timad drew his sword.

"Don't move," Serein said, pinning him down on the ground. *A refugee from the Old Kingdom,* she thought. *Right-handed. Mid-forties. Sloppy, rage-driven.*

"How can you serve them?!" the man spat in slurred Sarlyrian, each word cutting like a whip. "You're a whore for the murderer! You're a traitor to your people."

The black beast clawed at Serein's belly, and she whirled the attacker around, drawing her dagger. She pressed the blade against his throat, drawing a line of blood across his dirty skin.

"You're serving the man who slaughters us! You wear *their* colors!" the man hissed. "Darkness take you!"

"I'm no one's whore," Serein whispered, her yellow voice sharp.

The white voice laughed. *But aren't you? You're the prince's little pet, so you might as well roll over for your master.*

The man thrashed, trying to break free. Serein hit his nose with the pommel of her dagger. Blood ran down the man's face as he gasped for air.

"Serein!" Rameses said, grabbing her shoulder. "Stop! Don't kill him. Let the soldiers take him to the cells to question him."

Serein jerked away from his touch, shoving the man at the guards. The black beast continued to rumble, pacing around as it gnawed on her rage.

THE AFTERNOON WANED INTO EVENING. I'TIMAD'S WATCH ENDED, and Ilderim replaced him. The attacker had been carried off to the dungeons, but his sapphire voice still rang in Serein's ears. Servants brought dinner and drinks to Rameses' chambers, setting the dishes on the table. An orange tagine with chicken, raisins, and rice sat next to a basket of msemen bread smeared with smen. Olives and a salad with purple pickles, carrots, and chickpeas were set in front of

Rameses. A grilled fish coated in rosemary, za'atar, and preserved lemons stared at Serein with a shriveled eye.

Na'im and Na'il rested on either side of Rameses as he sat down. "Come, Serein. Sit," he said, golden voice struggling to carry a light tone.

Rameses opened a dark glass bottle of arak as Serein sat across from him, filling his goblet almost to the rim with cloudy white liquid. A tired look rested on his face.

The smell of the alcohol and anise stung the inside of Serein's nose. *Arak's stronger than wine. He plans to drink until today's a blurred memory. Is this the kind of king he'll be when he faces difficult situations?* she thought.

"I heard from the kennel master that you have been visiting a lot lately. How's your little tigress doing?" Rameses asked and set the cup down, scratching Na'im behind his pale ears.

"Does the attack on your life not faze you?" Serein asked, hands resting in her lap.

Rameses scooped up some of the chicken and rice with the bread. "I'm confident in my wali. Besides, you held a knife to my throat, and everything turned out well."

Serein rubbed the dark crescent marks in her palm. The bangles sat heavy against her scarred wrists, the cool metal growing colder. "What about the slaughtering of children for entertainment?" she asked.

He flinched, swallowing hard. Rameses wiped his fingers on a napkin and glanced at Ilderim, nodding. "His Highness wishes to be alone," Ilderim told the servants, who hesitated before filing out of the chambers.

Dread crept through Serein, slithering around her wrists, the teal *thud* of the door bringing a sense of finality. Rameses met her gaze, finger tapping the side of the cup. He swallowed, nervous energy tensing in his shoulders.

"There's something I want to discuss with you..." Rameses said. "I was going to wait to ask you this at a better time, but after today, I don't think it can wait." He paused, his gaze darting to her face as he drew his next breath. "I want you to enter the Aikhtiar."

Serein's limbs locked, the white ringing sound growing louder in her ears. The heat of the arena, blood, the roaring mob all hit her at once. The warden's lemon-colored shouts and the rattling chains. Sa's face as he tried to choke the life out of her.

Fighting to earn a title that puts me in the Murderous King's shackles. To serve and be used by him. There will be nowhere to hide from Sethos or Xansas.

Whore! The sapphire word rattled around with the screams of children.

"No." The single yellow syllable shattered the quiet.

Surprise overtook Rameses' features. "No? What do you mean no?" he asked.

Serein's hands clenched in her lap. "No. *Non. La,*" she said. "Do you want to hear it in other languages to help you understand?"

"Being a muharib is not the same thing as being an indentured servant. You have freedom in that position, a salary, accommodations. It's a position of honor, a contract job for a minimum of five years. I would provide you the entry fee of ten gold for the Aikhtiar—"

"I don't care about any of that," Serein snapped. "That's always been the plan, hasn't it?" *If he had told me this in the beginning, I'd have spit in his face. He lied when he said he wasn't hiding anything else.*

Rameses sighed, touching his ring. "Not entirely...After you told me about ships going to Bar Elenion, I thought about asking you later in the year to enter the Aikhtiar in order to gather more information about what my father is doing. Now, the competition's coinciding with the Sister Moons Festival in the month of Soron instead of at the end of the year."

"The agreement was to be your guard for six years in exchange for my freedom," she said through her teeth. "Then I'm to spy on your father. Now you're altering the contract again."

He shifted on the cushion. "I know this is a lot to ask, but please hear me out. Your contract with me would end the same time your service as muharib would. My father cannot make you serve beyond the five years. You will still get your freedom. I give you my word."

Anger flowed out of the cracks. "Spies and assassins don't get to retire. If I follow you down this path, I only see my death." *Rameses doesn't know the full price of what he asks. I know what the Murderous King would use me for,* she thought.

"This competition's now crucial to the plan," Rameses told her. "It's apparent now that you need to become my father's muharib to really learn what he's planning. As muharib, you would be working with the Golden Jackals and learn more about my father's plans. If there's information to be found, it will be in the Tower of Secrets."

"I'm still not interested," Serein said, standing.

The dogs raised their heads. "Serein, wait," Rameses said.

"Sit down," Ilderim told her, the ocher words serrated. "You weren't permitted to leave."

She glared at Ilderim. "Have me whipped, thrown in a cell, or executed. I refuse to take part in this."

Serein left Rameses' chambers without waiting for a reply, the cool night air wrapping around her. The shadows moved out of their hiding places as they closed in.

SEREIN INHALED DEEP BREATHS AS SHE STOOD IN HER CHAMBERS. *It never ends...Xansas saved me only to use me and rape me. Grasdan tried to break me and kill me. Rameses found me to carry out his foolish whims,* she thought, anger building as it carved its way out of her bones. *I can't be free.*

You're foolish not to take the opportunity, Xansas hissed in her ear. *Do you hesitate because you despise Sethos that much or because you've come to care for the prince?*

Serein spun around, fist slamming into the wall. A yellow cry ripped from her throat as everything she fought to keep locked away snapped its jaws, claws digging into her insides. Blood smeared the stone. She stared at the faded scar across her left palm and slumped to the floor, knuckles split and bleeding.

I can't serve Sethos. Not after all he's taken from me. I won't be used again.

Chapter Twenty-Seven
The Lion's Roar

BLUE SHADOWS MOVED ACROSS THE DOMED CEILING OF THE THRONE *room. Rameses stood before the carved throne, the white wood smooth like bone. Voices mixed together as the painted motifs moved on the walls. Plants grew in twisting designs, wrapping around the columns while birds flew toward the ceiling. Shadowy lions prowled around the room, eyes glowing.*

The chiming of Rameses' earrings cut through the air as he approached the throne on the raised dais. He turned and found his father standing behind him, sword in hand. The shadows crept in, dripping down the white walls.

"You think you are ready to sit on the throne?" Sethos asked.

"I only want what's best for Sarddon," Rameses replied, shivering as a chill traced its fingers up his spine.

Sethos approached, eyes glowing pools of gold. "You do not know the weight of the crown you will bear."

A younger Rameses ran past, laughing as his sandals slapped the floor. A shadow of Sethos chased after him, smiling. The lines in his father's face had been smoothed out, the gray in his hair gone. He scooped the boy up and tossed him over his shoulder, and they disappeared. His father's deep laughter twisted Rameses' heart.

Sethos lifted the black sword, pointing at something behind him. Rameses turned. Two children lay slumped on the throne, bodies torn and blood dripping in ruby rivers across the pale wood, empty eyes staring back at him.

The whispers grew louder until they became like buzzing flies. Rameses staggered back as the crimson pool spread under his feet.

"No," Rameses choked, whirling back to his father. "This is not the way I want to rule! Not by killing innocents."

Sethos reached out and cupped Rameses' face, his palm cool. "Every throne is stained with blood. To rule, the pride must fight. We fight to protect our own and ensure we survive." The stern voice softened. "Sharpen your claws, abnay. Your time is coming."

Rameses' eyes stung as tears pricked the corners. The blood lapped against his ankles, warm and carrying reflections of faces contorted in pain. The lions on the walls leapt down and circled Rameses, eyes flashing as they drew closer.

"No," Rameses whispered. "Stop this bloodshed, Baba. Please!"

Sethos' grip on Rameses' face tightened, claws extending from his fingers. "If you do not grow teeth, you will be devoured," Sethos said, his voice becoming a growl.

Sethos' skin melted away to reveal a tawny muzzle with a flowing mane. His claws dug into Rameses' cheek and neck. The painted lions clustered behind him, growling. Sethos' jaw opened, a maw of teeth lunging for Rameses' face—

Rameses jerked upright, hand going to his neck and feeling along his stubbly beard. Nausea burned the back of his throat, tasting of arak. A headache squeezed his head, eyes burning. Na'im and Na'il sat up at the end of the bed. They yawned and wormed their way up to him, licking his hands.

"Everything all right, Your Highness?" Ilderim asked as he opened the bedchamber door.

"I was having a nightmare," Rameses replied, throwing on a robe.

"Should I have one of the servants fetch coffee for you?"

"No."

Rameses shuffled past him and stood in the dark living chamber, staring out the open window. Stars winked between the veil of clouds drifting across the sky. A cool breeze touched Rameses' face where the phantom claws had dug into his face.

"I dreamed about those children, the ones my father put in the arena...It was not right. They were children. How are the deaths of children justified?" Rameses asked. *Why is my father embracing this madness? Has this cruelty been going on since the war began? Or has his grief become hatred? Was I too blind to see it before?*

Ilderim stood by the wall. "Many get caught up in the war, those who have no part in the fighting. Sarddon's enemies aren't women and children. There's no need for innocent bloodshed," he replied. "The war has been going on so long that people have begun to lose bits of their humanity. I believe grief and fighting can change a man and make him unable to see when he's gone too far."

Rameses worried his lower lip. "Do you think I'm making a mistake?" he whispered. *I don't want to force Serein to do this, but I cannot see any other way of uncovering the truth.*

"It's best to be cautious with this. Perhaps there's another way to utilize her skills rather than having her fight in the Aikhtiar," Ilderim told him. "I know you want to do what's best for Sarddon, but don't let that desire become desperation. Good men lose themselves that way."

"I fear Serein will not speak to me to discuss another plan. It took this long for her to begin to trust me."

"Give her time, sayyidi."

Rameses sighed, looking at the thin pale band around his finger left by his ring. "Things are moving faster than I expected. I fear that time is running out..."

Serein watched the dawn creep across the ceiling. Rosewood-colored calls from the elephants mixed with the melodic blue morning prayer of Saint Zaman. She flexed her hand, smarting pain running through her split knuckles.

If Rameses decides he no longer has a use for me, will he just throw me in a cell? Serein thought. *Perhaps this is the day I'll have to fight my way out.*

Serein slipped into a tunic and tan sirwal, running her fingers through her short hair. Grabbing a persimmon from the bowl, she took a swig of coffee and headed for the door, dagger tucked through the sash around her waist.

As Serein stepped into the hallway, she found Rameses dressed in an indigo qamis, dark hair tousled. The shadows of sleeplessness hung under his eyes as he leaned against the wall. Ilderim stood nearby, watching with a cool stare.

"Good morning, Serein," Rameses said, the edges of his gold voice rough.

"Why are you here?" Serein asked, clutching the persimmon. *Seems he didn't get much sleep. He wants to continue talking, so I don't think I'll be executed for disrespect yet.*

"You want to go that far back?" he asked with the shadow of a grin on his lips. "It was a night twenty-three years ago when Alkhaliq stirred up the passions of my mother and father."

Serein locked the door behind her, heading down the hall. Peach ringing followed. *Using humor to ease his discomfort. He's not ready to deal with difficult situations,* she thought, descending the stairwell.

Rameses fell in step with her while Ilderim walked behind them. "Most women would blush at that."

"Say what you need to say or leave," Serein told him.

Rameses cleared his throat, eyes dropping to his sandals. His index finger traced the lines of the lion's head ring. "I wanted to apologize."

Serein kept her eyes ahead, slicing off bits of the orange fruit with her dagger. Honey-like sweetness stuck to the inside of her mouth. Sunlight warmed her bare arms as they crossed through a riad. Rameses' expectant gold breath hung like a mist in the corner of her eye.

"Serein?"

She discarded the remains of the persimmon in the bushes, washing her hands in the fish-shaped fountain. Pink lilies bobbed on top of the water while thin blue and red minnows flashed beneath the surface. A bee buzzed near Serein's tattoo with stumbling blue flutters before drifting to the nearby jasmine flowers.

"I thought we were past this silence," Rameses said, voice straining. "Serein, let's talk about this, please."

Serein wiped the blade clean on her sirwal as they approached the kennels. *If he says my name one more time, I might just kill him to shut him up,* she thought as she maneuvered down the rows.

Dogs barked, the pistachio-green sounds bouncing off the walls. The kennel master appeared. "You're back," Salatis said to Serein, his powder-blue voice soft. He stiffened when he spotted Rameses, dropping into a bow. "Sayyidi. Marhaba."

Rameses gave him a thin smile. "Everything well with the hounds, Salatis?" he asked, sticking his hand into one of the kennels. A large black dog approached and licked his fingers.

"Yes, sayyidi. Bahiga's litter will grow to be healthy hunters," Salatis said, rising from his bow.

"And the tiger cub?"

Salatis gestured to the kennel down the row, his lotus tattoos creasing along his wrist. "Growing. Bahiga looks after it like one of her own. The tigress and her other cubs are healthy as well."

Serein crouched in front of the kennel with Bahiga and her pups. The tiger cub stumbled around, bumping into her smaller littermates. Serein reached through the bars, palm cushioning the tiger's head as it wandered toward the edge of the pen.

"You're attached to it," Rameses said as he stood behind her, but Serein gave him only silence. "Is this how it's going to be again? I apologize for upsetting you."

"Your apology doesn't mean anything because you're still going to try and convince me to do what you want," Serein replied.

"I think we should keep discussing that then," he said.

Serein opened the kennel and picked up the tiger. It floundered in her arms, letting out peacock-blue mewls before settling against her neck. Serein brushed past Rameses and Ilderim, nodding at Salatis.

"Serein," Rameses called after her. "You cannot keep running away from this."

Morning sunlight turned the palace domes fiery gold as she left the kennels. "The kennels aren't the place to talk," Serein replied. *Jackals everywhere. Anyone could be watching, listening.*

"Would you like to go somewhere private? My chambers?" Rameses asked, sandals crunching along the gravel as they crossed through the gardens.

"That wouldn't be a good place either."

He smirked. "Oh? Why? Are you thinking of improper things?" The grin wavered as she held him with a narrowed look. "Seems that joke was ill-timed..."

Her pace increased, and the peach jangling of the bells grew louder as Rameses tried to keep up. Servants stared at the tiger cub as they passed, bowing to Rameses. His gaze prickled along the back of her neck, fixated on the murderer's brand.

Serein stopped at the base of the tower, forcing Rameses to come to a halt. "If you keep staring, your Saints might blind you," she said. *Or I might gouge his eyes out myself.*

"I don't think that's how their justice works," Rameses replied as they climbed the stairs.

The sunlight collected in the stairwell through the small windows, glinting off her bangles. "*Fiat justitia ruat caelum,*" she told him, the words carving into the curved walls in pale-yellow strokes.

"I don't know what that means."

"'Let justice be done even though the heavens may fall.'" The cub let squeaked as they reached the top floor. "It was the saying of one of the ancient houses of the Old Kingdom."

"Sounds brutal. Almost vengeful."

"Vengeance and justice are often two sides of the same coin."

Rameses slowed as they approached her chambers. "Wait here," he told Ilderim. "I need to discuss things with Serein in private."

Ilderim's features hardened. "...Very well, Your Highness," he said, the ocher words carrying his disapproval.

He's leaning toward dislike now, Serein thought, unlocking her door. She set the cub down in the middle of the room. It staggered about, letting out a shrill cry. Orange footsteps drew closer, the peach chimes filling the doorway.

"Now," Rameses said, "let's resume our conversation from yesterday."

"I gave you my answer," Serein told him, blocking him from the chamber. "There's nothing more to say."

"Clearly, there's more to talk about on the matter," he said, arms folded across his chest.

"Nothing you're willing to listen to. You didn't even give a decent apology. Now, if you'll excuse me, Your Highness, it's my day off, and I'd like to spend it alone."

"But—"

The door shut, shattering the word in the doorjamb. Serein turned the lock and glanced back at the tiger cub.

"Serein, don't do this." Rameses' muffled words seeped through the wood grain in faded gold ripples. A few beats passed before Rameses left with a sigh.

Serein crouched down, touching the cub's soft nose. *This is already dangerous, sneaking around to gather secrets. If I make a mistake, I'll be killed—even if Rameses promises protection. I was already separated from you once, my Sun and Stars. I won't leave you again.*

You're growing comfortable here, volchitsa, Xansas whispered. *Don't forget that you're a wolf among lions. Always be on guard, or they'll tear you apart.*

Threads of pain worked their way through her split knuckles. *I can't bring Sethos down yet without endangering myself. Rameses' plan is foolish and poorly thought out.*

You're foolish to pass up an opportunity like this. I gave you steel to fight, not cower. You're just like me.

Serein felt his curved smile in her mind, the prickle running down the back of her neck. The snake brand felt hot, holding memories of pain in the faded white lines. *I'm not you.*

The cub wandered over to the table, bumping into the wooden legs. Serein scooped up the tiger, settling onto the sofa. Tiny claws dug through Serein's tunic as she stroked the black and white fur.

"Would you like to hear a story, Nala?" Serein asked.

Nala chewed on Serein's hand, tongue rough against her skin. Veins of gold and black stripes ran from the clouded eyes. A smile spread across Serein's face.

"There once was a girl soft as clay. A man came and cut her up with a black sword. Life and Death had a wager. In the end, Life won the girl. Death made her his servant while Life kept her fed. Another found her. He shaped and molded, forging her into a knife. On the outside, it looked like the work of his hands, but inside she became something of her own making."

Chapter Twenty-Eight
Ink & Blood

THE SWEET AROMA OF MINT TEA WAFTED THROUGH THE AIR, latticed shadows forming star patterns across the red and gold rug. Serein ran a fingernail along the grooves etched into the pommel of her dagger as she stood with Ilderim and five other guards. Rameses chatted with Amirah Fairuz as they sat at a table with a pomegranate tree painted across the polished wooden surface. Gold laughter wrapped around Fairuz's fluttering blue-green voice. Metal disks woven into her turquoise veil cast golden shards across her seafoam-green kaftan. Lujayn sat nearby with Fairuz's mother, a woman in a dark orange abaya with a round face and light brown eyes. They nibbled on honey-soaked baklava sprinkled with crushed pistachio and sugared apricot slices. The Malika smiled as her hazel eyes drifted to Rameses.

Seems this princess meets with the queen's approval, Serein thought. *The fact that she's a distant cousin must help.*

Servants came by and refilled their glasses, waiting with plates of sweets, fruits, and bread. Rameses glanced at Serein with an imploring look and creased brow before turning back at Fairuz as she asked him a question.

Ilderim shifted beside Serein. "How long will you continue to ignore His Highness' request?" he asked under his breath, the ocher words cutting across her vision.

"There's nothing else to discuss," Serein replied in a low whisper. "I only want to fulfill my contract." *And keep out of Sethos' sight as much as possible, and remain hidden from Xansas for as long as I can.*

"You're here to serve. It doesn't look good to refuse a request from the one who is employing you. You have a life contract to uphold," Ilderim told her.

"I'm here to protect the prince, apparently from himself."

The older wali cast her a sideways glance. "I think you misunderstand him. His Highness didn't ask you because he wants to use you. He trusts you and wouldn't have asked this of you if he didn't think you could succeed."

Serein's hand tightened around the pommel of her dagger. *He can't guarantee that I will,* she thought. *If I enter, Sethos could kill me before I even have a chance to fight. And if I won, he might have me murdered under mysterious circumstances. There's too much to lose. I don't want to die without seeing you again, my Sun and Stars.*

You're still thinking about what would happen if you accepted because you know it's the best option, Xansas whispered, white breath brushing against her ear. *Serve as the King's blade so you can use that same knife against him.*

"Do you have doubts about who you serve?" Serein whispered, watching the other guards around the room.

"Sarddon has always strived to enrich its people and be a place of peace. Our rulers have always arrived to uphold that ideal, but even good men can be led astray," Ilderim muttered, gaze resting on Rameses. "I believe Rameses wants to do better and correct the wrongs of this nation. Sarddon's future rests on him."

A future that can be tipped in your favor, volchitsa. *With one blade, you could decide the outcome of an entire kingdom. Send it spiraling into chaos.*

The umber sound of the afternoon prayer seeped through the open window. Lujayn rose from the majlis, skirts flowing around her. "Bahiyya, I would like you to join me for prayer in the kanisa before dinner tonight," the Malika said, her mauve voice warm as she kissed her cousin's cheeks.

Bahiyya gestured for Fairuz to follow as the two women left the chamber with two guards. "I am looking forward to dinner. The food from your name day diffa was exceptional, so tonight's meal should be equally delicious," she said, her dusty marigold voice high-pitched.

Fairuz gathered her skirts, bowing to Rameses before she left with the remaining two guards. Rameses nodded as he stood, his smile slipping from his face.

Sighing, he turned to Serein. "I'm going to go take a walk along the beach for a bit," Rameses said, tugging at the sleeves of his blue qamis.

Beach is secluded. The noise of the waves drowns out conversations from being overheard. He wants to talk again, Serein thought. *And there won't be a door to shut in his face this time.*

THE WOMAN RAN HER HANDS ALONG THE STONES OF THE RUINED castle. Her girlhood had been smoothed out and hardened by the years, marked by scars and muscle. Hidden in the barrier of trees, she set down roots, hoping the White Snake couldn't find her.

Worn rune marks were etched into the broken arches. Pointed leaves from the vines climbing up the wall brushed against her wrists as she pushed them aside to reveal clusters of red berries. Dappled sunlight shifted over the blue ink curling along her arm. She popped a berry in her mouth, tartness hitting her tongue before sweetness overtook it.

The amethyst colored wind curled over the broken ramparts. Bird calls bloomed through the tree branches in clusters of wine-colored petals, lavender stars, and sunlight-yellow rosettes.

A twig snapped, and the woman turned, searching the green shadows. She tucked herself into the corner of the wall with broken statues of humanoid figures and gnarled bushes. Quiet lilac-purple footsteps crunched through the underbrush nearby.

The woman darted through the fractured hallway, light pooling over cracked stones. "Where are you?" she sang, pale-yellow words drifting through the warm beams of sunlight.

Sunset-orange laughter bounced between the columns. The woman's heart swelled as the sound filled her veins with buzzing warmth. Blue whispers trickled into view, following the orange bursts.

The corridor ended in a curtain of voronwa vines, curling flowers with ash-gray and orange petals open among the broad leaves. Shadows darted on the other side as the woman neared the crumbling entrance, pushing aside the vines.

"PLEASE, JUST SAY SOMETHING, SEREIN."

Serein looked up as gold words sparkled in the sun, poking through her thoughts. The taste of berries and the sound of orange and blue laughter faded, leaving behind a hollow ache. Droplets of saltwater from the ocean spray hit her face as the breeze pushed against her headscarf.

Only a memory, Serein thought, sighing as she looked up at Rameses.

He and Ilderim had stopped in front of her. Rameses' mouth was set in a thin line, dark locks escaping his white turban. Rocky crags spilling across the sands contrasted with the pale walls of Alqamar Palace further down the beach. Earthen arches extended into the sea like grasping tentacles of a stony beast. Gulls floated along the amethyst air currents, burgundy cries staining their white feathers.

"I know you don't want to talk about this, but I need to," Rameses said.

"What else is there to talk about? I told you no," Serein replied.

"But I don't understand why. There's more risk involved in this, yes, but I know you're more than capable of winning."

"The risk is death." *Then I'll never see you again, my Sun and Stars.* The thought twisted its bladed edge under Serein's lungs.

Rameses' gaze drifted to the churning cerulean waters. Waves rolled and crashed with opaque purple roars against the shore, dragging what they could back into the depths with foamy fingers.

"That's not the only reason why you're not agreeing to this, is it?" Rameses asked.

"I agreed to be *your* guard. I agreed to look for secrets. I may be a criminal with a debt to pay, but we still have a contract. And it says nothing about doing this."

"Serein," Ilderim said.

Rameses put up a hand, stopping the ocher word. "She's right. I have asked more of her than what she originally agreed to," he said. "Stay here for a bit, Ilderim."

The wali nodded, watching Serein as she and Rameses walked toward the monstrous rock forms further down the shoreline. Caves bored into the rockface like dark eyes. Shadows fell over them, and the plated tops of the palace towers blazed against the sky. Date palms and dry pines grew along the slopes dotted with goats and windswept bushes.

Rameses stopped at one of the caves, turning to her. "Please, say whatever's on your mind," he told her, voice collecting in the rock outcroppings. "I only want to know the truth."

"Why should I believe you? So far, you've lied to me and keep changing the terms of the agreement," Serein said as sand skittered over her boots. "If you wanted a weapon or a spy, then you should have just said so, not pretend like we're friends or equals to get what you want."

"It was never my intention to use you as a weapon," Rameses told her. "I told you that I have no intention of using you to kill people."

"I've listened to you talk about how you want to be different from your father and how you think people should be treated, but you've been toying with me since you approached me at the Harpy's Chest with this *offer*."

"I understand why you're upset," he said, golden gaze softening.

Serein's bones trembled as the memories opened fresh veins of hurt and anger. The black beast lifted its muzzle, fangs bared. "No. You don't, so don't insult me. Upset doesn't begin to describe what I feel," she said. "You bribe me with gifts and try to pretend we're friends and then expect me to do whatever you want—expecting me be grateful for your *kindness*. You treat this like it's a game, moving pieces however you want to without thinking about the consequences."

"Serein—"

The ocean waves crashed with her rising rage. "You wanted to hear what I have to say, so shut up for once in your damn life and listen!" Sharp yellow words sliced through the golden silk. "You haven't seen war. You don't know what it's like to have your home set ablaze and watch those you love die. You haven't killed, stood face-to-face with Death itself, smelled it choked on it."

Rameses stared at her, hands clenched at his sides. Serein listened to the roaring of her pulse, blood molten and scars crawling.

"I was there. I watched Sethos tear apart women and children. He hunted his people who had magic, all in the name of his war. He burned my home and slaughtered everyone I ever knew. I've seen what he looks like covered in blood, so don't tell me that his actions can be justified. You've seen him slaughter children and call it justice. What other proof do you need?

"The secrets you're looking for are everywhere, but you don't want to face reality. You want some consolation that your father is still good to put your mind at ease. But you can't ignore what's been done. You don't need me to tell you what kind of man your father is. You've already seen him for what he is. Sethos could drown this country in all the blood he's spilled," Serein spat.

"Enough!" Rameses shouted in a burst of gold. "For Saint's sake, enough."

Rameses walked away a few feet out of the shadows, stepping past small tide pools. His shoulders tensed as he sucked in a breath.

"How did you end up on the battlefield? My father has not fought on the war front in thirteen years. You would have been a child at the time," he said, voice almost lost in the roaring of the waves.

"Don't ask questions you already know the answers to," Serein said. *My scars don't lie.*

Rameses looked back at her, face crumpling. "Those scars. Saints. Did my father...? The one on your chest. Did you get it..." His hand went to his mouth. "Saints," he muttered. "I'm so sorry. I had no idea..."

Seconds dripped into the surf, washing away like bits of broken seashells. Rameses twisted his ring. A golden sigh crumbled on the ground.

"I understand why you would not want to serve as his muharib, serve someone who has hurt you so much," Rameses whispered, walking back into the shadows toward her.

Serein held him with a stare. "You don't. Otherwise, you wouldn't have asked me to enter the Aikhtiar," she said. "Shifting kingdoms isn't a game. You hold the weight of lives in your hands, princeling. Becoming muharib is a death sentence for me, but you don't seem to care."

"I *do* care, Serein. This isn't a game to me."

"Then stop ignoring what's in front of you. You know what your father is and what he's done, so decide what you're going to do about it," Serein said. "Will you have me kill him?"

"No." He shook his head. "I would never suggest killing my father. I want to change this country, not bring it further strife." Rameses rubbed his hand across his mouth. "I know there's still good in him. I have to believe that he can be saved. He was kind and loving once."

It'd be easier if he just accepts what his father is and that he can't be allowed to live. Is it mercy or blind love for his father that will undo him? Serein thought.

It's the ones blinded by love that fall victim to blades. End the line, and there will be no more lions to hunt you, Xansas whispered.

"You have ideals of a better world," Serein said as a chill settled on her skin, "but do you have the resolve to carry them out? Either kill him or take his throne from him. You can't let your feelings blind you and prevent you from doing what needs to be done."

Rameses ran his thumb along the glittering emerald embedded in the lion's forehead. "Whatever he's done, I don't believe he deserves death. There has to be another way," he told her. "I know you despise my father, but becoming his muharib brings us one step closer to stopping him from hurting anyone else. To ending all this bloodshed so that what happened in the arena doesn't happen again."

Becoming muharib means I'll no longer be able to hide. Xansas will know where I am. If Sethos manages to bring the war to the northern continent, then there will be no place to run, no place where we'll be safe. His Steel Road threatens everything I'm trying to protect.

Gulls landed on the beach behind Rameses, squawking at each other as they fought over a fish caught between the rocks. The shimmering gray scales sparkled through the mass of feathers as the fish thrashed, glassy eyes watching Serein as its mouth gasped for air it couldn't breathe.

If you throw away this opportunity, you might not have another chance like this. You'll have to fight harder, and there's no guarantee that you'll ever get close to Sethos. You can become his shadow, the one that'll eventually strike him. Xansas' words closed in around her, white scales wrapping around her leg as they slithered upward.

Make him see the monster. You can show him the black heart of the Murderous King. Then he'll beg you to kill what he can't, Xansas whispered. *His soft heart can be used to your advantage. You need only reach out and take it.*

"Serein?"

One of the gulls dove in and grabbed the fish, carrying it away from the squabbling mass. The opaque purple waves washed away Rameses' voice, the foam dragging the golden syllables into the sea. *It's mutual survival. Rameses also stands to lose his life if his father suspects treason. As his guard, I still have protection, but all that is lost if I serve Sethos,* she thought.

Rameses reached into the pocket of his qamis, pulling out two scrolls. "What if your service was three years instead of six?" he asked. "You would not have to serve the full five years as my father's muharib."

Serein's gaze snapped to him. "Why should I believe you?" she said, salty air hitting her tongue.

"I swear to the Saints and Alkhaliq that I'm not lying." Rameses placed his hand over his heart, holding out the two scrolls to her. "New contracts with three years' servitude instead of six. Both copies have my signature and royal seal. This replaces the one you signed before. It will be known only to us. To everyone, it will appear that you're still here to serve for six years, but you will have your freedom in three years. Lawfully, my father will not be able to do anything about our contract because it's in my name. Only I can nullify or change it."

In the distance, the umber prayer rang out, the words of Saint Raz Nura bobbing along the waves. *"Though the desert heart may be cracked, the waters of forgiveness can make an oasis bloom."*

Serein stared at the wax seals along the scrolls. "You have a lot of faith in laws your father can choose to ignore," she told him. "The only way to ensure I'm free in three years is to seize the throne before that time's up."

Rameses tensed, his arm lowering. "I will not lie to you and say that the thought doesn't terrify me," he replied, tapping the scrolls against his open palm, "but I have already made my decision. I cannot go back."

"I've only been your guard for three months—half of which I spent recovering from injuries. Having me enter the Aikhtiar will make people suspicious," Serein told him. "Who else besides Ilderim knows that you want me to enter the competition? Does the captain know?"

The shadows of gulls flying overhead danced across the waters. "Uriah and I agreed it would be better if I didn't inform him of what's really happening, so that he will not be breaking his oath. Uriah will not betray me. If the true extent of my father's deeds comes to light, he will do what's right," Rameses said.

"Are you so sure about that?" Serein asked. "What will you do if the captain sides with duty over friendship? Will Ilderim still protect you when the lives of his family are on the line? You'll find that a person will do anything to protect what they love."

"I pray it will not come to that. I trust them," Rameses replied.

"It's going to take a lot more than prayers to take down your father." *Will Rameses be able to hold onto his morality, or will he lose himself and become like Sethos? How long will the captain be able to hold onto his friendship and his duty before one destroys him? Everything hangs so precariously.*

Rameses' shoulders tightened under his navy qamis. "I have a feared assassin, so I think I'm off to a decent start." His smile was rimmed with dark humor as he held the scrolls out to her again. "Please, take these. I will give you time to decide."

Serein took the scrolls, the vellum warmed by his hand. She saw the shadows of Sethos on Rameses' face. Behind the same gold eyes shone softness and hopeful light, different from the cold glint of his father's.

Three years. The thought hung so close that Serein felt it within her grasp, glowing with the warmth of hope. *For three years, I could be the king's dog, waiting for him to kill me or continue to be the prince's guard, hiding in the shadows. Could I endure it, or will it break me?*

Despite the risks, you know which path will allow you to achieve what you've longed to do, volchitsa.

She closed her eyes, breathing through the white noise. The orange and blue laughter floated past, tugging on her heart. Her thumb traced the faded scar across her left palm.

"I accept," Serein told Rameses, the words snagging in her throat as she opened her eyes. *I survived Xansas. I survived Grasdan. I survived Sethos. I'll survive this too. I'll make sure this plan doesn't fail so that I can get back to you, my Sun and Stars.*

Rameses blinked, mouth agape. "I didn't expect you to accept so easily," he said.

"I don't make this decision lightly. If you betray me or lie to me again, you'll find no peace. I'll make sure of it," Serein said, gaze boring into him.

Fitting the scrolls through her sash, she pulled out her dagger. Fear flashed in Rameses' eyes. The blade glinted between them, reflecting his creased brow and pursed lips.

"Why are you holding out your dagger?" he asked.

"You hold my life in your hands. Show me your resolve, that you understand what it means to carry the weight of another's life. This is my price."

He swallowed. "If that's what it takes, I will do it."

Serein drew the dagger along her right palm, a line of blood blooming along her skin. "By your blood, draw the link of binding to seal the agreement," she said. "I vow to uphold this agreement to uncover Sethos' secrets and ensure our mutual survival. Do you vow to do the same, Rameses Nasr ibn Sethos al-Amirmoez?"

Rameses took the dagger. "I do," he replied and cut a deep line in his palm. He flinched, hissing through his teeth.

She clasped Rameses' hand, blood running down their skin. Crimson droplets hit the sands, seeping down into the granules. Ocean spray misted the air, and rainbow fractals glimmered.

"In the sight of the Lights, our pact is forged. Blood to blood, signed on the earth. For as long as this deal lasts, we're bound. If either betrays the other, then let the heavens bring down their wrath. Look at the mark and remember your oath," Serein told him. "*Factum est alligatus.* It's done." *No going back. Only forward into whatever darkness lies ahead,* she thought, releasing Rameses' hand.

"You seem familiar with this. Do you often perform this ritual?" Rameses asked, staring at the bleeding wound.

Serein cut off two strips of her sash, handing one to Rameses. "No. It's only done for important agreements. Blood runs deeper than ink," she replied.

Unrolling the scrolls, Serein dragged a bloody finger across the bottom. She wrote her name next to Rameses' signature, the red ink seeping into the vellum. As her blood dried and the dull pain throbbed with her pulse, she felt Xansas' smile over her shoulder.

What will I look like at the end of this? Will you even recognize me when you see me again, my Sun and Stars? Serein thought, biting the inside of her cheek. *If I survive this, the money could help create a better life for us.*

"Thank you, Serein," Rameses said as he pressed the fabric against the cut, clutching his hand.

"I didn't do it for you," Serein told him, rolling up the scrolls and handing one to him. "If this fails, we'll both be dead. We'll need a believable lie as to why I'm entering the competition."

"Do you want me to weave an enthralling tale?"

She wrapped the strip of fabric around her palm, tying it tight. "Make it sound as believable as possible. We'll say that I'm entering because I want the money from being a muharib to search for my family. I was searching for them before I was sent to Grasdan. Il-Makah already believes I stayed in the Old Kingdom because of sentimentality, so the lie will have some weight."

Rameses nodded. "I think I can make a good story out of that. Something worthy of a novel."

"I doubt Sethos will shed a tear over it. It just needs to be believable enough to draw suspicion away from us."

"Why *did* you stay in the Old Kingdom?" Rameses asked.

Serein flexed her hand, the pain hot under her skin. "You must be suffering from blood loss because you've forgotten that you've already asked your question."

Rameses glanced at her split knuckles. "What did you do to your hand?"

"Went too hard with training," she replied. "Your idea lacks crucial details. We have three years to accomplish this, so it's time you learn what you're really up against and what it takes to bring down a king."

Chapter Twenty-Nine
Gathering Clouds

A FAT ORANGE AND BLACK LIZARD SCURRIED UP AN IVY-COVERED colonnade, eyeing Rameses as he walked through the garden. Bees drifted through the rows of flowering bushes as the morning mists evaporated under the sun. Three women in colorful djellabas passed him, smiling as they batted their eyelashes. His grin made them blush as they walked away.

Rameses blinked, smile crumbling as he twisted his ring. Serein's words and the anger in her eyes fueled Rameses' twisted dreams. *My father destroyed Serein's village, killed her family, gave her those scars,* he thought, the gnarled scar across Serein's chest burning behind his eyelids. *And I pushed her to serve him.*

He stopped, leaning against the railing. Pain dug into his palm, and he winced, turning his bandaged hand over.

Have I made a mistake? Does she hate him enough to kill him? With all that's been done to her, that rage is justified. But I can't let her kill him. Uriah would say not to trust her, but she made a pact with me. I have to trust that her freedom is worth more to her than revenge.

Sighing, Rameses headed for the barracks. He found Uriah bent over a well, wearing his usual contemplative look, brow slightly creased. Uriah splashed water on his face, his tunic and sword lying on the edge of the stone basin. A peeling sunburn ran across the back of Uriah's neck.

"Planning for the Aikhtiar already, sadiqi?" Rameses asked as he walked up.

Uriah turned, straightening. "Sayyidi," he said, bowing.

"Someday, I will order you not to do that," Rameses said, his smile stretched.

Rameses clasped Uriah's arm. "What are you doing here?"

"I wanted to talk with you." Rameses lowered his voice, the grin wilting.

Uriah slipped his tunic back on, gathering his hair back into a ponytail. "What's on your mind?" he asked.

Shadows from the clouds passed over them. "Serein's entering the Aikhtiar," Rameses said.

Uriah's eyes widened. "When did this happen?!" he exclaimed.

"She refused a few days ago when I first asked her, but she agreed to enter yesterday," Rameses said, touching his ring.

Uriah looked around at the guards by the barracks. "Why did you ask her to enter the competition? Why risk putting her so close to your father?" he asked quietly.

Rameses shook his head. "Things are moving faster than I thought they would. I know we agreed not to talk much about all this, but I wanted to let you know that this was my decision." He paused. "I saw the scar across her chest, and I know how she got it. I cannot...I cannot back down from my decision."

"Scar on her chest?" Uriah's brow creased. "When did you—"

"My father gave it to her. He killed her people during the war. Serein was there. She would have been a child. He attacked children, Uriah. Did you know that my father's been putting children in the coliseum?" The whisper twisted in Rameses' throat, lodging there as he tried to swallow past it.

Uriah's mouth formed a hard line, expression darkening as a faraway look pulled him back. "Some of the guards there have mentioned the most recent matches. I don't know how long this has been going on. It's making some people uneasy," he replied, swallowing. "How do you know Serein was attacked by the Malik? She could have gotten those scars anywhere."

"She told me. I saw the look in her eyes. So much pain and rage," Rameses said, flinching as a gull shrieked nearby and swooped at a cat. "It explains why she doesn't trust me. I'm the son of the man who destroyed her home."

Heavy silence expanded around them. "You remember how your father was after his brother was killed. Grief does something to a person. It changes them," Uriah muttered, gripping his stone pendant.

"But to kill so many people..." *I cannot say anything to Serein to undo what's been done. I cannot understand why my father would do something so horrible*, Rameses thought. *His heart was not full of malice before my uncle died. But do I really know my father at all anymore?*

Uriah crossed his arms. "Are you worried that she'll do something to the Malik?" he asked.

Blinking, Rameses glanced up at the clouds. "I made a blood pact with her, one that ensures our mutual survival in this. I don't think she will do something as reckless as killing him." *She wants to kill him, but maybe I can show her that there's another way of getting justice.*

The blood drained from Uriah's face. "You did *what?!*" he hissed.

"Serein said my word was not enough," Rameses replied, unwrapping the bandage to show the red mark across his palm. "She's putting everything on the line for this. I can at least do the same. I owe her that much. I'm the one who brought her here and asked her to take these risks. I just don't know if anything I do will be enough."

Anger flashed across Uriah's face as he grabbed his sword. "You don't owe her *anything.*"

Rameses wrapped his hand back up. "But I do," he said, "We need to have that drink soon before you're swamped with work from the Aikhtiar. You will have a long week ahead of you, helping out with the preliminary matches. Rajiya and Baqir have a bet going about when we will have dinner with them again."

Uriah's scowl softened. "I'm assuming she has something that needs fixing?" he asked.

"Cracks on the sidewall, but I think the longer we put off seeing them, there will be more things that need to be fixed," Rameses said as they left the barracks. "Let's go tonight. I'm sure you have a few hours to spare. I don't want to be rude since I already declined a meal from her before." *Just a moment not to see dead children and think about my father killing people. Maybe I should ask Uriah for one of those rocks he keeps in his pockets.*

"Fine. I suppose nothing will fall apart if I take a break," Uriah said, shoulders slumping. "This time, please don't get so drunk that I have to help you back to the palace."

Rameses laughed as they stepped under the marble arches leading to the riads. "Are you sure that was me? I don't seem to recall those times."

Uriah gave him a knowing look, eyebrows slightly arched. "It's hard to remember anything when you're dead drunk."

URIAH'S ANGER MOUNTED WITH EACH STEP HE CLIMBED TO THE top of the tower. *What's she planning? Is she just manipulating Rameses with stories about being attacked by Sethos?* Uriah thought. *She has to be doing this to get close enough to the Malik and kill him. Why else would she agree to serve someone she hates?*

He stormed into Serein's chambers, jaw clenched as words gathered behind his teeth. Serein and Rasima glanced up from the table, tea glasses in their hands. The Amirah sat with a dog-sized tiger cub in her lap. Rizwana folded clothes on the couch while Rasima's wali and handmaiden stood nearby.

Uriah stopped. "Your Highness," he said as he bowed, eyes darting to Serein. *Why's the Amirah with Serein? And a tiger? Is it a new pet of Rasima's?*

"Captain Stormheir, how nice to see you," Serein said, setting her glass down. "Want to join us for tea? You look parched from running over here."

"I...Can I talk to you? In private?" Uriah asked, forcing a steady tone through his teeth.

Serein arched an eyebrow. "Can you?"

His jaw twitched. "Now." *Saints, she's irritating.*

"Such manners," she said, standing. The tiger's ears perked up and galloped toward Serein, head butting her knee. Uriah stared down at the cub. "No need to look so stiff. Nala's not going to hurt you."

The tiger sniffed the air, turning her milky eyes to Uriah. "Why is there a tiger here?" Uriah asked.

"The prince gave her to me. Thought I needed company," she said as Rasima came over to grab the tiger, smiling at Uriah. "Scared of cats too?"

"That's *not* a cat," he said, stepping into the hallway.

"What would you like to discuss?" She followed him. "The weather? What a cat is? How has your life been? It feels like we haven't seen each other in a while."

Uriah slammed the door shut. "Don't," he snapped. "Why did you force Rameses to make a blood pact with you?"

"I didn't force him to do anything. He agreed to the terms. And no, we didn't drink each other's blood. That's uncivilized," Serein said quietly. "He's lied to me before, so I wasn't going to agree to such a dangerous thing without his assurance for my safety."

Uriah swallowed, irritation forming a knot between his shoulders. "Why did you agree to enter the competition?"

Serein tilted her head. "It's my best chance of helping Rameses and getting my freedom. I won't kill his father if that's what you're worried about. That's part of our agreement."

Blood pacts are serious things in the Old Kingdom, but will Serein really uphold it? She's killed people and probably done worse things. Would an oath really stop her from getting revenge? Uriah thought, catching sight of the red line across her right palm. His gaze darted to her chest for a moment before he looked away. *Rameses said he saw the scar on her chest, but how would he have seen that? He didn't...Not with her.* Uriah swept the thought away, reaching for the rock in his pocket.

"If watching my dagger helps you sleep better, then do so, but don't miss the other blades around you," Serein said and went back to her chambers, leaving Uriah alone in the hallway.

FRESH TADELAKT RAN ALONG THE CRACKS IN THEN SIDEWALL OF Rajiya and Baqir's house like muddy rivers. The early evening sun threw long shadows. Uriah wiped his brow, smearing ocher plaster across his sweaty forehead. His scimitar rested by the front stoop of the house. The smell of baking bread, lemon, and chicken wafted from the open window.

Should be dry enough in a few hours to repaint, Uriah thought, his gray tunic sticking to his back. *I'm sure Rajiya will find something else for us to fix.*

Rameses set the wooden scraper down in a bowl of paste, wiping his hands on a rag. His gray keffiyeh was tied back into a turban. He took a sip of the chilled pomegranate juice Rajiya left for them. A dog barked in the distance, and a group of children ran down the street.

"Well, that didn't take as long as I thought it would. My plastering skills have improved," Rameses said, testing a drying patch on the wall with his finger.

Uriah took off his keffiyeh, dunking it in the basin of water against the house. He wiped the wet cloth across his face and neck. "At this rate you might be able to build that library of yours by yourself," he told Rameses.

Rameses grinned. "I think building a structure is very different than repairing a wall."

Rajiya poked her head out the window, her loose green headscarf fluttering over her shoulder. "It's been so quiet out here that I thought you boys left," she said.

"And miss dinner?" Rameses smirked as he stood. "Perish the thought."

The woman leaned against the sill, flour dusting her hands. "Uriah's the quiet one, but for you to be silent for so long, something must be wrong."

Rameses touched his empty ring finger. "I was just focused on making sure the wall looked good. Didn't want to distract Uriah too much," he said.

"So, what's wrong? Is it a woman? That Ravanassë with the scars and the blue eyes perhaps?" Rajiya asked, and Uriah's head snapped to her.

She knows about Serein? Did Rameses bring her here?

"It's not about Serein. I'm fine, really, Rajiya," Rameses told her, waving his hand.

Rajiya snorted. "You're a terrible liar, boy. You'd best watch that woman."

The smile on Rameses' face faltered. "What do you mean?"

"Women like her have seen more than you know and won't put up with nonsense. You may have charm, Rameses, but I bet you that she can see right through it. Whatever you did, make it right."

"Why do you think I did something wrong?" Rameses asked.

Rajiya dusted her hands off, brushing back a gray lock of hair back under her headscarf. "I didn't live this long without being able to notice a thing or two," she told him. "You're just like Baqir was when he was your age. That man was a troublemaker. Still is."

Rameses glanced over at Uriah, wearing an incredulous look. "Uriah, have I ever done anything wrong before?" he asked.

Uriah sighed. "Please, don't ask me to lie," he muttered.

"Fine, I suppose I have gotten into my fair share of trouble," Rameses said, throwing his hands up. "But I swear to the Saints I'm better."

"Probably because Uriah keeps you in check," Rajiya said, craning her neck to admire the side wall. "You boys did a fine job. Dinner will be ready soon. Baqir should be back with the paint in a bit. That man— no matter where he is in the city—can always tell when food is ready."

She ducked back inside. Uriah grabbed his glass and downed it, tart sweetness quenching his dry throat. Rameses leaned against a dry corner of the wall as he stared at the bandage across his palm.

"So, what *is* actually wrong? You wanted to come here, but you've barely said anything," Uriah said, squinting against the sunlight. *Could he be having second thoughts about Serein entering the Aikhtiar?*

Rameses looked up at the gulls flying overhead. "How can I not have known?" he muttered.

"Not have known what?"

Rameses paced between the two houses, fingers twisting together as he wrung his hands. "Known what my father's done when he went off to war. It couldn't only have been Serein's village. All this time, I have pretended that the things I heard were just rumors..."

Uriah stared at the ground as nagging shame scraped against his spine, whispered voices swirling with the heady smell of water. He rubbed his shoulder as tension built underneath the old injury, radiating upward.

"This crown will soon pass to me, along with all the blood and sins that come with it," Rameses said, staring down the street as he stopped pacing. "I'm starting to dream about everything. I see those children in the arena."

Uriah walked over and placed a hand on the Rameses' shoulder. "You aren't responsible for the war or what's happened since, Rameses," he said.

"Do you ever question everything you thought you knew and the mistakes you might have made because of it? That those mistakes can be forgiven?" Rameses muttered.

Guilt stabbed Uriah's chest. He grabbed the piece of black tourmaline around his neck. Their shadows grew longer as the sun descended over Oyon. "I have..." Swords sliced and red sprayed the air, bodies lying in fields behind Uriah's eyelids. "Many times since I got back. Things become muddled in war. It's easy to blur the lines. I'll always live with the weight of my choices, but I believe that when this is all over, that there will be peace." *I have to believe it...*

Because you're afraid that everything you fought to protect was a lie. The whisper rose in the back of his mind, curving with a grin. *Because what are you without your oath? If there's no honor or justification for it, then you're just a murderer.*

Uriah slammed the thought out, teeth grinding together as his jaw clenched.

"I know you don't agree with all that's happening and don't want to betray my father," Rameses said, "but you still believe in him as I do. I cannot ignore what I saw or what Serein's told me. This is the only way I can maybe begin to make a difference."

Uriah met his gaze, arm dropping to his side. "I'll stand by you. Always. You know that. I want the truth too, but I can't do things your way. I don't want to entrust something like this to someone like Serein," he said.

"I know," Rameses replied with a wan smile as dishes clattered inside the house. "Now, I really do need a drink after so much heavy talk. I think Rajiya has a bottle of mahia somewhere."

Rameses is taking too much on, Uriah thought as Rameses walked back to the house. *He doesn't need to start losing sleep over nightmares too...*

Chapter Thirty

Old Friends & New Enemies

SEREIN'S EYES DRIFTED OVER THE DUSTY SCROLLS ON THE SHELVES. Designs for palaces, courtyards, common areas, and buildings across Oyon and Sarddon were housed in the Royal Archives' map room. The closed door kept the musty air and whispered secrets from the guards outside and the archivists milling through the rest of the Archives like ants.

This is where Rameses probably got a lot of his old maps from. Perhaps there's one in here that shows if the Royal Archives has any more hidden rooms, Serein thought, brushing dust from the dark sleeves of her wali uniform. *Maybe after the guards leave for the evening, I can sneak back in and see what else is lying around here.*

Rameses stood hunched over a raised drafting table covered in building designs and room layouts, charcoal staining his fingers. He drew an intersecting line with a wooden ruler, mapping out an interior section of a library. His tongue poked against his cheek. The shadows from the lanterns ran down his yellow qamis like dark creases.

"What do you think of this so far?" Rameses asked Serein, golden words rolling across the large parchment.

Serein peered down at the sketch. "The layout is simple enough to understand, but you should probably ask an actual architect. I could only tell you which areas look the easiest to sneak into and where a person could hide," she replied.

Rameses looked at her. "An interesting perspective. Most of our libraries and spaces like the Archives are laid out in a dodecagon shape, but I think I want to do something different."

He's been talking to me about drawing the exterior of this library he wants to build, but his design ideas keep changing. Perhaps he's waiting for divine inspiration.

Rameses set the charcoal stick down, rubbing the black residue from his fingertips. "How did your evening go last night?" he asked as he turned to her.

"Nothing too eventful," Serein replied. "The Grand Vizier and the Finance Minister had a lengthy conversation about the Steel Road after the war meeting. Mostly about new taxes to implement to fund the project and what resources could be taken from the Old Kingdom and Ginjarr for the construction of new garrisons."

Serein reached underneath her armor and handed him a few folded papers. They crinkled with light plum-colored rustles as Rameses unfolded them, looking over the list of figures, supply quantities, and sketches of the Steel Road's route from Oyon through Locklin Forest.

His brow creased. "Where did you get these?"

"Umar's study. It was on the way to the kitchens, and I was going there anyway." Serein crossed her arms. "I didn't steal these. They're just copies. I didn't find anything else yet that connects Umar to a conspiracy against Salman or to the war, but with his connections and how close he is to Sethos, he has to know something." *No doubt any important correspondences and journals are kept hidden in his chambers. Another search for another day.*

Rameses slipped the papers under the library sketch. "How did you get into his study?"

Serein gave him a thin smile. "Picked the lock. I haven't gotten a key made yet, but word in the kitchens is that the keymaster has a drinking problem, so it might be easy to find the mold for Umar's key," she replied.

"That seems a bit risky, Serein," Rameses told her.

Serein walked toward a shelf with a plaque reading "Palace

Gardens" below a section of stacked folios. "I'm making up for lost time. Rizwana kept me informed of the gossip happening, but most of it wasn't useful to our work. I won't be able to get much listening through walls," she said. "Picking locks and looking through Umar's chambers is easier than trying to follow Kamau."

"Do you think he knows much?"

"He's the King's closest guard. He probably knows who that woman is and what Sethos is searching for. But I won't know for sure without eavesdropping on him or going through his chambers."

"Considering what happened last time you encountered him, it's best to stay away from Kamau for now."

Serein sighed. "The only major thing I found was a record of Nasr's illness and death I found here," she said, moving to the section containing maps of the city.

"When did you come to the Royal Archives?" Rameses asked.

"Back in Airen," Serein replied.

"When you were injured?"

Serein turned around. "I wasn't so injured that I couldn't hide out in the dark for a few hours. What I read led me to believe that your cousin's illness may not have been natural. It's possible that it was intentional."

Rameses tapped his ring. "That could mean someone was targeting my uncle's family. Did you find anything else that might support that theory?"

"No, but I managed to find a hidden room on the second level that may prove useful. It wasn't on any of your maps, so I think that it was a recent addition," Serein said.

Rameses shifted, glancing at the door. "Have you investigated this hidden room?" he asked. "What do you hope to find there?"

"It'll probably be old, rare books, maybe something about magic or the plague," Serein said. "I found one book that they missed that talks about the history of Sarlyria. It's written in ancient Sarlyrian. The sections I've been able to translate talk about the creation of the world and the Lights. I can't tell yet if this is a book about Sarlyrian mythology or history. It might have some insight into magic and what your father's searching for in Bar Elenion."

"I think I'm more impressed that you found a book you want to read," he said, smiling. "Once you have translated it, please lend it to me. There are so few books here on Sarlyria and the Ravanassë, so I'm eager to learn more and make sure it's not lost."

Most of the stories have been lost with the tribes scattered and broken, she thought. *I only know a few stories from my mother and the ones I've picked up in my travels. So much lost that can't be regained.*

Rameses leaned back against the table. He opened his palm and stared at the healing cut. "There are a lot of competitors, dignitaries, and performers from across Cemiyon coming for the Aikhtiar. There are also a lot of women entering this year. Perhaps they heard about you being a wali and were inspired."

"But Sarddonian women still won't be able to enter, will they?" Serein asked.

"The Aikhtiar doesn't forbid women from entering, but it's still difficult for Sarddonian women to enter. The only rules are that the use of poison and magic is forbidden," Rameses told her. "In the three hundred years that the Aikhtiar's been happening, I think there have only been a few women muharib. The last one was at least a hundred years ago."

"I might as well continue to defy your country's traditions a bit more while I'm here." *Small shames and humiliations will cut Sethos deeper than any knife.*

Rameses laughed, walking around the table. His hand trailed across the sketched lines of the building. "Kamau, Hisein, and Uriah will be testing the competitors during the preliminary matches at the beginning of Hlon in two weeks," he said. "Usually, all the Malik's current muharib handle the testing, but Ezio's still at sea, so Uriah will fill in for him."

"I've fought two out of the three," Serein said, tugging at her left bangle. *Against the captain, I have an advantage. Kamau's swings are powerful, as my ribs remember. Hisein's unknown. I've heard from the servants and guards that he's dangerous with a sword and has a cruel streak. Fitting for the leader of the Scourge.*

Rameses looked at her. "How are you feeling about this?" he asked, gold voice dipping as if he was approaching a wounded animal.

"Today, I'm feeling hungry," she replied.

He sighed. "I mean about the Aikhtiar and becoming my father's muharib..."

Serein's eyes narrowed. "You've been asking me the same question for the past few weeks. I don't have time to let my personal feelings get in the way." *He thinks I'm some injured woman now. He's been using that pitying voice that makes me want to slap him.*

Rameses turned his ring, worry twisting through his shoulders. "I know you don't want to talk about it, but I only want to understand you more, Serein," he said. "How did you end up on the battlefield where my father was?"

The old ache returned to her chest, turquoise screams and the smell of smoke stirring in the musty room. Serein drove a knife into the encroaching emotions, watching them writhe. "It wasn't a battlefield. It was my home," she whispered. "Sethos and his men burned our houses. Those who hadn't succumbed to the plague tried to flee, but they couldn't outrun the horses. We were running, and he cut us down."

A surge of pain escaped its confines. Rameses stilled, eyes on her scars. Serein wanted to pry herself out from his stare, but she stood unmoving.

"I'm sorry," Rameses said, swallowing. "I'm sorry that you lost so much and suffered so greatly."

"I don't want your apologies. What I want is for you to stop asking me how I am. We have to focus on how to stop your father." *The jaws of the lion are closing. It's too late to run,* Serein thought, rubbing the flaking scab across her palm.

Serein waited in the shadow of the arena as people crowded around the three sparring rings set up for the Aikhtiar's preliminary rounds. The month of Hlón came with its heat, making everything shimmer as if the city were melting. Hot sand slid over her sandals, bare arms resting against the warm stone wall. Her tunic stuck to her back, an amethyst breeze cutting through the dusty haze.

She studied the competitors passing by. Bronze-skinned

tribesmen from Zhao with dark hair and bright clothing. The dark skinned warriors of Ginjarr, some men and women with shaved heads and tattoos and others with locs. Fair-haired men from Sinabrac with tanned skin. Sarddonians with flowing robes and keffiyehs. Serein spotted a handful of women from Edolas with hair shaved along the sides and wound in long braids, ears pierced.

Surprising to see Edolasians here with the tensions between Sarddon and Edolas. Could it be related to the ships heading to Bar Elenion? Or do they enjoy fighting that much that it doesn't matter if it's a competition hosted by an enemy kingdom? Serein thought. *If an Edolasian woman becomes muharib, maybe Sethos will die of shock and save me the trouble.*

Serein caught a glimpse of Uriah's red hair. A burly Edolasian woman stepped into the ring with him, standing a bit taller than him. Her blonde hair was shaved along the sides and tied back in a long ponytail. A black tattoo curled along the right side of her jaw and up her temple.

A man bellowed Serein's name, the wine-colored word bruising the air. She pushed through the crowd toward the recorder flanked by four guards under the shade of a canopy. Crates sat behind him as another man counted the collected entry fees.

"You Serein?" the man barked as he looked up from a list of names scrawled on a long scroll of parchment.

"Yes," she said, brushing sand granules off her palms.

"Ring three," he said, pointing to the roped circle on her left. "You'll have three minutes to stay in the ring or hit your opponent three times. Cross over the line or get hit three times, you fail. Leave any weapons here until you're done."

Serein unstrapped the dagger from her belt, and one of the guards placed it on the crates with other weapons. They glanced at the bangles but didn't say anything. Serein maneuvered through the crowds and found the ring with a timekeeper overseeing the match. She grabbed the wooden sword sticking out of the sand, testing its weight.

General Hisein al-Daivari tossed aside his broken sword, picking up another from the barrel of weapons. His hooded eyes followed her, a sharp glint appearing in the hazel depths. His sweaty brown hair was slicked back. Flecks of sand stuck to his tawny skin.

Muscles hardened by battle shone with sweat, long scars running across his bare chest.

The Golden General. Rameses mentioned that he'd returned two weeks, but I didn't see him around the palace. Probably too busy in the brothels and taverns, Serein thought.

The black metal bands of Hisein's silver haya bracelet caught the sunlight. "A Ravanassë woman. Don't see many of your kind here," he drawled, words dipped in blue twilight. "I'll try not to aim for your face. Wouldn't want to add another scar to your collection."

Serein smiled. *Right-handed. Thirty-five. Oyon accent, but not a noble. Sounds like the accent from the slums. Based on how the female servants spoke about him, he gets his way through money, power, and intimidation. Being muharib pays for his lavish lifestyle and that gilded armor he's known for.*

"Begin!"

Hisein rushed at Serein, sandals kicking up sand. He jabbed at Serein's middle, driving her back to the edge of the ring. A wicked light overtook his features, sparking in the depths of his eyes. Seconds fell into the sand, melting under the sun.

Uses brutal force and speed. Not overly cunning. Quick to anger. Rameses said he won the Aikhtiar ten years ago by breaking his opponents' bones and beating them within an inch of his life, Serein thought.

Hisein swung the stick, and it hissed through the air with a reedy blue color. Droplets of sweat slid off his skin, catching in the sunlight. Hisein's expression changed as she dodged, shifting like ocean tides as the calm veneer morphed into irritation.

Serein's weapon passed close to Hisein's face, and he deflected. Cursing, he lunged at her. Through the barrage of assaults, Serein spotted cracks in his defenses. She pushed him back toward the edge of the ring. Hisein's sword passed by her head as she ducked. Aiming her weapon upward, the wood cracked against his jaw in a dark blue burst. Hisein staggered back, clutching his face as the onlookers gasped. She struck his side, his ribs, and the underside of his arm.

"I believe that's three, General," Serein said. *A cruel core disguised under his attractiveness. Men like him are easy to read. Without cunning, he's like a rabid dog.*

"Stop!" the timekeeper shouted.

Blood ran from Hisein's nose, staining his teeth red. "You

Ravanassë bitch!" Hisein seethed, face twisted with rage. His eyes landed on the bangles. "A servant?! Who's your master?"

Serein dropped the stick on the ground, sauntering away. "I have no master."

SEREIN RETRIEVED HER WEAPON, KEEPING HER HAND CLOSE TO IT. The interior tunnels of the coliseum were crowded with contestants and onlookers sitting on benches or standing in the wide hallways. Colored swatches of conversations clung to Serein headed to a quieter antechamber with a basin of water and a metal pump. Two Edolasian women sat on a bench in the corner of the room, speaking apple-red and steel-blue Edola. The blonde woman shot Serein a look, her smile wavering before she glanced back at her companion. Serein recognized the taller one as the woman who fought against Uriah.

They don't seem upset, so they must have passed the preliminaries, she thought, splashing her face with the cool water. *Guess I'm not the only one.*

An opaque blue whistle rang whizzed past Serein as a burly Zhao warrior stalked toward her on heavy orchid-colored footsteps. The sleeves of his yellow and green deel were rolled up to expose a red dragon coiled around his right arm. His black hair was braided down his back, and a mustache shadowed his upper lip. Pale band marks ringed the middle three fingers of his left hand as it rested on the pommel of the dao sword hanging at his side.

"You marked the Golden General," he said. "He must've been distracted because he fought a woman." The Common Tongue carried a thick Lóng Shé accent that rippled like blue waves.

Right-handed. Mid-thirties or so. His tattoo marks him as a tribe leader — the Shan tribe, judging by his clothes. The ring marks around his fingers on his left hand suggest he uses emei piercers as well as swords. Not a common weapon. Has an ego. An arrogant man, she thought, drying her face.

Serein went to leave, but the man leaned in close, blocking her path. "If you'd like some tips on how to fight, I'd be happy to teach you," he said. His gaze slid over to the two Edolasians who quieted.

"I doubt you have anything to teach me that I don't know already," Serein said.

"Little blue eyes has a mouth. What else can you do?" he asked, hand edging to her waist. "I'll make it worth your while. Few women have said no to Fang Qu."

Her skin prickled under his touch. Ramming her knee into the man's groin, Serein grabbed him by the collar of his deel and slammed him against the wall. Fang's head hit the stone as his legs gave out. She pressed her arm against his windpipe, the edge of her dagger hovering against his cheek. The other Zhao men shouted at her, going for their weapons.

"No," she said, glancing at Fang's companions. They hesitated as they saw the dagger against Fang's face. "Or would you like me to teach you what else I know how to do? Castration perhaps?"

Serein pointed the blade at his groin. "You're all talk!" Fang hissed, spittle landing on his thin mustache.

Serein gave him a steely grin. "Do you want to test that?" With one last shove, she pulled away, leaving Fang gasping for breath.

"I'll tear you apart!" Fang snarled as she walked away.

The competition hasn't even started yet and there's already so much excitement, Serein thought.

The Edolasian women followed Serein down the tunnels, the metal toes of their boots hitting the ground in leafy-green and ginger-colored clacks. Serein kept her hand near her dagger.

"You surprised me," the taller blonde one said, her apple-red voice throaty. "One so small brought that cur to his knees."

Serein glanced over her shoulder. The woman grinned down at her, the inked whorls along her right jaw creasing. A few scars trailed along her thick arms. Silver piercings adorned her ears. On the nicked breastplate was an embossed rearing horse. A double-headed axe with the four-armed Mother Goddess etched into the blade was strapped on her back, and a small hand axe hung from her left side.

"I'm Salveig," she said.

Right-handed. Early thirties. Skilled with axes—the Edolasian weapon of choice. Has money, judging by the silver piercings and the decorative work on the axe blade. Tan lines suggest she spends a lot of time outside, probably in the army or cavalry, Serein thought.

Salveig gestured to her shorter, brown-haired companion with a shield across her back. "This is Ragnhildur."

The shorter woman with a black band tattoo ran around her right bicep nodded to Serein. Freckles ran across the bridge of her nose, round eyes the color of chestnuts. A short axe hung on her right side with a broad knife.

Left-handed. Looks to be in her late twenties. A shield-maiden based on the large shield and the tattoo band. Shield-maidens are usually only for nobles and the upper class, so Salveig probably isn't a common warrior.

"What's a Ravanassë from the Old Kingdom doing here?" Salveig asked, hazel eyes going to the bangles around Serein's wrists. "Although it seems like you don't have much of a choice."

"There's no rule that prevents indentured servants from entering. I figured this was a chance to gain power and wealth, along with my freedom," Serein replied. *Assuming this all goes according to plan.*

"I look forward to seeing how you fare, *palaúlfa*," Salveig said as she and Ragnhildur left.

At least there's someone who doesn't want to bash my head in. Fang Qu will be a problem. Most of the Zhao I've met have been pleasant, Serein thought as she navigated through the crowded tunnels to the exit. *Fang may be a prick, but his skills aren't to be underestimated. Most clan leaders don't get their positions because they ask nicely.*

Serein stepped out into the streets into the chaos of the city. The peach jangling of bells made her look up. Three women lounged against the trunk of a date palm near one of the coliseum entrances, surrounded by a crowd of men. Indigo scarves wound around their chests and flowed out behind them, thighs showing through the slits in their sirwal. Ornamental bangles snaked around their wrists and ankles, light dancing across the metal disks sewn into their clothes.

The curvy woman in the middle wore a see-through veil over her face, her long black hair twisted in an elegant braid. Her round nose and warm brown skin almost made her blend in with the Sarddonians. The woman's heart-shaped face pulled at a thread of memory in Serein. A rose-colored laugh bloomed around the woman, and Serein froze.

Years slammed into her as she was thrust back to the dark nights of the mountain hideout where she grew up. Shared tears and rosy laughter—her only friend in a world of shadows and steel.

"Eneca?" Serein called. The woman whirled around, lips spreading into a silent gasp as she spotted Serein. *Eneca's alive?! And here in Oyon?* she thought, heart leaping.

"Serein?!" the woman exclaimed.

She rushed across the square, sweeping Serein into a hug. Cinnamon and honey wafted off her. Eneca stood a foot taller, her skin soft and unmarred. Serein smiled, tears pricking her eyes.

"Am I dreaming?" Eneca said, cupping Serein's face as they broke away. Her brown, kohl-rimmed eyes flashed. "I heard rumors you were captured and killed."

"The Lights deemed me worthy to live," Serein told her, Sarlyrian wrapping around them as the Common Tongue fell away. "I arrived here almost five months ago."

Sadness darkened Eneca's face as she studied Serein's scars. "Oh. Your face...What's happened to you? Who did this to you?"

"You don't need to worry about me. How did you end up in Oyon?"

Eneca dropped her hands. "Xansas sent me here not long after you escaped. One of his contacts, the Aanisah, bought my contract six years ago," she said, words falling like rosy petals. "I've been paying off my debt for her training."

The warmth in Serein's chest cooled. "You weren't there when the soldiers found the hideout?" *Seems neither of us was able to get away from our pasts.*

"The hideout was discovered? Was Xansas captured?" Eneca asked, a tremor of hope rising in her voice.

Serein shook her head. "I told the Sarddonians about Xansas and the Bone Vipers when I was in prison. I thought they would've captured him, but I didn't know he escaped until I came here. I thought it was the only way he could finally be stopped."

"You did what you had to do. If the Bone Vipers are scattered, then Xansas won't be able to find you." Eneca scanned the streets before giving Serein a worried look. "You haven't told me what you're doing here. What about...?"

"That's a long story." Serein's grip tightened around Eneca's hand. "There's so much I want to share with you."

"Tomorrow night?" Eneca asked. "The Faten in the Gold District. Ask for Zahra. That's the name I go by."

"Do you remember the codename I used to use?" Serein asked, and Eneca nodded. "I'll come under that name. May the Lights give you safety."

Eneca kissed Serein's brow. "Let Life protect you, and Death never find you."

"*Vade in pace.*"

"*Vade in pace,*" Eneca repeated and slipped back into the shade as two guards appeared, dispersing the crowd of men gathered around the courtesans.

She's alive, Serein thought. For the first time in years, she felt a flicker of happiness taking root.

Chapter Thirty-One
The Faten

Sleep pulled at Uriah as he walked up the street toward the palace, his arms and back sore from the second day of preliminary fights. The sea breeze cooled the sweat along his skin, and he pulled his rida' closer. The smells of cooking meat and smoke from the food stalls wafted around him. A few passing guards saluted him, and he nodded to them.

Firoz is taking care of the guard rotations for the south side of the city, and the squads set to be at the coliseum are arranged, Uriah thought, rubbing his beard. *There are still preliminary matches for another four days.*

A hooded figure slipped through the night, leaving through the hidden door along the wall. Darkness obscured their face as they darted between the houses. Uriah stopped, exhaustion evaporating as suspicion snapped in place.

Uriah changed directions as he followed in the shadows. *Why's someone leaving through the secret door? Only Rameses and I know about it.*

The figure wove through the streets, heading to the wealthier pleasure houses of the Gold District. The color of the buildings changed from ocher to a deep vermillion. Uriah slowed, pulling the cowl of his rida' over his head. Prostitutes leaned over balconies, and some sauntered through the streets. Laughter and singing bled through latticed windows and walled courtyards.

Uriah kept to the side of the buildings, watching from across the street as the figure stopped in front of a brothel with the word "Faten" hung across the entrance in elaborate, gilded script. *Is it really a servant slipping out to a brothel? These are too expensive for servants to afford. Why would they use that door to leave the palace?*

Serein's blue eyes and scars were unmistakable in the torchlight as she turned her head and slipped inside. Uriah pressed against the wall, scowling at the door.

What the hell is she doing here?

A GUARDS SHOWED SEREIN THROUGH THE FATEN. WOMEN DRESSED in colorful scarves danced in the middle of the room, every movement ensnaring the gaze of their audience. Men and women smoked from ghalyans, smoke curling around them in gossamer tendrils. The smell of cloying incense and tobacco thickened the clouds of colored voices.

I hope Captain Stormheir's enjoying all the pleasure houses have to offer. I wasn't sure if he would actually step foot in this part of the city, Serein thought. *If he follows me in here, then I'll really be shocked.*

The man with the thick beard stopped at a room at the end, two dark blue raps painting the door as his knuckles hit the wood. "Enter," a plum-colored voice said.

Serein stepped into a study where a woman in a silver and purple kaftan reclined on a plush couch. Two burly men armed with scimitars stood against the wall. Smoke rose from the ivory pipe between the Aanisah's long fingers adorned with gold rings studded with gems. Her dark hair was swept on top of her head. A key hung around her neck. Lines like dry riverbeds ran from the corners of the woman's eyes, cutting through the vestiges of beauty on her face.

"Another girl?" the woman asked, waving her hand dismissively. Her dark blue haya bracelet shifted on her thin wrist, the ivory bands flashing like teeth. "Too scarred. Send her back to the Tafall District."

"I'm not here to work. I'm here to see Zahra," Serein replied and pulled out a heavy bag of coins from underneath her rida'. *Right-handed. Forty-four. Vices are money and power, as well as expensive tobacco. A woman with powerful friends and secrets that could bring down kingdoms. She has connections to Xansas and has most likely been in her profession most of her life. She won't hesitate to leave my body in an alley if she feels like I've crossed her. There are powerful people in Oyon's underworld, and no doubt this woman has sway over many of them.*

The woman raised a delicate eyebrow, gaze darting from the coins to Serein. "I don't recognize you, Ravanassë."

"Zahra mentioned that if a woman named Lupa came here to let her know," the guard told the woman, his light gray voice wavering.

The Aanisah tapped out the ashes of the pipe into a glass dish. Uncrossing her legs, she stood. "Lupa, was it? A lover?" she asked.

"Acquaintance," Serein replied. *There's a chance she knows who I am. Not a lot of scarred Ravanassë women here. I don't know if she's still in contact with Xansas. If she is, I've made a dangerous choice coming here, possibly putting Eneca in danger. The money will keep her quiet. For now.*

Sentimentality has always been your undoing, volchitsa. *That's why you ended up in Grasdan.*

Serein suppressed a shiver as the Aanisah took the purse, hefting it in her hand before giving Serein a satisfactory nod. A vulpine smile slid across the woman's face. "Zahra should be finished with a client soon," she said.

The Aanisah headed for the crowd around the staircase, and the guards straightened. Fear rippled in their gazes as they dropped their eyes, the crowd making a path for her as she moved like a shark through a shoal.

"My little Zahra is quite popular. A succulent flower in the desert," the Aanisah said.

Some find out too late that beautiful flowers aren't always safe, Serein thought. *No doubt she also uses Eneca's "other" skills when she needs to remove someone. The Thanatos Flower is both a beautiful and deadly weapon.*

The Aanisah tipped her chin, and the guard by the door stepped away. She knocked on the door. "Zahra, darling, you have a visitor."

Feet shuffled on the other side of the door, magenta bleeding under the crack. "Give me a moment," Eneca said.

A few moments later, a man stepped out, fixing his silk robes. He glanced at the Aanisah, face paling as he bowed and hurried down the stairs.

"Go in. Try not to be too long. Otherwise, I'll have to charge you extra," the Aanisah said. "The guards will take your weapon during your stay here. For safety reasons."

Serein unhooked her dagger and placed it in the guard's outstretched hand. The sharpened bones remained hidden in the folds of her sash and the kebab skewer in the seam near her trouser pocket.

The Aanisah reached for Serein's chin and tipped her face up. "Your eyes are stunning. Half-bloods always have such unique eyes. You could've ruled this world if you had looks," she said.

"I've no interest in ruling anything," Serein replied, skin prickling.

The Aanisah released her and turned back down the hall. "Everybody wants to rule the world in one form or another. Few have the will and the means to do it."

"Come in," Eneca said, the rosy words cutting through the perfumed, plum-colored haze of the Aanisah's voice.

Golden light spilled from the lamps hanging from the ceiling. Eneca sat on a rumpled bed, fixing her sheer robe. Serein felt roughened hands holding her down, the taste of overly sweet wine on her tongue.

He's not here, Serein thought, digging her nails into her palms as she closed the door.

Eneca's face lit up, and she flitted across the room on soft green footsteps to hug Serein, black hair curling over her shoulders. "It's good to see you, Ser," she said, arms tight around her.

The rose-colored Sarlyrian swept away the memories, bringing Serein back to the room they shared when they were younger, telling stories at night and forgetting the dangerous world lurking around them.

"I caught you while you were working," Serein said, the tension draining away.

"I'm always working. I rarely have time to myself unless I make a fuss to the Aanisah," Eneca told her as they broke apart.

"That woman's a real pleasure. Guess she isn't sending the Thanatos Flower out tonight."

"The Aanisah sends me to clients from time to time, but she prefers that I keep most coming back." A hollow light cast a glaze over Eneca's eyes. "Does she know who you are?"

"I don't think so. I paid her enough to buy her silence at least."

Serein pulled a smaller purse from her robes, handing it to Eneca. The gold coins slid against each other in dark blue *clinks*.

"You don't need to do this," Eneca said.

"You can't hide the shadows under your eyes with kohl, En. This should at least be enough for you to ask for a day to rest. I'm sorry I can't do more," Serein whispered. *I don't have enough to help buy her freedom yet. I owe her so much. She stayed behind, so I could escape.*

Eneca took her hand. "What happened wasn't your fault. Xansas was looking to have me work here long before you left. He sent me here so that you wouldn't be able to find me. To hurt us both."

"You helped me escape and risked so much. I should have taken you with me. Let me do this small thing for you. I also have this," Serein said and held out a small cloth bundle. "You still like candied nuts, right?"

Eneca opened the pouch and smiled at the sugarcoated pistachios. "You still know me after all these years." She wrapped her arms around Serein again. "Still the same."

"A few more scars than last time, several pounds lighter, and maybe a bit taller," Serein said, grinning.

"Still thoughtful and resourceful, O sister of my heart," Eneca replied.

Serein chuckled. "You've been spending too much time with Sarddonian poets."

"A few have written some lovely poems about me. I'll have to show them to you. Some are quite good, but others give me a good laugh."

Eneca put the bundles on her vanity. Tucked behind bottles of perfume and pots of makeup, a small fabric square with a dark skinned woman embroidered on it caught Serein's eye. The woman stood in a desert, arms lifted as water swirled around her.

"Interested in the Saints?" Serein asked, spotting a copy of *Twisted Boughs* next to the image of the Saint.

"One of the women here, Lina, made it for me when I first arrived here," Eneca replied. "Raz Nura is the Saint of Water, originally a prostitute before she discovered she had magic. Many brothels around here and in the Tafall District have shrines and murals of her. Lina told me that she serves as a reminder that even the imperfect can be used for divine purposes."

"I wonder how many of the Saints might have just been Sahriminhas," Serein said.

Eneca shrugged and gestured to the cushions by the windowsill. "They remind me of the Lights in some ways."

Serein eased down onto a blue velvet cushion. "And the book? *Twisted Boughs?*" she asked. *Seems that book's popular.*

Eneca sat beside her. "One of the girls lent it to me. It's an entertaining read. Have you read it?"

"It wasn't to my liking."

Serein peered through the lattice window screen at the street. Uriah stood tucked in an alleyway, staring at the Faten. His hand went to his necklace, tension rolling off his squared shoulders.

The captain must have some choice words ready for me if he's going to stand there the whole time, she thought. *All the assumptions that must be running through his head. I'm amazed he's not blushing.*

"Something caught your eye?" Eneca asked, peering through the leaf cutouts of the screen. "That red-haired man across the street? Don't see many Wendish here. Is he dangerous?"

"You don't have to worry about him. He's mostly harmless," Serein replied. "He followed me because he thinks I'm up to no good."

Eneca arched her eyebrows. "You have a lot to tell me. What color is his voice?"

"Green. Like a forest."

"That must compliment his hair. How do you know him?"

"He slammed my face into the ground the first time we met."

"Now I *have* to hear your story," Eneca said. "You were always such a good storyteller."

"I haven't had much time for stories," Serein replied with a sigh. "Have any Bone Vipers come to the city?"

"I haven't seen anyone. Why? Are you worried that Xansas will find you?" Eneca asked, her rosy voice lowering.

Serein's knuckles whitened, hands curled into fists. "I keep hearing his voice—like he's *still* here. He knows someone betrayed him, and it won't take him long to figure out it was me."

"I haven't heard anything about him being in the city. I'll keep my ears open." Eneca squeezed Serein's hands. "If you haven't seen him yet, he probably doesn't know you're here."

Dregs of old fear resurfaced. "It's only a matter of time." *He doesn't forgive or forget. He will come after me.*

Eneca moved closer, and her fingers brushed against the bangles. "Oh, Serein..." She ran her thumb across the metal. "I'm so sorry. This...is the symbol of the royal house? What do the Sarddonian royals want with you?"

"The prince wanted me to serve him. It was the bargain for my freedom," Serein said. "That's where I'll start my story."

Uriah tapped his finger against his arm. His discomfort mounted, heartbeat catching in his throat each time a scantily-clad woman approached him. He kept his gaze averted, one eye on the Faten. *It's been almost two hours. What's she doing in there?* Uriah thought. *She's not...is she?*

A white-haired man with pale skin passed by him, dressed in a gray rida' that obscured his face. Uriah returned his scowl to the Faten's entrance.

Did Rameses tell her about the door? What if she's been leaving the palace regularly? Why come to a place like this—

"Waiting for someone, Captain Stormheir?"

Serein melted out of the crowds beside him, cowl shadowing her face. "Saints!" Uriah hissed, reaching for his weapon. "What are you doing here?"

"Meeting an old acquaintance," she replied.

"In a brothel?" he asked.

"Is that what that place was? That explains why everyone wore so little clothing," Serein said, walking away. "I'm shocked you stalked me here."

"I didn't stalk you!" *She knew I was tailing her. She's not trying to hide that she's in a place like this.*

"Really?" He felt her condescending smile before he saw it. "What do you call following me so late at night?"

Uriah caught up to her. "What was so important that you had to sneak here in the middle of the night? How do you know about the secret door?"

"Rameses told me about it." She glanced back at him as he pushed past a group of laughing men in the middle of the street. "I came here for a story," she said.

"A story?" Uriah repeated, eyes narrowed. "You're lying. I'm going to find out what you're hiding "

"If I were hiding my activities from you, you wouldn't have been able to follow me. It was enjoyable to watch you squirm outside the brothels. I can't wait to hear the rumors that will circulate."

Uriah glanced around at the people shuffling through the streets, his hand on the sword. The neat buildings of the Gold District wrapped around the palace like a glittering collar, private riads visible behind carved walls as they cut through the interior of Oyon. Lamps burned in the streets, stretching out their shadows. Alqamar Palace drew closer as it gleamed against the night.

"When will the official listing of the competitors be released?" Serein asked.

"It'll be announced in a week and posted outside the coliseum. Those who passed will receive an invitation to a feast at the palace before the Aikhtiar begins," Uriah told her. "You'll be expected to attend."

"I think I'll spend the evenings in my chambers. Nala's better company."

He shot her a sideways glance. "Nala?"

"You and the prince like to repeat everything I say. It makes you seem unintelligent," Serein told him as they approached the palace walls. "Being alone with one's self is often more appealing than being in a room full of those who despise you."

"It's your fault if no one likes you."

She opened the gate to the servant's entrance along the palace wall, walking past the doorkeepers. "You mean my charming personality and wit aren't endearing?"

The causeway stretched before them, the reflecting pools catching the light from the torches and the braziers. The crescent moon hung against a bed of stars. Birds and frogs called from the gardens as the warm night wrapped around them.

Uriah made a noise halfway between a sigh and a groan. *Out of all the women in the world, Rameses had to find this one,* he thought.

"The preliminary matches will force you to get some sleep," Serein said.

"I sleep," Uriah retorted.

"So, those shadows beneath your eyes are just part of your complexion?" she asked.

"Why do you care? You hate me."

Serein threw back her cowl, climbing the stairs to her tower. "Did I ever utter those words?" she asked.

Uriah stopped at the bottom step. "Then why harass me?"

"You're just so easy to tease," Serein said, her voice bouncing down the stairs. "If you follow me to my chambers at this hour, more rumors are bound to grow."

Uriah *tsked* as he stalked back down the corridor. *It's like she lives to make my life miserable,* he thought.

Chapter Thirty-Two
Releasing the Arrow

on her tongue. Her gray veil fluttered back down as she lowered the cup, glancing across at Eneca. The gold flecks in Eneca's brown irises sparkled through the eye slits of her purple veil, the skirts of the violet abaya pooling around her. Morning sunlight streamed through the lattice covering of the teahouse. The patio filled with colorful conversations—cinnamon-colored laughter, soft blue murmurings, quick chocolate-brown questions.

"I still can't believe you're participating in the Aikhtiar," Eneca said, rose-tinged words falling across the geometric-patterned top of the low table between them.

"No one's more surprised than me, but the offer of my freedom was one I couldn't ignore," Serein replied as the pale-yellow syllables collected beneath the veil. "There's a feast at the end of the week for everyone who passed the preliminary matches."

Eneca reached for a hole-riddled beghrir, spreading apricot jam and honey across the spongy pancake. "I attended a party at the palace with a shahrban a few years ago. I'd never seen so much food or fine clothes in one place before."

"They're definitely overwhelming with all the colors," Serein said.

"Do you trust the prince?" Eneca asked as she took a bite of the pancake. "From what you told me and what I've heard over the years, he's not like his father."

Serein traced the healing cut along her palm. "We are aligned with a similar goal," she said. "Trusting him is another matter. I don't think he'll throw me to the Jackals, but he might let something slip unintentionally. It's safer if he doesn't know everything. For his sake and mine." *No one else can know about you, my Sun and Stars.*

"Will you ever tell him?" Eneca asked, sipping her coffee.

"With Xansas still alive and Sethos in power, no," Serein replied. "If I become muharib, he'll know exactly where to find me."

"Why not ask the prince to protect you? With his resources, couldn't he help?"

Camels passed by on the street, bells chiming in dark peach tones as they hung from their saddle blankets. "It's hard not to see danger everywhere. The last time I let my guard down..."

"You and I both know the past isn't easily forgotten," Eneca said. "This is a new part of your life, so why not adapt to it?"

"How have you adapted to living in Sarddon?" Serein asked.

Eneca's gaze softened, and she moved her cushion closer. "The climate isn't too different from where I grew up near the Olsen Desert. One of the guards, Rahet, is kind to me. He doesn't tell the Aanisah everything I do outside the Faten. There are women there I consider friends. But I still dream of a life beyond all this."

"How do you feel about farming? I know of a nice place in the Sava Forests where no one could find us. The locals are nice."

"Farming?" Eneca laughed. "I thought I might open a bakery somewhere. I remember my mother making bread when I was little."

Serein took an orange slice from the yellow dish in the middle of the table. "Might be good to learn something other than how to kill someone. I've learned some embroidery. It's basically the same as stitching wounds," she said, peeling away the rind.

"Now you can add a nice little flower next time you get cut," Eneca told her.

A mother tugged her daughter after her through the street while a cat darted out of their way. Gulls alighted on the rooftops, beady eyes scanning for scraps of food to snatch.

"I want to do what I can to help you, En. You deserve to have a life not controlled by someone else. I've always regretted not taking you with me..." Serein said, tart citrus juice seeping across her tongue.

"It was my choice to stay behind," Eneca replied, taking Serein's hand. "You wouldn't have been able to get away if I'd been with you. I never regretted that decision."

Serein squeezed Eneca's fingers. "You helped me, and now I want to help you. I heard the pay as a muharib is pretty good. What else am I going to do with all that money? I can only buy so many weapons before people start noticing."

The corners of Eneca's eyes crinkled. "I know what you're trying to get back to. That's a more worthy goal."

"O sister of my heart, how could you be blessed with such beauty yet not see your worth? Shall I write you a poem and show you?" Serein asked.

"The assassin poet. There's a new title for you," Eneca said and chuckled. "I'm glad you can find a bit of happiness here."

Serein took a sip of tea, staring out at the street again. More people moved about as the cool air began to evaporate. "It's hard to think that I could find happiness again. Grasdan ripped almost everything from me," Serein muttered and reached for a beghrir, slathering it in thick cream. "Everything I care about gets threatened. I don't want to lose anything else." The words stuck to her throat, making it hard to breathe.

Eneca broke apart a honey-drizzled sfenj, the cinnamon dust sticking to her fingers. "But even Xansas can't destroy love. He can only make you afraid of it and what you stand to lose, not what you can gain. You have far more to gain than you have to lose."

"When did you get so wise, En?"

A smile sparkled in Eneca's eyes. "I learned from you."

THE SUN YAWNED AS IT SANK LOW INTO THE SKY, DRAWING THE soft edges of dusk with it. Rameses nocked an arrow, pulling back the taut bowstring with three fingers. White fletching kissed his cheek as he let the arrow fly, grinning as it struck the center ring of the hanging target. He turned to Serein standing a few feet away. Her stillness made her resemble the garden statues, black and red robes wrapped around her like shadows. Na'il and Na'im lounged by the bench nearby, the cream-colored canines sprawled out on the grass.

"Impressed?" Rameses asked Serein, lowering the bow.

"You're better with a bow than I am," Serein said.

"Did you just compliment me? I'm honored," Rameses told her, dusting his hands off on his long tunic. "If you really want to be impressed, my horseback archery is quite good. The last week of the Aikhtiar, I will be participating in an archery competition."

"Will it be a challenge for you, or will they just hand you the victory?" Serein asked.

"Oh, how you wound me." He placed a hand over his heart. "The competitors are some of the most skilled archers in the kingdom. I would not use my station to disgrace them. If I win, it will be because I earn it. I used to enter competitions, but I have not been able to for the past couple of years."

Rameses ran his fingers through his hair, rolling his shoulders.

"My father always wanted me to use a sword, but I didn't like the feel of it. I like the bow because you have to wait and think before releasing the arrow. You have to look at your target before shooting."

Serein glanced around the riad. "Both can kill regardless."

"True, but I hope I never have to take a life," Rameses told her. The smell of jasmine wafted from the high trellises around the courtyard. Swaths of pink and orange turned the palace domes a soft peach color. Sand shifted beneath Rameses' sandals as he walked to the bench, reaching for his waterskin. His turban rested next to a book Serein had returned to him.

Rameses sat down, bare arms glistening with sweat as he took a sip of water. Serein went over to the targets, gathering the arrows before dumping them in his empty quiver.

"I heard that you managed to wound Hisein during the preliminary matches. Were you showing off?" Rameses asked. *I doubt she likes the idea of having to serve beside a man like him.*

"A small revenge for him underestimating me," Serein said, the ghost of a grin on her lips.

"There will be a lot of people at the diffa this week. Hopefully, you will not run into him anytime soon," Rameses told her.

"One might question if having so many fighters in one room is a good idea."

"More loose lips to listen to. Perhaps you will find another lord to enamor with a tragic story. There will be plenty of foreign dignitaries to choose from." Rameses winked at her. "Have you given any more thought about looking into Hasim? He asked about you the other day when I was by the stables to see Jabbar. He was in the city to check on some of the mares that are ready to foal."

Serein's footfalls were silent on the sands. "Sending him letters would be the easiest thing, and if he insisted on meeting in person, I could hide my face with a veil," she replied, looking up as a nightjar flew past. "Still, it's risky."

The arrows clacked together as Rameses slung the quiver over his shoulder and walked back to the target. "When have you ever shied away from difficult things? You survived Grasdan, cracked ribs, and a bruised nose. You even put up with Uriah's moods. Sending letters should be easy."

She chuckled, the sharp edges softening.

Rameses paused, wanting her mirth to last longer, but instead asked, "What else have you been doing with your time?"

Her mouth pursed, guarded steel passing over her eyes. "I'm looking into the records of the healers," Serein replied.

"Have you been following anyone else? That may yield more than the infirmary records," Rameses told her as he stroked the fletching of the arrow.

"Small steps, prince. The darker secrets are hidden deep, so you have to dig a little bit at a time," she said. "The healers keep meticulous records. A few have been serving since your grandfather's time, so they might have kept records of the king's condition and his family through the generations. Your father's injuries were most likely recorded somewhere."

Rameses adjusted his stance. "How are you going to explore the healers' records? Are you planning on getting sent to the infirmary again? I would prefer that you not get injured anytime soon."

"Your concern melts my heart."

He released another arrow, the shaft grazing the one already in the center. "Rasima's quite taken with you, and I don't want to see her upset over you being injured again. She talks about you often. I think she wishes you were her sibling."

"A poor choice," Serein said.

Rameses' arm slackened as he looked at her. "Do you have any siblings?" he asked. *Serein will not admit it, but I think she likes Rasima. It's good for her to have moments not filled with worry.*

"No. Most of the people in the tribe were like family. I had many cousins growing up. We all lived in the same house with my grandparents, aunts, and uncles," Serein told him, her expression unchanging as stillness surrounded her.

"Sounds like you had a big family," Rameses said. *One my father probably killed...*

A faint shift rippled through Serein's blue eyes, vanishing as she blinked. "I don't remember much, but it was always noisy and warm."

"Was your friend from your tribe? The one you mentioned at my mother's diffa," Rameses said.

"No. She wasn't a Ravanassë," Serein replied. "She was from the west, near the Olsen Desert. We grew up together in the Bone Vipers."

"Was she an assassin like you?"

"Not like me, but she had her own way of killing people." Another arrow struck the target. "Those faces you drew, were some of them your family?"

Serein's eyes followed another bird that flew from the branches of a nearby olive tree. He saw her mind wandering to a memory as he nocked another arrow. "Some. The rest are just faces," she told him.

When will she trust me enough to talk more about her past? Rameses thought, the X-shaped scar across Serein's chest burning in his mind. *She doesn't want me asking how she's doing, but I know those memories must cause her deep pain.*

Rameses' arm wavered before he released the bowstring, the sharp *twang* kicking up his thoughts. The arrow struck the wooden circle on the edge of the center ring. The sky darkened as blues and purples unfurled, sweeping up the edges of sunlight. Torches sprang to life along the palace walls. The nighttime prayer of Alkhaliq rang out from the towers of the Royal House of the Saints.

"I suppose that's enough practice for today. Don't want to wear myself out before tonight," Rameses said.

"Expecting company?" Serein asked.

His lips tugged upward. "I made arrangements with Yasmine so we could talk. She's been on business with her father these past few months."

She arched an eyebrow. "I'm sure you'll be doing a lot of *talking*."

"We do. Usually afterward. I think business excites her more than anything else."

"Seems your good looks and charm don't work on every woman. At least not for long," Serein said.

The dogs lifted their heads, tails wagging as Rameses patted their heads. *She didn't ask for anything when I asked her those questions. And she didn't stop me when I asked more than one,* he thought, watching Serein retrieve the arrows. *I think she will enjoy the surprise I have for her to use in the Aikhtiar.*

Chapter Thirty-Three
Reminders of the Past

WAVES OF COLORS WASHED OVER SEREIN AS SHE STEPPED INTO THE audience hall. Her black and red guard robes cut through the elegant dresses and fine outfits of the guests like a dark shadow. Guests showed off the finery of their countries in silks and brightly dyed fabrics, ornate headdresses and hats, and glittering jewelry. Warriors transformed, the festive attire masking the dangerous air they carried in their movements.

Ginjarrians and men from Sinabrac mingled with people from Zhao, while the Edolasians remained in their own pockets of conversation. The Sarddonians made up most of the crowd. Snippets of conversations flowed past. Rough Ginjarrians dialects, orotund Edola, rippling and dulcet Lóng Shé, rolling Sarddonian constants.

Two hundred and twenty fighters, Serein thought. *It won't be easy to win.*

Music drifted from the other end of the hall, accompanying dancers in yellow kaftans. Sethos spoke with a group of Zhao men, his black and gold qamis and white mantle with the roaring lion seeming to absorb the light from the hall. Serein caught the flash of gilded armor as Hisein stood near the Malik with a cluster of women. Yellow bruises dabbed the side of his face.

Will that be my fate? Tagging along at the Murderous King's heels like a dog? she thought, feeling the lamb bone and the kebab skewer tucked inside her sleeves. Her dagger hung from her belt, hidden under the folds of her robe. *Two people to avoid tonight. The queen and the younger siblings aren't present tonight. Probably best not to have them among such dangerous people.*

Serein headed to the massive table at the front of the hall that supported a whole roasted camel on a silver platter stuffed with eggs, almonds, dates, lemons, and rice. The smells of tangy za'atar spices, ras el hanout, and cumin swirled in the air as Serein selected marinated chunks of chicken and lamb, and rolled them into a piece of msemen bread.

I would've preferred to stay in my chambers tonight, but I should at least assess my competition. I can always count on the food to be good at least. The night could take an interesting turn, and I may need something other than my sharp wit to fend off those who won't be pleased to see me.

Gray footsteps cut through the swirling hues, and Serein turned to meet Uriah's stern face. He wore his armor and red city guard robes with its white sash. His scimitar and dagger hung at his sides.

"What are you wearing?" Uriah asked, his green voice saturated with disapproval.

Serein smoothed out the front of her robes, brushing away crumbs. "Clothes. Or was I not supposed to? Is it *that* sort of party?" she replied.

Uriah crossed his arms, a scowl forming. "*Carreg cryau fi.* Wear what you like. It's not my problem."

"Really? Because it seems like you came over here to comment on my attire. Do your duties include protecting the kingdom from clothing disasters?"

"You're not on duty tonight. The least you can do is pretend to enjoy the feast. It's almost like you're afraid of social gatherings."

Serein grabbed a glass of pomegranate juice from a passing servant, the filigree on the ruby-colored glass sparkling under the lantern light. "I was forged in blood, bones, and steel. Few things scare me," she replied.

Uriah shook his head, muttering as he turned and stalked off.

Will the Vale be here? If this all gets to be too much, maybe I can slip away to the gardens and check. I doubt I'll run into Hasim tonight.

The music's tempo increased, rippling lines of marigold from the santurs and emerald beats of the tombaks dancing overhead like living serpents. Female Zhao acrobats with faces painted white and dark hair coiled in flower shapes dangled from red streams of fabric hanging from the ceiling, bodies bending around the fluttering coils. Their red, white, and gold outfits shifted like birds' wings.

"You're not wearing a dress." Serein glanced up as Salveig approached, towering over her. The woman's apple-red voice tilted upward with mirth as her accent clung to the Common Tongue. "You look like you're dressed for battle."

The Edolasian wore a flowing blue velvet dress with cutoff sleeves and a white fur mantle. Her braided hair hung over her shoulder, blue ribbons woven into the pleats. Ragnhildur followed beside her, wearing a green and gold gown.

"This suits me better than a dress," Serein said.

Salveig took a sip from the cup of wine in her hand, hazel eyes sharp. "I heard that you serve the crown prince of Sarddon as his guard. Were you forced to do it against your will?" she asked.

"Seemed better than dying in prison," Serein told her, licking the tart juice from her lips. *Wonder how many other rumors about me she's heard.*

The black tattoo on Salveig's jaw wrinkled as her mouth curved. "I have heard about Sarddon's custom of purchasing a person's life contract and using them as indentured *servants*. What did you do to find yourself bound to the Sarddonian prince?"

Serein grinned. "Now, Salveig, we've only just met. Where's the fun in sharing all our secrets now when we have a whole month of fighting to get to know each other better?"

Salveig nodded, the beginnings of a thin smile forming on her face. "I like you, and I don't even know your name."

"Serein."

The Edolasian nodded, turning her gaze to Uriah as he stood across the room. "That red-haired man you were talking to, what's your relationship with him?" Salveig asked.

"An occasional sparring partner," Serein replied.

"I enjoyed fighting against him during the preliminary matches.

It's been a while since I've met someone who could match me," Salveig said.

"He's shy around women. A smile from a pretty face will make him blush." *I doubt the captain would be able to handle a woman like Salveig,* Serein thought.

"A virgin? That's unexpected." A smile entered Salveig's voice.

"The Wendish are quite conservative when it comes to sex. They believe in keeping themselves pure until marriage. It's part of their devotion to the elemental deities."

"Still, he has fire in him, and he'd make a great soldier of Edolas. Like one of the Mother Goddess's berserkers."

"Sounds like you want to carry him off to join your army," Serein said.

Salveig followed Uriah's movements with hungry eyes. "I'd need to test him with real steel first. I think I'll start tonight," she said as she and Ragnhildur walked away.

Like prey for a wolf. Good luck, Captain Stormheir, Serein thought and headed back to the food table.

Light brown footsteps tickled the edge of Serein's vision, a dark shape appearing. "Ah, Serein, so good to see you," came the soft onyx voice from behind.

Seems I can't eat in peace, Serein thought, turning to face Il-Makah as he stood dressed in a dark qamis with white feather embroidery. *His little shadow isn't around. Or his pet.*

The corners of the spymaster's eyes crinkled as he smiled. "Lovely diffa, isn't it? Inga went to fetch some food," he said, hands folded together in front of him. "I'm glad to see that you've healed from your injury. Fractured ribs are nasty things."

"It wasn't the worst injury I've received," Serein replied.

His eyes went to her throat. "I heard that you entered the Aikhtiar. Are you not content serving the Amir?" Il-Makah asked.

"I think I might do better in a position with more excitement. The prince said I could serve the rest of my contract as a muharib if I wanted to." *What does he suspect? No doubt he and the King have their suspicions.*

"You're an ambitious one. Perhaps as a muharib, His Majesty will send you my way. The Golden Jackals would benefit from your skills." His gaze drifted to the people passing nearby, watching with a thin smile. "Well, I'll let you enjoy the party. May the Saints bring you luck in the Aikhtiar."

Il-Makah nodded before melting into the crowd. Serein finished her drink and handed the empty glass to a servant. She grabbed more chicken and bread before retreating to a half-hidden corner of the hall behind maroon curtains. Sethos appeared again with Kamau and his guards, Hisein nowhere to be seen.

Serein licked grease off her fingers, blending into the shadows. Among the swirling bodies, a tall, lithe woman with a dark braid moved like a ghost. Both women stared at each other, tension freezing the air. She wore a walnut-colored dress with a white bodice. Her sharp face and pudgy nose hadn't changed in seven years, brown eyes calculating.

The breath caught in Serein's throat, and the edges of the room blurred. *Mayte's here?! I didn't see her name on the list of competitors. If she's a competitor, she must have used a false name,* Serein thought, stomach turning to stone. *If the Brown Adder is here, then Xansas knows where I am. Is she here to kill me? I need to get out of here. Did he send anyone else? How many other Vipers are lurking in the palace?*

Thoughts slammed into Serein, a phantom hand closing around her throat. Mayte disappeared into the crowds, leaving behind a chill in the air. A cold sweat broke out across Serein's skin. She searched the faces for bright green eyes and sharp features, heart twisting.

A shadow fell over Serein as General Hisein blocked her way, hazel eyes glinting. Wine-colored robes brushed over his gilded armor. The smell of alcohol rolled off his breath, the yellow bruise staining his jaw. Beauty and anger fought on Hisein's face.

"You," he seethed, his reeking twilight-blue voice dripping down her front.

"Ah, General Hisein," Serein said with a smile. "That bruise seems to be healing nicely." *Wonderful. An angry, drunk man,* she thought.

"You think you can talk to me that way, half-blood?" Hisein snapped. The words slurred, knocking together like blades.

Hisein grabbed Serein's wrist. She dropped the food as he twisted her bangle, crushing the bread underfoot. Anger pushed against

Serein's chest, skin prickling at his touch. A few people passing by glanced over but quickly looked away when they recognized the Golden General.

Serein's left hand inched toward her dagger. *Drive the bone through his eye and the skewer through his throat,* she thought, watching the veins in Hisein's throat bulge. *One slash across the throat would be quicker, but it might be more satisfying to hear him scream.*

"I thought the Amir had better taste than some scarred bitch. And a filthy Ravanassë at that," he said. "Does he show you favoritism when you warm his bed?"

"Is that how you got *your* position? Warming the King's bed?" Serein asked.

"Watch your tongue!" Hisein spat, gripping her face. "I could have you whipped for such insolence"—he leaned in closer—"so you should be thankful that I'm a tolerant man."

Yes, and as calm as a wildfire. "I suggest you take a step back, General," she said, sliding the dagger from its sheath.

"Or what?" Hisein sneered, nails digging into her cheek. "You have no power here. *I* can have you punished at my command. You're nothing. You're just a Ravanassë savage. I've dealt with your kind before."

His nails dug into her cheeks. "Did you know that the Warden of Grasdan has four fingers on his right hand? He used to have five, but then he stuck his hand too close to something dangerous. Will you still be able to wield a sword with only nine fingers? Or eight?"

Hisein's jaw twitched, and he pushed her back behind one of the curtains against the wall, breath hot on her face. "Your threats are empty."

Serein's fingers tightened around the dagger's hilt. "If you know that I'm the prince's wali, then you also know who I really am. I can do a lot more than bruising your face, General."

"Some assassin pulled from the cesspits of Grasdan. So what? Being the Amir's servant won't help you through the Aikhtiar. A real sword will cut that smile off your ugly face."

"Does the emptiness inside you keep you up at night? All the women and drinks in the world can't drown out that nagging feeling that you'll always be the son of a prostitute. A twisted monster masquerading as a general. I've killed generals before. That gold armor won't protect you."

Serein saw the moment blind rage took over, and Hisein's features melted into fury as his grip tightened. Peach chimes approached on orange steps behind him. "General Hisein, is everything all right?"

Hisein whirled around, eyes landing on Rameses and Ilderim. "Yes, Your Highness," he said and dropped into a bow. "I was only reprimanding your servant. She's being disrespectful."

Rameses glanced at Serein, fingers tight around the goblet in his hand. She slid the dagger back into its sheath out of sight. "That cannot be right. Serein is a courteous, upright woman who would not dare show disrespect to someone as esteemed as yourself," he said, his smile carrying an unspoken warning. "Let me worry about my guards, General."

Hisein straightened, swaying a bit. "My apologies, Your Highness."

He threw a dark look at Serein as he marched off, his bristling rage hanging in the air.

Serein glanced at the crushed food on the floor. *I was looking forward to eating that. I should've hit him harder,* she thought. *Or gutted him where he stood.*

"Are you all right? Did he threaten you?" Rameses asked, staring at the red marks on her face. "Did he hurt you?"

"No," Serein said. "He *did* ruin what I was eating. Seems he's still upset about the bruise I gave him." *I need to get out of here. There are too many people, too many dangers.*

"Hisein has an ego and a bad temper to match," Rameses told her. "You should be careful. I have heard stories about what he does when he gets angry. Tell me if he does anything to you."

She rubbed her chin, touching the small crescents left by Hisein's nails. "You're confusing me with someone who needs your help."

Rameses sighed, sipping his wine. "Why are you wearing your guard robes?"

"They're more comfortable," Serein replied.

Fang appeared through the crowd with three other Zhao men beside him. He locked eyes with Serein, his opaque blue conversation dying. Glaring, Fang made a crude gesture at her. Serein smiled at Fang. His features twisted, arms tense cords.

"Who's that?" Rameses asked. "He doesn't seem happy to see you."

"Another competitor. I pinned him against a wall and threatened to castrate him," Serein replied.

"You seem to be doing a good job at making enemies." Rameses glanced up as one of the acrobats unwound herself from the coils of the red fabric before stopping above the partygoers.

"It's a special skill of mine."

Rameses followed Serein to another corner of the audience hall. "Uriah tells me that you went to a pleasure house the other night. When he said that, I wondered why *he* was there, but Uriah's married to his work and would never cheat on that. So, what *were* you doing in a place like that?"

Serein glanced at the doors leading out of the hall. "I'm sure you've already come up with some theories." *I need to slip the prince and leave,* she thought. *I don't know if Mayte's here to kill me or if others were sent. Xansas will be coming soon, and I need to prepare. I'll have to warn Eneca. She may know something. I don't want her getting caught up in whatever's coming.*

Rameses broke into a grin. "It's probably best that I don't share them. He says you met an acquaintance," he said. "Is that a code for...?"

Serein stared at him. "I went to talk with a friend," she answered.

"I thought you didn't have any friends," Rameses said, leaning in.

"I do know people who aren't wanting to kill me," Serein said and brushed past him.

"Where are you going?"

"Back to my room." *I need to make a plan before Xansas finds me,* Serein thought, the black emotions bubbling up as she looked for Mayte among the partygoers. *I'll never be safe until he's dead. And now I have Mayte to deal with.*

Rameses moved in front of her. "Come now, Serein. Stay," he said. "You cannot tell me you were meeting a friend at a pleasure house and not go into details. I might go mad trying to guess the truth."

"It'll be a fun guessing game for you. Help cure your boredom," Serein replied.

A group of Zhao warriors clapped and cheered as one of the dancers was tossed into the air and caught by her partner, her yellow skirts fluttering like flower petals. Serein glanced past Rameses as Uriah walked over, cheeks a splotchy red. His hair had been freed from its ponytail, and he pulled it back with hurried fingers.

"You look flustered, Captain Stormheir. Is that sunburn, or are you blushing?" Serein asked. *Seems his interaction with Salveig went well. He's still got his clothes on, so it looks like she didn't get too far. I would've loved to have seen their conversation.*

"Shut up!" Uriah snapped, green words bristling as he looked over his shoulder.

"What's got you so perturbed, sadiqi?" Rameses asked, grasping Uriah's shoulder.

"...These women came up to me. Edolasians," Uriah said, clearing his throat as he tugged at his necklace.

"Ah! Finally, someone who's not thwarted by your scowl," Rameses said with a laugh. "So, what kind of women were they?"

"Intimidating ones. The blonde looked like she wanted to devour me. Or fight me. I couldn't tell..." Uriah muttered.

With Salveig, it's probably both, Serein thought, catching sight of the Edolasian across the room with Ragnhildur.

Rameses looped his arm around Uriah's neck, his wine sloshing in the cup. "A woman scares *you*? She must have been something. You should try talking to her."

Uriah coughed. "I don't think she's interested in talking..."

"She wants to skip right to the bedroom?" Rameses asked, his smile broadening.

Uriah's ears reddened. "I don't intend to run into her again. Or her friend."

"You're fortunate to have two women interested in you," Rameses said, turning to Serein. "So many women have tried to win Uriah's attention, but unless their names are Duty or Honor, he has no interest."

"Salveig isn't coy," Serein said through her laughter.

"You know her?" they asked, green filled with worry while the golden voice piqued with interest.

"We talked after the preliminary matches. She asked about you, Captain Stormheir. Edolasians prize strength above all else, and she thinks you're strong," Serein told Uriah. "You should be honored."

Uriah scowled. "Did you tell her I was interested?!" he snapped.

"You caught her eye all on your own. Edolasians are very straightforward and stubborn."

"Seems you're in a bit of a bind, Uriah," Rameses said. "Serein, do you have your eye on a man?"

"No." *Not for the reasons he thinks. The people I have my eyes on are the ones I'm planning to kill and those I want to avoid,* Serein thought.

"Do you want to think that response over a little longer?" Rameses asked.

Serein glanced at him. "No," she said.

Rameses raised an eyebrow. "Well...a woman perhaps?"

"No."

Rameses frowned. "Not a single person interests you? I find that hard to believe. I bet you left a long line of broken hearts in your wake."

"I have better things to do than spend my nights with lovers." *Like plotting Sethos' death and surviving long enough so I can leave this place.*

A hush fell across the room, heads turning toward Sethos as he faced the crowd. "Welcome, fighters and honored guests," the Malik said in a booming voice, splattering the walls red. "Over the next month, you will train and prepare yourselves for the Aikhtiar. Fight with all your strength for glory and honor. Tonight, eat, drink, and celebrate!"

Chapter Thirty-Four
The Moon-carved Viper

A HEADACHE POUNDED THE INSIDE OF SEREIN'S SKULL, THE SILENT hallway offering solace in the late evening hours. She didn't see Mayte for the rest of the night but felt the prickling of unseen eyes along the back of her neck. *With Mayte here, Xansas will be close behind —if he's not here already. I don't have much time to prepare,* Serein thought as she glanced around the empty hallways, gripping her dagger.

Serein called for Nala as she stepped into her chambers, but the cub didn't appear. Pink scratching and peacock-blue cries came from the other room. Serein approached the bathing chamber, Nala's yowls coming from the other side of the door.

Why is Nala in there? Did Rizwana accidentally shut her in? she thought, reaching for the door handle.

A prickle ran up Serein's spine as a hand grabbed her throat, metal cutting her neck. The cold point of a dagger poked against her ribs as an arm encircled her waist, pinning her arms to her sides. "It's been a long time, Serein," a white voice whispered.

The dagger dug into Serein's skin, a trickle of blood running down her skin. Her heart thrashed against its bone cage. "*You!*" she hissed. *No! He can't be here! Not yet!*

Adrenaline broke through the fear, and Serein slammed her head back, skull colliding with his jaw. The dagger scraped against her stomach as she twisted around. The hand left Serein's throat and clamped on her wrist, wrenching it behind her back as she tried to pull her blade free. Pale green eyes cut through the darkness, hair slipping from the cowl around his head. Her nightmares became flesh, bone, and terror as Xansas Regor, the man carved from the moon, stood before her. He caressed her cheek, touching the scars with callused fingers. The claws of the Viper's Teeth over his knuckles glinted, the serrated tips of the bagh nakh coated in an oily sheen. His knife hovered near her face.

Serein jerked back, and her shoulder shrieked in pain, the joints in her arm straining. "No," she whispered.

"I've missed your face terribly, my *volchitsa*. Is that how you greet me after all this time?" Xansas asked, holding her fast.

The black anger fought the mounting fear. "You took everything from me!"

His eyebrows creased. "Took from you? I *gave* everything to you. *You* ran away and had to be punished. Grasdan was to teach you, but it seems you didn't learn much."

Realization ripped a hole through her, legs weakening. *He was the one who sent the soldiers to find me. Was he there in that town?!* She swallowed. *He knew where I was this whole time. I never escaped from him...*

"Still, I made sure you were safe in prison."

"Safe? They tortured and beat me, put me in a fighting pit, and tried to burn me alive!"

"That wasn't supposed to happen, but there are things even I can't control," Xansas said. "I made sure you were kept alive. Why do you think you weren't executed when the soldiers found you? I had someone alter the sentence, so you could live. My contacts there made sure you were fed and not killed. Who do you think killed that Golden Jackal? You told him what I looked like, gave away my secrets, undoing everything I did to protect you."

Numbness spread through Serein's limbs, the dagger slipping from her grip. "They were supposed to kill you," she said, swallowing. *That's what happened to the information I gave Nizar. How did Xansas get a hold of that information before it got to Il-Makah? Does he have a spy within the Jackals?*

He tilted his head, smiling. "They nearly would have if my contacts hadn't informed me they were coming. I planned to return for you, but you killed some of my men, and I didn't know if you were dead. But the princeling got you before I could."

His fingers traced Serein's lips, moving down her throat as the edge of the dagger brushed against her cheek. Nala's cries turned to growls on the other side of the door. Serein gripped his arm as she struggled to stand, nails digging into the pair of black and white snakes inked along his skin. Serein tried to kick him, but he avoided the attack, jerking her arm back further.

Her lips tingled, jaw stiff. *Poison? No...Snake venom. It was on the Viper's Teeth.* Serein's heart pounded in the back of her throat. *Not a high dosage. Diluted cobra venom. Causes nerve and muscle numbness.*

"Does the prince treat you well?" Xansas asked. "He may try to mark you as his"—anger flashed in his eyes as he glared at the bangles—"but you'll always be mine."

Xansas pressed his face against her hair, inhaling. *No. Fight it. If I stop moving, he'll take me. I can't go back.* Serein jerked her head away, legs trembling as they gave out.

Xansas caught her. "The night's young, so why don't we enjoy our reunion, *volchitsa*? It's been seven years. I want to see what you've become."

He threw Serein on the bed, straddling her legs. White hair spilled down his shoulders as he pushed his dark cowl back, sharp face split by a smile. A thin snake-shaped bone earring hung from his right ear. Thin scars crisscrossed his throat, and a long line extended down his right cheek. Hanging around his neck was a leather pouch on a thick cord.

Serein spat in Xansas' face, and he wiped the saliva off his cheek. "You didn't seem to be enjoying the party. Did you say hello to Mayte?" he asked and slipped the dagger from her fingers, putting it out of reach. "You stopped wearing dresses for me. Yet you wear them when *he* asks."

Her breath caught, too afraid to leave her lungs for fear that he'd smell the terror. *How long has he been here?! Since the Malika's name day? How did he get into the feast unnoticed?*

"These robes don't suit you either," Xansas said.

He dragged his knife through the robes, tearing the fabric to the collar. He flicked aside the tatters with the blade to expose her scarred skin. Serein bit her cheek, screaming at her body to move. Xansas touched her stomach, and she flinched. His fingers wandered over the scars and the pink burn tissue. He ripped the rest of the robes from her arms, his eyes trailing over the inked leaves and vines.

"That's new," Xansas said. "Your collection of scars has increased. Grasdan couldn't break you."

Serein folded herself deep into her bones where he couldn't reach her, away from the memories of blurry nights and overly sweet wine, sharp knives and screams, and hands that took, the smile that hung over her as she cried. *I can't break. I can't pass out,* she thought, the edges of the room melting.

Xansas' finger moved along the lines to Serein's throat. Coldness spread across her skin, dizziness pushing against her skull. She inhaled a sharp breath as his mouth found hers, pressing, hungry. She bit Xansas' lip, but he didn't pull away. Salty blood stuck to her tongue as she wrenched her face to the side.

Keep fighting. I have to kill him. Fight. Move! Serein screamed at herself. *Go for his throat, rip it apart with my teeth. This venom will wear off soon.*

"You've always had a singular focus. You're willing to walk through the darkness to achieve your vengeance. I've always loved that about you because you're like me," he said, red smearing his mouth as he laughed. "I have a proposition for you. We can be partners again like we once were."

"Never," she said, the word slurring. *Who has he been hired to kill?*

He cradled Serein's face in his hands. The handle of his knife pressed against her cheek as he left a streak of red across her jaw. "You think running away changes things? You're still a Bone Viper. You will always be one," Xansas told her. "I've been hired to kill Sethos, but before that, I'm to find secrets about the King, his plans, everything. I know you have been digging into his life since you arrived here."

How does he know that? Serein thought, head spinning. *Does he know that Rameses is looking into his father's activities? If he as spies here, that puts us in greater danger.*

Xansas traced the red scar along Serein's neck, sucking away the breath coiled in her throat. "We can bring this kingdom down and make the white stones cry blood. Wouldn't you like that?" he asked. "We could destroy the King together, make him pay for what he did to you. You've dreamed about that since you were young. I can give you that dream if you return to me."

Serein blinked, trying to keep her heavy eyelids open. "I'd sooner die!" she shouted, slashing at his face with yellow-bladed words.

Xansas' smile died. Fear stabbed Serein as the dark anger rose in his eyes. "Do you know how long I searched for you?" he asked, gripping her chin. "It's hard to forgive you for what you did, leaving and betraying me."

Keep breathing, Serein thought, eyes darting to the dagger just out of reach. *Even the bones could blind him. One strike to stun. Enough time to kill him.*

"While you are wrought of steel, you do have a soft spot. Eneca. I know she helped you escape. No doubt you know she's here. A loose thread that can still be cut if needed."

Serein saw the flash of Eneca's round face splattered with red, her brown eyes dulled with death. She tried to quell the thoughts, but Xansas' green eyes burrowed their way under her skin, undoing every scar he touched. His fingers moved across the X-shaped scar, tracing the lines. His callused fingertips trailed to her stomach and followed the silvery stretch marks, inching to the waist of her trousers.

"Tell me, *volchitsa,* what happened to the child you were carrying?"

His words split Serein open. A choked cry escaped in a broken yellow sound. Xansas' grin opened wider as her mask crumbled. He held the buried secret—her pulsing heart in a white cage—ready to crush it.

"You thought you could hide the changes of your body from me? I trained you better than to make mistakes. I thought you'd kill the child once it was born, but then you ran away." Xansas' pale eyebrows creased, pain crossing over his features. "I searched for you, but you hid from me. When I finally found you, you didn't have the child with you."

"It died," she whispered. *You'll never find them,* Serein thought, fingertips twitching as the numbness left. *I'll kill you before you find them.*

"You should know better than to lie to me." His voice dropped low as he sat up. "Was it a boy? Or was it a girl?" he asked, each question pushing deeper toward the truth. "Maybe when I find our child, I'll train it to become an assassin to follow in our footsteps. Or perhaps I'll kill it."

Blood roared in Serein's ears, and the numbing weight of the venom cracked. A sound tore from her chest as the black beast rose with her. She slammed into Xansas, raking her fingernails across his face. Grabbing the dagger, Serein slashed at Xansas' throat, but he knocked her hand aside. The blade cut his chest as she staggered. She found the lamb bone in the torn fabric of her robes, driving the point into his arm until it snapped.

Blood ran down Xansas' face as he backed away. Serein swayed on her feet, robe hanging in tatters. "You don't know how happy this makes me, *volchitsa*," he said as he pulled the piece of bone from his arm. "You bare your fangs at me, and I can see what you're becoming. You don't know how much I love you, Serein Che—"

Green shouts blurred in the air, footsteps gray thunderclouds. Uriah appeared, sword drawn. Surprise broke across his face before he lunged at Xansas.

The assassin covered his face with the cowl, dodging as the scimitar clashed against the wall in orange sparks. "I'll be back for you, my *volchitsa*," Xansas said, slipping onto the balcony and jumping over the railing.

Uriah cursed, holding the rope tied around the railing as it went limp. "I'm not yours," Serein whispered.

The world spun, a cold sweat breaking out across her skin as she fell. Uriah rushed to catch her. She jerked away from his touch, swiping the knife across his neck. Xansas' blurry face burned behind her eyelids.

"Don't touch me!" Serein yelled.

A trickle of blood ran down Uriah's throat as the blade nicked his skin. "Serein! Stop," he said, voice sounding far off in the white fog of Xansas' voice. "Lower the blade."

Serein's eyes narrowed, Uriah's face coming into focus. The beast growled before slinking back into the darkness, taking the last bits of her strength with it. She lowered the weapon and slumped against the bed.

Gone, but he'll be back.

Uriah grabbed a sheet to wrap around her. "What happened?" he asked.

"Xansas," Serein mumbled, eyes struggling to stay open. *Can't pass out. He'll come back and take me.*

Uriah sheathed his sword. "Xansas Regor?!"

Feverish heat scattered Serein's thoughts. Her head lolled against the side of the bed, tremors running through her limbs. *I couldn't kill him. I failed again...*she thought, tears freeing themselves as her eyelids drooped. *Xansas can't find you, my Sun and Stars. I can't lose you.*

Uriah shifted, and Serein tensed, eyes opening again. "What happened?" he asked, the rolling words growing fainter in Serein's ears. "Did he...?" He swallowed, looking away. "You need a healer."

Serein's fingers dug into the sheets as she forced herself to stand, the ground shifting under her feet. "No."

Uriah raised his hand but didn't touch her. "Serein, please. You don't look well."

"That's the first time you've said 'please' to me..." The words stuck to her tongue, sloughing past her lips.

He placed a hand on her arm, and Serein flinched, pointing the dagger at him. Uriah stepped back as she staggered to the bathing chamber. Nala darted out of the room before Serein slammed the door shut.

SEREIN SAT IN THE BATHING POOL, TREMBLING AS SHE FOUGHT THE venom and fear. Her skin turned red the harder she scrubbed, trying to remove the burning touch of Xansas' hands. Blood dripped into the water, tiny rubies dissolving off her body. The armor Serein had worn for years splintered, leaving her with bleeding wounds.

His touch won't come off. I can still feel his hands, Serein thought, tears running down her cheeks.

Serein. She shuddered at the white voice, biting on her knuckles to stifle a scream. *You're a weapon, and weapons don't weep.*

Her name on his lips—her true name—squeezed like a noose. The name she thought she could entrust to him became a weapon against her, reminding her that she couldn't escape.

He always knew. I can't escape. There's nowhere I can go. Everything I did was for nothing, she thought.

Xansas' hands closed around her neck. *I'll always find you.*

The rag fell from Serein's hand as she pulled herself out of the pool, water dripping on the floor. The ground beneath Serein's feet cracked, pale-yellow breaths crumbling as the edges of her vision blurred. She vomited into the water, opaque purple splashes rippling out. Chunks of food sank into the murky depths as threads of saliva dangled from her lips. Mouth filled with bitterness, she crumpled on the floor.

Her reflection stared back at her from the blade on the ground. "He has to die," she whispered, grabbing the weapon.

Cold steel plunged into her shoulder, stabbing the snake through the head.

URIAH LOCKED THE BALCONY DOOR AS NALA PACED AROUND, growling. He touched the cut on his neck, red coating his fingers. *She could have slit my throat...*he thought, looking at the spots of blood on the floor.

The whip marks and scars across Serein's body crisscrossed behind Uriah's eyelids as he blinked. Almost every inch of her had been marked, faded lines intersecting with more recent wounds.

She couldn't have gotten all those wounds in Grasdan. Some of them looked much older. Did Xansas do all of that to her—

Serein's cry sliced the quiet. Uriah ran into the other chamber, hand on his weapon. Blood ran from her shoulder as she dug the dagger into her flesh. He froze in the doorway, staring at the whip lashes across her back. A burn mark wrapped around her side, pink flesh cutting across tawny skin. Her scars stood out like pale stitches. The leafy tendrils of the tattoo curled around her shoulders.

"Luca...Astra," she moaned. "I'm so sorry. *Mea culpa.*"

Uriah pried the slick dagger from her hand. The snake's branded head was perforated and bleeding. "What are you doing?!" Uriah asked, throwing the sheet back over her.

Serein hunched against the side of the bathing pool. "He always finds me. I can't escape..." she whispered, staring at the floor.

His eyes went to the X-shaped scar on her chest, blood growing cold. Rameses' words came in a rush—*"My father gave it to her."*

Uriah swallowed, his mouth dry. Blood seeped through the sheet, and he grabbed a towel, tucking the dagger through his belt. He bent down and dabbed at the wound. Serein jerked away, tensing.

He pulled his hand back. "Press this against your wound while I get a healer," Uriah told her. *She's afraid. What has that man done to her to make her so scared?*

"Don't tell the prince," Serein said and grabbed his arm, her hand a shaking vice. "No one can know."

"I can't do that. Rameses needs to know that Xansas was here." She flinched. "The royal family is in danger."

Tears stained her cheeks, eyes wide. "No one can know about this. I swear I'm not working with *him*. Please!"

Uriah hesitated. "I...I can say I came to your chambers to find you violently ill, but I can't promise that people will believe me."

Serein released him and sank to the ground, trembling. Uriah adjusted the sheet around her bare shoulders. "I'm sorry, Luca, Astra," she murmured.

Her whisper made Uriah stop. "Who are Luca and Astra?" he asked.

"*Liberos meos.*"

The Sarlyrian words rippled through his memories. He had heard them in the screams of mothers while on the war front. His ears still burned with the sounds, nightmares echoing the cries.

Liberos meos—my children.

"Your children?" Uriah repeated. "You have...children?" *Is she rambling? She can't have children. She can't be...a mother?* he thought, blood seeping down his neck.

Serein tried to stand, slipping on the slick floor. Uriah caught her. Fragile murmurings slipped out, mixing with the tears hitting the floor. Uriah picked her up and carried her out. Nala mewled at him, bumping into his legs.

"Where are they now?" Uriah asked.

"Far away," Serein said, and he set her on the bed. Her eyelids fluttered for a moment before she jerked upright, blue eyes filled with a wild gleam. She darted for the edge of the bed, but he grabbed her arm.

"Stop! You're injured!" Uriah snapped.

"No!" Serein cried, nails digging his hand as she scratched him. "I can't! He's here! I have to—"

"He's gone. Xansas isn't here!" he told her.

Serein thrashed in his grip, teeth bared. "He'll get them! Xansas —I can't let him! He'll kill them!"

"Serein!" Uriah gripped her shoulders. "You said they're far away. Your children are safe." Serein stopped and slumped against the pillows, shivering. "I'm going to get a healer. I'll have guards posted outside your door."

"No guards. No one can know!" Serein told him, voice cracking.

Uriah waited for her to bolt or lunge for a weapon. "Fine. No guards. I won't say anything."

Serein met his gaze. "Thank you." The words were so soft that he almost missed them.

She curled into a ball, turning away from Uriah. The whip marks stretched across her back, the three thickest ones where the skin had been torn away and poorly stitched up. Old bite marks stood out among the blade and lash marks. Nala clawed her way onto the bed, nestling against Serein.

Uriah pulled the sheet over Serein. He touched the bleeding cut along his throat, the scratch marks on his hand stinging. *Who are you, Serein?*

Chapter Thirty-Five
Open Scars

URIAH STOOD OUTSIDE SEREIN'S DOOR, STARING AT THE DARK wood grain. Every moment he held onto her secret, the heavier he felt. The scratches on his hands stung as he flexed his fingers, dark red marks cutting across his pale skin. He touched the scabbed cut on his neck as the leather cord rubbed against it.

I have to tell Rameses about this, Uriah thought. *She told me not to, but Rameses will wonder why she isn't at her shift tonight.*

The door opened, and Uriah straightened. Rizwana stepped into the hallway with tattered clothes and bloodied sheets bundled in a basket.

"The healer's still with her," Rizwana said, brushing loose strands of hair under her headscarf.

"How...how is she?" Uriah asked, clearing his throat.

"She's sleeping. Her fever's broken, but she's still vomiting. Kept muttering in her sleep. I couldn't understand a word of it," she said. "What happened?"

Uriah's hand rested near his sirwal pocket where the rock was. "Food poisoning."

Rizwana fixed him with a stare. "I might not be as perceptive as Serein, but you can't fool me—not with bloody clothes and her wounds—but I'll keep my silence." She covered the bloodstained clothes with a blanket. "I've seen women like her in my village."

"Women like her?"

"She's been broken and has spent a long time piecing herself back together. You'd better keep whatever secret she entrusted you with to yourself and tread lightly."

Serein wandered the carved tunnels of the Tenebris Mountains. Torches popped in the wall sconces. Light blue footsteps bounced behind her as she passed the various rooms, scattering like rabbits. The hallway opened into a cavernous training room, the floor streaked with old blood and blade marks. White whispers hissed through the air. The smell of oil and leather wrapped around the shadows of her childhood.

The room crumbled away until Serein faced a dark wooden door, the grain black as night. Her throat clenched as she went for the handle, but the lock held.

No. No. No, her pulse shouted as she pounded on the door, a scream lodged in her throat.

The door swung open, and a thirteen-year-old girl in an emerald dress stood before her, blue eyes sharp and filled with the knowledge of how to take a life but unaware of how much would be carved out in exchange. She bore a small scar along her chin. She swept through Serein into the room, the door closing with a final teal groan.

Serein reached to grab the girl, but her limbs locked. Xansas stood by a table, mouth peeled back into a grin. The girl smiled as he held out a glass of wine. White fog slithered from his mouth, knives disguised in false promises. Serein tried to shout, but a vice wrapped around her throat. The girl sipped the wine, her eyes on Xansas as he distracted her from the poison spreading with each sip.

The glass slipped through the girl's fingers, shattering in a sharp ruby crash. Xansas took her as she tried to fight. A dark gleam rose in his eyes as he bent his mouth to hers, fingers digging into her hair. A cloying sweet smell overlapped with the scent of iron and sage.

"I do this to make you stronger," he said, the white sentences wrapping around her like writhing ropes.

Fingers squeezed Serein's throat as she was spun around. Xansas held her, the black and white snake tattoos along his arm hissing. The taste of poisoned wine burned her throat, and the world blurred in bleeding colors.

"You can't leave, volchitsa,*" Xansas said, tearing her clothes. "We're just starting."*

SEREIN STARED OUT THE DARK WINDOW. HER THOUGHTS CRAWLED out, sluggish and fuzzy. The aches from her shoulder traveled through her arm. Nala pushed against Serein's palm, licking her hand.

"The color's back in your face," Rizwana said, lapis voice floating across the room as she set out dinner. "I brought you some tea and bread to settle your stomach."

When Serein regained consciousness, Rizwana had been by her side. The maidservant had cleaned the room, removing the bloodstains and any traces of Xansas' attack. Her brown eyes spoke of her silent knowing and understanding.

My head feels like it's full of sand. And I've finally stopped vomiting after almost two days, Serein thought, licking her cracked lips. *Even with that small amount of venom, I was powerless...*

"Do you need anything? Poppy milk for the pain?" Rizwana asked, smoothing out the front of her white gandora. "Can I get you something to help you sleep? You were having a nightmare."

"No, I'm fine." Serein said. *How much did I say when I was poisoned? Rizwana cleaned the bloody sheets and stayed to take care of me and hasn't said a word about it. It's been a long time since someone's done that for me. She reminds me of my mother.*

Rizwana's round face creased with concern. "I know you don't talk about your past, but if I can help you, please let me know."

Serein managed a weak smile. "Thank you, Rizwana, but the past isn't something I want to remember." *The past isn't something that can be fixed with words.*

"I'll be back in the morning then," Rizwana said, hesitating before she left.

The silence crashed down on Serein. Each shifting shadow made her heart race. She found the sharpened training dagger tucked inside a slit in the mattress. The kebab stick was nowhere to be found.

How'd he get into my chambers? Climbing up the balcony from a lower level? Mayte or his spies must have helped him gain access to the palace. Rizwana and I should be the only ones with the key to my room, she thought, pain pulsing with her anger. *This room is no longer safe. Nowhere is.*

The memory of Xansas' touch brought a fresh wave of nausea. A knot grew inside her chest, teeth carving fresh lines of pain across her skin. She remembered Uriah's worried and horrified expression sharpening as he took the weapon from her bloodied fingers. Dizziness pushed against Serein's skull as she got up. She threw on a clean robe and sirwal. Nala sat up and let out a soft peacock-blue noise. Checking the locked balcony door, Serein left with her scimitar at her side.

Captain Stormheir knows something he shouldn't. No one else can know about Astra and Luca.

SEREIN POUNDED ON THE DOOR, GLANCING DOWN THE HALL OF the officers' quarters as the dark blue sound ran along the wood. Silence answered her. She knocked again and heard the frustrated green sigh on the other side. The door opened. Uriah's red hair hung loose as he stood in a gray tunic and black sirwal, brow furrowed. His irritation shifted to confusion, the scar across the bridge of his nose flattening.

"Serein?" She shoved past him and slammed the door shut with a teal *thud.* "What—hey!" Uriah snapped, whirling around. "What are you doing?!"

She scanned his orderly chambers. Armor sat on a wooden dummy, Uriah's sword at its side. The bed was against the left wall near the bathing chamber, a trunk of clothes sitting at the end of it. Different colored rocks sat on the edge of his desk near the papers while three shelves full of stones hung along the wall behind it.

"Nice place. Cozy. Much cleaner than the prince's. I think my chambers are bigger than yours," Serein said, turning to face him. *He likes rocks. His chosen deity seems to be the earth elementals. The Wendish keep totems linked to the elementals for protection. Explains the rock in his pocket and the one he wears around his neck. Seems he turned it into a collection, or he's really worried about his wellbeing,* she thought.

"What are you doing here?" Uriah asked.

"You have something of mine, and I'd like it back," she said.

Uriah stiffened, eyes darting to his desk. "Are you going to hurt yourself again?"

Shame twisted in Serein's throat, shoulder aching. "No." *He saw everything. All it took was seeing Xansas again, and everything unraveled.*

Sighing through his nose, Uriah went to his desk and pulled out the cleaned dagger, handing it to her. Red nail marks ran along his hand, the skin scabbed over in places.

She slid the weapon through her sash. "I'm here to finish our conversation from the other night. You know something you shouldn't. It's only a matter of time before you talk, and I can't have that." *No one was supposed to know about my children except Eneca, Titus, and Abelia. Now their safety is at risk.*

He swallowed, glancing at her sword. "You were rambling and feverish. Half of what you said didn't make any sense. I couldn't make out much of what you were saying."

"Don't lie to me. I may not have been fully coherent, but I remember enough to know that you heard things you shouldn't have."

His shoulders tensed. "Are you here to make sure I don't say anything?"

"The only way to ensure that would be to kill you, but I think people would notice if you went missing." *He knows. I can't change that. I don't remember everything I said, but he knows about Luca and Astra now. He's seen my scars. Why did it have to be him, of all people, who found out?* "Have you spoken to anyone about what happened the other night?"

"Rameses was wondering why you didn't appear for your shift. I...I told him that you were ill and that he shouldn't bother you," Uriah told her, eyes never leaving her weapons. "He didn't push it, but you know he'll stop by your chambers, asking questions. I made sure the healer won't say anything either."

"Rizwana can handle the prince," Serein said. *Of course Rameses would start questioning where I was. The healer is another loose thread I'll have to watch. Things are getting too messy,* she thought. "You want to know about my past and what Xansas is doing here. I can give you answers."

Uriah crossed his arms, arching an eyebrow. "I'm not giving you paints in exchange for answers," he said.

"What I want in exchange is for you to help me catch Xansas in secret and keep what you know about what you saw and heard to yourself."

Clever, volchitsa. *You're going to use his concern to manipulate and use him to track me down? You haven't changed,* Xansas' white voice crooned in the back of her mind.

"Why?" Uriah asked. "Keeping quiet about this will only make it easier for Xansas to get into the palace again. Are you still working with him?"

Fury surged, and Serein slammed Uriah against the wall, hand around his throat. "I want Xansas dead," she said, wearing a smile doused in rage.

Her fingers dug into the fresh cut on Uriah's neck. He sucked in a breath as he wrestled against her grip. Serein released him, shoulder throbbing.

"What the hell was that for?!" Uriah asked, rubbing his throat where her fingers left red marks.

Serein looked around. An amethyst-colored thread of wind drifted across the floor and curled beneath the tapestry of a roaring lion and a shield on the opposite wall. *A draft. There's a secret passageway in here. I remember seeing this on a map. This passage goes from here under the barracks to the armory.*

Serein walked to the tapestry, pushing it aside. She felt along the wall, fingertips trailing along the mortar between the stones until she felt the draft again.

"Shut up and follow me," Serein said.

"What makes you think I'm going to go anywhere with you after what you just did?" Uriah snapped.

"If you want answers, then you'll come with me," she told him. Serein pushed the stone, and a section of the wall swung inward with a silver-white grating noise to reveal a dark tunnel that curved downward. *Guess we'll have to see if this tunnel is still intact,* she thought.

"What did you do? How long has that been there?" Uriah asked in disbelief.

"You've never noticed that there was a secret entrance to your chambers?"

"No..."

"You'll have plenty of time to explore the mysteries of your chambers later." Serein paused in the doorway. "For what it's worth... I didn't mean to cut you. I'm sorry."

Uriah's eyes widened as he stopped, arms hanging at his sides.

Killing him would have saved me the trouble of having to reveal the truth, but it seems I'll need an ally to stop Xansas, Serein thought, turning toward the darkness. *Adapt and find a way to survive.*

URIAH STAYED CLOSE TO SEREIN AS THEY LEFT THROUGH THE secret door into the city. Underneath her hood, Serein peered around a corner before stepping out of the dark alley. The hum of voices and the cooking sounds in the Gold District grew louder as they turned down another street. Serein's eyes darted to every person they passed.

"Are you sure you shouldn't be resting?" Uriah asked. *I've never seen her so on edge. The other night she was ready to slit my throat when I touched her.*

Lantern light illuminated the irritated look on Serein's face. "If you ask me that one more time, I'm going to slap you," she said. "I'm fine."

"Two days ago, you had a fever and stabbed yourself. That doesn't sound like someone who's fine," Uriah told her. *She was crying and barely conscious. Now she's acting like nothing happened,* he thought, unable to erase the broken woman lying on the floor.

More people filled the streets, the faint sound of music drifting between the houses. The familiar vermillion buildings of the pleasure district appeared. Serein skirted to the side of the street to avoid clusters of people who laughed and drank. Women in sheer clothing tried to approach Uriah, but he kept his head down, heat creeping up his neck.

"You can't be serious," he muttered as they approached the Faten.

"The brothel? Why are we here, Serein? Are you visiting that *friend* of yours?"

Serein rolled her eyes. "You're welcome to wait outside. Or entertain yourself elsewhere, but if you want me to tell you anything, you'll shut up and follow me," she said.

Uriah lingered by the doorway as Serein stepped inside. *What am I doing here? What if she doesn't have children? Those tears seemed real, and she seemed genuinely afraid...*

Swallowing, Uriah entered the Faten. Sultry laughter danced around him as women in shimmering badlahs twirled through the room. Men lounged on the majlis and cushions around low tables, women draping off them. Uriah felt heat rising again across his skin.

"Try to look like this isn't your first time seeing a woman," Serein whispered, approaching a guard. She handed the man a sack of coins and her weapons, glancing at Uriah. His hand tightened around the sword hilt. "Hand it over before you draw attention. You'll get it back."

Uriah took his weapon from his belt, eyes narrowing at the guard as he took the scimitar. The man tossed Serein a piece of wood with a red flower painted on it, jerking his chin toward the stairs. The steps creaked under their feet, and Uriah tried not to think about what was happening behind the closed doors they passed. Serein handed the chip to a man at the top of the stairs.

They stepped into the dim room at the end of the hall, the door hinges creaking shut behind them. A woman in a sheer, midnight-colored gown turned, the silver threads woven into the fabric shining. Cascading brown hair rimmed her round face, skin a warm swarthy color. The shadowed curves of her ample hips and thighs pressed against the robe as it clung to her.

A wide smile hung from Serein's face, full of warmth. *This is who Serein's been meeting with?* Uriah thought, trying to keep his gaze from lingering on the woman.

"It's good to see you, Ser. I was worried when I received your letter," the woman said as she embraced Serein.

"I didn't mean to worry you. I had to speak with you," Serein replied and winced.

The courtesan pulled away, head tilted. "Are you injured? What happened?"

"I'll be fine, En."

"Why can't you just ever admit when you're hurt? I'd worry less." The courtesan glanced at Uriah. "This is the one who followed you the last time, isn't he? The green-voiced captain?" the woman asked. "He's handsome up close."

Uriah looked away as her warm brown eyes melted his insides. "Is...is this who you came to meet?" he muttered, clearing his throat. *Green-voiced? What's that supposed to mean?*

"Yes. Zahra as she's known in Oyon," Serein replied.

Cinnamon and rose-scented perfume caressed Uriah's face as the courtesan moved closer. "A pleasure, Captain Stormheir. You can call me Eneca. If you ever want to visit, let me know. Any friend of Serein is a friend of mine," Eneca said and touched his arm.

Uriah stiffened and backed away. Eneca laughed, and red crept up to his ears. "How...how do you two know each other?" he asked, keeping his eyes on Serein.

"We grew up together," Serein told him.

Another assassin? he thought.

Serein threw back her hood. "Her killing method is something I doubt you'll wind up ensnared in, so you can relax."

Serein's scarred skin contrasted with Eneca's softness. Their matching smiles left him unsettled. "Don't tease him," Eneca said and gestured to the cushions by the closed window. "Come, sit."

Uriah sank down, scanning the room. "Why did you bring me here instead of talking at the palace?" he asked.

Serein's smile was replaced by weariness. "It's safer to talk here," she told him, glancing at Eneca as she settled beside her. "Xansas is here. He finally found me."

Chapter Thirty-Six
The Price of Trust

SEREIN WATCHED ENECA'S EXPRESSION CHANGE, A TREMOR OF FEAR coursing through her. "*Lumina adiuva nos,*" Eneca whispered, her rosy breath wilting. "When did this happen?"

"He was waiting for me in my room," Serein replied, hands curling into fists.

Eneca placed a hand on Serein's uninjured shoulder, moving closer. "How did he find you?"

"He had people in Grasdan keeping him informed. Xansas probably has others in the palace and in Oyon," Serein said.

Eneca's expression darkened. "How did he find you?" she asked.

Serein swallowed. "I don't know," she muttered. "I saw Mayte the other night in the palace. She's a competitor in the Aikhtiar. I should have expected him to not be far behind."

"Who is Mayte?" Uriah asked, his verdant question surrounding her like a forest.

Serein leaned against the wall. "The White Snake's pet. She's another assassin we grew up with. One that's completely devoted to him."

Uriah frowned. "Why didn't you tell me that you spotted an assassin at the feast?" Anger laced his voice.

"I didn't have a chance."

"Really? You couldn't say, 'I saw an assassin in the palace. Here's what she looks like.'"

Serein glared at him. "And if I had told you, then what?" she snapped, knuckles whitening as she clenched her hands. "What would happen if you told the king that Xansas was in the palace? I'd be questioned and watched, which puts Rameses at risk. If the king finds out that his son is trying to uncover his secrets, what will you do then? You didn't want to know about Rameses' plans, so you don't get to question how I do things."

Eneca's warm palm rested on Serein's arm, the steadying presence drawing her back. Serein inhaled to cool the anger stirring in her chest.

"Xansas has been hired to kill Sethos, but he needs secrets before killing him and wanted me to get them. Whoever hired him wants to know what Sethos is really doing," Serein said.

Uriah's expression darkened as he watched her. "This is a serious threat. How can you expect me to keep quiet about this?" he asked.

Serein rubbed her shoulder, the lines of the snake brand burning. "The fewer people who know about Xansas, the safer things are for Rameses and me," she replied.

Uriah touched his necklace. The music from downstairs drifted through the door as loud maroon and straw-colored laughter seeped through the floor. The muddled colors melted across the rug of Eneca's chamber, crumbling into the swirling pattern of birds and flowers.

"Do you really think the two of us will be able to stop him before anyone finds out?" Uriah asked, breaking the silence. "Xansas got into your room and poisoned you. He...he could've seriously hurt you."

"He can't hurt me anymore than he has." Serein looked at Eneca. "He knows we've been meeting. I don't want to put you at risk, En."

"Don't worry about me," Eneca replied, taking Serein's hand. "I would helped you a thousand times over to get you away from that monster."

Serein's shoulders fell, the heaviness pressing on her. Overhead, the flame of the amber-tinged lantern flickered. Small shadows in the shape of stars danced on the walls. *Can I really protect her? Or Luca and Astra? Will we ever be safe from him?* Serein thought. *There's so much he can take from me.*

"What about your children? Aren't you worried he's going to go after them now, too?" Uriah asked, and Eneca's gaze snapped to him.

"Xansas couldn't know about them. Serein left before he could find out she was pregnant," Eneca whispered.

Serein plucked at a loose thread on the cushion. "He knows. He always knew. But he thinks there's only one," she muttered. Eneca's face fell, worry creasing her smooth face.

"Where are they?" Uriah asked. "Do they know you're alive?"

"Safe with people I trust where he can't find them. I was able to get word to them when I was released from Grasdan," Serein said, looking at the faded scar along her palm. *If Xansas gets to them, I won't be able to survive.*

"How?" A suspicious tone slid into Uriah's voice.

"I have my ways, Captain Stormheir. Be assured that it poses no threat to you or the crown."

Uriah shifted, hands resting on his knees as he let out a heavy sigh. "How did you get separated from your children?"

"I went into one of the nearby towns. Xansas must have found out from one of his contacts and told the soldiers I was there. That was the last time I saw them before I was sent to Grasdan..." Her voice came out in a yellow whisper as the memory cleaved down to the bone in a flash of swords. *They'll be seven this year. Two years, lost. There's no guarantee if I become muharib that I'll be able to return to them without being discovered. And if I do, how would I be able to leave them again?*

The rugged edges of Uriah's face softened. She sensed the next question on his breath. Her stomach clenched, her grip around Eneca's hand tightening.

Don't say it.

"Who is the father?" Uriah asked, the green question dropping like a stone.

"They have no father," Serein said, spitting out the words.

The flickering light shifted across Uriah's face. "Shouldn't

Rameses know about them? Wouldn't he be able to help keep you and your children safe?"

"No. We'll be hunting a viper, so it's best not to bring along anyone who could get hurt. You want to protect him? Then keep him in the dark about this."

The irritated sigh rattled to the ground like fallen leaves. "Fine." Uriah threw his hands in the air. "How do you propose that we go about finding Xansas? What about this Mayte? Does Xansas want her to become a muharib so that he can get close to the Malik?"

"Mayte won't give Xansas up even if you interrogate her," Eneca told Uriah, hands resting in her lap.

"I doubt she's skilled enough to win. More likely, she's a distraction," Serein said, glancing at the dark sky beyond the latticed window. "If she realizes that you're following her or Xansas, she'll just tell him, and they'll hide." *Xansas said he wanted me to help him willingly, but he could force me to join him if he made sure I had no other option. If he knows about what Rameses and I are doing, then he could expose that.*

Uriah sat up straighter. "How do you know that Xansas won't move sooner?"

"He's as patient as he is cruel. He likes to inflict as much pain as he can before the killing blow. Xansas said he'd come back for me before he kills the king. There's still time before he makes a move."

"I'll do all I can to find out about who hired him and if there are any other Bone Vipers in the city," Eneca told them. "If Xansas and the Aanisah are meeting, I'll send word."

The next time I see Xansas, I'll kill him. He can't be allowed to live, Serein thought.

A dark blue knock cut through the room, and Serein stiffened. "Seems our time's up," she muttered, standing.

"Please take care of yourself, Ser. I don't want to lose you again," Eneca said as she rose.

"I'll try. May the Lights give you safety, En," Serein told her.

"Let Life protect you and Death never find you," Eneca replied, pulling Serein into an embrace.

Serein closed her eyes for a moment before they broke away. "*Vade in pace.*"

"*Vade in pace*," Eneca finished. "We'll stop him."

Serein let the thought of hope bloom, trying to shield it from the growing darkness. Uriah watched her with unspoken questions poised on his lips. Eneca turned and smiled at him as she touched his arm, causing red to creep along his cheeks.

As Serein headed for the door, she heard a rose-colored whisper behind her. "Watch over her, Captain Stormheir. Otherwise, you'll have me to worry about."

Dragonflies danced across the lake's surface, blue buzzing trailing off iridescent wings. Sunlight turned the waters into shimmering platinum. Flowers and grasses bent in the breeze, carrying the last warm smells of summer.

The woman sat on the shore, a piece of paper resting on a board across her lap and a stick of charcoal in her hand. Two small children splashed in the lake, sunset-orange and sky-blue voices catching in the trees surrounding the small glen like flocks of birds. The woman's scarred mouth broke into a smile as she captured the scene on the paper, pressing it between the pages of her mind.

The girl kicked water at her brother, soaking him. She dove beneath the surface, away from him, before resurfacing, wet hair plastered to her face. The boy looked down at himself, round blue eyes turning to the woman.

"I'm all wet, Mama," he said, sloshing over to her.

The dragonflies darted away, the opaque purple ripples disturbing the reeds they sat on. "So you are, my Sun," she said.

The boy crouched down by the shore, watching the red and blue tetras dart by his toes. He scooped up a handful of silty rocks and a purple water hyacinth. Mud and water dripped from his fingers as he held them out to the woman.

"Thank you, Luca," she said, taking the gifts. She set the rocks next to her, slipping the flower behind her ear. "I'm going to bring you and Astra something special tomorrow."

"What is it?" the boy asked.

"It's a surprise," the woman said, scooping him up in her arms as she covered him in kisses.

Blue giggles brushed her cheeks as the cool waters lapped against her feet.

Small, damp hands grabbed her, soft palms warm against her scars. The woman stood, swinging the boy around in the air. Her drawing lay in the grass, speckled with water droplets. The woman stopped, pulling the boy close as she pressed her nose against his. Within the forests filled with the sounds of her children laughing, she forgot the prowling gold lion and the slithering white snake that haunted her past.

Chapter Thirty-Seven
Glass & Blood

THE NIGHT GREETED SEREIN AS THEY LEFT THE FATEN, whispering secrets on the amethyst-colored wind. *If Xansas is watching, he'll know who I'm with. He's most likely watching the Faten, and his people inside the palace have seen me. Anyone could be watching. Servants, guards, anyone,* Serein thought, turning down an alleyway. *People I trust even.*

"Just who is that woman to you?" Uriah asked, the verdant words drawing her to a stop.

"Eneca's the closest thing I have to a sister. She helped me escape from Xansas," Serein replied.

"Did Xansas hurt her too, the way he hurt you?" His voice was quiet.

"She suffered in different ways at his hands."

"How old were you when he...?" Uriah asked, green eyes catching the light of nearby lanterns.

Serein tensed, biting back the memory. She had known the pain of a blade, what it felt like to draw blood and take a life. But she hadn't been prepared for the agony in her own body, the sight of her blood, and the betrayal as the face she trusted filled her nightmares.

"Serein?"

She sucked in a breath. "Old enough to know that I was too

young for him to have taken what he did from me. Eneca was the only one who knew what had happened. I was too naïve to see what Xansas really was until it was too late." *And I was too weak to stop him,* she thought, shame punching a hole in her gut. *I had the chance to, but I couldn't.*

Moths fluttered near the glass panes of the lanterns, throwing dancing shadows on the walls of the alley. People passed in the street as grabbed food from the stalls.

"What were you doing on my hall that night?" Serein asked. "Why were *you* of all people there?"

"I..." The green word hung in the air as Uriah swallowed. "I wanted to talk with you about the Aikhtiar. I heard you scream, so I ran to see what was wrong," he said, shoulders stiff. His finger twitched as his hand hung at his side.

"You wanted to talk about *that* in the dead of night?"

Uriah scowled. "Are you upset that I was there to stop Xansas?" he snapped. "Don't say that you were handling things because you weren't."

"Do you want me to bow and thank you?" she shot back, mouth twisting into a sneer.

Anger flared in Uriah's eyes, jaw tightening. "I'm not asking you to thank me. I promised I'd keep your secret and help you. What more do you want?" Uriah asked. "How do I know you won't suddenly turn on all of us if it means saving the lives of your children?"

Opaque blue laughter cut through Uriah's words, drawing closer as three other voices mingled together as slurred Lóng Shé bounced down the street. Serein turned to see Fang at the end of the alleyway with three other Zhao warriors.

"We need to leave. Now," she hissed.

"Why? You keep dragging me places without any explanation, and I'm getting tired of it," Uriah said. "Saints, you're irritating!"

Fang's gaze landed on Serein, his grin morphing into a sneer as he stopped. His familiar yellow and green deel stood out among the ocher buildings. Fang advanced toward her, the three men staggering behind with daggers and short swords at their sides. One held a bottle of alcohol in his left hand, his right near his knife.

He has friends. Those men were at the feast the other night.

"Did you ask your master if you could be out this late, little blue eyes?" Fang asked, his braid trailing down his back.

Serein's hand rested on her dagger. *Maybe punching him in the face will make me feel better. We have to leave before this escalates into a fight,* she thought.

Fang turned his gaze to Uriah. "I see you open your legs to anyone. Does your master know you spend your nights with another man?" he asked. "Either he's too stupid to know that his woman is sneaking out, or he cares so little about you."

Uriah lunged past Serein, face livid as he punched Fang in the jaw. He shook his hand as the man reeled into the wall, curses filling the alley. *So much for avoiding a fight,* Serein thought. *Four men. Right-handed. Drunk. A skilled with knives and swords. Probably the martial arts forms of the plains tribes. They're all from the same clan, so they have strong loyalties to protect their chief.*

Fang clambered to his feet and sprang at Uriah. One of the men drew a knife, preparing to rush at Uriah's unprotected side. Serein shot between them and wrenched the man's hand around. The weapon clattered to the ground, orange spreading across the hard packed earth. Serein kicked the knife away, shoving the assailant down. His head smashed against the stones, and he went limp. Her shoulder throbbed as blood trickled down her arm.

A wave of dizziness crashed against her, the edges of the alley spinning. *Not now!* she thought, shaking her head.

The second man shouted, his crackling orange voice filling her vision as a knife gleamed in his hand. Serein ducked to avoid the attack. Pain ran up her arm as the heel of her palm connected with the man's chin. Her fist connected with his stomach, and he vomited on the ground as he staggered back.

Uriah and Fang grappled on the ground. A cut bled along Uriah's forehead, blood running down one eye as he fought to hold Fang's dagger away from his stomach. Fang yanked the necklace from the captain's neck, the black stone clattering across the ground.

"I'm Oyon's Captain of the Guard, and I order you to stop before I have you arrested!" Uriah shouted, green booming off the alley walls.

Red streamed from Fang's lip. "And I'm the Ascended Emperor!" he sneered, kicking at Uriah's leg.

Cursing, Uriah stumbled and hauled Fang up, trying to wrestle the weapon away. The third Zhao man ran toward them, shouting. Serein rammed her fist into her opponent's throat before grabbing the other man by his braid, yanking him back. He howled as he fell, his pale red voice pooling across the ground.

Fang threw Uriah back against the wall, slashing at his face. Uriah ducked, going for his scimitar. Serein slammed into Fang and knocked him off balance. He whirled around, teeth bared as sweat shone against his skin.

"You want to die so soon?!" Fang hissed, opaque blue seeping through his teeth.

"You're welcome to try," Serein said as the pain from her bleeding shoulder dripped onto the street. *I could always kill them here, but that would draw unwanted attention.*

Serein heard the pale red shout again, and she turned in time to see a wine bottle hit the back of Uriah's head with a ruby *crack*. Uriah's eyes rolled back, and he collapsed on the ground.

Great, Serein thought as Fang brought his blade down on her.

THE WORLD CAME AT URIAH, DARK AND UNFOCUSED. PAIN radiated through his skull in time with his pulse.

"...Any time now, Captain Stormheir."

He blinked, finding Serein crouched over him. A folded rida' was bunched underneath his head. Groaning, Uriah tried to sit up, but a white-hot stab dug behind his eyes.

He grabbed onto the pieces of his scattered memory as they slipped out of reach. *What the hell? What...happened?* he thought.

"It's best not to try and move for a while," Serein said.

Uriah moaned, touching a lump on the back of his head. His hair was sticky with blood and alcohol. He tasted a coppery tang in his mouth. "Where...What happened?"

"You were struck with a bottle and then hit your head on the ground. I carried you here to this alley after the city guards came."

"You carried me here?"

Serein dabbed his head with a wet cloth. "Half-dragged."

"What about those men? What happened?" Uriah asked as Serein withdrew her hand. "Did you get hurt?"

"My wound opened up again, but I'll be fine," she replied, flecks of red splattered along her neck. "Fang and his men ran when the guards showed up. He'll have a nice black eye from that punch you threw."

"How will I explain this? Why did I let you drag me out here?"

Serein rolled her eyes. "If it means that much to you, I can say I went a little too far during a late-night sparring session."

Grunting, Uriah pushed himself up, the cloth falling into his lap. His hand went to his neck, finding his necklace gone. "No..." *Where is it? My pendant...*

"So, you losing to me in a fight is worse than admitting that you were attacked in the street?"

The pain came back in full force, making him stagger into the wall of the alley. Nausea roiled in his stomach. "Shit."

"I bet if you try cursing more, you'll walk straighter," Serein told him. "You should take it slow unless you want to"—Uriah doubled over, retching into the dirt—"throw up." She sighed. "Lovely."

Uriah blinked, the splattered contents of his stomach blurring as his vision doubled, thoughts sloughing away. She grabbed him by his arm and dragged him to his feet. "What are you doing?" Uriah rasped, wiping the saliva from his mouth.

"Making sure you don't collapse in the streets. If you'd like me to leave you here, I can," Serein replied.

Uriah stumbled beside her. He swallowed the sour taste of bile. The buildings thinned, and the palace wall came into view. He bit the inside of his cheek to keep the nausea down. Serein dragged him through the secret door. Each step made the sky spin.

"How...?" Uriah mumbled, sweat trailing down his neck. "The door only opens one way."

"I find that if you mess with something enough, you can get it to do what you want. Even a door that only opens one way," Serein replied, shutting the door behind them.

Vines and plants shifted like writhing limbs, the smell of flowers overpowering. The shadows of the barracks darted by as they passed.

Anise and alcohol stung his nose. *We're at the palace already?* Uriah thought, looking around.

"Breathe. Don't pass out," Serein told him. "If you're going to vomit again, don't do it on my trousers."

"Just stop talking. Your voice hurts my head," Uriah moaned.

Serein readjusted her grip on his arm and rounded the corner of the armory. The door creaked as they stepped into the dark room. Uriah squinted at the hanging tapestry with the roaring lion poised over the shield and swords, the fabric rippling as Serein pushed it aside.

"Why are we in the armory?" Uriah asked.

"I see the memory loss is setting in. This is a shortcut. We went this way when we left," she whispered beside him.

Flashes of recollection dislodged from the pounding fog in Uriah's head. A section of wall behind the tapestry swung open to a dark passage. Musty air wrapped around them as they stepped in, the door closing behind.

"Keep your hands on the walls and walk slowly," Serein said, letting go of his arm.

"I know how to walk," he grumbled, the stones smooth against his palms.

"You also know how to fall. I'd prefer not to drag you the rest of the way."

He stumbled forward, navigating the thick blackness. *Just keep walking.* Uriah latched onto the thought while the rest were swept away.

"You coming to my chambers the other night. I..." Serein said, pausing. "Thank you."

Uriah tried to find her face in the darkness, unsure if he imagined the words. "What did Xansas do to you?" he asked. *How can a person look so enraged and broken at the same time?*

She nudged him forward. "Another story for another time."

Uriah's eyes fluttered close, chin slumping against his chest as he leaned against the wall. The darkness cooled the pain threatening to crack open his head. The ringing grew in his ears. Serein grabbed his arm and jostled him, slapping his cheek.

"Don't fall asleep," Serein said, and his eyes snapped open. "We're almost to your chambers."

Uriah heard her move past him, gripping his arm to keep him upright. Faint light broke open the darkness as the wall opened. A wave of dizziness slammed into him as he staggered forward. Serein took his arm again, dragging him over to his bed. Uriah groaned as he slumped forward, gripping the headboard.

"I'm going to get a healer. Stay awake, or you might not wake up," he heard Serein say as he sat against the pillows.

"Why keep things hidden when Rameses wants to help you?" Uriah asked.

She stopped. "I keep things hidden to protect my children so that nothing can be used against me. If anything happens to them...I don't know what I'll do," she muttered. "I can't risk Rameses knowing. I don't want to trust you, but I have no choice."

"Uriah? Are you here?"

Uriah looked up as the door creaked, and Serein stopped. Dryness spread through his mouth, tongue sticking to the roof of his mouth. *No. Not now. I don't want Rameses to ask questions about this,* he thought, excuses scattering like leaves as he clamped down on the nausea.

Rameses stepped into the chamber with Ilderim, confusion spreading across his face. "Serein? What are you doing here? I thought you were sick. Rizwana told me not to disturb you when I tried to see you," he said, smoothing the sleeve of his blue qamis.

"I'm fine. Something at the feast didn't agree with me," she replied, stepping away from the bed.

"Oh. I see. Am I interrupting anything?" Rameses' gaze shifted from Serein to Uriah. His eyes widened as he stared at their blood and torn clothes. "Is that blood?! Saints, what happened?!"

"Rameses...It's not what it looks like," Uriah mumbled, shame riding another wave of nausea as he attempted to sit up.

"We were in the city and ran into some trouble," Serein said. "He was struck in the head after we were attacked and passed out."

Rameses' brow furrowed. "Attacked? Are you hurt?"

Serein straightened her robes. "The blood's not mine. Captain Stormheir, on the other hand, requires a healer."

Bells chimed as Rameses moved his head. The sound tapped against Uriah's head, poking the lump with sharp jabs. "What were you doing out in the city?"

"Telling stories."

"What were you two *really* doing?" Rameses asked.

"Meeting with a courtesan. Any other questions?" Serein replied.

Uriah closed his eyes against the voices pressing in around him. *Stop talking. I'm going to vomit again,* he thought, slumping against the pillows. His hand went for his necklace again, fingers grasping empty space. *Where's my necklace?*

"I'm going to get a healer. Ask him questions, so he doesn't forget things. And keep him awake," Serein said, glancing at Ilderim as he gave her a questioning look. "I'm well enough to return to my duties tomorrow," she told him.

"I'll add you to the morning guard," Ilderim replied.

Uriah watched Serein leave through the cracks of his eyelids. *I can't tell Rameses...but how can I lie to him? Maybe I'll pass out before I have to talk.*

"Are you all right, sadiqi?" Rameses asked.

"No...My head feels like it's going to explode," Uriah groaned. Rameses disappeared into the bathing chamber and returned with a wet rag. Uriah flinched, cursing as Rameses dabbed the back of his head.

"Saints! How hard were you hit? This looks like a lot of blood," Rameses said.

Uriah pushed his hand away. "I have work to do. You don't...need to do that."

Rameses placed a hand on his shoulder. "I think that will have to wait. Lieutenant Firoz can take over for you," he said, continuing to mop up the blood from Uriah's hair. "Next time you decide to go out and raise hell, you should take me along. Seems I miss all the interesting things."

"It wasn't like that," Uriah told him through gritted teeth. "I didn't mean to start the fight. Serein wanted to talk. Then these men attacked us."

"Talk?" Rameses repeated. "About what? Was there also really a courtesan?"

"She was going to tell me about him." Uriah sucked in a sharp breath, trying to keep his eyelids open. "Saints...I lost my necklace."

The pressure on the back of his head stopped. "You're not making sense. Him? Who are you talking about? Is this about Serein?"

Questions built up behind Uriah's eyes, forcing the pain deeper into his brain. "She didn't want me to tell you," Uriah said.

"Tell me what?" Rameses asked as he sat on the edge of the bed.

Uriah felt the knife against his throat. The tears on Serein's face. The soft, painful whispering that cracked her cold expression. Her scream and rage. Everything crashed together in slashes of blue and faded scars.

His eyes flew open, ears ringing. "Serein's...not who we think she is."

SEREIN GLANCED OVER HER SHOULDER AS A HEALER RUSHED OUT OF the infirmary, glass vials clinking with ruby ripples in his bag as he headed to Uriah's chambers. On her walk over, she had cleaned off the blood from her face and hands in one of the riad fountains. Serein walked to the table filled with vials of ointments, salves, and tinctures. Lantern light made the glasses shine. Smoke drifted from the censers hanging throughout the sickbay chamber, giving off the smell of cloves, sage, and rosemary. A few people occupied the beds, their sleeping breaths quiet.

Uriah's necklace was in her pocket, the cord stiff with dried blood and alcohol. *I'll have to stitch the wound up when I get back to my chambers,* she thought, her shoulder throbbing. *I'll also have to find the healer that tended to my wound from the other night and keep a close eye on them.*

Bright yellow footsteps shuffled toward her. "May I help you?" A crisp sage-green voice broke through the quiet. A rotund healer in a blue gandora approached, her round face framed by a goldenrod-colored headscarf.

"I'm looking for something to stop bleeding, help with nausea and dizziness, and some herbs for headaches. I usually see Healer Sajjad. Is he here tonight?" Serein asked.

"He's not, but I'll go look for some medicines for you," the woman said.

"I'd also like some frankincense and ground charcoal. I'm still recovering from food poisoning from the other night, and I get these headaches sometimes. Also, if you could bring me some catgut and a needle."

The healer nodded and walked to a back room near the greenhouse where shelves of medicines were stored. Serein snuck behind the shelves to Sajjad's study. She slipped into the unlocked room, finding the candle and matches she'd hidden behind a stack of dusty books a few weeks prior.

Glad to see Sajjad doesn't have the time to clean his study, Serein thought, lighting the candle.

Shadows spread across the piles of papers and folios on the bookshelves. Serein scanned the stacks of health records of Sarddon's royals until she found the ones with Salman's name on it. Dust drifted off them as she flipped to the back. A detailed sketch of Malik Salman's body took up a whole page with notes of his injuries and death written in Sajjad's looping script.

The injuries were grievous, so there was no need for the healers to check for poison before death. His son's illness and death might reveal if someone was intentionally making him sick. Serein cut the pages out with her dagger, doing the same with the folios for Salman's wife and child. She slipped the pages into her sash.

As the candle guttered, Serein glanced at the stacks of scrolls containing the examinations of plague victims. They filled the top shelf next to jars of darkened flesh with thick wax seals.

She swiped a scroll from the top, listening for movement on the other side of the closed door. *I'll have to return another night. There must be other records here or in the Archives. Maybe in that hidden room.*

Serein tucked the scroll into her robes, snuffing out the candle. Darkness plunged around her as she hid the candle and matches. Serein heard only the quiet sounds of sleeping on the other side of the door and left the study. A man in one of the beds stirred but didn't wake.

The healer returned a few minutes later, carrying a few vials and sachets of dried herbs and powders. "It took a while to find some frankincense, but I found a little we can spare," she said, placing the items on the table. "If you have a wound that needs stitching, I can do that."

Serein put the medical supplies in her pockets. "I've gotten good at patching myself up. Thank you for your help," she replied. *I'll need to gather some more ingredients to combat any poisons Xansas might use. I'll have to see what antidotes I can find in the city. I can't be unprepared again.*

Chapter Thirty-Eight
Mouths Full of Secrets

RAMESES STARED AT THE CEILING, THE DARKNESS MOVING IN THE corners of his bedchamber. He had been hesitant to leave Uriah with the healer, but Ilderim's urgings to get sleep and his own exhaustion won out. The hurried mumblings Uriah whispered about Xansas kept Rameses up.

Xansas was in the palace, Rameses thought. *He attacked Serein. Uriah said she was sick, but it's more than that...*

"Serein's...not who we think she is."

He rubbed his eyes, the smell of orange soap clinging to his skin. Na'il pressed in close, licking Rameses' cheek. Rameses pressed his face into the soft fur, fingers moving over the dog's side.

What did Uriah mean? What does he know? I will have to talk to Serein and get some answers, he thought. *Uriah said he promised Serein not to tell me something. What are they keeping from me?*

A knock on the door startled Rameses, and he jerked upright. Na'il and Na'im lifted their heads, letting out low whines. "Sayyidi," Ilderim said, "are you awake?"

"Yes," Rameses replied.

"There's a messenger here for you. His Majesty wants to see you in his study."

Rameses' stomach clenched as he raked his fingers through his hair. "Did he say why?" *It's not even light out. Is this about Serein, or does he already know about Xansas?*

"He didn't say."

Sighing, Rameses grabbed his sandals and straightened his qamis, brushing off dog hairs, before stepping out of his bedchamber. Concern was etched on Ilderim's face. The indigo night lightened as the moon shifted in the sky. Rameses tried to dislodge the weight of fear trying to mold itself around his lungs as he left his apartments. The quiet gave room for his thoughts to grow as they spilled into each other, creating a ball of twisting threads.

He smoothed out his tousled hair as he stood outside the doors of his father's study, swallowing the nervous flutter in his throat. Rameses rubbed the cut across his palm. *Breathe. Don't give him reason to suspect anything,* he thought as the doors opened.

Sethos sat behind his desk in a maroon qamis, lantern light flickering. The smell of coffee hung thick in the air. His guards stood at attention around the chamber, Kamau watching from the corner. Documents lay across the desk as Sethos dipped his quill in the inkwell. Rameses tried to read some of the writing but caught only a few words and sentences as his father moved them around.

"You wanted to see me, Father," Rameses said, arms still at his sides. *He's up early. Is it more proposals for the Steel Road or something to do with his searches for tombs? What work does he do in the evening that I'm unaware of?*

Sethos glanced up, taking in Rameses' disheveled appearance. "Word has reached me that your wali has entered the Aikhtiar," he said, putting the quill down.

"Yes," Rameses said, pulling the story together in his next breath. "Serein told me that she had been looking for her family before she was thrown in Grasdan. As my wali, she does not necessarily have the freedom to look for them, so I suggested that maybe she enter the Aikhtiar. The muharib salary would allow her to start her search again, to see if they are still alive." *Move the pieces carefully, Serein would say.*

Sethos titled his head, his mouth forming a hard line beneath his beard. "Why would you allow such a thing after spending so much time to seek her out for your guard?"

"She mentioned that she had family members from her village that were scattered during the war. I thought this would be a good opportunity to help her find them."

Sethos' eyes narrowed as he rested his elbows on the desk. "And you believe her?"

"Il-Makah suspects that she might have stayed in the Old Kingdom after she left the Bone Vipers because of someone. I think it was because she was trying to find her family before she was thrown in Grasdan."

"I find it hard to believe that she is a sentimental woman," Sethos said. "Your heart is too kind, abnay."

"She appeared genuine," Rameses told him. "I know her skills are not being fully utilized at my side. I hate to see talents being wasted. She would be more useful to you."

"Why would I need another assassin when I have the Golden Jackals?" his father asked.

"Il-Makah has looked into her and has not found anything to make you question her loyalties. I heard he has shown an interest in Serein and tried to ask her to join the Jackals." *He doesn't know about Xansas yet. I don't know whether to be relieved or fearful. If he finds out an assassin is after him, he will probably kill Serein despite my protests.*

Sethos rested his hands on the desk. "Hisein distrusts her. She could not stand against Kamau. Seems she would make as poor an assassin as she does a guard."

"Hisein only distrusts her because she beat him in the preliminary round. Serein has proven her skills and will continue to do so. Ask any of the guards she spars with. She fought off an attacker and has not neglected her duties. Her fight with Kamau was not a fair one, but she still managed to fight while injured," Rameses replied. "I do not question her abilities or her loyalty."

"Yet your guard is currently not here," Sethos said, shifting through a few papers. "She did not appear for her shift."

Rameses ran his thumb over his ring. "She got ill after the feast. Something did not agree with her. She will be back to her duties in a few hours." *Does he suspect that she's been sneaking around? How closely is she being watched?* he thought, swallowing the dryness sticking to his throat.

"A woman muharib will make our enemies laugh," Sethos said, sipping his coffee.

"I think they will be too scared of the threat of death to do much laughing. Her name is known, and that fear will be a powerful tool," Rameses replied.

Sethos pursed his lips. "Seems you are finally starting to sound like a ruler." He glanced back at the papers on his desk. "We shall see if she can claim victory or if she dies trying."

Notes of pride broke through his father's sternness. It wiggled under Rameses' ribs, warming him for a moment before the cold realization swept it away. *He's only proud that I sound like him...Play the game. Be the son he wants.*

Dawn streaked the sky as Serein walked to Rameses' apartments, pink and orange bleeding into the violet. Songbirds filled the riad with delicate coral and periwinkle notes. Serein knocked on the door of Rameses' living chambers, and orange footsteps shuffled on the other side. Rameses wore the same blue qamis from last night, his hair disheveled. Anger burned in his gold eyes.

Rameses let Serein through. "Sayid, give us a moment," he said to the wali in the room.

A serious talk so early in the morning, Serein thought, bowing. The wound on her shoulder was stiff from the fresh stitches and ointment. *Same clothes from last night. Looks like he didn't get much sleep. He's upset about something. Is it about fighting in the streets or because he knows about what happened the other night?*

Sayid and the three servants in the room bowed and left. Remnants of breakfast lay on the table by the majlis sofa, the smell of coffee lingering in the air. Na'il and Na'im lounged on the rug in the middle of the room. Their ears perked up, tails wagging as Rameses headed to his bedchamber. Stacks of books teetered in the corners of the chamber. The dogs slipped in and bounded onto the large, unmade canopy bed before Rameses shut the door behind Serein.

"How is the captain? Still in the land of the living?" she asked.

Rameses sighed and faced her, shadows collecting on his face from the lanterns suspended above. "Uriah's fine. The healer said he has a concussion," he told her. "Why didn't you tell me that Xansas broke into your room?"

"It wasn't something you needed to know," Serein replied, keeping her face impassive. *He told Rameses. If Rameses knows about Luca and Astra...I will be too exposed,* she thought.

"That *is* something I need to know, Serein. He's a threat to my family and you," he said, the gold words edged with whispered anger. "You and Uriah came back bloodied, and then I find out about Xansas in your room. I'm already worried enough, and now I feel like I'm about to lose my mind.

"Uriah said you were poisoned and barely conscious when he found you. You should have told me what happened, not lie to me. I could put more guards outside your chambers to protect you. Xansas is dangerous—"

Serein gave a cold laugh. "He got in despite all the soldiers. I know how dangerous he is," she said.

Rameses sighed, running his fingers through his hair. "I thought we were past keeping these kinds of secrets from each other. You told me that you didn't trust me because I kept things from you, yet you're doing the same thing. Trust goes both ways. Uriah said that he promised not to say anything. What else are you keeping from me?"

"Xansas has been hired to kill your father." Rameses stopped pacing. "I didn't tell you because I didn't want anyone else finding out. It would bring suspicion down on me and what we're doing. Things are already difficult, and no doubt your father watching me more closely now that he knows I've entered the Aikhtiar."

Rameses walked over to his bed and sank down on the mattress. The dogs padded over, licking his hands. "Is anyone else in danger?" he asked, twisting his ring.

"Xansas is the type of man to kill anyone who stands in his way, but for right now, he's not making a move against anyone but Sethos," Serein said. *Rameses doesn't know about my children. Seems Captain Stormheir didn't tell him everything,* she thought, relief easing the tightness in her chest.

He looked at her. "How do you know this?"

"Xansas told me. He's also looking for secrets before he kills your father. He didn't come to kill me—he wants me to work with him."

"Would you have ever told me?"

"I would have told you when you needed to know. Xansas won't kill Sethos until he has what he needs first."

"Do you think I cannot keep a secret?" Rameses asked.

"You're not an exceptional liar. You have too many tells," she replied.

"I'm better at keeping secrets than you think," Rameses said, frowning.

"You don't have to say anything to give something away." Serein pointed to his ring. "When you're anxious or upset, you twist your ring and avoid eye contact."

Rameses stopped and looked at the lion's head around his finger. He dropped his hands into his lap.

"Will you be able to keep your mouth shut when you're faced with pain? Do you know what it's like to have your skin ripped off? To have whip marks that keep splitting open each time you move?" Serein asked. "You may have every intention to keep a secret, but you give things away without realizing it. Don't be naïve and think that Sethos will spare you if he realizes the treason you're engaged in."

"I know we don't see eye-to-eye on everything, but you're not to lie to me about things anymore. Or does the oath mean nothing to you? You can't keep me in the dark. I know the risks involved in this," Rameses said, standing.

His anger is justified, but I can't tell him everything. He can shout and whine about how unfair I'm being, but it's not safe for him or me.

Exhaustion seeped through the anger in Rameses' eyes. His stern look faltered, a sigh deflating him. "My father spoke with me this morning. He wanted to know why you're entering the Aikhtiar. So, I told him the story," Rameses said.

Serein stiffened. "And what was his reaction?" she asked. *Does the King know about what happened the other night? Does he know about Xansas already?*

"He finds it hard to believe that you would want the position so you could look for your family, but he didn't ask any more questions beyond that," Rameses told her. "He doesn't seem to know about Xansas. I didn't tell him about that because I knew what he would do to you if he knew."

The fine line is disappearing. Sethos will never trust me, she thought. *He'll either kill me before the end of the Aikhtiar or after. This story will only buy me time, not remove his suspicions.*

This is the price you pay for trusting them, volchitsa. *Now, you'll become another casualty of this war, and you'll never see your children again.*

"Were you afraid Xansas would find you? Is that also why you didn't want to enter the Aikhtiar?" Rameses asked, his voice softening.

"I knew if I entered the Aikhtiar, he would find out where I was," she muttered. "The next time I see Xansas, I'll kill him." *That's the only way to make the nightmares stop.*

"It makes sense that you would not want to be found by a person like that," Rameses said. "But is killing Xansas the best option? Would it not be better to capture him and uncover what he knows?"

"He's dangerous and can't be left alive. I won't let him harm you or your family." *Sethos is mine to kill.*

"Do you want to move to a different room or have guards posted outside? It'd be safer for you if you were living in the guard quarters in the Royal Wing."

She shook her head. "That won't help. He knows where I am, no matter where I go. If a high tower can't keep him out, then nowhere is safe. All I can do now is work with the captain to find a way to stop him." *I'll need more weapons. Maybe sleep in the rafters now that I have rope. Better than a cold prison floor.*

"How are you going to do that?" Rameses asked.

"I don't know yet. I'll find ways to track him down without attracting the suspicions of the Jackals. Maybe find out what information he's trying to uncover," Serein said, pulling out a sheaf of papers from underneath her armor. "I found these in the infirmary. Records of the deaths of your uncle, aunt, and their children. It's not much, but it does record Nasr's disease. Whoever hired Xansas may be looking into the same things we are."

Rameses took the papers, flipping through them. "When did you have time to get these?" he asked.

"When I went to get a healer last night. I've been there quite a bit, so I know the layout well. Healer Sajjad has many things in his study, and he doesn't always keep it locked."

Rameses went over to a stack of books by his bed and slid the papers into the fifth tomb in the pile. "Was that part of your plan last night?"

"No. I was going to do it another night, but the captain complicated things," Serein said. "I didn't think he would throw the first punch to defend your honor."

"Uriah doesn't hesitate to protect what he cares about, but it's rare to see him get into fights," Rameses told her with a breathy chuckle. "What *were* you really doing with Zahra the Night Flower? I have heard of her beauty, but I have never laid eyes on her."

"She's a friend. We grew up in the Bone Vipers together. She knows Xansas as well as I do, so I wanted to see if she had heard anything."

Rameses raised an eyebrow as he put his earrings in, the bells jingling. "She's an assassin too? I'm a bit afraid to know who else you might be friends with," he said. Rameses went over to the low bench covered in books and sketches of buildings. He lifted a polished wooden box from under the pile. "I wanted to give you these next week when the Aikhtiar begins, considering all that has happened, I think it's best you have these now."

Serein took the box and opened the lid. Two long khanjars rested on the maroon lining. Their hilts were made of black lacquered wood decorated with silver inlay of two moons. White filigree decorated the dark curved sheaths. A blue sheen reflected off the metal blades as she unsheathed them.

Twin Sarlyrian steel daggers. Excellent craftsmanship, she thought. *This is the "Sister Moons" set I saw in the Copper District market.*

"Do you like them?" Rameses asked, golden words falling into the box like coins. "I managed to track them down from the same merchant."

Her gaze flicked up. "I haven't had a set of daggers this nice in a long time. I had a set of vambraces with hidden blades a long time ago," Serein replied. "I like these daggers a bit more."

"Are you telling me that you also want a set of hidden blades?"

"Perhaps."

Rameses smiled. "I will see what I can do."

A horse, maps, weapons. The Lights are equipping me to complete my plan —tools for revenge handed to me by Sethos' son, Serein thought, attaching the new daggers to her belt. *These blades will kill Xansas nicely.*

Rameses' gaze lingered on her face. "You look tired," he said.

"I've been busy confronting someone I hoped never to see again, so sleep has been eluding me," she replied. *Not to mention the Aikhtiar, finding Xansas, trying to uncover all the horrors Sethos has committed, and the memories I don't want to revisit...*

"I don't know how you and Uriah do it. I have not gotten any sleep tonight. I'm going to need a lot of coffee to make it through the day," Rameses told her. "Please, take care of yourself, Serein. You've been through enough."

Chapter Thirty-Nine
Hisses and Whispers

 peering through the carved openings in the wall. Fang swung a sword at his opponent, bruises from the other night painting his face. On the far end of the arena, Salveig and Ragnhildur stood with a group of Edolasian men, their loud laughter breaking through the sounds of clashing swords.

Even drunk Fang was strong. If I fight against him again, he'll try to kill me, Serein thought, noting the few guards around the coliseum and the other competitors further down the tunnels. *Best stay out of sight for the next two weeks until the competition begins.*

The back of Serein's neck prickled as familiar olive-green steps approached. "I didn't think I'd see you again, Mayte," Serein said in Sarlyrian, turning to the taller woman behind her. "Did you come over here to catch up and tell me all I've missed these past seven years? Or are you trying to spy on me? If that's the case, you're not doing a very good job."

Mayte's sharp face was hardened with years of anger. Dark freckles stood out against her olive skin, brown hair tied in a braid. A short sword hung at her side along with two side sheaths lined with knives. The faded curve of a brand on her collar bone appeared beneath the rough-spun fabric.

"Master Xansas wanted you to know he was coming," Mayte replied, muddy-brown voice high and reedy. It carried the rugged accent of the people who lived near the Tenebris Mountains.

"Were you expecting him to pat you on the head and tell you what a good girl you are? You seem disappointed that he didn't kill me," Serein said, the familiar hilt of the dagger against her palm keeping her grounded.

"It's more than you deserve after what you did. Xansas told me not to hurt you. If he hadn't, I'd kill you myself," Mayte said under her breath.

"Kill me?" Serein laughed. "Is that why you entered this competition? Because you thought you'd have a chance to beat me, Mayfly?" *Her loyalty has gotten more twisted, more delusional. That makes her dangerous. No doubt that brand is a snake. If it's recognized, the Jackals will make the connection.*

Mayte's hands clenched, scowling down at Serein. "Don't call me that!"

"What was that, Mayfly?" Serein asked, tilting her head. "I couldn't hear you with your head so far up Xansas' ass." *She's still short-tempered. Makes her sloppy and uncoordinated,* she thought, keeping her hands near her weapons.

Mayte's lips curled, scrunching her pudgy nose as she reached for the knife at her side. "Always so arrogant. Xansas saved your life, took you in, trained you, and you betrayed him." Her voice rose and splattered the air with muddy words, drawing looks from three Ginjarrians walking by. "You had all Xansas' affection, yet you ran away. You adored him, and then you turned against him."

"Are you just here to whine about how you never got what you wanted?" Serein asked. "Listening to you complain makes me want to stick a dagger in your arm to give you something to complain about."

"Don't pretend to be a victim when you went to him willingly," Mayte snapped as the knife caught the sunlight. Her voice bounced off the concave ceiling, making a nearby guard glance over in their direction.

Serein blinked, sucking in a breath as shame unfurled its burning claws. "If you don't want half of Oyon knowing who you work for, then shut up and put that knife away," she told Mayte. "Xansas didn't take in orphans out of the goodness of his heart. Whatever life he promised us was a lie. He only wanted to use us for his own gain." *I need to get away from her before I break her neck. She's drawing too much attention.*

Serein got up from the bench and walked away, feeling Mayte's glare on the back of her neck.

"You can tell your *master* that the next time I see him, I'll sever his head from his spine." Serein stopped by the gate leading out to the street. "And I'll do it for free."

DIAMOND SHADOWS FLICKERED AS THE FLAME BEHIND THE ORANGE glass panels danced. Serein reached for another scroll, the smell of musty paper and dust hanging in the hidden room. Twelve shelves reached up to the low ceiling, scrolls spilling over each other as she continued shifting through correspondences from the frontlines, records of the purging of magical texts and the Sahriminha, and textbooks on magic.

Sethos probably has other records hidden in his study. Since this room exists, it's possible that there are more, Serein thought, skimming the text. *I keep finding texts written by Scholar Ithamar. I'll have to ask Rameses if that name is familiar or find a record of him.*

She stopped at a passage about the year of Sethos' invasion written in Ithamar's neat handwriting.

3 Atyaur, Hlón 577

Tensions along the borders have continued to grow as Sarlyrian troops gather near the Locklin Forests and the Baltha Gorge. King Haza is stationed in Savas with Vale and Elven armies while the other Immortal Kings remain in Caew-im-dwinath. It's estimated that 15,000 stand ready while the bulk of their forces remain centralized at the Citadel and Ygris.

Malik Sethos has been sending false information about Sarddonian troops heading to Locklin to draw the Old Kingdom armies to the border. Admiral Ezio continues to amass his fleet in the north and the south. Sinabrac vessels have brought our number to 150 ships. They prepare to sail in a

month's time to the northern and southern coasts of the Old Kingdom.

Serein blinked as the words settled behind her eyelids. *Sethos drew the Sarlyrian troops to the border so his ships could invade from the coasts. They couldn't break through the contingents along the Locklin Forests,* she thought.

27 Cantaar, Soron 577
A sickness has been spreading through the Old Kingdom, killing the Immortals. Our reports say it starts as a fever that causes weakness, open sores, and bleeding from the eyes, nose, and mouth. The infected exhibit intense agony. Once symptoms occur, death happens within three days. Within weeks of our troops approaching Locklin, it was reported that a third of the Sarlyrian troops had died. This sickness—this plague—has quickly spread across the Old Kingdom, and many of our troops fear catching it. Other reports claim that the Immortals are unable to use magic. Many of our healers who used magic have noticed their abilities dwindling.

Memories of bloated bodies and blood-stained faces appeared as Serein read. The opalescent magic that thrummed through the earth vanished in the wake of the dying, leaving behind a hollow emptiness. Serein remembered the tear-stained faces of her grandparents and people of the village as, one by one, they succumbed to sickness and fear.

4 Lemenyaar, Calina 577
As our forces continue to push through the armies around Locklin, it's been observed that the Immortals suffer the brunt of the sickness. Several dozen deaths have occurred within our ranks because of the plague—a few being healers skilled in magic. The infected soldiers were identified as Sahriminha. The link between those infected by the sickness and those who remain unaffected seems to be magic. This was tested with

captured Fae soldiers. When exposed to the sickness, they died within three days while our troops remained healthy.

Sethos planned the war around the plague decimating the Sarlyrian armies and magic disappearing. Drawing the troops to the borders ensured the disease would spread faster. He knew this would happen before the war ever began, Serein thought. *But how did he get it to spread from the Old Kingdom first? Did someone cast the spell for him? Sethos wasn't affected by the plague, so he doesn't have magic. Or he was protected from it somehow. The plague has to be tied to Sethos and seemed to stop spreading after he returned to Sarddon. But how did it affect magic so strongly to make it disappear? What kind of spell has that kind of power?*

Serein rolled the scroll up, tucking it into the folds of her robes. The lamplight sputtered.

So many of Ithamar's works are here. For some reason, his records have been hidden away. There must be something here that was deemed too dangerous for the public eye. If that's the case, there's a good chance Ithamar is dead or in hiding.

Serein pocketed a few more parchments, straightening the room so that nothing appeared out of place. Her gaze drifted around at the shelves full of texts still unread, feeling the answers seeping from the pages.

Chapter Forty
The Marks of Memories

S EREIN LET OUT A FRUSTRATED YELLOW CRY AS SHE SLASHED upward with her daggers. The courtyard filled with the trilling of insects and distant conversations of guards around the barracks. Mayte's muddy voice continued to echo around in her head for days.

Mayte's a thorn in my side, but she's not the one I need to kill, Serein thought, streaks of dark orange arcing through the air. *Still, I need to deal with her. Follow her, see where she's staying and how she's staying in contact with Xansas. I think it's time to reach out to some of my old contacts here in Oyon.*

She inhaled, and the fire died down to a dull glow. Nala lay near a hay bale on the edge of the sparring circle, licking her paws. Torches burned, hissing with bluish-purple whispers as sparks tried to reach the indigo sky.

Am I slipping? I keep missing things and seeing Xansas where he's not. Why can't I get his voice out of my head? Serein sliced downward as her shoulder ached. *Men can be killed. I'll kill him, and I'll be free.*

The sand crunched gray behind her, and she whirled around to find Uriah in a pale tunic and sirwal. A scruffy red beard clung to his face, the shadows under his green eyes fainter.

"I'm surprised to see you standing," she said.

"I'm fine," Uriah told her, his verdant voice roughened with exhaustion.

Serein turned on her heel, twirling the dagger. "You need to work on being a convincing liar. Your movements are slow, and you're still in pain."

Uriah's brow furrowed as she sheathed the weapons and circled him. "What are you doing?"

"Walking. Does that make you nervous?"

Serein darted behind him and tugged the string from his hair. Uriah's hand went up but grasped only empty air as his ponytail came undone.

"Stop that!" Uriah snapped, wincing.

Serein danced out of his reach, dangling the hair tie in front of him. "That was too easy. You usually put up more of a fight," she said.

"I said I'm fine!" Uriah snapped, jaw clenched.

"Yet I'm not convinced." *It would be a gift from the Lights if the concussion made him forget about Luca and Astra. But I never get that lucky.*

Nala rose and bounded over to Uriah. He jumped back, keeping his hand on the hilt of his sword. The tiger sniffed his knee.

"If she chews on your hand, it means she likes you," Serein told him.

Uriah lowered his hand, hesitantly touching Nala's head. She stood on her hind legs, stretching her paws up to his chest. He staggered back as Nala took his hand in her mouth. Uriah winced, trying to pull away.

At Serein's yellow whistle, the tiger cub released him and went to Serein. "You didn't tell him," she said, scratching Nala's head.

Uriah wiped his hand on his trousers, inspecting the bite marks. "I did tell him..." he said, glancing up. "I told you I wouldn't lie to Rameses."

"But you didn't tell him everything. Why?" Serein asked.

"I thought you didn't want anyone to know about your...about them," he told her, right index finger twitching. The scratch marks had healed into pink lines across his hand.

"You have my thanks." *Seems he's got some honor.*

"That's twice you've thanked me."

"Three times, but you probably forgot since you hit your head."

"Did Rameses talk to you already?" he asked.

"We reached an agreement yesterday about what he needs to know," Serein said as she reached into her pocket, tossing the necklace to Uriah. "You might need this since your luck doesn't seem great."

Uriah caught it, turning the pendant over in his hands. "I thought I lost this," he muttered, twisting the cord between his fingers. "You had it?"

"I grabbed it after it fell. I saw the rock fall out of your pocket, but the guards arrived before I could get it," she told him. *Little good it did protecting him.*

Uriah slipped the pendant into his pocket. "Thank you."

A breeze rippled through the warm air, cooling the sweat on her skin. Clouds floated across the half-moon hanging in the sky. Nala rolled around on the sand, dust collecting in her white fur.

"You keep a rock in your pocket, one around your neck," Serein said, "and the rocks on the shelves in your chamber. Are you that concerned about your wellbeing, or have you taken your devotion to the earth deities a little too far?"

"How did you...?" Uriah asked, rubbing the back of his neck.

Serein held the hair tie out to him. "I never thought of you as someone who collected things besides scowls and paperwork."

"You're making fun of me." Uriah snatched the hair tie back. "Haven't you ever collected anything?"

"Just scars." *And a lifetime of painful memories.*

"What about your drawings and paintings?" Uriah asked.

"They help to keep me focused. Nothing more," Serein replied.

Uriah sighed, crossing his arms. "Should you be out here by yourself? Aren't you worried that Xansas will come for you again?"

"Are you out here to make sure I'm protected? A man with a concussion makes me feel so much safer," she said. "Hiding in my room serves no purpose. I'm better off spending my time preparing to face him again."

· · ·

THE COLORED CALLS OF VENDORS CLASHED TOGETHER AS SEREIN navigated through the bazaar. As the Sister Moons Festival and the Aikhtiar approached, the city buzzed with anticipation. Stalls with flowers and sugary treats brightened the streets. A Zhao woman in pink and green robes tended to birds in wooden cages, the kaleidoscope of hues flooding Serein's vision as she walked by.

It's been years, but some of Eneca's contacts said he should still be around, Serein thought, adjusting the gray headscarf covering her face.

She rounded a corner across from the glassblowing building with a stall selling lanterns and lamps. White and ocher buildings with chipped murals were stacked onto each other. A thin man with a pointed beard in a brown tunic and tan sirwal leaned against a crate between the buildings, scratching a tabby behind its ear. Years had shaped his round, boyish face into chiseled angles, but his dark brown eyes remained the same.

"You're doing well, Faysal," Serein said in Sarddonian as she approached. "Still fond of cats." *Looks like he's been doing other work besides being an informant. He did say he wanted an honest trade one day. Seems he chose glassblowing,* she thought, taking in the faint burn marks on his sun-darkened arms and hands.

The man turned, his brow creased. The cat jumped down, tail twitching as it ran away. "Who are—" he began, the smooth emerald-colored words dying as Serein pulled back part of her scarf. His eyes widened, turning the color of tea in the sunlight. "You! I thought you were dead."

"Here I am. Very much alive."

Serein inspected a green and yellow glass lantern hanging from the thatched cover of the shop. The blurry reflections of people and animals on the street behind her passed over the lantern's polished surface. The metalwork of tiny stars and flowers on the outside glowed in the sunlight.

Faysal's gaze darted around before he stepped into the stall. "What are you doing here?" he asked under his breath.

"I'm in the city for a while, but for a different reason than before." The twenty-eight brass bands along his haya bracelet caught the sunlight. Two different colored leather straps were woven together. "You got married."

He touched his wrist, a smile appearing. "A few years ago. Her name's Akilah."

"Still doing your other work?" Serein asked.

"Yes. I work mostly with the other glassblowers here and help at this shop when they need me, but for the right price, I can do some listening," he replied, looking down the street.

Serein pulled out a folded piece of paper and passed it into his palm. "I've got work for you then. I need you to keep an eye on this woman. Mayte. She's dangerous and highly skilled. She's staying at the Alrraha Inn near the Tafall District," she said, picking up a small hand lantern. The shopkeeper watched her, nodding to Faysal.

"Is she like you?" Faysal asked when the shopkeeper returned to the inside of his shop.

"In some ways, so be cautious. See where she's going, who she's talking to. If you see her or a man with white hair and green eyes, make sure you aren't seen."

Faysal pocketed the paper. "I'm never seen."

"This is why I like you." Serein held the lamp in her hands. "Your skills could put the Golden Jackals to shame."

"Thought about joining them, but the mask doesn't suit me."

"Three gold for the first half, the other half when the competition is over," Serein replied. "We'll meet at the usual location every two days. Do you remember where that was?"

"I do." Faysal nodded, brushing dust from his arms. "A female Aikhtiar competitor. I heard there are quite a few this year. The Amir has a woman guard too."

Serein slipped three gold dijils to Faysal along with a few silvers for the lamp. "He seems like an eccentric man."

"I don't worry too much about the royals. Got more important things to worry about." Faysal ran his fingers over the lion heads on the coins as he slipped them out of sight. "I'll track down the mark this week. Expect an update by Ennaar."

Serein headed back to the palace through winding back alleys. *Ennaar. A week before the Aikhtiar begins,* she thought. *Xansas doesn't know about Faysal. I'll utilize every advantage I can use to bring him down.*

THE HEAVY DELIRIUM LIFTED, SHARP CLARITY SLICING THROUGH. Aches flared across the girl's body, her head pounding. She stared down at her nakedness, dark bruises and cuts fresh along her arms. Teeth marks stood out on her breasts, and splotches of blood stained her skin like wilted flowers, thorny vines running along her legs in red, sticky streaks.

Everything crashed into her. The White Snake's face, his body crushing hers, mouth hungry, the heat and pain, poisoned wine. Her green dress lay discarded on the floor. A yellow sob rose in the girl's throat, vomit burning her throat.

The door opened, and the White Snake entered, holding a set of clothes and a cup. The girl scrambled off the bed and pressed herself against the wall. Each step the man took drove the feverish memories into her chest like a knife.

"What did you do to me?" she whispered.

"Do to you?" he said, white words stirring up hazy memories. "Nothing you didn't want."

"Stay away from me!" she yelled, tears salty on her lips.

She spotted a knife hanging on the wall and lunged for it, holding the trembling point at him. The White Snake set the clothes on the bed. The knifepoint pressed against his chest as he stood in front of the girl.

"You're still feverish, Serein," he said. "The poison's still in your system. You've been sick for days. I've been taking care of you."

The smell of bitter herbs, a cool rag against her skin, his voice whispering in her ear, fingers tracing her scars. "No..." A spot of red bloomed through the White Snake's shirt as she jabbed the dagger into him. "No!"

He stared at her, smile cutting the dark. "How ferocious, volchitsa. But not vicious enough. You're not ready to kill me yet."

The girl vomited, the dagger slipping from her hand. The White Snake hauled her to the bed, and she thrashed. He released her and held out the cup of liquid.

"Drink," he told her.

She wiped saliva from her mouth. "No. Don't touch me!" the girl shouted.

"Drink, or I'll force you to."

The girl stared at the cup, stomach twisting as the taste of wine stuck to her tongue. Her heart slammed against her chest as she took the cool cup.

"This is to avoid any mistakes. They only weaken you," the White Snake said. "Get dressed and clean yourself up. We'll continue your training tomorrow."

The girl hurled the cup at him. He dodged, the ceramic shattering against the wall in a ruby-colored burst. "No. You..."

Shame slithered around her, scales scratching her flesh. She tried to spit out the words, but the truth lodged in her mouth. The White Snake took the girl's face in his hands, the black and white snake tattoos along his arm reaching for her.

His thumb pressed against the corner of her eye, wiping away a tear. "Tears don't suit you, volchitsa," *he said.*

She shoved him back, grabbing the clothes as she scrambled away. Her fingers fumbled with the tunic and trousers she slipped into, trying to hide from his burning green gaze. The girl sprinted out of the room down the familiar corridors of the citadel, bare feet slapping against the hard floor. She crashed into her room, locking the door. Sobs cracked her open, spilling everything out she collapsed in her bed.

A candle sprang to life, and the scarred girl flinched. Rose-colored breaths filled the room as a girl with long dark hair sat up in the bed against the opposite wall.

"What happened?" the Poison Flower asked, getting up and shuffling over.

"I...h-he did something to me," the scarred girl said through the strangled breaths. "I drank something and then...I can't remember."

A sad look crossed the Poison Flower's face as she pulled the girl to the small bathtub in the corner room. "My father did the same thing to me when I was seven." Her rosy words were quiet as she wiped away tears and blood. "I remember the knife and the blood on my hands, and my father's still body."

"I didn't want him to," the scarred girl choked. "I couldn't stop him. I had a knife, but I couldn't ..." She doubled over, stomach clenching as she vomited liquidy bile.

A warm hand rubbed her back, the quiet presence bearing everything she couldn't. "It's not your fault."

"I didn't know..." Pale-yellow words dissolved into cries as the scarred girl curled into herself, ready to crumble.

SEREIN WATCHED THE SHIFTING SHADOWS, LISTENING TO THE amethyst-colored *tap tap* of the wind against the shutters. Dim lantern light clung to Rameses' chambers, keeping the night at bay. *Xansas has a weakness, but why can't I see it?* she thought, digging through her memories as they sliced her. *I can't go back with him...I don't know if I'll be able to escape again. I have to make a move before he does.*

She took a deep breath, fingers tight around the hilt of her dagger.

Focus on what I know. Right-handed. Thirty-three. From Saxum, where conditions are cold and harsh. Pale complexion makes him more likely to move at night and avoid the sun. No family. Skilled with daggers, throwing knives, swords, the bagh nakh. Uses poisons. Contacts across the world. Patient and cunning.

Rameses' orange footfalls cut through the dim as he shuffled into the living chambers. A sheen of sweat coated his throat, hair tousled, and robes rumpled. Na'il and Na'im padded after him.

"Can't sleep, Your Highness?" she asked.

"Do you have nightmares?" Rameses asked, gold words quiet.

"I've lived one for most of my life. I have plenty of things that keep me up," she replied.

Na'il and Na'im panted at Rameses' side, tails wagging as he rubbed their heads. "How do you...stop them? My dreams are not always clear. A lot of them are of the arena and those children...Sometimes I see my father. Lately, they seem to end in death."

"Perhaps you should talk to Captain Stormheir about nightmares instead," Serein told him. *Is the pressure getting to him?*

Rameses rubbed the back of his neck. "Uriah's not much of a talker," he said. "I just want them to stop, and I don't know how to do that."

"Find how to fight it. I find that literally fighting it helps," she said. "Whatever guilt you're dealing with, you'll have to come to terms with it, or it'll eat you alive." *Make the fear into a weapon.*

"Does that usually work?" he asked.

"If you are that bothered..." Serein muttered, sighing, "then you can talk to me about it."

Rameses glanced at her, eyes widening. "I guess I should get us some coffee then."

PART III

THE SMILING RAGE

Chapter Forty-One
Hunting Snakes

THE SCARRED GIRL SWUNG THE SWORD, ORANGE SPARKING AS IT connected with another blade. Her brown-voiced opponent, the Brown Adder, shifted and disengaged. She came at the scarred girl's left side. The weapons danced while the man with moonlit skin watched.

The scarred girl saw the swings and changing movements of the Brown Adder but couldn't counter fast enough. Every bruise and cut told her to move faster and strike harder. White words pointed out her failings, the tight scar across her chest a reminder of her weakness. The black blade glowing while flames flashed, her mother's turquoise scream.

In that split second, the Brown Adder broke through the scarred girl's guard and slammed her into the ground, the blade cutting her skin as the sword pressed against her throat. Smiling, the Brown Adder turned away, seeking the White Snake as he watched.

Fear crept in, fear that he'd return her to the same field of carnage he'd saved her from a year ago because of her weakness. The scarred girl gripped her sword and lunged at the Brown Adder's unprotected back, kicking her knee. A mud-colored cry escaped from the Brown Adder as she stumbled, putting her sword up to block.

Don't stop until she bleeds, a dark voice whispered.

Hand clenching, the scarred girl punched her opponent in the throat, *sending her to the ground. She stepped on the bigger girl's wrist. "Yield," she said, holding her blade under the Brown Adder's chin.*

Anger and tears formed in the older girl's eyes. "I...yield," she gasped.

The scarred girl pressed the blade down harder before standing.

"Mayte." The pale voice snapped through the air, stillness settling around the room. "Do you know why you lost?" the White Snake asked. "Your mistake was not finishing off your opponent. You left yourself open, and Serein seized the opportunity to gain the advantage."

The man looked at the scarred girl with a smile. Warm pride stirred in her chest.

"Never turn your back on an opponent. We don't fight fair. We don't leave any alive."

"Yes, Master Xansas," the Brown Adder muttered and hung her head.

"The technique was sloppy, but you did well, Serein," the White Snake said, placing a hand on her shoulder. "I think you've trained long enough with Nero and Adara. I'll be training you personally from now on."

The Brown Adder stopped. "But Master Xansas, I—" The man's narrowed gaze silenced the brown-voiced girl.

"You've been training longer than Serein. Such a failure isn't acceptable, Mayte. Continue to work until you no longer forget the basics," he told her.

The Brown Adder flinched. Her chilly glare did little to dampen the scarred girl's spirit as she clung to the warm fluttering in her chest. She would earn the right to hold the blade entrusted to her—become strong enough to strike down lions.

SEREIN PEERED AROUND THE CORNER AS PEOPLE FILLED THE darkened streets. The links in Uriah's chainmail under his robes clinked orange-red next to her. The buildings of the Tafall District slumped, wearing the years in cracked plaster. Bright tapestries with a black and white moon hung from windows and over the streets. Smoke from cooking fires and sewage mixed together in the slums.

Eneca's note said Xansas was seen at the Sand Fox Inn, Serein thought, stepping into the street, the hood of her tan rida' pulled up. Uriah followed behind, his gray footsteps stiff.

Sighing, she grabbed his arm, looping hers around it. "What are you doing?" Uriah hissed, his forest-green words jagged as he tried to jerk away.

"Trying not to look suspicious," she replied. "We're here on a stroll to return to our rooms. Should I kiss you to make it look more convincing?"

His scowl darkened, muscles tensing. "Don't you dare."

"Then stop complaining. Act like you're drunk or something." Uriah looked away, jaw tightening. Serein led him down an unpaved road marked with wheel ruts and churned up by hooves and countless footprints.

The Sand Fox Inn was a pale beige building with small windows like glowing teeth, smashed between tenements and a thatch roofed sooq. The square lay empty except for a few people slumped by the well in the middle. Horses were tethered nearby, tails swishing.

Serein pulled closer to Uriah, swaying a bit as they approached. He stiffened. "Keep your head down. Laugh or something," she said through her smile, snatching a glance at the darkened window. *Second floor, fourth room on the left.*

Uriah wrinkled his nose, a protest forming on his lips. He let out a strained green laugh.

She giggled, pulling him closer. "We'll have to work on your acting skills. That was the least convincing laugh I've ever heard," she whispered as they stepped into the inn.

Dingy orange light seeped from the lanterns. Crumbling motifs of faded flowers and geometric patterns painted the walls. People sat around tables, eating and chatting. Serein's eyes darted over the faces, reading their movements and colored voices.

She laughed as she led Uriah toward the stairs, the weight of her daggers resting at her sides. "Have you considered that this might be a trap?" Uriah asked, the stairs creaking in watery blue crosshatches.

"That's why you're here as backup," Serein said. *Most likely, it's a trap or a false lead. Mayte hasn't been seen in this area either,* she thought as they stepped into the empty hallway.

"We should have brought guards to surround the place at least," he muttered.

"The point is not to draw attention. A squad of guards isn't subtle."

Serein unwound her arm from Uriah's as they passed the worn doors. A gravely blue laugh, fuchsia snoring, pale green and dulled orange conversations. No light appeared under the crack of the fourth door, no white voice slithering through the air.

She pressed her ear to the wall, hearing only silence. Uriah gave her a questioning look, hand resting on his sword as he glanced at the door. Serein tested the handle and found it unlocked. She drew her dagger as the door swung open.

A bedroll lay in the corner of the small room next to a low table pushed underneath the window. On it, a folded piece of paper rested, a mocking white smile in the dark. Uriah's green sigh seeped through the air.

Too easy. He wanted me to find this place, she thought, anger seeping through her fingers. She picked up the note with the hem of her rida'.

"Why are you picking it up like that?" Uriah asked.

"Xansas once poisoned me with paper that had been coated in a powder made of monkshood sap," Serein said. "It was to teach caution and to build up a tolerance to poisons."

Xansas' handwriting slashed across the page, each slant of the grouped lines a fresh cut on her skin. The lines of scars along her right arm tightened.

"It looks like a bunch of lines," Uriah said as he looked over her shoulder.

"It's an old language from the Saxum region in the Old Kingdom. Filo Lingua. It uses lines for its alphabet," Serein said. "We used it to send secret messages." *Carved it onto my skin. He taught me lessons I can never forget.*

"What does it say?"

"It says, 'Not yet.'" The sharp smell of lemons wafted off the paper. *That's not the real message. He left me something else.*

Serein folded the paper and slipped it into her pocket. Her stomach knotted as she glanced around the room. Faint boot prints scuffed the floor, the mud still damp.

"He was here recently. Left less than a day ago," she said.

"How did he know we'd be coming?" Uriah asked.

"He has spies. It was probably a test to see how quickly we'd come running. Xansas will have other places to go to avoid detection," Serein replied, sheathing the dagger. *What will he do next? Appear in my room again? Find me in an alley?*

"Now what? He knows we're coming. We can't run around in circles like this. The Aikhtiar begins in a week, and I'll be busy monitoring the city," Uriah said as they left the room.

"Your guards can search the city. You don't need to say that they're searching for Xansas, just a man with white hair and pale skin who's very dangerous."

"I'll see what men I can spare, but we're spread thin with the festival. The Golden Jackals are going to catch wind of this."

Which Xansas knew when he decided to ambush me. What else is he going to do? The yawning unknown consumed the ground beneath her, Xansas standing across the abyss. *I can't see his next move.*

"What do you plan to do next?" Uriah asked, his forest-green voice irritated.

"I'll think of something. See if Eneca can find anything else out," Serein said. "During my matches is when he's more likely to show up to watch. You'll want to make sure you have men watching every exit and entrance they can."

Uriah tugged at his necklace. "Do you think he'll try and kill the Malik during the competitions?"

She shook her head. "He won't make a move yet, not until he has the information he needs. Xansas likes to play with his prey before he destroys it."

SEREIN LIT A CANDLE ON HER DESK, THE FLAME DANCING AGAINST her yellow breath. Shadows stretched across her bedchamber, Nala's peacock-blue breathing rippling off the bedsheets like small waves. Serein unfolded the paper, fingers covered in the edges of a headscarf. She chewed on the inside of her cheek, the flame glowing through the paper. The Sarlyrian words revealed themselves, filling the page.

I knew you'd come for me, volchitsa. We are alike in that. You think you have a place here, but you'll see that the only place for you is with me. Consider this a peace offering. I know you're gathering secrets for the prince. I know how the previous king and his family died. Few from that night are still alive, but there is one who escaped—one who knows the truth about how Sethos gained his power. A healer's assistant. Masud al-Nazari. He'll be found in time, and we can do it together. I offer you this choice freely. I'm not your enemy. Until then, I'll enjoy our game.

Masud al-Nazari, Serein thought, the smell of heated lemon juice wafting from the page. *I've seen that name before in some of the records in the infirmary. How did Xansas find this out?*

You can't stay away from me, volchitsa, Xansas whispered in her ear. *You've always been hungry for answers. I can give them to you.*

Serein held the paper closer to the flame, ready for the orange tongues to consume the words. She stopped, pulling it away. *If this is true…this person could have the answers about what happened. What else has Xansas found?*

Serein folded the letter and tucked it into the slit in the rug underneath her bed. Xansas' presence stalked the shadows of the bedchamber as she closed the curtains, locking the balcony door.

Too many threads. Will they strangle me, my Sun and Stars?

Chapter Forty-Two
Growing Shadows

"Citizens of Oyon!" Sethos said, his blood-red voice cutting through the sounds of the coliseum crowds. "The day has come for the Malik's Aikhtiar to begin. A hundred and ten matches will commence the festivities of the Sister Moons Festival this week. May Alkhaliq and the Saints pour out their blessings on us!"

Sethos raised a golden goblet to the sky, the sun turning it into a burning scepter. The crowd roared. Tapestries with two moons flapped in the hot amethyst-colored wind as they hung from the open dome.

Serein stood by a gate leading to the tunnels underneath the coliseum stands as the first two competitors entered the arena. Sweat collected under her vambraces and cuirass armor. The Sarlyrian blades at her sides were comforting as other combatants crowded the corridor. She glanced up at Rameses as he sat next to Sethos, his expression unreadable.

She searched for a flash of white hair in the crowds. *I know Xansas is here,* she thought, squinting against the sunlight. *Does Mayte know that I found one of Xansas' hideouts? If they are meeting, it's probably not frequently. Faysal said that her routine hasn't been suspicious.*

The matchkeeper stood beside the two men, inspecting their

weapons. A winner was decided if the opponent yielded or was unable to fight. Bright auburn horn bursts rang out to start the match. Heat shimmered around the combatants.

"Who do you think will win?"

The apple-red question made Serein turn. Salveig grinned at her, Ragnhildur following beside her.

"The man Jinzo from the Black Isles," Serein replied. "His opponent, Tau, has an old injury to his right leg that causes him to move a second too slow. He won't be able to keep up with Jinzo's attacks."

Salveig's teeth flashed as she smiled. "Sharp eyes," she said, staring at the scar across Serein's throat. "Who tried to kill you?"

Serein tasted fire and blood as she blinked. "Someone who didn't do a very good job. One day I'll show him how it's done."

Jinzo swung his sword upward, and Tau dodged. They exchanged blows until Jinzo knocked his opponent back onto the sands, disarming him. The crowd roared as the bell rang, the dark peach toll ending the match.

"You could win decent money betting on these fights," Salveig said. "I'm interested to know what you think my weaknesses are."

Salveig won't be easy to fight, Serein thought, glancing at the battleaxe across the woman's back. *Most likely she's been trained for battle from a young age, as most Edolasians are. And if she could hold her own against Captain Stormheir, then she'll have strong attacks and defenses.*

"I heard there will be some of Sarddon's famous horse races in between the matches. I'll have to see how they compare to Edolasian races," Salveig went.

"You should see the camel races. That's an interesting sight," Serein replied.

Salveig leaned against the wall, burly arms crossed. "Camels are strange beasts. They don't look like they would be very fast," she said. "This country seems to have no shortage of interesting things. I wonder how the Sarddonians will react when they see women fighting."

. . .

LONG SHADOWS RAN FROM THE LATE AFTERNOON SUN AS SEREIN stepped out into the heat. The energy of the crowds in the packed stands continued to pollute the air with noisy color. Sarddonians filled most of the seats—families with young children, old men, and women—while Ginjarrians, Edolasians, and people from Zhao and Sinabrac intermingled with them.

Amidst the cheers, jeers aimed at Serein struck the sand like colored arrows. *Seems I'm not exciting enough for them,* she thought, rolling her shoulders. *I do love seeing the look on people's faces when I defy expectations. I hope they bet lots of money on my opponent.*

Marcello del Piero Giordano waved at the crowd, smiling beneath his round helmet. Gryphons and sea serpents decorated the breastplate of his half-plate armor, the chainmail sleeves stopping at his elbows.

The matchkeeper inspected their weapons before returning them, satisfied that no poison was on them. He went over the rules, wine-colored voice cutting through the noise of the crowds. The man turned and left the arena.

"I've heard about you," Marcello said as he faced her with a crooked smile. Rolling indigo words accented the Common Tongue with rolling *r*'s and throaty vowels of his Sinabian accent. "You're the one who marked the Sarddonian general. Although, judging by all those scars, you don't seem to be that great at fighting."

Right-handed. Thirties. Skilled with a rapier and in the Passero-style fencing common in Sinabrac. Confident. Uses quick thrusts and constant movement to tire opponents before breaking through their defenses, Serein thought, fingers resting on the hilt of her daggers.

Marcello lowered the helmet's visor, his sky-blue eyes standing out against the shadows. The auburn horn bursts rang out. He drew his rapier with its frilled silver hilt with swallow and vine designs. Serein shifted, feinting left as Marcello rushed forward. The thin blade glinted off the sunlight as he thrust at her with quick strikes. Each riposte forced her back, the whisper of steel passing close to her cheek.

Quicker than he looks. If he had another weapon, he would make for a formidable opponent, she thought.

Marcello smiled as he aimed at her abdomen, a sandy blond curl sticking to his temple. "Careful," he said, shifting for another attack, "or you'll end up with another mark for your collection."

Serein moved in close with her dagger in hand and brought her left arm around, slicing the inside of his left thigh with her right dagger. Red stained his brown trousers, spotting the sands. The sword slipped from Marcello's fingers as he let out a cry and stumbled, the indigo-colored sound rattling inside the helmet. He tried to knock her off balance, but she dodged and kicked his sword away.

Marcello raised his hands and aimed a punch. Serein blocked and shifted left to counter, cutting at the underside of his gauntlet straps. Marcello twisted around, swinging another fist at her face. His face struck her shoulder as she darted to the side and kicked the side of his left knee. Marcello staggered forward, and she punched his exposed throat. The shouts of the crowd shifted from excitement to a mixture of anger and disbelief.

Gasping, Marcello bent forward. Serein slammed into him, driving him onto his back in the sand. Picking up the rapier, she plunged it downward before he could scramble up. The sword opened a ribbon of blood along his throat. The bell rang across the arena in a resounding peach tone. Cheers and boos washed over Serein in a sea of colorful noise. She sheathed her dagger and turned away, skin prickling under the hundreds of eyes trained on her. Marcello grabbed his sword and limped out of the arena in the opposite direction.

I'm too exposed here, she thought, scanning the crowds.

Uriah stood by one of the arena gates inside the interior of the coliseum. "Should I be honored that you came all this way to watch my match?" Serein asked Uriah, pushing through the combatants waiting in the tunnels.

Sunlight turned Uriah's hair copper, the light bouncing off his armor. "I'm just doing my rounds," he said, the forest-green words following her.

Guards stood by the stairs leading up to the upper levels of the coliseum, saluting to Uriah as he passed. *Stairs are being watched, but there's a possibility that Xansas will use the chaos of the crowds to slip through,* Serein thought and found an empty side room.

The metal pump over the basin of water creaked bright orange as Serein lifted the handle. She splashed cool water on her face, brushing wet strands of hair back. Voices hummed through the ceiling and walls like hives of bees.

"Find any troublemakers in the stands?" Serein asked.

Uriah shook his head. "A few rowdy drunkards, but nothing out of the ordinary," he said.

"Probably best to make sure the guards are watching the stands on the days my matches happen."

"There are guards at every stairwell and entrance. He won't be getting past us," Uriah told her.

Serein glanced at him. "Let's hope that's true." *If Xansas is here, he probably has ten different plans of escape. Could Mayte be helping him move about the coliseum? Does Xansas have some of the city guards in his pocket?*

Uriah pointed to the ornate sheaths at her sides. "Where did you get those daggers?"

"They're a gift from the prince. Sarlyrian steel," Serein replied and walked out of the room.

"Serein! There you are."

Rasima raced toward them, her violet voice flying around her. The Amirah's blue abaya with white lace cuffs fluttered like birds' wings. Her golden eyes were visible through the slit of her white veil. Karam and another wali followed behind Rasima, keeping people at bay. Laia looked around, sticking close to Rasima.

Jasmine and honey perfume clashed with the smell of sweat, sand, and iron. "You were so fast! I could barely follow what was happening," Rasima said.

"Your Highness," Uriah said, bowing. "What are you doing here? Your parents don't usually allow you to attend such events."

"I came to see Serein's match. Rameses said I could if I stayed near the guards," Rasima said, turning to Serein. "Are you going to stay and watch the other fights? Can I watch with you?"

"I was going to get some food and head back to my chambers." *And continue to hunt Xansas and think of ways to kill him. My usual evening,* she thought, tugging at her left vambrace as an itch crept underneath. *It's best that the princess not remain here. No doubt Sethos will find out, and I'll get in trouble.*

"You're leaving? What if there are instructions about the next matches?" Uriah asked.

"I'm sure you'll fill me in," Serein said.

Picking up the hem of her abaya, Rasima followed. "Wait! Come get food with me and enjoy the moussem for a bit," she said. "There are moon cakes made only for the festival. It's a chewy pastry with coconut cream in the center, and powdered sugar, so it looks like a tiny moon. I know you don't like sweets, but I think you should try it."

Amber sunlight stretched out the shadows of houses and buildings. Colored tapestries with silver and black moon designs flapped in the breeze. Musicians played in the square while women danced with scarves in their hands. Festival markets filled the sooqs, vendors selling garments and woven luck charms shaped like moons. Bright flowers from different regions of Sarddon were twisted into murals around koubbas on street corners.

Rasima brushed against Serein's arm, excitement brimming in her eyes. "The Sister Moons Festival is one of my favorites. I love the food and the lantern lighting that takes place every night. They say that there used to be two moons in the sky—two sisters. The pale moon loved a man who died. After his death, she kept crying for all the world to see. The dark moon came to comfort her sister, gradually covering her in darkness as her grief grew. When the sister's grief wanes, she becomes full and bright again, but her heart's still heavy with sorrow, so she doesn't stay full long, but her sister's always there."

Colored streamers were strung over the streets, tendrils of black, white, green, and orange snapping in the wind. Children ran past while old men lingered in the shade by ocher houses. Rasima and Serein passed a mural of two women holding a moon in their hands one painted white and the other painted black with contrasting eyes.

"Have you ever been to a festival like this?" Rasima asked, looking up at her.

"I've been to many. The Dragon Festival in Zhao, the Tempest Festival and Summer Solstice celebration of Edolas," Serein replied, the smell of honey-spiced lamb and bowls of couscous wafting from a nearby stall. "I went to one where human sacrifices were offered to the gods of volcanoes to appease them. It happens in the far corners of the Black Isles."

Karam shot Serein a glare. "That sounds terrible, but now I want to know more about it," Rasima said.

Serein glanced at the rooftops. The brand on her shoulder felt tight. "I've also been to one in Sinabrac where they paint goats and let them run through the towns," she said. *It's not safe on the streets. He'll be watching every place I go, everyone I'm with.*

"Why?" Rasima asked, walking over to a vendor selling round cakes dusted with sugar. The vendor bowed, face breaking into a smile as Rasima ordered two, handing one to Serein.

"It's to protect livestock from elemental spirits that mean to harm them," Serein replied, powdered sugar clinging to her fingers.

Rasima stared up at Serein, waiting and watching. Serein took a bite of the moon cake.

A smile entered Rasima's eyes as she lifted the edge of her veil. "Isn't it good?"

"It's not bad." *It's too sweet,* she thought as the coconut filling coated her mouth. *Luca and Astra would like this. I wonder if they still like sweets. Abelia has probably been spoiling them these past few years.* A pang of sadness mixed with the sugary sweetness.

Azraq traders led their camels through the crowded square. The blue robes of the nomads cut through the dusty streets. Bags hung from the humped backs of the camels, bringing with them susurruses of the desert. Karam pulled Rasima close to keep her from being knocked about, Lala hovering near him. They walked closer to a wall with a faded mural painted on it. The dusty eyes of Saint Zubaida watched them, sand swirling around her hands.

"You mentioned that Edolas has a Tempest Festival. What's that?" Rasima asked through a mouthful of moon cake.

"It's to celebrate the four-armed Mother Goddess," Serein told her as they walked down the street.

Rasima licked sugar from her lips, eyebrows creasing. "Four arms?"

"She had six, but she threw one of her right arms into the sky to create the valkyries and threw one of her left arms into the ocean to create the berserkers. Each arm represents an ideal of Edolasian culture—strength, protection, nature, and family."

"You've been to so many places and met all sorts of people," Rasima said.

The Amirah's eyes drifted to the bazaar down the street. She stopped by one of the stalls and selected an indigo scarf, handing over a few silver coins to the shopkeeper. Karam's scowl and the other wali kept people back while Laia assisted Rasima with her purchases.

"For you," Rasima told Serein and held out the scarf. "The color suits you."

Serein tucked the scarf into her sash. "Thank you." *It'll be useful if I need to blend in. If I continue to win fights and become recognizable, it might be harder to move through the city unnoticed.*

"What are the festivals like in the Old Kingdom?" Rasima asked, her violet voice tossed about in the sea of conversations around them.

"The festivals vary depending on the region and cultures. The Ravanassë adopted many festivals the Immortals celebrated, everything from young women coming of age to when humans first received magic," Serein told her, fingers sticky with melting sugar. "Most people in the tribe had Vale ancestry, so we celebrated many of the Vale festivals about the Lights and Mirarnediad creating the world."

Serein's mind drifted to Kona, the beginning of spring marked by flower bundles and breads with floral designs. Her mother braiding her hair as they prepared for the twelve-day festival celebrating the creation of the world. The side of the houses were painted with floral designs, and the dresses and tops for the women and girls were embroidered with plants.

"My village had a festival every winter to celebrate the season of rest. There were large bonfires and all kinds of soups and hot dishes. It was usually snowing by then, so the village had snow sculpture competitions. There was also a competition to see who could produce the most elaborate blanket patterns."

Rasima's eyes widened. "Snow? I've never seen snow. Rameses said it snowed a few times when he was younger. What's it like?"

"It's like ice but softer and finer. The flakes have unique shapes if you look closely enough. It's cold, and when it covers everything in white, there's a peaceful silence around it. *I didn't think I'd ever miss snow,* Serein thought.

"How did you get all your scars?" she asked, gold eyes tracing over Serein's scars.

The violet questions continued to thread around Serein like ribbons. "By living," she replied, the moon cake sticking to the roof of her mouth. "Death is easy. Life is greedy. It'll claw and bite at you the more you cling to it."

"But life isn't all about pain. There are good things. There's joy and love," Rasima told her. "Do you have anything in this life you're truly living for?"

"Vengeance." *Astra and Luca. Too many things threaten them,* Serein thought, cradling the fragile warmth close in her chest.

Rasima stopped. "Who do you want to get vengeance against?"

"One took my family and home from me. One tortured me for years and had me thrown in Grasdan. Another forced me to fight and tried to kill me."

"A person who seeks revenge follows a path of ruin. You dig a grave not only for those who have wronged you but for yourself," Rasima told her.

"I've already counted the number of graves I need," Serein said, swallowing the last bite of the moon cake. "I don't need the words of your Saints to remind me of the cost."

Serein lifted her gaze, heart seizing as she met the familiar bright green eyes under the shadow of a dark cowl. Xansas smiled at her from across the bazaar. People flowed around him as if he were a ghost.

Her hands went to the daggers. *He's here! He's been following me, and I didn't notice,* she thought as she prepared to rush through the crowd.

Rasima took Serein's right hand, holding tight to the scarred fingers. The touch jolted Serein, ripping her eyes away from Xansas. "Are you all right, Serein?" Rasima asked.

Serein looked back to the street, but Xansas had vanished. Cold fear squeezed her lungs. She gripped Rasima's hand, biting the inside of her cheek. "We should head back to the palace. People tend to get rowdy when festivals happen," Serein said. *He's seen Rasima. I shouldn't have come here with her. She's at risk.*

"Oh. I was hoping to show you the lantern lighting that takes place at sundown. People write their prayers on paper lanterns that they release into the air by the ocean. It's like a million stars rising from the city the whole month," Rasima said as they left the sooq. "We can watch it from the palace wall."

Violet breath brushed against the scars. Serein wanted to pull her hand away but found it still clasped in the warm, firm fingers.

"That sounds nice," Serein muttered, scanning the faces passing by. *A path of ruin was easier to walk when there was no one else who could get hurt besides me.*

THE LIDLESS GAZE OF THE FULL HARVEST MOON WATCHED OVER Oyon, pink and orange bleeding across the sky as the sun waned. The nearby House of the Saints unfurled long black, white, green, and orange ribbons from the tops of archways and towers.

Xansas watched the street below from the shade of a thatched roof, face hidden in the folds of his scarf. The surprised look on Serein's face when she spotted him, the rage burning in her eyes, made his heart race. Serein maneuvered through the streets with a young girl beside her, their hands clasped together. Serein cut through the crowds, searching—searching for him.

He had watched from the roof until Serein disappeared, tracing the scar along his right cheek. A sigh escaped as Xansas settled back against one of the wooden beams of the covering. He pulled out a knife, his smile reflected in the blade. He cut twenty-seven lines into the wood—some short, some slanted.

Xansas rubbed his chest where Serein's dagger had cut. His arm ached where Serein had stabbed him with the bone. *Does the little princess remind you of our child? Did you have a girl?* Xansas thought. *Or do you see yourself in her? You're still clinging to your sentimentality,* volchitsa.

He opened the pouch around his neck and pulled out a piece of fabric with an embroidered flower on it. A thick lock of dark brown hair, a small emerald piece of a dress, and the broken lamb bone were rolled up in the fabric. He held the embroidery cloth to his nose, the smell of argan filling his nose.

A group of children raced down the street below, laughing. *I can't wait to meet our child, Serein. Does it have your eyes? I'll find where you've hidden it,* Xansas thought, running his finger along the flower design. *Then we'll be together again.*

Chapter Forty-Three
Mutual Survival

MAYTE STALKED INTO THE ARENA, LITHE AND PREDATORY. THE knives along her belt glinted in the sunlight. Her opponent was a tall Sarddonian with a scimitar. Serein shifted as she stood behind Rameses. Sethos watched the matches in the royal viewing box with his usual stern expression. Hisein glared at Serein as he and Kamau remained behind the Malik.

Xansas' face appeared in each moving shadow, every flash of white making Serein's heart race. *How long before he decides to come for Rasima to get to me? Or Eneca?* she thought, the dagger handle digging into her palm.

I warned you about attachments and how they leave you exposed. The white laugh mocked her on the breeze.

The dark peach toll carried over the excited shouts of the spectators. Mayte lunged forward, knives drawn. She avoided the swing of her opponent's sword, mirroring Xansas' viciousness and defense-eroding techniques.

THE GIRL GRIPPED THE KNIFE, THE BLISTERS ON HER FINGERS PAINFUL. Soft hands turned callused with a year of training, childhood traded for steel. She lunged at the White Snake, swiping with an orange arc. He feinted left, aiming his blade at her stomach. She rolled away, her foot connecting with his knee as she kicked, but he remained standing.

"You're still weak on your left side," the White Snake told her, blades scraping together in colored sparks.

The girl spun as he swung, the dagger hissing by her ear. Each clash reminded her of the king cloaked in gold and blood, a sky filled with ravens, and the sightless blue of her mother's eyes. Grabbing the White Snake's arm, she twisted, trying to ram her knee into his stomach. The black and white snakes tattooed on his arm rippled with his muscles.

The White Snake disarmed her and grabbed her wrist, the knife clattering on the ground. She released him and kicked her fallen weapon up, catching it in her left hand. The man's eyes widened, mouth curling in a grin. He twisted the girl's arm behind her back and forced her to her knees. The dagger touched her throat, the whisper of steel kissing her skin.

"What was your mistake?" asked the White Snake.

"I didn't anticipate your movements, Master Xansas. I saw an opening and rushed in," the girl replied, pale-yellow breaths clouding around her.

"Always anticipate. Read your opponent's movements." He released her. "Do you like using two weapons?"

She stood and turned around. "It felt better having two weapons."

He handed the girl his dagger, the scars along his neck dancing like silver threads as he swallowed. "We'll work on that then," the White Snake said. "I saw you tried to utilize your fallen weapon. That could become a deadly surprise attack."

The girl stared at the weapons, excitement fluttering. She saw the Murderous King's blood running down her hands.

The White Snake tipped her chin up. "You have the potential to be a great assassin, Serein. You might even surpass me one day."

Mayte sliced into the arm of her opponent as she broke through his defenses. The man's painful lime-green cry streaked the air as he raised his sword to block another attack.

Mayte has better control her left hand but hasn't mastered using dual weapons. Fast and eager for blood. The Adder's hardly changed, Serein thought.

Rameses looked up at Serein as he lounged on the raised

cushions in the viewing box, a goblet of wine in his hand. "The competition's fierce this year, and it's only the second day of the Aikhtiar," he said in a quiet voice, the golden words sparkling. "Are you feeling confident about your odds?"

"Everyone has a pattern and a certain way they fight. Knowing how to read a person gives you the ability to predict their movements," Serein told him.

"Did you like watching the lantern lighting with Rasima the other night?" he whispered.

"It was nice." Serein watched Sethos out of the corner of her eye. *I couldn't enjoy it because I worried that Xansas would be watching.*

Rameses glanced at his father, adjusting his white turban as the peach chimes sprinkled down from his earrings. He lowered his gaze and twisted his ring.

"It'd be wise to keep Rasima away from the coliseum. She's safer in the palace," Serein said.

"Have you seen Xansas since then?" Rameses asked.

"No. Captain Stormheir has his men combing the city. I won't let anything happen to her." *I won't be able to find Xansas without Sethos finding out. Too many people could get hurt. He will come after people here to get to me,* she thought, seeing Rasima writhing in agony as Xansas stood over her with blood on his hands.

The bell rang out, ending the match. Mayte stood over her unconscious opponent. His tunic was torn, and bloody patches seeped across his skin. She stalked across the sands, blood dripping from her knives.

So many threads, volchitsa. *Which ones will I pull? Eneca? The princess? How about the prince and his captain? Your children? I'll tear everything away until you're left alone.*

Serein shivered, the air thin in her lungs. *I have to give him no place to hide. Keeping it a secret is no longer an option,* she thought. *I won't be able to hide after this either.*

STARS POKED THROUGH THE SKY, THE COLORS OF OYON DRIFTING upward like clouds of smoke. Serein darted across the rooftop, keeping Mayte in sight as she followed her from the coliseum to the

Tafall District. A large city square opened up, crowded with people grabbing dinner from nearby stalls. Mayte crossed the street below, glancing over her shoulder. The shape of a short sword was visible underneath her dark cloak.

Faysal said Mayte leaves to train in the coliseum after the matches before returning to the Alrraha Inn around sundown. It'd be too risky to have predictable movements. That routine is to throw off anyone watching, Serein thought, leaping over to a low building.

Mayte turned down a winding street, her tall frame cutting through the shadows. The dark outline of gallows and a stone chopping block in the execution square stood like bowed sentries. Hanging lanterns strung across the streets cast dusky amber light over the buildings. The inn was painted with murals of Saint Esmail, the Saint of Earth, raising the walls around Oyon.

If she's sending messages to Xansas or meeting with contacts, she's doing it in a way I'm unaware of. There are no signs of the usual codes the Bone Vipers use.

Serein dropped behind a low wall when Mayte stopped and looked back. A cat yowled in the distance, the bright peacock colored sound cutting through the night. Mayte continued toward the Alrraha Inn.

She launched herself onto the balcony of the closed teahouse across from the inn. The still-warm bricks scraped against her palms as she scaled the side, hauling herself onto the roof. Serein crouched behind the low wall, peering through the leaves cut into the worn stones.

If you kill her, you won't have to worry about her. Xansas' voice trickled up the back of her neck.

Serein shivered, hand resting on her dagger. *Mayte will slip up. She always does,* she thought. *Between Faysal and Eneca's contacts, answers will shake loose.*

WATER DRIPPED ONTO THE TILE FLOOR AS URIAH STEPPED OUT OF the bath, hair plastered to his head. He grabbed the towel off his bed, patting his skin dry. The blue hours of the early morning bled through the closed curtains.

The second week of matches starts tomorrow. We've been searching, and still no sign of Xansas, he thought, brushing his hair back off his face. *That was too close a call, having Xansas near Rasima. I don't know how much longer I can keep this from the Malik...*

Uriah left the bathing chamber and found Serein sitting on the edge of his desk, her dark robes blending in with the shadows. He froze, standing with only the towel in his hands.

Serein arched an eyebrow, blue eyes catching the lantern light. "Seems the armor *does* come off," she said

His thoughts raced, face hot as his mouth began working again. "What the hell are you doing in my room?!" Uriah shouted. He grabbed the tunic and trousers on his bed and ran back into the other room, the door slamming behind him. *I thought I locked my door. Or did she come in through the secret entrance?*

"Waiting. I knocked, but I heard no response," Serein replied.

The sound of her laughter made his ears burn more. "And you decided to come in?!" he seethed, throwing on his clothes.

"It's not like you haven't barged into my room before," she said.

Uriah stood in the doorway, scowling. Water dripped from his hair, dampening his shirt. He tried to hold her gaze but wilted, staring at the dark blue rug beneath his feet. "What do you want?" he snapped.

"I can't stop laughing. You *actually* jumped. I didn't think your face could get any redder," Serein said, chuckling.

Anger surged through his chest, rising above his embarrassment. Heat burned his cheeks. "Leave!" he told her, glaring.

Serein's mouth settled into a grin. "We've both seen each other in various stages of undress. No need to be so bashful."

He stiffened. "I didn't mean to—"

"I didn't come here to see you naked. I came to discuss something with you."

Serein glanced at the shelf hanging on the wall with rocks arranged according to color. Twisting around, she shifted through the papers on his desk.

"Say your piece and leave," Uriah said. *What's so important that she has to be here at this hour?*

Serein turned back to him. "I think you're cranky because you're not sleeping well," she said.

"My lack of sleep is because I'm managing a city and hunting Xansas," he hissed, throwing the towel around his shoulders. "How much longer do you think we can keep this hidden? I don't have much to go on besides a man with pale skin and white hair."

She reached into the sleeve of her robes and held up a piece of paper. "This will help in your search," Serein told him.

Uriah walked over and took the paper, unfolding it to reveal the face of Xansas. Sharp green eyes stared back at him, his features angular and hair long and white. A black and white snake drawing was sketched beside his face, marked as a tattoo on his right arm. Xansas' physical descriptions were scrawled on the side of the paper in Serein's straight handwriting.

"Why didn't you give this to me sooner? Why didn't you tell the Golden Jackals what he looked like while you were in Grasdan?" Uriah asked, and her face darkened. *Serein doesn't get rattled. This really worries her if she's asking for help*, he thought, taking in the slight wrinkle along her scarred forehead.

She inhaled through her nose. "I did tell them, but Xansas killed the Jackal who interrogated me in Grasdan. He destroyed any information on him so that no one else knew what he looked like. I suspect he has someone within the Jackals working for him," Serein muttered, uncrossing her legs.

Uriah's gaze snapped to her. "Are you sure?" *That does explain why no one knew what he looked like. If he has spies within the Jackals, who else might he have working for him?*

"He had people within Grasdan, so he likely has people everywhere, which is why we need to move carefully," Serein said. "Exposing Xansas will force him to make a move or lie low long enough for us to come up with a different plan. He won't be expecting me to tell Sethos about him."

"You're fine with telling the Malik?" Uriah asked.

Serein's eyes snapped to his face, her mouth set in a hard line. "No, but there's too much at risk to keep this a secret any longer."

"What if His Majesty asks me why I didn't bring this information to him sooner?"

Serein blinked, the stillness settling over her again. "Tell him there had been reports about an assassin with a Bone Viper brand, and you wanted to make sure your sources were accurate," she said. "You wanted to question me further before making your move, and once you gave me the description, I confirmed it was Xansas. Make it appear that you were being cautious and thorough. You will probably be reprimanded, but he won't execute you."

Uriah swallowed. "You said that if Sethos knows why Xansas is here, that it'll make things dangerous for you and Rameses," he said. "I want to catch Xansas too, but I know you stand to lose more. I don't want to prevent you from seeing your children again or do anything that puts them in danger. I'm not heartless."

Loud ringing grew in Uriah's ears. Faces flashed in a blur of swords and blood. Mothers fleeing with children, soldiers giving chase. Echoing screams cut into him, the smell of water clogging his nose as bodies swirled in the dark depths.

*I'm sorry. I didn't...*Uriah swallowed, biting his tongue. *I'm not there. That was the past.* The waters stilled as the memories retreated into the darkened corners as he sucked in a breath.

Serein's gaze seemed to pry his thoughts from his head, finding the secrets he didn't utter. Uriah glanced away from the steel in her eyes, afraid she would see what lingered beneath the depths of his mind.

"I never thought you were heartless. Just a man of duty and honor, two things that don't always align," she said. "You've made your mistakes, as have I."

Uriah rubbed his damp stubble. "Is this really what you want to do?" he asked, straightening the papers on his desk. "You have...you have Luca and Astra to think about." *She thought she wouldn't see her children again and was prepared to die.* Her skeletal appearance from the Harpy's Chest with sunken, defeated eyes flashed across his mind. *She won't throw away a chance to get back to them.*

"More eyes, more Jackals, high risk of imprisonment, and death. Feels like most of my days. There are no good options, but it's better to catch him off guard any way we can. Il-Makah is already looking for enemy spies in the palace. I'll handle Rameses to make sure he's prepared for when his father questions him."

Serein glanced at the shelves of rocks again. The indigo light outside began to turn a shade of violet, and Uriah heard the distant sounds of the guards leaving their barracks.

"I do this for them," Serein said. "Everything I've done for the past seven years has been for them. There isn't any other choice except to trust that you'll help me stop Xansas."

"And how did those words feel coming out of your mouth?" Uriah asked.

She gave him a razor-sharp smile. "Like chewing on glass."

Uriah folded the paper and waved her off his desk. She moved aside, and he slipped the paper into a secret compartment in one of the drawers.

"Why didn't you try to stop Xansas before you were sent to Grasdan?" Uriah asked.

Serein remained still. "I ran away because I was afraid of what he would do to me if he knew I was pregnant. I thought I could hide somewhere he wouldn't find us. But he still did," she told him, voice low. "Xansas won't leave Oyon without me. If he kills the king, I won't be able to get back to them. I can't risk losing any more time."

He crossed his arms. "You're offering yourself as bait? That's a terrible idea," Uriah said. "What if the Malik thinks you've been hiding information from him this whole time when I tell him about Xansas?"

"Then this might be the last conversation we ever have." Serein's words carried a sense of finality as they hung in the air.

Uriah sighed, glancing back at her. "I'll pass the picture along to be copied," he said. "What about Mayte? She should be removed from the competition. You said yourself that she's dangerous."

"Let me deal with Mayte. If you arrest her, that'll draw more attention to me. She won't give Xansas up," Serein said. "I have someone watching her."

"What do you mean you have someone watching her?"

Serein walked around his desk to inspect the armor on the training dummy on the other side of the chamber. "One of my old contacts is still active in the city. He's been following her for the past few weeks. I'll make sure she doesn't win and that she's no longer a threat."

"There's no guarantee that you'll win the final match." *How many contacts does she have in the city? When has she had time to meet with them?* Uriah thought. *Is she planning on killing Mayte?*

She glanced at him over her shoulder, head tilted slightly. "You'd best start praying that I make it through the match if you're that worried about me."

"I'm not worried about you," Uriah grumbled. "What will happen to your children if you die?"

"They're being cared for. The people watching them will continue to do so, even if I never make it back. That was the agreement before I ended up in Grasdan," Serein said.

"I'll make sure the Malik knows you aren't involved with Xansas and are helping to capture him," Uriah said, staring at the faint scratch marks across his fingers. "Rameses has faith in you so just...keep protecting him and Rasima."

Serein stood in front of his desk, her hands hidden beneath the dark folds of her robes. "You might make me swoon with all these declarations of feelings and grand statements," Serein said.

Uriah jerked his head up. "You're the one who decided to come to my chambers," he snapped. *She's never going to let me live this down. She's so aggravating and cryptic and...strange.*

"Well, I'll be sure to announce myself next time so you can make yourself presentable," she said.

Heat crawled under Uriah's skin again. Serein reached into her pocket and placed a ruddy-colored rock onto a stack of papers. The edges were worn, its surface luminous under the lantern light.

"What's this?" Uriah asked, glancing at it.

"A rock. Can't you tell?" Serein replied. "If you don't want it, I'll take it back."

Uriah sighed, the scowl releasing from his face as he turned the rock around in his hand. "I'll keep it. Thank you for this...and the drawing." *Almandine. A stone of protection to the Sarddonians. Does she know that? Is she trying to be nice?*

"I find great pleasure in undermining Xansas. I want him to feel the same helplessness that I've felt for so many years," Serein said, a dark chill clinging to her words. "When you decide to tell the king about Xansas, let me and Rameses know."

"I plan to do it in the next few days," Uriah said. *Gives me time to get my story straight and prepare myself for the worst.*

She moved toward the tapestry on the adjacent wall, pushing aside the thick fabric. The door swung open, musty darkness sweeping into the chamber.

"I can't get over how embarrassed you got. Perhaps I should tell Salveig what she's missing. She'll find you even more desirable and might try to sneak into your chambers," Serein said.

"Just go!" Uriah seethed through his teeth.

Serein grinned at him as darkness swallowed her up, the door swinging shut behind her.

I don't understand her. I doubt I ever will, Uriah thought, staring at the stone on his desk.

Chapter Forty-Four
False Security

RAMESES WATCHED THE MOTHS DANCING AROUND THE LANTERNS. Purple bougainvillea swayed in the balmy night breeze, dangling from the arched pergola. Guards stood around the garden, armor glinting from the four lit braziers.

Servants moved around the table filled with tagines of chicken and lamb, plates of fluffy couscous with golden raisins, baskets of flatbread, and bowls of olives, pickled vegetables, hummus, and sun-dried tomatoes with harissa and lemon juice. Sethos lounged on plush cushions. Lujayn sat beside him, reaching for a piece of flaky chicken b'stila.

Rameses and Rasima sat around a raised, square carrom board. The board had a hole in each corner and a smaller square painted in the middle. At the center was a six-pointed star surrounded by black and white disks, one red one resting closer to Rameses' side of the board. Rasima chewed on her lower lip, fingers hovering over the round piece with a lion painted on it. She had pushed her black veil back, ringlets of dark hair falling past her shoulders.

"Don't take too long, Rasi," Rameses told her with a smile as he sipped his wine.

"You're trying to make me mess up," she said, flicking the disk. It bounced off a white piece, knocking it into one of the corner holes.

"Or I'm just encouraging you to succeed."

Rasima grinned as she picked up a sticky piece of honey-spiced lamb. Rahim ran around between the servants, laughing. He held a lion and an elephant figurine in his hands, waving them through the air. A servant darted out of the way, clutching the basket of bread as he almost tripped.

It's been a while since we have had dinner together like this, Rameses thought, the tension coiled in his chest loosening.

He glanced at his father, the hard lines of the Malik's face softening as the hint of a smile appeared. A pang of sadness hit Rameses, muddling with the images of the sword coated in blood and the screams of children.

What will he do once he finds out about Xansas? Will he blame Serein? She and Uriah want to handle this, but there must be something else I can do, Rameses said, chewing on a piece of rosemary-crusted tuna in a lemon dill sauce.

"Akhun?" Rasima's voice broke through his thoughts, and he glanced back at his sister. "It's your turn."

"So it is," Rameses muttered. He flicked the striker piece, and it slid between two white pieces and a black one, hitting the black disk to the right.

Rasima gave him a curious look. "You weren't trying," she told him, taking a sip of sweetened almond milk.

"Yes, I was. You just are doing better than me tonight."

Rameses settled back as Rahim ran by again, the boy's small red turban askew. His brother stopped, peering at their game.

"Rameses, Umm said I could learn archery. Will you teach me?" Rahim asked.

Glancing up, Rameses smiled at him. "Of course. I can let you use my old bow if you would like," he said.

Rahim's grin pushed dimples into his cheeks. "Can I ride Jabbar?"

"We will see. Let's start with shooting an arrow first."

Rahim ran around the table toward their parents. "Baba! Look!" he said as he jumped on Sethos' back, holding the elephant in the Malik's face. "Umm got me an elephant!"

Sethos set his goblet down. "I see," he said as Rahim climbed into his lap. A smile broke through his father's stony expression, and Rameses stopped. "What will you get next? A tiger?"

The boy tilted his head. "An eagle." Rahim flapped his arms. "Or a dragon!"

Sethos laughed. "A dragon? That is an unusual request, abnay."

Rameses swallowed a lump lodged in his throat. *Does Ummi know what he's done?* he thought. *Does he think of the people he's hurt? How can he look at his children and not think of the ones he's killed? How can he have done such horrible things yet love us?*

"Rameses?" Rasima jostled his arm, her brow knitted together. "Are you all right?"

"Yes," he said, managing a smile as he blinked.

"You have been acting strange lately. What are you thinking about? Is it about the man who attacked you?" Rasima asked, voice quiet as she scooted closer.

"No. I have a lot on my mind with different trade meetings and potential bride interviews. You don't need to worry about me, Rasi," Rameses told her, flicking one of his pieces across the board. It knocked two black disks into the left corner hole. "You should be worried about me winning because I think that put me ahead of you."

His sister frowned, letting out a huff. "That's not fair," she muttered.

"Sounds like you are intimidated that I might win." *She cannot know what's going on,* he thought. *I don't want Rasi caught up in all this.*

One of the Malik's Guard approached Sethos, bowing. "Your Majesty, Captain Stormheir says he wishes to speak with you about something urgent," the man said. "Something for your ears only."

Sethos' expression shifted, the hard mask returning as he lifted Rahim from his lap. "Take the children through the gardens for a bit, delam," he told Lujayn.

The Malika's mouth pursed as she took Rahim's hand. "Come along, Rasima," she said, the silver threads of her white headscarf glowing. Her guards followed, taking one of the hanging lamps to illuminate the path.

"Let's go to the fishpond for a bit," Lujayn said to Rahim.

"You too, Rameses," Sethos said.

Rameses downed the last of his wine and followed Rasima and Karam to the gardens with Ilderim. He looked at Uriah as he stood at the edge of the lantern light. Uriah nodded at him, his expression difficult to read in the shadows.

Is he going to tell my father about Xansas? Rameses thought as he lingered behind the rest of his family, stopping several yards from the pergola.

Rameses watched through the almond trees as Uriah bowed to the Malik, voice quiet. Sethos turned to him, face hidden from view. A few minutes passed, and his father's shoulders tensed.

"What are you doing, Rameses?" Rasima's voice almost made him jump.

"Just wondering what they are talking about," he replied, eyes darting to her.

"Your Highness, we should stay with Her Majesty," Karam told Rasima as he waited by the path.

"Just a moment," Rasima said, craning her neck to peer through the tree. "You have been acting strange tonight, akhun. What's bothering you?"

"Why do you think something's bothering me?" Rameses asked, keeping his hand away from the ring.

She took his hand. "Because you are quieter than usual, and you seem tired."

Rameses sighed. "I have been having nightmares as of late." *If she knew the things our father has done and what he's capable of, it would frighten her. Rasima will find out eventually, but I want to protect her from harm for as long as I can.*

Sethos gestured to a servant who headed into the garden. He approached Rameses, bowing. "His Majesty would like you to return to the pergola," the man said.

Rameses stiffened, worry twisting into a tighter coil in his stomach. Rasima cast him a questioning look, and he swallowed his nervousness behind a smile. He patted her head as he followed the servant back to the pergola.

Does he know? Does he suspect something? Rameses thought, trying to slow his anxious heartbeat.

Uriah stood with his hands at his sides. Rameses sat down at the table across from his father as a servant refilled his goblet. Sethos took a sip from his cup, mouth a hard line beneath his beard. He wore the same calculating look Rameses knew from war meetings when he encountered an issue on the battlefield.

He's displeased, Rameses thought. *Serein said keeping me in the dark about certain things was to protect me, but everything's becoming precarious.*

"Leave us," Sethos said to his muharib and the guards around the pergola. "You may stay, Captain Stormheir."

Rameses' heart pounded as Ilderim and the other guards left, scenarios running through his head. The seconds dug under his skin, threatening to crack his stiff limbs.

"It seems there is an assassin in Oyon. Xansas Regor, the man your wali used to work for," his father said, voice steady. "Were you aware of this, Rameses?"

"Wrap the lies in strands of truth. Tell it to yourself enough times that you believe it so that others will too."

"Serein let me know last night that Captain Stormheir had been following some leads about Xansas being sighted in Oyon but that he had not been officially sighted," Rameses replied, reciting the words Serein told him to say. "Uriah approached her for help once it was confirmed."

"I want to know why this information was not relayed to me weeks ago," Sethos said.

Rameses went to touch his ring but stopped, remembering Serein's words. He reached for his goblet of wine to wash down his unease. The chilled wine slipped past the knot in his throat.

"I wanted to see if the rumors had merit since there hasn't been any mention of the White Snake near Sarddon for almost two years. I had some guards searching for him the past few weeks, but they weren't able to turn up anything. Serein gave me this drawing of him," Uriah said, holding out a sketch out to Sethos. "It matches the vague description we got from people in the city and what little the Jackals know about him."

Rameses caught a glimpse of the man's angular face with a scar, sharp green eyes, and white hair. *The White Snake,* he thought. *I was expecting him to look more monstrous. He looks normal.*

"I have this sketch circulating Oyon, and the Golden Jackals have copies as well. I alerted Il-Makah as soon as I confirmed it was Xansas," Uriah said.

Sethos stared at the drawing, setting it down on the table. "I find the timing suspicious. Her becoming muharib would bring more danger to us," he said. "I want her watched more closely."

"Serein is loyal to the crown. She values her freedom and knows that if she is involved in your death, she will be killed," Rameses told his father. "I do not think that she has any involvement with the Bone Vipers anymore. If anything, she wants to hunt Xansas down."

"You seem so sure about this, abnay, but you forget who our enemies are. She is still one of them, and you are unwise not to have any distrust toward her."

Sethos touched the scar across his face, face darkening as he closed his eyes. Rameses remembered seeing the gash cut across his father's face, Sethos' tears as he sat beside the wrapped body of his brother, the red trim of his white qamis like bleeding wounds. Sethos' mask vanished, exhaustion seeping through the cracks. In the flickering lantern light, Rameses thought he caught a flash of pain in his father's eyes.

Would he have injured himself on purpose? Rameses thought, the whispers of doubt swirling around him in the night air. *How far has he gone to get what he wants?*

"Assassins have come before and failed, but we cannot let our guard down," Sethos said, opening his eyes and looking at Rameses. "You find my actions harsh, but I do it to protect our family and everything we have built. Everything is held on a tenuous line. One moment of weakness or misstep could plunge Sarddon into chaos."

"I understand, Father," Rameses told him, glancing at the tabletop. "I want only the best for Sarddon as well."

"Captain Stormheir, continue to search the city. The Golden Jackals will be looking into these rumors. Next time, do not delay with such information. You have served this city faithfully for years, so it would be a shame if you were no longer able to do so."

Uriah bowed his head, fingers touching his forehead. "Yes, Your Majesty," he said, his hand resting near his pocket where he kept the rock.

Sethos' stern gaze snapped to Rameses. "You must be careful as well, Rameses. No more shirking your guards. I do not want you leaving the palace any more than necessary until this matter is resolved."

Rameses' mouth tightened. *Of course, he knew. What else does he know?* he thought. *For now, we have avoided the worst. We will see what comes next.*

URIAH WIPED SWEAT FROM HIS EYES, GLANCING UP AT THE STANDS through one of the carved arena windows. The people shifted like a living sea while vendors sold kebabs, fruits, and drinks in the stands. *If Xansas is watching in the stands, he's well hidden. Or Serein's wrong, and he's nowhere near here,* he thought, spotting the guards positioned throughout the crowds.

His gaze went back to the arena as Serein darted past her opponent's arcing sword. The bluish sheen of the Sarlyrian dagger cut through the air, deflecting Husam's attack. She circled the man, jabbing at his side she continued to push him back. The crowd cheered, fewer jeers raining down on Serein as she dodged. The sounds hummed through the interior tunnels of the coliseum.

A hand on Uriah's shoulder jostled him, and he stiffened, hand going to his sword. "Enjoying the matches, sadiqi?" Rameses asked as he came up beside him with Ilderim and I'timad.

Uriah relaxed, glancing at Rameses. "What are you doing down here?" he asked. "You have a better vantage up there in the viewing box." *And it's safer there than down here in the crowds and tunnels.*

Rameses sighed. "I needed to get away from my father for a bit," he replied, glancing up to the royal viewing box. "Things are still tense since last nights' dinner."

I still have my head, so it went as well as it could have, Uriah thought. *No doubt more Jackals will be watching Serein. Will they be watching me now?*

"How's your head?" Rameses asked.

"I'm fine. Most of the headaches have stopped, and the light doesn't hurt my eyes anymore."

"The rest was probably good for you." Rameses stared at the back of Uriah's head. "Saints, I almost passed out when I saw you covered in blood and nearly unconscious. It was a pretty grim scene."

Uriah lowered his gaze. "I didn't mean to worry you."

Rameses patted his shoulder. "It's not your fault. There's not much else I can do but worry about my friends." He glanced around down the hallways before flashing Uriah a grin. "Are you down here waiting for that Edolasian and her friend?"

"No. I haven't seen either of them, and I don't want to run into them," Uriah said, frowning.

Rameses laughed, watching the fight as he sat on the stone bench. "I'm sure they're lovely once you get past all that armor," he said.

Uriah rolled his eyes.

"There are more guards than usual here today," Rameses went on, his tone losing its lightheartedness as his smile thinned. "Seems my father is taking this threat seriously."

"There's a chance that Xansas could be here today. Serein said he might show up to watch her matches," Uriah said.

Rameses touched his signet ring, nudging the band with his thumb. "Is it too much to hope that he could be caught today and that this can all be over?"

"I have my men spread through Oyon looking for him."

Serein disarmed Husam, cutting a deep gash along his arm. Sweat shone on her skin, arm muscles tensing as she lunged with another lightning-fast strike. The crowd roared as Husam dodged, clutching his injured arm. The man fell to the ground, screaming as Serein landed another blow. Blood seeping from his cut leg, he threw a weak punch at Serein, and she struck his head with the dagger hilt. The man crumpled into an unconscious heap, the bell proclaiming her victory. A healer rushed into the arena to attend to Husam as Serein sheathed her weapons and left.

Uriah touched the line on his neck, the edge of Serein's blade a fresh memory on his skin.

"You and Serein have been spending more time with each other these past few weeks," Rameses said.

Uriah shot him a look. "It's nothing like whatever you're insinuating," he grumbled.

Rameses' grin returned. "I'm just happy that you two are getting along. Months ago, you were ready to kill her. Who would have thought you two would be working together."

It still doesn't make sense to me, Uriah thought. *Working with an assassin to protect the Malik from another assassin. And helping to protect her children. Like something out of one of Rameses' novels.*

THE SHADOWS OF THE STAIRWELL WRAPPED AROUND SEREIN AS SHE climbed the tower, amber sunlight cutting through the small windows. A faint sunburn warmed the back of her neck. Sweat stiffened her hair, the tunic sticking to her back.

No sign of Xansas again. Am I being too paranoid? Serein thought, rubbing her eyes. *No, I know* he's watching. He wants to see me and for me to know I can't escape his gaze.

Tiny dots danced across Serein's vision as she blinked, reaching the top floor. Movement at the far end of the hall made her stop, hand going to her dagger. Il-Makah glanced in her direction as he waited near her chamber, a book in hand. His smile unfurled as he shut the tome, back straightening.

Serein kept her steps even as she approached. *Why is he waiting outside my chambers? Does this have to do with the king finding out about Xansas?* she thought, insides twisting.

"Ah, good evening, Serein. I heard about your match today," Il-Makah said, his feathery onyx words swirling in the air. "Seems you've been progressing quite efficiently."

"Not watching the matches personally?" Serein asked, stopping by her chamber door. Her gaze went to the book Il-Makah held, the green cover worn. *Poetry by Ibn el-Idrissi. Odd choice for a spymaster.*

He sighed, his hands folded in front of him. "There's so little time to leave the palace. The festival and the Aikhtiar bring so many new people into the city. People that need to be investigated to make sure they aren't threats." Il-Makah's sharp hazel eyes watched her, blades hidden in his soft voice. "It seems that your old master is in Oyon. I find this very interesting, as does His Majesty."

Serein met the spymaster's gaze. "Captain Stormheir told me a Bone Viper assassin was spotted and wanted my help identifying him. Based on the description he gave me, I determined it was Xansas," she told him.

"The sketch you provided is most helpful. After all these years, the White Snake now has a face," Il-Makah said. "Shame we didn't have one sooner."

"Did you come here to ask me about Xansas?" *He's suspicious about why he didn't get the information from my interrogator in Grasdan. If he suspects that Xansas had a hand in it, he'll wonder why.*

The corners of his lips curled upward, wrinkles creasing the edges of his brown skin. "I had hoped you would be back earlier, but it's a bit late to discuss such matters. You're probably tired from your fight and your wali duties," Il-Makah said, rubbing his bald head. "I won't trouble you with questions tonight, but I hope you will join me for tea soon. Perhaps after the Aikhtiar."

"I'll be happy to assist the Golden Jackals in any way I can," Serein told him.

Il-Makah tapped the book across his leg. "You've been most helpful aiding Captain Stormheir to track Xansas down. You must despise the White Snake greatly if you're willing to betray one of your own so readily."

"An assassin like that doesn't come to the city for sightseeing. He poses a threat to the crown, so it's my duty to identify and stop threats. I have no love for Xansas." *I have to get to Xansas first before the Jackals do. I have to be the one to kill him. If he feels cornered, he may attempt to expose me and force me to work with him.* Serein clamped down on the slithering thought, driving a blade through its head before it could latch on.

"Your loyalty's commendable. I'm eager to hear more about your thoughts on tracking Xansas down." The spymaster tucked the book under his arm. "I look forward to your continued victories, Serein. I'd like very much for you to become muharib and work alongside us."

Winking, Il-Makah brushed past her on quiet tan footsteps, melting into the darkness. As his footfalls receded, Serein pulled the key out of her pouch and unlocked the door.

Yellows and oranges from the sinking sun coated the walls as Serein stepped into her chambers. Nala's head lifted as she lounged on the majlis, black-tipped ears swiveling. Serein ran her fingers through the tiger cub's fur, loose white hairs dancing in the air.

Sethos knows now, so I have to be careful, Serein thought, kicking off her boots. *Sneaking around will be more difficult since Il-Makah is paying more attention. I'm still breathing, so I have time to think of what to do next.*

A folded piece of paper lay on the bed, half of Xansas' face staring at her as she stepped into the bedchamber. Serein stopped. Her hand went to her daggers. The silence was colorless as she checked the bathing chamber.

Someone's been in here. Nala's fine, so it must have been someone she recognized, Serein thought, approaching the bed.

She undid her sash and unfolded the wanted poster with covered fingers. Xansas' writing burned against the parchment. Cold dread bubbled up, fingers tightening around the dagger.

I'm impressed with your drawing of me, volchitsa. I was even more surprised when I saw my face across the city. You've made it difficult for me to move around and see you. I was planning to deliver this note myself, but the palace guards have increased. Instead, I had one of my friends deliver it to you. Have you enjoyed digging into the king's secrets? There's so much that's waiting to be uncovered. We could uncover so much more together. It'd be better than spending your time with the princesses and bowing to the whims of princes. Or aiding the red-haired dog of the crown. They'll turn on you if they know your true intentions.
I look forward to watching your matches.
I'm sure you'll make me proud, Serein.

Who is he using to get into my chambers? The door was locked. Did Rizwana leave this? I followed her and found nothing to suggest that she would be working with Xansas. Was Il-Makah in here? He's more than capable of picking a lock and locking it again. If he was in my chambers, did he see this? Or is he the one who left this?

A chill crawled through Serein's veins as she crumpled the letter between her fabric-covered hands. She felt Xansas' smile hovering behind her, white breath hot against her ear. Her breath hitched, skin prickling.

Rizwana and I have the only keys to this room unless there's another I don't know about. He must be using a servant. Or is it a Jackal? They would be the only other ones with keys to all the palace rooms, Serein thought. *It'll be tricky to set a trap without harming Rizwana, and Nala isn't big enough to be a threat. Perhaps I can change the lock somehow.*

Serein unlocked the balcony doors and tore up the wanted poster, watching the pieces drift away in the breeze. She returned to the dim chamber, nails digging into her palm. Each yellow breath fought with the fear trying to climb up her ribcage.

If Sethos knows what I'm doing, I'll have to run. Xansas will be able to come after me without anything to stop him, she thought. *He can't win. Not after everything he's done. If he wants ruination, I'll bring it down on him.*

Chapter Forty-Five
Sister Moons

SEREIN WATCHED THE YELLOW-ORANGE RIBBONS OF SOUND streaking through the air as the arrow left Rameses' bow. Jabbar's hooves kicked up vermillion clouds as he cantered around the large sandy riding arena lined with archery targets. Rameses' arms flexed as he nocked another arrow with gray fletching. The horse turned and galloped down the line, arrow after arrow finding its mark in the center rings.

A few city guards stood outside the fenced ring as people led horses from the stables. Date palms grew around the blue-painted houses of the Gold District, drooping leaves laden with fruit. Birds darted from the trees to the rooftops, swooping to gather ripe fruit and bits of fallen feed from the stalls.

Xansas won't be out here in the heat of the day, but no doubt he has people watching, Serein thought.

Rameses sat back in the saddle as he slowed Jabbar, his white keffiyeh flapping in the wind. He patted his horse's neck and dismounted, hooking his bow to the saddle.

"Not a bad round," Rameses said, gold words shimmering on his smile. "Still a bit slower than I would like, but there's still time before the archery competition."

"Have you ever done this competition before?" Serein asked as the sun burned through her maroon headscarf.

"Not in the Aikhtiar. But I have entered plenty before and done quite well, even won a few," he replied, sweaty hair curling around his ears. "You have seen me practice, so you know that I not only cut a handsome figure on a horse but that my aim's spectacular."

"Seems you've mastered humility as well," Serein said. "Do you want me to give you a kiss next week for good luck?"

He threw his head back and laughed. "I would probably fall off my horse if you did that."

Rameses led Jabbar out of the ring, letting him drink from a water trough. Dusting himself off, Rameses took a sip from his water skin and sat down in the shade of a palm tree.

"Still no luck with your search?" Rameses asked under his breath, wiping away stray droplets from his beard.

Serein noted people walking by and the conversations rising in colored clouds around the stables. "Nothing so far, even with the additional guards and wanted posters," she replied. *Xansas has ways of moving through the city unseen. Could he be using tunnels under the city? A few contacts back in the day mentioned using them as part of Tafall's underworld market. Rameses hasn't found any maps of the old city yet. I should ask Faysal what he knows.*

"Isn't it better that he has to hide? Means he's less likely to make a move without exposing himself," Rameses said, blinking.

"It's always best to know where snakes are. When they're hidden, you don't know when they'll strike," Serein told him.

Rameses nodded, standing. "Seems we are both encountering dead ends. I tried looking for any reference of Scholar Ithamar but have not found anything. If there's a death record, perhaps it's in the House of the Saints."

"Assuming he wasn't buried in an unmarked grave or thrown in the ocean." *More buried secrets. Likely there's no trace of Masud al-Nazari either.* Rameses stroked Jabbar's nose and led the horse down the street.

A flock of birds flew overhead, their shadows skimming the buildings. Serein met the gaze of a brown-haired man passing by. His hazel eyes flashed blue, features shifting for a split second as an opalescent thread curled around his face with a delicate cadence. He melted into the stream of people as Serein stopped.

Was that the Vale from the queen's diffa? Or are there more Immortals hiding in the city? she thought, hand near her dagger. *If it's the same one, is he following me?*

"Everything all right, Serein?" Rameses asked, pulling on Jabbar's reins to stop the horse.

"Have you ever considered the rebels?" Serein replied, lowering her voice.

"As allies? I disapprove of their methods," he said as they continued walking. "They don't seem interested in peace. I don't want to bring further violence to Sarddon."

"Is this because they attacked you?"

He pursed his lips as Jabbar's tail swished. "No. They have attacked innocent people over the years. Innocent villages, traders trying to make a living, soldiers that have surrendered. The last major attack was in Oyon four years ago that killed fifty people. Do you think it's wise to seek out a group that wants to overthrow my father?"

"They want to take back their home from the man who destroyed everything. Their cruelty is a result of oppression and desperation. They could have knowledge about what Sethos is doing, especially if there are spies already in the palace." *They have to know something. It'd be wise to keep an eye on them, especially if they're following me.*

"Perhaps, but I thought you wanted to be cautious about this. Involving rebels seems like an unnecessary risk," Rameses told her, casting a sideways glance, "so I'm surprised you would consider it."

Serein gave him a sharp grin. "Well, I thought my life needed more risk and excitement."

Past a sooq full of pottery stalls, a group of people gathered around a square where a stage was set up. Black, white, and gold banners with moon designs rippled in the wind. Two women moved across the stage, one dressed in a white abaya with metallic whorls and the other in a matching black one. White paint rimmed the eyes of the woman in black, while the one in white had black around hers. A man in green circled the woman in white. The three performers danced around each other against a star-studded background. Shining yellow trills from a ney and the strummed chartreuse notes of an oud wove together in the air.

"Plays about the Sister Moons are popular this time of year. There are several popular theater troupes that perform. The Alriysh Alraaqis group will be putting on a show during the last week of the Aikhtiar. It's worth sticking around to see," Rameses told Serein as they stopped to watch.

The melodic voices in sparkling blue and ruby-red sang over the crowd. The Sister in white spun toward the man in green, handing him a golden lantern. Their song rose and ebbed like waves, crashing lyrics of love and longing:

"Though apart, my heart still knows your song,
In my breath, bones, and blood.
Though the night may be long,
The stars will lead me to you, my beloved."

Something burrowed into Serein's chest, drawing out a memory preserved in the pages lined with flower petals and paint. Astra and Luca standing in the lake, splashing as they chased dragonflies and blue tetras. She had sketched the lines quickly, trying to capture the fleeting moment before it darted away on iridescent wings.

"There's a very good poem about the Sister Moons I enjoy," Rameses went on, gold poking through the tapestry of the song. "I could lend it to you sometime if you like. This version of the story is one most people haven't read and has a bit of information many thought lost. It has a lot of surprising twists and turns."

The smell of lake water and grass lingered in Serein's nose. "That *does* sound intriguing," she muttered.

The man on stage staggered, clutching his chest as red streamers poured past his fingers. He collapsed to his knees, the pale Sister weeping at his side. The cadence of the song shifted, dipping as grief settled into the voices.

If all this works out, I'll return to you in a few years, my Sun and Stars. And I don't intend to be separated from you again, Serein thought, old scars tightening with dull aches.

The scarred woman was shoved forward into the familiar room. Her shackles chafed against her wrists. Dark blood crusted her fists, bruises blue and black flowers on her skin. The woman's back ached from recent whip marks. The noise of the fighting ring came like blows. Red fists, blue jabs, green hits, everything blurring together into a cacophony that shouted for blood.

She watched the other prisoner. A young man with empty eyes and sallow skin, wearing the same marks Grasdan gave a those chained inside its wall. Any youth he had was drained away, leaving a hollow shadow of a person.

Every fight was for survival. Win and receive extra food, the slight favor to avoid the whip. The warden watched next to an archer, his lemon-yellow voice calling out bets. Again and again, the woman found herself with bloody fists, standing over an unconscious body. Fight or die. Over and over until...

A guard lengthened the chains attached to the woman's shackles, the green sound snapping through the haze swirling in her head. She wrapped the chain around the guard's neck, unsheathing his dagger. His strangled mango-colored cry was silenced as she sliced his throat. The body dropped, and the black beast in her chest snarled.

Death moved beside the woman, picking up the guard's soul. "Do you want to die this way?" Death asked, silver words caressing her cheek.

Shouts and steel turned toward the woman, blood roaring in her ears as she locked eyes with the warden. She plunged into the chaos as armed guards rushed at her. Her blade burrowed into a man's soft hazel eye, bloody tears and dark pink screams running down his face as he broke away. The archer fired, and she yanked a man forward by his arm, the arrow finding its home in his chest. The warden pushed his way toward the door.

A hand grabbed her arm, and she whirled around, fist connecting with cartilage. She stabbed his leg and grabbed his head as he fell, twisting. Bones gave way with dark amber snaps. An arrow struck her arm with a yellow orange thump. She winced, red haze coating her vision.

Breaking the shaft in half, the woman followed the warden, leaving bloody footprints on the floor. Sweat stung her cuts. A sword blade gave an orange hiss, and she ducked. A stab to her bearded attacker's armpit dropped him, a red smile carved across his neck as the woman silenced him.

Guards filled the corridor as alarm bells rang out, their peach tolls pounding through the walls. Two men blocked her way. The scarred woman threw the dagger, and it sank into the right guard's arm. The second man hesitated as she closed the distance. She grabbed the short sword at the injured man's side, driving it into the other's groin and slashing downward. The black beast rumbled as it fed off the smell of carnage.

The woman's labored breaths spilled down the front of her shirt, arms trembling as she stumbled. A blade cut her leg, the dull pain breaking through the rushing thoughts. Whirling around, she slashed at his face, a howling apricot-orange sound ripping from the man's chest.

Kill him. Kill him. Kill him, the beast chanted with the alarm bells.

The woman turned a corner, three guards blocking her way. Two lunged at her, wrestling her to the ground. Numbing pain ran through her arm as her elbow struck the stones. She slashed and hacked at anything close—hands, arms, legs, armor. The dagger cut deep into the inner thigh of one of the men, spilling blood across her. The yellow scream built in her throat as she tore herself free. Another slash tore across her back, and she staggered.

Another arrow struck her leg, and she hit the ground. The dagger was pried from her hands. A sapphire crack broke through the ringing in her ears as a whip raked across her back. Fresh veins of pain opened, spilling fire across her skin. Orange and blue laugher flashed across visions of green forests as small hands held hers. Rage burned through her bones, unable to keep despair at bay.

"I should have killed you when you arrived here," the warden said, his dark amber footsteps drawing closer.

Tears escaped as fingers dug into the woman's face, nails scraping her lips. Her teeth snapped down, biting into flesh and bone. Screaming and thrashing, blood slick across her tongue, she jerked her head back. A punch rattled her jaw, and she released the warden's finger as it dangled on the end of the joint.

"You bitch!"

Metal glinted and cold pain carved across her throat, the warden's blood dripping on her face. Death cradled her face as Life appeared beside him, a grim look on his face.

"Here we are again, child," Life said, his bright yellow words melting as the darkness came. "What will you choose this time?"

SEREIN ROLLED TO HER FEET, RAISING ONE OF HER DAGGERS TO block an attack. The orange clash sparked as she kicked out, striking her opponent's ankle with her foot. Dubaku let out a yellow-green groan, stumbling over the arena sands.

She's not going to let up. Her strikes are quick, but the shorter weapon gives me the chance to get in closer, Serein thought as the Ginjarrian's curved khopesh slashed downward. *If she stabs me with that hooked edge, it won't end well for me.*

Serein grabbed a handful of sand as she parried with her dagger's spine. The bronze rings around the Ginjarrian's throat glinted, her bald head shining with sweat and painted with white bird designs. An eagle pendant hung around Dubaku's neck, hitting the scales of her armor.

Serein threw the sand in the woman's face as another slash came for her midsection. *Captain Stormheir would disapprove of my methods, but fighting isn't always elegant,* she thought, slashing upward with the dagger and reaching for the second Twin at her side.

Dubaku dodged a second too late, the rippled steel of Serein's blade cutting a line along her cheek. The Ginjarrian squinted as she disengaged, swiping at the grit in her eyes. Serein rushed forward, feinting right.

A flash of white in the stands caught Serein's attention, and her attack slowed, the shouting of the crowds growing distant in her ears. She scanned the spectators but saw no sign of Xansas.

He's not there. The city guards are in the stands, and everyone knows what he looks like, Serein thought, twisting away from her opponent's sweeping sword. *He won't have anywhere else to hide.*

With a yellow-green shout, Dubaku lunged with a series of quick thrusts and swipes. Serein moved on the balls of her feet. She caught her dagger in the hooked end of the khopesh, jerking the weapon forward. Serein's fist struck the Dubaku's jaw, knuckles striking hard bone. Spit flew, and the woman staggered, eyes rolling back before she collapsed on the sands.

Sweat stung the corners of Serein's eyes as she glanced up at Sethos. The shadows of his viewing box obscured his features, but she felt his burning, gold eyes on her.

Two more fights to go, she thought. *Two weeks for Sethos to make a move.*

Serein sheathed her daggers, shaking out her stinging hand. The tolling of the match bells punched peach holes through the colored cacophony of the spectators as their excitement cascaded down the walls. A healer ran out into the arena to check on the unconscious Dubaku.

A few Edolasians offered their congratulations and slapped Serein on the shoulder as she passed. She nodded, ignoring the prickling along her skin left by their touches. Orchid-colored footsteps crept up from behind, and she whirled around to face Fang.

His dark brown eyes narrowed, lips pulled back in a sneer. The bruising around his face had faded into pale-yellow shadows. His three clansmen flanked him.

"Best watch yourself," Fang hissed, opaque blue words serrated. "You won't have your red-haired friend to help you in the arena."

"I won't need his help dealing with you," Serein replied with a dark smile, hand resting near her weapon. "You bleed like every other man."

Fang's shoulder bumped into hers as he stalked past.

He's making no effort to hide his hatred. It's easier to deal with the visible disdain rather than the hidden rage, Serein thought, brushing her sweaty hair back.

"You're earning me a good deal of coin, *palaúlfa*," the familiar apple-red voice said. Salveig pushed through the throngs toward her, followed by Ragnhildur.

"Partaking in the Sarddonian pastime of gambling?" Serein asked.

Salveig unhooked the dark waterskin from her side, holding it out to Serein. "It's not gambling if the odds are in my favor. Betting on you is the smart choice. Everyone who doesn't is a fool."

Serein took the waterskin, cool water quenching her thirst. Salveig's gaze followed Fang as he walked out into the arena, the roar of the crowds pouring down on him.

"I've heard rumors that he's a distant cousin of the Ascended Emperor," Salveig said, jerking her chin at the arena, "but with how many wives the emperors of Zhao usually have, half of the country probably has royal blood. Their royals love to spout that they're descended from dragons."

"Worried about a Zhao serving the king of Sarddon?" *Having a muharib with royal connections might be useful to Sethos. Another way to possibly find a way into Bar Elenion. Does the king know about Fang's ancestry, or is it just a coincidence?* she thought, putting the stopper back in the waterskin before handing it back to Salveig.

"It hasn't happened before, but given the way things are now, the thought worries me," Salveig replied. "Have you been to Zhao before?"

"Once or twice. Fú Lián is an impressive place. The City of the Floating Lotus wasn't easy to get into since it sits in Sky Lake patrolled by ships. Still, it's not impossible." *Killing a Zhao prince wasn't that impressive since the Ascended Emperor has about a hundred sons. Still, makes for an interesting story.*

Salveig's hazel eyes darted to Serein, sunlight reflecting off the silver earrings. "Seems you've been all over the world," she said.

"My work kept me busy. No shortage of people to kill," Serein replied, crossing her arms.

"Would you go back to it if you had the chance?" Salveig asked.

"No. There are other things I'd like to do with my life." *A life without you, my Sun and Stars, is no life at all.*

Chapter Forty-Six
Story of a Thousand Horses

THE SMELL OF ALCOHOL AND SWEET SMOKE CLOGGED THE AIR OF the tavern. Serein tapped the side of her untouched cup of wine as she sat next to Salveig and Ragnhildur. Small braziers were lit under tall ghalyans packed with fragrant mu'assel. Banded cords snaked from the pipes, puffs of smoke rising as patrons smoked. Raucous colors seeped through the hazy atmosphere.

Salveig poured more dark wine into a cup, dipping a chunk of bread in a dish of red harissa. A basket of puffy coriander bread sat next to a plate of cured meats and meatballs, pickled vegetables, and hummus.

"My deepest apologies," Ragnhildur said, her soft periwinkle voice dripping into her drink. "I failed to achieve victory today."

"Failure isn't the end but a chance to improve. You made it through four weeks of fighting and made the Mother Goddess proud," Salveig replied and clapped her on the back, her apple-red laugh booming across the table. "This may not be Edolasian mead, but it should help."

Serein scanned the faces in the hazy room. *They celebrate victory and defeat. Edolasians love to celebrate everything,* she thought.

"You haven't touched your drink," Salveig said, turning to Serein. "Don't care for the wine?"

Xansas' curved smile reflected in the liquid in the earthen cup, his white, alcohol-laced breath burning in the back of her mind. "I find it best not to cloud my senses," Serein said and pushed the drink toward Salveig.

Salveig grabbed the cup. "You're missing out. It's nothing compared to a nice ale, but no sense wasting it," she replied, knocking the contents back.

"I'm honored that you've invited me to join you tonight instead of the other Edolasians."

"Who said I won't go drinking with them later? The night's young." Salveig laughed as she slammed the cup down.

"So, what's a member of the Edolas nobility doing in Sarddon?" Serein asked quietly.

Salveig's hazel eyes turned to Serein, the smile fading. "What makes you ask that?"

"I know enough of the Edola tongue. You may talk like a soldier, but sometimes your speech changes, becomes more refined. Ragnhildur has a band tattoo and carries a large shield, as Edolasian shield-maidens do. Only the nobility has shield-maidens."

"I suppose I didn't hide my identity as well as I thought. I'm the second princess to the Olhouser throne, Salveig Brynhildur Dahl, daughter of the former queen of Edolas, Inga Unnur Dahl."

"I've been speaking with royalty. Should I curtsy?" Serein gave a tilted smile. *Edolasian royalty on Sarddonian soil. Could it have something to do with the ships trying to get to Bar Elenion? Did someone from Edolas hire Xansas?*

Salveig's earrings sparkled under the light as she slapped her knee. "I can't remember a time when anyone has curtsied to me. I don't think we know how," she said.

"Why would someone like you be here for the Aikhtiar?" Serein asked.

"Given the tensions, I'm sure it looks suspicious. I'm here for the fighting, and I'm interested to go against fighters from across Cemiyon, especially you, *palaúlfa*," Salveig said and reached for her half-full cup of wine. "When I heard the prince had a woman guard, I wanted to see for myself since the Sarddonians have such disdain for women fighting."

Serein grabbed a piece of coriander bread. "What will you do if you win?"

The Edolasian smiled as she drained her cup. "Let me tell you a story. When I turned fifteen, I said that if any man wanted my hand, he'd have to prove himself through combat against me. If he lost, he would give me two acres of land and five horses. So many have tried to best me that I've lost count. Fourteen years later, I have over a thousand horses and two hundred acres of land for them to roam on."

Alcohol kissed Salveig's cheeks, leaving red marks underneath her tan skin.

"You see, I have no need for more wealth or a new title from a foreign king. I just want to fight and see who can beat me," Salveig said, reaching for the earthen tumbler of wine. "The red-headed captain...I'd like to fight seriously with him."

"I doubt Captain Stormheir's considering marriage to anyone besides his work," Serein told her. *She'd probably try to wrestle his clothes off. The look on his face would be priceless.*

"Perhaps I can change his mind." Salveig emptied the pitcher and frowned at it. "We'll need another."

Ragnhildur got up, drawing stares from the patrons as she moved toward the barkeeper.

"Have you seen the capitol city of Olhouser? Forests and fields of sunflowers stretch on for miles." Salveig waved her hand. "This place is so damn hot. And bare. Like it's dead without magic. The air here's different without it."

"When I went to Edolas, it wasn't for sightseeing. The city is a wonder, though," Serein replied. *The northern continent feels more alive than this one. I could even see magic through the ground at times,* she thought. *Could Sethos destroy magic in the northern continent too? Is that his end goal?*

Salveig leaned forward. "People are fearful that what the king has done will spread, that more war is coming because of the ships attempting to reach Bar Elenion," she muttered, the slurred apple-red words dripping into her wine. "The people of Zhao are restless. No one knows what's happening beyond the Fog. Most of the Immortals cling to the Silver Shores and don't venture much outside

Illamatras anymore. Most people aren't allowed to pass through the city into Bar Elenion."

She may know more about what the king's attempting to do in Bar Elenion, Serein thought, watching a dark look enter Salveig's eyes before she blinked it away.

Salveig rested her chin in her hand, head tilted. "It's strange that *you* would want to fight in a competition like this after what's been done to your people."

Serein shrugged, taking a goat meatball and dipping it into the harissa. The spicy sauce burned her throat a bit. "I have my own reasons for fighting. Money and power can be useful weapons."

The Edolasian nodded. Another pitcher was brought over as Ragnhildur returned. "Drink up. Tomorrow, we fight!" Salveig shouted, a few drunk patrons echoing her cheer.

Salveig broke into song, wrapping a muscular arm around Ragnhildur's neck. The Edolasian melody filled bar with undulating red, and other men added to the sound, their voices mixing like churning waves:

"Eyes affixed on wild seas
Where the Mother Goddess' berserkers arose
On crests of breaking surge and crying breeze.
My heart belongs to the ocean's throes."

Serein's mouth curled into a smile. *When was the last time I heard someone singing like this? Feels like a lifetime ago.*

THE MOON WAS EATEN TO A YELLOW HALF AS SEREIN WRAPPED THE blue scarf around her head. The crowded streets faded behind her as she approached the palace wall. Guards passed by as she clung to the shadows, eyes on the secret door. Once the colors of their footsteps vanished, Serein darted across the street.

I might be able to explore the hidden room tonight. There are a few scrolls of Scholar Ithamar I haven't read yet, she thought, reaching for the door. *Maybe finish a few more chapters of* The Illumination of Sarlyria *before the sun rises.*

Teal groaning cut through the darkness as it swung open. She darted back, reaching for her dagger. Rameses slipped out, draped in a gray rida' and wearing simple robes. A sack was slung over his shoulder and his earrings gone.

"Dangerous for a prince to be wandering the streets alone at night. There are assassins at large," she said, and Rameses jumped. *What's he doing out this late by himself?*

"Saints! Serein?" Rameses asked, relaxing.

"What are you doing out here by yourself? Didn't your father forbid you from wandering the streets on your own?" Serein asked and moved her hand away from her dagger.

"He did, but I'm not on my own. I have my guard with me now. Rizwana said you went out for drinks with the Edolasians, and I was going to look for you," he said.

Serein arched an eyebrow. "You were going to wander the city, looking in taverns for me?"

Rameses laughed, the gold sound bright. His dark hair curled against his forehead under his hood. "Probably not every tavern, but I thought I would follow the sound of loud drunken laughter. Edolasians are not known for being quiet. It's fortuitous that I ran into you here."

He gestured for her to follow as he readjusted the sack, smiling. *I shouldn't be out here with him. Too many eyes are watching. Vipers, lions, and jackals are lying in wait,* Serein thought, glancing around. *I guess I won't be doing any reading tonight.*

Serein sighed, following him. The smell of roasting meats and smoke wafted around them, the warm glow of the fires stretching out the shadows. Yellow trills and marigold strings danced in the air as an emerald drumbeat exploded into bright shards. The sounds grew louder as Rameses and Serein passed a gated courtyard lined with palms and purple and white bougainvillea.

People clapped as a man and woman were carried out to the center on decorated seats, glittering jewelry catching the lantern light. The man smiled at the woman clothed in a green and gold takshita and a draping headdress with beads and trails of golden silk. Rouge painted her cheeks, gaze resting on the man. Cheers rose from the guests as the procession came to a stop and the seats were lowered.

A wedding. Gold and green for wealth and blessings, Serein thought, the sounds fading as they walked by.

"This way," Rameses said, pointing to a street on his left.

Serein stared down the sloping street as it cut between the dark buildings. "Taking me down another alley to test me?" she asked.

"Humor me, Serein. I want to talk for a little bit," Rameses replied. "You seem quite friendly with those two Edolasian women who are interested in Uriah."

"Only Salveig has her eye on him. They don't seem interested in bashing my skull in. I suppose that's friendly enough," she said.

"Did Salveig say why she's interested in Uriah?" Rameses asked.

"She wants to test him for marriage." *Hopefully, he owns two acres of land and some horses.*

He laughed, his rida' billowing out as a sea breeze swept through the street. "The poor fellow. I have heard Edolasian women are rough lovers."

Rameses approached a stall and picked up a stout bottle, pointing to a platter of steaming maaqouda. The shopkeeper handed him four fritters in a small reed basket as Rameses slid a few copper dijils into his weathered hand. He readjusted the sack over his shoulder as he tucked the bottle under his arm. Rameses held a maaqouda out to her. The hot potato fritter burned her fingertips, the smell of cumin and turmeric wafting out as she tore it open.

"That Fang is a force to be reckoned with. Today's match was especially brutal," Rameses said to Serein, blowing on the maaqouda. "Why did he cut off that man's hands during his match today?"

"It was to humiliate him," Serein replied. "The belief in Zhao is that one can't enter heaven unless their body is intact. Fang did it so that the man couldn't find rest and would be forced to wander the Void, condemned to madness for eternity. Most people of Zhao wouldn't do such a thing since it goes against their beliefs, so Fang's behavior is unusual. Some of the nomadic tribes are more brutal than others," she said. *A perfect muharib for the Murderous King. Vicious and cruel.*

Rameses grimaced as he tore off a piece of the fritter. "You should be careful then. He already seems to despise you and will most likely try to kill you," he said.

"He'll have to get in line. There's already a long line of people ahead of him."

The city sloped down to the docks, arches carved with wave motifs. Sand swallowed up the streets as the houses dwindled at the edge of the beach. The opaque purple roar of the ocean lapped against the shore, leaving a dusting of froth on the dark sand. Moonlight bled across the waters like oil. People gathered on the beach with torches and paper lanterns. Children stood around their parents, small faces illuminated by the glow of candles. Couples held hands as they sat on blankets, writing out prayers on slips of paper. Men chatted around bonfires as music filled the air with colorful tones.

"This is a long way to go to talk. Thinking of going for a late-night swim?" Serein asked as they navigated through the crowds.

"Not tonight, but if you're interested, I can take you to some of my favorite spots," Rameses replied.

In the distance, Alqamar Palace's towers reached for the sky, soaking up the moonlight along its white stones. Caves dotted the shore like roughened eye sockets half-buried in the sand. Rameses pulled himself onto a jutting lip of a shallow cave, holding a hand out to her. She took it, suppressing a shiver, and hauled herself up beside him. Below, the churning sea stretched toward the dark horizon. Shells and small fishbones deposited by birds and crashing waves littered the ledge.

Rameses settled on the ledge, legs dangling over the edge. He dropped the sack beside him and pulled out a small pouch of pistachios and a small glass lantern. Striking the flint, a tiny spark caught and lit the wick. Serein brushed aside loose rocks as she sat.

He opened the bottle and took a swig before holding it out to her. "It's prickly pear juice," Rameses said.

Serein's nose wrinkled as the smell of alcohol hit her. "That's been fermented."

"Yes, but it's more juice than alcohol. Not too sweet. Try it."

Serein grabbed the bottle, sloshing the contents around. "If you're trying to get me drunk enough to loosen my lips, you'll have to do better." Sniffing it, she took a small sip. The tart and sweet flavor left a warm trickle down her throat. *Not bad,* she thought, handing it back to Rameses. *Not poisoned.*

"I know better than to try and trick you," Rameses said, head tilted back to the sky. He cracked open a pistachio, popping it into his mouth. "You know...I don't think I have seen you drink alcohol."

Serein picked up a broken seashell near a rock and turned it over in her palm. "It's not to my tastes," she said and tossed the shell out of the cave. *Killing the problem works much better than drinking it away,* she thought, inhaling the salty tang of the sea.

"I figured you would enjoy drinking," he said.

"Because I kill people and was in prison?"

Rameses shrugged. "We all have a preconceived image of what a person is like based on their occupation," he said.

Serein reached for the bag of nuts, scooping a few into her hand. "A spoiled prince with little regard for anyone but himself. Considerate only when it suits him. Charming, handsome, smooth talking, overly optimistic," she told him.

He smiled as he rubbed his beard. "You said I'm handsome."

"Don't read into it," Serein said, rolling her eyes as she split the shells apart, pulling out the green nuts.

"But you're not fooled by appearances since you have that uncanny ability to read people," Rameses said. "The rest of us are not so good at reading people. That's why we talk and build relationships so that they trust us and tell us things."

Pistachio shells fell into the sea below as Serein discarded them. "If you did less talking and more observing, you'd learn a lot more about people."

Rameses sat up, arms resting on his knees. "You will have to teach me."

She popped a few pistachios in her mouth. "You can start by shutting your mouth."

"Hilarious," Rameses said. "Why don't you like alcohol?"

The memory came unbidden, slamming into her. The green eyes hovered over her, and nausea stung her stomach. "I got drunk once and blacked out. When I woke, I didn't remember anything. I don't like not knowing things," Serein replied. "Did you bring me out here just to talk about my drinking habits?"

432

Rameses set the bottle down and reached into the sack, pulling out two bags made of thin blue paper and a charcoal stick. "I thought I would show you more about Sarddonian culture. The prayer lanterns are an important part of the moussem for the Sister Moons. It's said that this was how the Light Sister used to communicate with her lover. It's now become a way of sending prayers to the Saints."

Rameses pushed aside the bag of nuts, laying out a few slips of paper. Two small candles rolled over the uneven rocks, stopped by a handful of thin reeds. Serein looked over the small tin of acacia gum glue, fire starter materials, the small knife, and the spool of twine.

"Crafting isn't what I thought I'd be doing tonight," Serein said. *Embroidery and lantern making. I'll have new things to show you, my Sun and Stars,* she thought, picking up a few reeds.

"Glad I can still surprise you," Rameses said, gold sprinkling into his lap. "So, you'll build a frame out of the reeds, gluing them together with the acacia gum."

He began constructing the rectangular frame, sticking the amber-colored resin around the joints. Rameses slid the paper bag over the frame, connecting it by poking holes in the ends and tying them down with bits of twine. The candle sat in the middle of the frame's bottom on a large glob of resin. When it was finished, Rameses held it up with a grin.

"Not bad for a rough construction. Imagine what I can do with a little more time," Rameses said, watching Serein as she copied his design.

The acacia gum stuck to her fingers. "Did you do this often as a child?" Serein asked, light plum-colored creases shuffling off the papers as she picked them up.

"Many times. When I was younger, we would gather in the riads by the Royal House of the Saints and light lanterns. I once wished for a pet roc, but my cousin told me that they no longer existed. I cried." His voice drifted, a memory grabbing his attention. "My father used to join us back then...Now, we don't do it as much. Usually, it's just me, Rahim, Rasima, and my mother."

What did Sethos pray for? Forgiveness for his sins or was it for power? Serein thought, setting down her finished lantern.

Rameses held out a slip of paper to her, the charcoal stick leaving black smudges on his fingers. "You write a prayer and attach it before lighting the lantern."

Serein raised an eyebrow. "You don't strike me as the praying sort," she said.

He picked up the bottle of prickly pear wine, taking a sip. "I'm not as devout as my mother, but I still believe in the Saints and Alkhaliq. I try to lead an honest life and say my prayers. I do a cleansing ceremony every few months so that when I die, and my heart is put to Alkhaliq's white flames to burn the impurities, there will be more good remaining than bad. There's a library in the Heavenly Palace in the Eternal Oasis that contains all the information that was, is, and will be. I would like to read for all eternity, so that thought keeps me living a righteous life."

"Only you would think an eternity of reading is heavenly." *The library sounds like the Halls of Nolmë, the Light who collects all the knowledge of the world.*

A smile crossed his lips. "I can think of no greater pleasure in the afterlife."

"I'm sure you did a lot of things you needed to be forgiven for," Serein said.

Rameses smiled. "I got into my fair share of trouble. I would not say I was a hellion, just adventurous. My mother would make us go every week to the cleansing ceremonies when I was younger. The bitter herbs we had to eat made me want to throw up."

"What do you do for this cleansing ceremony?" Serein asked.

"The Houses of the Saints have a special room with a pool," Rameses said. "You have to recite your sins and eat bitter herbs. Then you say the writ of forgiveness twelve times and submerge yourself twelve times in the water. Then you're given a piece of honeycomb to eat in remembrance of Alkhaliq's mercy."

Does Sethos seek forgiveness for the crimes he's committed? Would there even be enough water to wash away the oceans of blood he's spilled? Serein thought as the charcoal stick left orange curls on the paper.

Rameses swirled around the last bit of drink. "Do you want the rest?" he asked.

Serein shook her head. She rolled up the scrawled prayer and tied it to the bottom of the lantern. Dark forests flashed behind her eyes, sunlight filtering through the branches. A lake shimmering and a house resting in the shade of a massive tree. Two children splashed in the waters, sky-blue and sunset-orange laughter sparkling through the air. Their faces faded in and out of focus, and Serein's throat tightened.

"What did you write for your prayer?" Rameses asked, sweeping away the memory.

"That's a secret for me and whatever holy ears receive it," Serein replied.

Rameses snapped off a piece of twine, folding his slip of paper. Opening the glass lamp, he lit the candle wick from the flame. The lantern glowed in his hands. His eyes followed the floating light, sadness swimming in the golden pools.

The lantern floated into the air, joining the hundreds of glowing embers rising over the ocean. Heat bled through the paper as Serein released it. Her fragile prayer rose out of reach as it drifted to join the stars. A soft warmth curled in her chest, longing to float away with the lights.

*Three years. Assuming I survive this Aikhtiar. If I survive Xansas...*she thought, the ocean crashing below in opaque purple bursts. *I'll get back to you, my Sun and Stars.*

She caught Rameses staring at her, the shadow of a smile resting on his face. "You continue to surprise me," he said, his robes billowing around him. "You're very different from who I thought you would be."

"What are you expecting me to say in response to that? 'You've changed my heart, and I didn't know what friendship was until I met you'?" Serein asked, wiping the charcoal residue off her fingers.

"If you said something like that, I think I would need to be checked by a healer to make sure I was not hallucinating. I'm not expecting you to respond. I just wanted you to know."

Ocean spray dampened the hem of Serein's robes. A thin smile crossed her face. "I'm less likely to hold a dagger to your throat, although some days the thought is tempting."

"I'm pleased that you think of me so often," Rameses said with an airy laugh. His shoulders slumped, staring out at the ocean.

The waves continued to crash in the distance, rushing at the cliff face and shattering into white foam and cold droplets. "Your prayer was for your father," she said. "You want what remains of him back, but that won't undo what he's done."

Rameses glanced at his palm, rubbing the faded red mark from their blood pact. "I have to believe he can be forgiven. You have changed. The same has to hold true for my father."

Sethos chose to become a monster. He likes the taste of power too much to give it up.

And you chose to become the blade that will kill him, becoming a monster yourself, volchitsa, Xansas said. *Will you turn into the beast your children will fear?*

Serein pulled her robes tighter, standing. "It's getting late. Ilderim and your other wali are probably tearing apart half of Oyon looking for you."

Rameses gathered the materials and shoved them back in the sack. He cinched the pouch of pistachios and picked up the empty bottle. "I didn't just pray for my father. I also prayed for your safety," he said, meeting her gaze. "For what it's worth, I hope your prayer is answered too."

Serein glanced back at the caves. "It's probably best not to return to the palace the way you came if you don't want your father finding out. I have a feeling that the secret door won't remain secret for long."

Rameses looked back at the palace. "Did you find some new way to get in?" he asked, holding up the glass lantern.

Serein climbed down from the rocky ledge, boots sinking into the sand. "It's not a new way. More like a way that's been forgotten," she said. "Best put out that light."

Rameses' brow scrunched. "Why?"

"Because we don't want to be seen."

Chapter Forty-Seven
Secrets of the Dead

SEREIN FOLLOWED THE CRAGGY CLIFFSIDES AS RAMESES BLEW OUT the light, coming to a dark opening hidden behind a jagged slope of rocks. Cool ocean breeze whipped around her as she scanned the palace wall for guards.

"The tunnel is slippery and dark, so watch your step," she told Rameses as she pushed open the rusted gate. It let out a teal scraping noise.

"Where does this go?" Rameses asked, following her through the opening.

"To the catacombs," Serein said.

Shadows closed in around them as Serein navigated the catacombs, hands traveling along the damp walls. The muffled purple sound of the ocean rolled around the corner as the tunnel curved. Water dripped between the cracks in the ceiling, trickles melting into the damp ground. The stone coffins became sealed holes in the rocky walls marked by worn plaques with eroded names. Rats skittered unseen with pink and coral trails.

The faint glow of a lantern seeped around the corner, and Serein paused, Rameses bumping into her. "Sorry," he whispered as she put a hand up. "What's wrong?"

"Someone's here. Probably one of the acolytes they send down here to copy the death records in the archives room." She nodded to the closed door further down the hall. "Keep quiet, and we shouldn't have any problems."

"And if we're caught?"

"The goal isn't to get caught or be seen, but I'm sure you've become a convincing liar these past few months. You'll find a way to sweet-talk whoever we encounter."

Serein and Rameses crept past the door, faint trickles of pale purple shuffling seeping out from under the door crack. The lantern light stretched down the corridor, throwing their shadows over the tombs. Candles burned on the ledges, smoke from the censers curling through the musty air.

Teal groaned at the far end of the catacombs, the sound bouncing down the stairs. Serein froze as footsteps echoed in the staircase, quiet voices drawing closer. Her eyes darted around as she pushed Rameses back toward the corridor.

"Someone's coming," she whispered. *At least five. Why would that many acolytes be down here? It's not part of their usual prayer schedule.*

"What do we do?" Panic rose in Rameses' voice, the contents of his bag rattling.

As the footsteps grew louder, a door opened in the direction of the records room. "We need to hide." Serein dragged Rameses toward the tombs.

"Where?" Rameses asked.

Serein went to the large tomb with a cracked lid bearing the names "Allamu" and "Raqiyah," moving aside the larger chunk that was already askew. Jagged silver-white scraping clawed at the air. The dank smell of rot and mildew escaped, the dark outline of two shrouded shapes lying in the bottom visible in the low light of the lamps.

"In here. Now," Serein told him as the voices drew closer.

Rameses paled. "We cannot hide in there!" he said, voice rising. "That's a—"

"Just get inside before we're caught," Serein hissed, pulling the edge of her headscarf over her nose.

Swallowing, Rameses peered through the opening in the tomb, muttering a prayer. Sethos' blood-red voice seeped down the stairs with dark purple and sienna footsteps, and Serein's heart pounded in her chest.

"Hello?" A pale green voice drifted down the corridor.

"Rameses!" Serein said through her teeth as the sounds closed in around them.

Rameses climbed into the wide tomb, clutching his bag to his chest. Serein tucked herself in beside him, bones shifting beneath them. She ignored the dull pain poking at her side and Rameses' legs pressing against her. His frantic gold breath filled the space between them as she shifted the lid back over the opening, plunging them into darkness. Faint threads of light bled through the cracks and fell across the gaping skull next to Rameses' face. It peered through its torn shroud, the dried flesh stretched over the bones.

Rameses flinched, knees bumping into Serein's legs. "Saints—"

Serein clamped a hand over his mouth, his warm breaths tickling her sweaty palm. "Breathe through your mouth quietly," she whispered, yellow words trickling onto the bones beneath them. "Don't throw up." *It'd be better if he passed out. He'd make less noise.*

Armor shifted in orange-red creaks, boots hitting the ground in yellow-orange, sienna, bright white, and pale red colors. Shadows passed over the tomb, and Rameses sucked in a breath.

"Hello? Is anyone there?" a man with a pale green voice asked. "Oh, Y-your Majesty. Forgive me! I didn't know anyone was here."

Rameses stiffened. "A bit late for most acolytes to be awake," Sethos said, red voice rumbling through the crypt a few yards away.

"I was just copying the death records, Your Majesty. Can I assist you with anything?"

"No. I wish to visit my brother. Leave for a bit. You can return to your work when I am finished. I will not be long. My guards will escort you out."

"Of...of course, Your Majesty."

Hurried footsteps passed by, followed by the guards. The stench of death seeped through the fabric of Serein's headscarf. Something shifted by Serein's leg and muted coral squeaks sparked in the darkness. Tiny claws caught on her trousers as a rat crawled up onto her leg. Rameses jerked as a second one appeared on his shoulder.

Goosebumps ran across her flesh as she grabbed his shoulder, grip tight in silent warning. *Great. Rats. This keeps getting better.*

Silence crept in as seconds filled the tomb, turning into quiet minutes. Rameses shut his eyes as Serein removed her hand. Her limbs ached as her muscles remained tense, free hand sliding to her dagger. The rat scurried over her hand, moving up her arm.

Why is Sethos down here? If he doesn't leave before the rats start trying to eat us, this may turn into a very dangerous situation, she thought, sweat coating her palms.

A Silver-white grinding sound and a red grunt broke the quiet. "I am sorry about this, akhi. This is not how things were supposed to be," Sethos said, his usually steady voice cracking.

What's he moving? Serein strained to hear. The rat moved near her ear, whiskers tickling her cheek, and her grip tightened around the dagger. *Breathe. Being discovered by Sethos is worse than rats.*

Loose bones shifted as another rat crawled out of the skull's mouth, paws gripping stained teeth. Rameses' eyes opened, a sharp, gold gasp escaping. Serein's hand shot out and covered his mouth again Sethos' dark purple footsteps approached. The lantern light was swallowed up by shadows, and her heart leapt. Her breath stilled, fingers digging into Rameses' skin.

Now's your chance. End him now and leave his body for the rats to eat, Xansas hissed.

Two rats skittered out through the larger cracks, and the quiet green whisper of a blade leaving its sheath turned Serein's blood to ice. A blade struck stone in an orange burst, and a pained coral squeal followed.

"Wretched creatures," Sethos muttered, red words dripping through the cracks in the tomb lid.

The Malik's footfalls dissolved into tense silence, every sound of his boots against the stairs loosening the coiled knot in Serein's chest. A few minutes later, the acolyte's green muttering passed by, followed by a teal creak.

Rameses moved, his nervous breath trembling. "Serein..."

"Not yet," she said through her teeth, giving him a sharp look. Rameses trembled as the rats continued moving over them.

Serein counted the minutes on her breath as goosebumps ran

along her skin. When the shroud of silence grew thick in her ears, Serein reached into the pouch at her belt and pulled out the tiny square mirror, angling it up through the larger crack. Shadows from the flickering flame moved across the crypt. No guards. No Sethos. Empty.

She pulled her hand back, putting the mirror away. "Stay as quiet as you can," Serein whispered, shoving the lid aside. Dust and the scraping sound fell on her like dirty snow.

Serein climbed over the side and shook off the stillness. Rameses jerked upright, swatting the rat off his shoulder as he stumbled out with jerking movements. He swiped at his robes as the rat skittered away. His head snapped back to the corpses in the tomb, chest heaving as he backed away. Sweat shone on his skin, dust, flakes of dark mold, and bits of death shrouds clinging to his clothes. Rameses braced himself against the wall before doubling over, vomiting up golden groans and chunks of food behind the tomb.

She stiffened, looking around as she grabbed his arm and pulled him toward the shadows. "Quiet. Breathe, Rameses." *Hopefully, no one will see the vomit.* A rat darted out, sniffing the mess on the ground. *Maybe the rats will take care of it.*

Rameses leaned against the wall, gagging as he shivered. Serein dragged the lid back in place. "Saints..." he gasped, eyes glistening as he wiped his mouth with the back of his hand. "I was on corpses. The stench..." Rameses clamped his mouth shut. "How are you fine?"

"You get used to the sight of death in its many forms," Serein muttered, dusting herself off. "Did you enjoy getting acquainted with your relatives?"

Rameses let out a strangled sound. "Those were my grandfather's relatives, a great-aunt and uncle, I believe...I never met them. Does this smell ever come out of clothes?"

Serein glanced at the dead rat on the ground, its blood spreading across the stones. Crackling flames whispered in her ears, the smell of burning wood and flesh overtaking the incense. The burn mark on her side twinged. She blinked, watching as Rameses stared off at something unseen.

He's a child of light, volchitsa. *He can't survive in darkness like we can. His soft heart bleeds too easily.*

"Does your father usually come down here?" Serein asked.

"I..." Rameses swallowed, clearing the tremble from his voice, "I don't know. After my uncle was buried here, I cannot recall him ever visiting his tomb. It seemed too painful."

Serein glanced at Salman's crypt, noticing the disturbed dust on the lid and bits of fine grit around on the ground. *It sounded like Sethos was moving something around the tomb. Was there something inside he hid with the corpse?* she thought. *I didn't think to check inside, but I should have. Am I missing answers that are right under my nose?*

Glancing around, Serein approached the tomb. With a grunt, she pushed the heavy stone slab aside. The silver-white scraping noise rumbled like low thunder in her ears. *Hopefully the acolyte won't hear...*

"Serein!" Rameses said. "What are you doing?! Haven't we desecrated the dead enough?"

"Your father saw fit to disturb your uncle, and I want to know why," Serein replied, arms burning as she moved the lid.

The noise faded through the catacombs, and Serein peered into the tomb. Empty darkness stared back, water stains and patches of mold covering the inside.

"Either your dead uncle is prone to midnight strolls, or his body has been removed," she said, straightening.

Rameses came over, brows knitted together. "I don't understand...He was buried. I remember the funeral. I saw the bodies," he muttered. "This doesn't make sense."

"Did you see their faces?"

"I..." Rameses' brow creased as he paused. "They had been wrapped in shrouds because of how bad their wounds were...so I never saw their faces."

"There's no guarantee then that your aunt and uncle and their child were actually buried here. Those bodies might have been substitutes." *Does this mean that Salman wasn't killed? Or that his body never made it to this tomb?*

A flicker of hope colored Rameses' face. "Do you think my uncle's death was staged?"

"I don't know. I believe they were killed, but for some reason, your uncle's body isn't where it should be."

Her words deflated Rameses, his shoulders slumping as his

fingers went to where the ring usually was. Serein moved to the tombs of Nasr, and Muminah and Zaid. The dust remained undisturbed, the tar-like seal unbroken.

"You're not going to open those tombs, are you?" Rameses asked.

"They look unopened, but now I wonder if there are bodies in them," she replied. *If they're empty, then that creates more questions. Sajjad had notes on their wounds and deaths, so he had to have seen their bodies. Unless he's in on this. But Sethos doesn't let those who know too much live, so it seems more likely that the former king and queen were killed, and their corpses moved later. But why?*

Rameses let out a shaky gold breath. "Please...not tonight. I think we should head back. I want to bathe and wrap my head around...all this."

Serein met Rameses' gaze. His eyes swam with confusion, hands trembling as he wrung them together. *There's a lot more going on here than I thought. If Salman's body isn't here, where did Sethos put it? And what was he keeping in this tomb instead?*

Chapter Forty-Eight
The Wolf & the Mayfly

THE GROUND SCRAPED THE SCARRED GIRL'S SKIN AS THE WHITE Snake's knife hissed, orange slicing the air as it slashed her arm. Green eyes cut through her hopes of freedom as he snatched her in the night. Around her, the shadowed faces of assassins formed an inescapable ring. The pretty face of the Poison Flower as she was held back by the large assassin with one eye, her rosy words trying to reach the scarred girl. The tall Brown Adder with a pudgy nose who had seen the girl flee watched from behind the White Snake, her smile twisted.

"After everything I've given you, you tried to run," the White Snake hissed, white voice an edged weapon.

The girl jabbed at his side, her knuckles connecting with his ribs. His pale face twisted as he grabbed her arm, wrenching her aside. Each pale-yellow breath was a desperate whispered prayer that couldn't escape the stone walls of the mountain citadel.

Blinding pain seared through the cuts, tongues of fire radiating under the girl's skin as she sank to her knees. The air dragged its nails across her face, the shifting of her clothes like thorns as poison made its way through her veins.

The White Snake grabbed the scarred girl, and she screamed, his touch like fire. Voices slurred, becoming a rushing river she wanted to plunge into to cool her burning body. Her clothes ripped as the White Snake forced her down. A glowing orange viper hovered above, the smell of burning iron *stinging her nose. It shimmered before striking her shoulder. Burning flesh, yellow screaming, fiery tears, blinding pain.*

"Bring her to my room." The white words followed the girl into darkness.

The days bled together in threads of agony. Cool hands traveled over the girl's scarred skin, bringing relief from the burning. In the darkness, she longed for the cold bliss, but through the cracks of consciousness, nauseating terror arose. The white voice brushed her ears with lulling tones, kisses trailing her throat.

"You will always be mine, volchitsa. *You can run, but I'll always find you."*

She grabbed hold of her fear, anger sharpening it into a knife. When lucidity greeted her, she carved into the moon's face, a red curtain unfurling down his cheek. The moon unwound into a snake, fangs dripping and green eyes blazing.

His hand clamped over her mouth, hair hanging like snowy threads. "This is why you are a wolf. Vicious even when injured. This is why I love you," the White Snake said, coiling around her. Ruby drops fell onto her face, mixing with her tears.

Something black stirred inside the girl, forming teeth and claws. It growled promises of blood and steel that would one day crush the head of the viper, his death already signed on her skin.

SEREIN BLINKED AGAINST THE SUNLIGHT AS SHE ENTERED THE arena. Mayte stalked out from the opposite side, anger dripping off her movements. Mayte's hand rested on the short sword at her side, thick leather vambraces running up her arms.

Serein scanned the spectators. *He won't pass up an opportunity to watch his two assassins fight each other,* she thought, the sun burning her skin.

The matchkeeper checked their weapons, turning over all the knives Mayte had.

"Well, Mayte, is this everything you hoped for?" Serein asked, the pale-yellow Sarlyrian drifting across the sands.

"Shut up," Mayte snapped, her muddy brown voice rising with anger as she gripped her sword.

"Already losing your composure, Mayfly?" Serein jeered.

"Don't call me that!" Mayte spat.

The matchkeeper left the arena, and the dark peach sound of the starting bell rang out. Mayte swung her sword, moving fast across the sands. Serein dodged as the glint of a metal came from her right in a flash of orange. She focused on the small knife in Mayte's left hand. The blade scraped against Serein's raised vambrace as she twisted away.

Serein unsheathed her right dagger, swinging it upward in an arc. The tip nicked Mayte's cheek, drawing a line of blood. She jabbed her elbow into Mayte's diaphragm before skirting away. Mayte threw her knife at Serein's face. The orange whistle passed by Serein's ear as Mayte lunged.

She has the smaller hidden knives beside the ones across her chest. Vambraces, trousers, boots, sheath strapped around the back of her waist.

Mayte drew her sword, connecting with the back of Serein's dagger. She kicked at Mayte's knee before she could reach for another knife. A muddy brown hiss rattled out. Serein deflected the sword as it came back around, sweeping Mayte's foot out from underneath her.

The excitement of the crowd spilled out into the arena as Mayte hit the ground. *Don't want to drag this out. I can remove Mayte and have one less obstacle,* she thought, pinning Mayte down, knee on her stomach, and boot on her sword hand.

If you want to remove a threat, you have to kill it.

Mayte spat in Serein's face, eyes brimming with rage. *She watched me leave, knowing what he'd done, and still betrayed me. I could have escaped if it hadn't been for her,* Serein thought, blinking to dislodge the memory trying to claw its way up. She felt the fiery pain on her skin and the brand burning her shoulder.

Mayte's free arm was a blur as she tried to land a blow. She grabbed Mayte's wrist, and a dull pain needled through the burned scar tissue. Glancing down, Serein saw the small knife dug into her side. She rammed her fist into Mayte's nose, cartilage crunching under her knuckles. Specks of blood flew through the air as Mayte howled as she threw Serein off, pulling the knife free.

Serein backed away, her hand coming away red. Blood ran down

Mayte's face as she scrambled to her feet, sword raised and the bloody knife in hand.

The Brown Adder has fangs. Not a deep wound. Minimal blood loss. If she'd been allowed to use poisons, this would've been a bigger problem, Serein thought.

You were distracted, Xansas said.

"Not so perfect, are you?" Mayte sneered, wiping blood off her mouth.

Mayte charged, sword aimed at Serein's stomach in a whirl of fury and flying weapons. Steel flashed as Mayte jabbed at Serein's arm. The arena wall drew closer as Serein danced backward, deflecting the attacks. The taunts and excited shouts of the crowd rang in Serein's ears.

Serein leapt up as Mayte swung her sword, reaching for the metal ring embedded in the wall above her head. The blade hit against the stones as Serein swung herself around, kicking Mayte's chest. Serein pushed off the wall past Mayte, plunging her dagger into the assassin's right shoulder.

Serein righted herself as she landed behind Mayte, brown screaming smeared across the air. "What do you have that I don't?!" Mayte snarled, blood running down her arm as she tried to keep her sword raised. "Xansas told me I'd become a great assassin and that he was proud of me. Then he only looked at you! It was always about you!"

Mayte sucked in a rattling breath, her lips quivering as she staggered. *You're special, volchitsa, because you refused to die. Born from despair, you rose from it. And you didn't break.*

The blood rushed through Serein's ears as her stomach twisted. She grabbed Mayte's right wrist as she went to draw another throwing knife, kneeing the assassin in the stomach. As Mayte doubled over, Serein struck her in the jaw and forced her into the ground, knuckles throbbing. She yanked Mayte's arm upward, slamming her foot down above the elbow. The bone snapped, and Mayte screamed.

"Do you think he'll still want you after you lose?" Serein asked, the pale yellow Sarlyrian dragging across Mayte's face.

Mayte glared at her through the tears and blood. She grabbed another knife with her left hand, thrusting forward. Serein smacked Mayte's wrist aside and kicked her down, boot pressing against her injured arm.

"You think I wanted nights of pain? That I wanted to be poisoned and cut?" Serein whispered, the dagger blade pressed against Mayte's face. "I trusted him, and he drugged and raped me. I escaped, but you told him I fled! If you had wanted me gone, then you should have kept your mouth shut."

"I wanted him to kill you," Mayte hissed through her teeth.

The anger bubbled over as Serein stared into the murky brown. She cut Mayte's cheek, crimson smearing with tears. Mayte squirmed as Serein pressed her knee into her chest.

"If you want to be like me, you need more scars," Serein said, dragging the dagger along Mayte's arm.

The white laughter echoed in Serein's ears. *See? You're just like me,* volchitsa. *Vicious and cruel. I've taught you well.*

Serein's throat tightened, rage dripping past her teeth as she swiped the blade across Mayte's throat. Blood spurted back on Serein's face as a gurgled scream pierced the air.

She stood and wiped the dagger on her trousers. "Now you're just like me, Mayfly," Serein muttered.

"I won't let you hurt him," Mayte choked and clutched at her throat, voice a crumbling whisper.

"I'll do more than hurt him. I'm going to kill him," Serein said, slipping the Twin back into its sheath.

The match bell rang, peach knells slamming into her. The wound in Serein's side throbbed with each step, blood trickling down her leg. A few guards and two healers rushed past her into the arena.

Xansas doesn't tolerate failure. He'll probably kill Mayte himself or abandon her, Serein thought, stepping into the shade of the coliseum's interior.

She ducked into one of the side rooms and leaned against a nearby water pump. A stream of cool water burbled out in opaque purple ripples as she cranked the handle, splashing her face to wash away the blood and grit. The adrenaline drained away, leaving a bitter aftertaste.

Serein's heavy yellow sigh crumpled to the ground. She sat on the bench and unstrapped her cuirass armor. The tunic stuck to her skin, a patch of crimson bleeding through.

I let my emotions get the better of me...

Uriah's gray footsteps approached. He stared down at her, arms crossed. Sweat beaded across his forehead underneath his white keffiyeh, a layer of dust clinging to his uniform.

"The look on your face suggests you're disappointed, Captain Stormheir," Serein said. "Seems you've forgotten that I'm a killer."

"Were you trying to kill her?" he asked.

The green voice seeped into her shadow. "If that was my intention, she wouldn't be alive," Serein replied. "Mayte failed, and she's a liability to Xansas now. He may try to kill her since she's compromised. Killing her might have been kinder."

You shouldn't leave any alive, volchitsa. Xansas' voice wrapped around her, his strong grip on her shoulder.

Uriah glanced out of the room. A pair of Ginjarrians in red armor laughed as they walked by. "They'll take her to the nearby House of Healing. I'll be sure to have guards there to watch her and take her in once she's recovered," he said.

"It's only a matter of time before someone recognizes the brand on Mayte. Be careful with her. She's unpredictable when she's desperate."

The healers rushed by with Mayte on a stretcher, guards flanking them. A rag was wrapped around her throat to staunch the bleeding.

I would've ended up just like her...I was just like her. Serein's stomach twisted. *She clings to the delusion that he loves her because, without it, she'll have nothing left.*

Serein lifted her shirt to reveal a shallow wound along her burned side. She dug into her belt pouch and pulled out a folded cloth. Dunking it in the water, she pressed it against her side, trails of red dripping onto the ground.

Uriah's gaze lingered on the burn marks, questions gathering in his eyes like clouds. "You need to get that wound looked at," he said, gesturing to her side.

"It's not one of the worst ones I've received," Serein replied, lowering her shirt. "A few stitches should do."

Serein wiped her hands on her trousers as she tucked her armor under her arm. She got up and headed down the corridor, the dull ache spreading up her torso.

If Xansas was here, would he show his face to let me know he was watching?

"Where are you going?" Uriah asked, following after her.

"To the inn where Mayte's staying," she replied. "I'm going to sneak into her room and see if there's anything useful before Xansas gets to it or the Jackals discover where she's been." *Questions will be asked about our connections once the Jackals catch wind that Mayte's a Bone Viper. She isn't much of a threat right now, but she could still say something that might incriminate me. Have I already been backed into a corner? Too much is happening too quickly...*

"Is that a good idea to do with your injury?"

"You can always come along and keep watch, O knight in shining armor."

Uriah rolled his eyes, muttering in Wendish. Music floated through the streets from stringed instruments and drums like colorful fish darting by, broken by the chatter from the nearby bazaar. Sellers sat on rugs along the side of the street, selling decorative pots, woven tokens of the Saints, colorful woven baskets, and wooden toys. Floral fragrances and the scent of spices wafted over the smell of horses tied by the square's fountain.

Orange-red shavings rolled off Uriah's chainmail. "Will you be fine to walk back to the palace?" he asked.

Serein pressed the cloth harder against her side. "All she did was put a knife in my side. I've had my throat slit and my ribs fractured. The slit throat was hard to come back from."

"How are you able to joke about that?"

She glanced at him. "It's better than drowning in despair. I have these scars to remind me that I've lost too much to stop moving forward. The past always finds a way to track you down no matter how far you try to run. I tried hiding for five years, but the shadows found me anyway."

Uriah fell silent, his right index finger twitching as he adjusted his white sash. Serein stopped to check the cut as the blood stopped oozing out.

"I know you despise Xansas, but why would Mayte be so devoted to a man like him? Why would anyone follow him?" Uriah asked, green words spinning in the wind like leaves.

"Most of the people he found, children and adults, were crushed by the war and were searching for something to live for. He gave us purpose," Serein said, lowering the edge of her tunic. "His cruelty wasn't hidden—some even respected it because he was effective and allowed them to be monsters without shame."

Serein licked her dry lips.

"Xansas made us believe that we'd never feel powerless again. I never saw that man afraid. I felt like I had a choice to do something and had the skills to fight back. That was before I realized what he really was."

She ducked down a side street, the domes of Alqamar Palace shining in the distance. Exhaustion carved through her, making each step heavier.

*I should talk to Eneca. Mayte shouldn't have been able to rattle me so much...*Serein thought. *There are too many things I need to deal with. Finding missing bodies. Xansas. Mayte. What Sethos is hiding.*

"Uriah, I thought I saw your red mop. Keeping the city safe?"

The bright orange voice pattered down the street behind Serein like a bounding cat. They turned as Rajiya walked up, the basket on her hip filled with vegetables, a dead chicken, and bundles of spices.

"Where's Rameses gone off to?" she asked, reaching up to kiss Uriah's cheeks. He gave a sheepish grin.

"He's uh busy," Uriah told her, finger twitching at his side.

Rajiya fixed him with a look as she adjusted her green headscarf. "I'm sure he is." Her gaze darted to Serein. "Seems you two know each other. Are you the scarred Ravanassë competing in the Aikhtiar I hear people talking about? The one who was with Rameses?"

Serein shifted. "I suppose I am. Unless there's another one I don't know about," she said.

"Are you planning on walking through the city with blood on your clothes and a bleeding wound?" Rajiya asked, pointing to the red stain on Serein's tunic.

"It's not a deep wound," Serein said. "It's stopped bleeding mostly."

Rajiya let out an exasperated sigh. "Serein, was it? You seem like a smart woman, but it's wise not to reject help when it's offered. I'll stitch you up and give you some tea and a meal."

She shooed Serein forward, handing her basket off to Uriah. *Seems I can't say no to this woman,* Serein thought. *I don't want to stay out in the streets too long where Xansas' eyes can follow me.*

Rajiya hummed as she led them through the city, the bright orange melody fluttering like butterflies. The house with plants growing on its rooftop came into view. Baqir kneeled underneath the lemon tree, waving as he spotted them. Rajiya took her basket from Uriah.

"See if Baqir needs any help," Rajiya told him.

Uriah nodded, casting Serein a look before climbing the steps that led up to the roof. Rajiya ushered Serein inside the house.

The smell of herbs and bread greeted Serein as she stood in the seating area. A low, round table decorated with carved birds separated the cushion-covered section from the kitchen. Pots, cups, tagines, and bowls filled the shelves carved into the wall over the stone counters. Herbs hung to dry by the open window, and a glazed blue bowl full of fruit was tucked into the corner next to bottles of liquids, oils, and spices. A squat clay oven with stacks of wood sat in a side room attached to the kitchen. Faded tapestries with the names of the Twelve Saints around a white flame hung around the living area.

"Head over there," Rajiya said as she set the basket down, pointing to a back room behind a dusky blue curtain, "and I'll get my supplies together."

A staircase next to the room led to the second floor of the house. Serein stepped into the small bathing room with a copper tub, two short stools, and a chamber pot. Zellij tiles pressed into the walls caught the light from the narrow window. Muffled gray and yellow footsteps shuffled overhead, and bottles clinked from the other room like ruby-colored splinters.

Cozy. I can see why Rameses likes coming here, she thought.

A few minutes later, Rajiya appeared carrying a tray with three glasses. One had dark liquid and the other two were filled with the familiar steaming, mint tea. In her other hand was a bowl of cloth, catgut, needles, and vials.

"Sit," she said. "Show me your wound and drink this."

The stool dug into Serein's tailbone as she lifted her tunic. Rajiya's sharp brown eyes took in the wound, her expression unchanging as she touched the mass of scar tissue. Serein resisted the urge to jerk away. Rajiya dunked a cloth in the basin of water before wiping the area clean.

The medicinal supplies and steady composure suggest she might be a healer, Serein thought, sniffing the dark liquid. It gave off an herbal smell mixed with aniseed and honey.

"It doesn't taste the best, but the honey in it should make it palatable. Just some herbs and spices to help with the pain and keep away infection. The tea will help it."

Serein downed the contents, the bitterness still detectable through the taste of honey, ginger, and cloves. Rajiya opened one of the vials, rubbing thyme oil around the wound.

Ginger. Honey. Cloves. Aniseed. And...something else bitter and woody tasting. Serein examined the silty contents at the bottom of the glass.

"Not too deep. Few stitches should patch it up," Rajiya said, pulling up the other stool as she balanced the bowl in her lap. "This'll sting."

Serein set the empty glass down and sipped from the other cup of tea. The sweetness coated her mouth and washed away the lingering aftertaste of the concoction. "I don't feel anything in that area anymore," Serein muttered, watching as Rajiya threaded catgut through a hooked needle.

"Seems like you've had quite a life."

Dull pressure pressed against Serein's side as the needle pierced her skin. "You don't seem put off by so many scars."

"When I was younger, before the war, I was a healer. Spent most of my time traveling to different towns. Did that for many years and then when the war started, I went to the front for a year. Saw all kinds of wounds. After a while, you learn to bury your shock," the older woman replied, tugging on the string to close the wound.

"What made you retire to a life here?" Serein asked as the last stitch was tightened.

Rajiya straightened, cleaning off her blood-slicked fingers in a bowl of clean water. "Too much death. And I missed my husband. I felt that I did more good here. I don't practice now, but I have what I need to heal the occasional ailment and scrape."

Dipping her fingers in a small tin, Rajiya smeared a waxy ointment smelling of honey and myrrh over the wound. Serein moved onto the second cup of tea, the warm liquid hitting her stomach.

"Keep it clean and try not to move too much. Not sure how feasible that'll be with you fighting in the competition."

"I'll try my best not to get stabbed again," Serein told her as she stood. "Thank you for the tea and the stitches."

A smile crossed Rajiya's face as she gathered her supplies. "I'm sure you're tired, so I won't keep you long. At least have something to eat, so you don't pass out," she said. "Another cup of tea won't hurt either."

Serein grabbed the tray with the empty glasses and followed her into the kitchen. Rajiya lifted the metal teapot from a bed of ashes and raised it high over one of the cups. The stream of tea frothed in the glass and left a layer of foam on the top. Setting the kettle down, she uncovered four braided pastries with darkened edges on the counter.

"I made these last night. Trying out a new recipe I learned. Hopefully, these"—she pointed to the stuffed pastries and held the tea out to Serein—"aren't too spicy."

Serein stared at the golden pastries with crimped edges before taking one. Lamb, carrots, and chunks of potatoes covered in a thick gravy filled the inside of the golden bread as she took a bite. The spice of the peppers burned the back of her throat. Rajiya as she unpacked her basket, placing the chicken on a dark cutting block.

"Odd for a Sarddonian to be making Ravanassë dishes," Serein said. *This tastes almost like a salteña. Why is she making Old Kingdom foods? Was it from her time on the front? This is more from the northern region. Did she serve there?*

Rajiya shrugged as she grabbed a bowl and began plucking the chicken. Dusty gray feathers came free in her fingers. "I had a chance to sample some of the local dishes during the war. Learned a few that I liked," she replied.

Still strange. An interesting couple the prince and the captain have found, Serein thought, wiping her greasy fingers off on her trousers.

Rajiya's orange humming drifted to the floor, notes clinging to the small feathers that scattered off the counter. Uriah opened the door as he and Baqir stepped in. Baqir gave Serein a gapped-tooth smile, his hands moving in quick gestures as he signed. Serein followed along with his question.

"He's asking if you're all patched up," Uriah said, standing in the doorway.

"She'll live. Nothing my special ointment won't cure," Rajiya said, signing back. "Come, have some food and tea, Uriah. Next time you see Rameses, tell him the next bet Baqir and I have is that we'll see him in three months."

Baqir set about pouring more tea, filling the room with the smell of mint and sugar. Serein swallowed the rest of the pastry, the unknown taste in the herbal drink floating up in flashes of snowy winters and her mother preparing cups of tea. *Cat's claw. That plant only grows in the Old Kingdom. Why does she have so many Old Kingdom herbs and spices?*

THE FRESH POULTICE GAVE OFF A PUNGENT SCENT. FIVE NEAT stitches held Serein's wound shut. Eneca handed her a red glass of lemon verbena tea, the outside decorated with gold sunbursts. She shifted the cushions as she sat, smoothing the hem of her yellow gandora.

Serein sipped the tea, the lemony scent strong in her nose. "The tea's good," she told Eneca, the hot liquid burning her mouth as she sipped it too quickly.

"While I'm flattered, I know you didn't come all this way for tea, Ser," Eneca told her, her rosy voice soft as she moved closer. "It's about your fight against Mayte, isn't it?"

"I went to search her room with the captain and found it empty. Xansas must have gotten there first and removed anything incriminating before the guards found out where she was staying." *Did he know she would lose and take preemptive measures?* she thought. *He's done with her and wants to erase her existence.*

"But that's not what's really bothering you," Eneca said, tilting her head.

A heavy yellow exhale left Serein as her fingers tightened around the glass. "I almost killed her. I wanted to, but I didn't...I couldn't," she muttered. "After all she's done, it should've been easy to kill her. That's what *he* would have done."

Mayte's twisted face appeared streaked with blood, and Serein blinked it away, hands tightening around the glass.

"You're not Xansas," Eneca said.

"It didn't feel like that when I broke her arm and cut her throat. I wanted her to feel pain," Serein replied, gazing out the latticed window.

"But you have something Xansas doesn't. Remorse and the capacity to love."

"I'm afraid that when Luca and Astra see me again, they won't recognize me. I already lost two years with them, and to endure another three..."

Eneca curled beside Serein, arm looped through hers. The scents of cinnamon and honey mixed with the lemony tea.

"If they knew all the things I've done...When they were first born, I didn't want to hold them. I couldn't. Touching them felt unbearable. Like I was corrupting them. I couldn't stop imagining *his* hands."

"I can't say what'll happen, but I don't believe love is such a fragile thing. You never stopped loving them when you were separated. You made sure they knew that," Eneca said.

Serein swallowed. "When I was in Grasdan, there came a point where I wanted to die. For the first year, I tried so hard to escape. Waited for the right opportunity, but every plan failed. There was no way to escape." The words broke apart in her mouth, tears escaping the corners of her eyes. "I was ready to leave them because I was so tired of living."

"You can't blame yourself," Eneca murmured, squeezing Serein's hand. "There were nights where I couldn't see a way out." She paused, the rosy petals catching in her curling, dark tresses. "But then you appeared, alive, and I had reason to hope again."

Serein turned to look at her. "Aren't we quite the pair?" she said with a strained smile. "Two assassins with bleeding hearts." *Can vengeance and love exist in the same heart? Revenge won't bring back what was lost, but it will prevent any more suffering at the hands of Xansas and Sethos.*

The edges of Eneca's mouth crinkled. "Seems despite all our steel, we still bleed and cry."

Serein squeezed Eneca's hand back. "I'll free you from here one day. I'm not going to leave you behind again, En. I promise."

"I know you will, sister of my heart," Eneca said. "Your children are proof that you have good in your life, and you'll see them again."

When this is all over, Serein thought, closing her eyes.

The house by the lake beckoned her, orange and blue laughter following the two children with blue eyes. Warmth fluttered in Serein's chest, pushing against her throat.

Chapter Forty-Nine
Axe & Dagger

THE MUSTY SMELL OF DECAY AND MELTING TAR LINGERED IN Serein's nose despite the argan oil wafting off her skin. Mummified corpses filled the space in the back of her mind—the mother holding the wrapped remains of her infant child, and the son in repose, both staring back from their disturbed rest. The released sighs of their open crypts left more questions, the answers out of reach in the quiet of the early morning.

If the queen's body and the remains of her children were buried, why was only Salman's missing? Serein thought. *Rameses will be relieved that most of his past relatives are where they should be, even more so that he didn't have to venture into the catacombs again.*

Serein blinked the catacombs away. Ink dried on the parchment in front of her, bearing the weight of unspoken secrets within the Wendish words. Plum-colored rustles curled around Serein's fingers as she folded the paper, sealing it with a blob of wax.

If anything happens to me, this will ensure my children remain safe.

The letter felt heavy in her hand as she walked to the other chamber. Rizwana finished pouring tea from the kettle as Nala tugged on the hem of her white gandora.

"Enough of that!" Rizwana snapped, nudging aside the cub with her foot. "I already gave you a treat."

Nala's ears swiveled as Serein approached, abandoning Rizwana as she bounded over. The tiger gazed up with cloudy eyes.

Rizwana set the teapot down and turned. "I have a favor to ask you," Serein said.

"What is it, miss?" Rizwana asked, lapis voice dancing through the beams of sunlight.

"I need you to give this letter to Captain Stormheir if anything happens to me. It's meant for his eyes alone. Hide this somewhere only you know where to find it," Serein told her, holding the letter out.

The hazel eyes widened. "Are you worried about something, miss? Are you in danger?"

"I don't know what will happen during the last two days of the Aikhtiar. There's something he needs to know if I die." *It's a risk, but there's no one besides him and Eneca who know about them.*

Rizwana took the letter. "What should I do with this if you survive?" she asked.

"Hold onto it. I'll let you know if I need it back. For now, I trust you to keep it safe."

The paper disappeared into her apron, and Rizwana stepped forward, taking Serein's scarred hands. Worry etched across her round features, dark eyebrows creased.

"You don't have to tell me everything about your life, but if you think you're in danger, please tell me," Rizwana said.

"Death and danger have been my friends since I was young. I'm not afraid of Death, but there's something I need to protect," Serein replied. "I trust you with this letter."

"I'll light a lantern and pray for your safety in the competition."

"Thank you, Rizwana. You've been kind to me, and I'm grateful for that."

Rizwana squeezed Serein's hands. "You've come so far from the lice-infested skeleton that arrived here months ago. It's amazing what a little tea and a haircut will do."

Serein nodded. "I have a question for you," she said. "You and I are the only ones with keys to my room, correct? Has anyone else been up here?"

Rizwana tilted her head. "You and I have the only keys. No one else has been assigned to your chambers. Why do you ask?"

"There was a note left in my bedchamber, and I don't know who it was from," Serein told her. *If someone else is coming in here, they haven't done anything yet. Il-Makah most likely also has a copy of the key. I trust Rizwana, but there's still always the small chance she's being used. At least if she tries to read the note, she won't understand it because it's written in Wendish. If the Jackals get a hold of it though...*

Rizwana frowned. "I didn't leave a note for you. Does it have something to do...with what happened the night of the Aikhtiar diffa?" she asked in a low voice.

"I hope not. If there's a way to switch the locks discretely, please let me know," Serein said.

"I will see what I can find out, miss," Rizwana replied as she gathered up her skirts and headed to the bedchamber.

Serein took a sip of tea, staring out the window. *There's nothing that can be done now. I need to focus on my fight with Salveig today. She won't be swayed by emotions like Mayte,* she thought. *I don't think she'll kill me, but who's to say that she won't get overexcited.*

THE ARROW STRUCK THE PAINTED TARGET, THE RED RIBBON around the shaft fluttering. Serein watched Rameses nock and release another as he went down the row, Jabbar kicking up vermilion clouds in the arena. Colored tassels hung from the high-backed cantle and ornate bridle. Rameses' checkered keffiyeh snapped in the wind, white qamis bright against his black horse.

Twelve archers performed various maneuvers to fill the time between the two matches, earning points based on their ability to hit the bullseye of the targets scattered around the arena in the quickest amount of time. Other arrows with different colored ribbons dotted the targets, red tasseled shafts consistently embedded in the centers.

Rameses released his last arrow, the crowd cheering as he rode around the arena, grinning. He raised his bow as the next archer came out.

The heat lessened, the air charged with the pressure change as the amethyst-colored wind picked up. *Seems his boasting wasn't unfounded,* Serein thought, glancing at the gray clouded sky. *A storm's coming. I don't think I've seen it rain since I arrived in Oyon.*

A shadow fell across her, and Serein turned. "Excited for our match?" the Edolasian asked, apple-red voice eager. Ragnhildur stood beside her, brown hair braided into two coils pinned against her head.

Salveig's lamellar armor was polished, nicks running along the sewn plates. The metal bracers bore the insignia of an eagle, a leather pauldron strapped across her right shoulder. The double-headed battleaxe was strapped across Salveig's back, a small throwing axe and broad dagger hanging from the corded belt.

"I could hardly sleep," Serein replied, flashing her a grin. The wound along her side ached when she moved.

The curling tattoos along Salveig's cheek creased. She tilted her head, the long braid swept over her shoulder. "Nervousness or excitement?"

"Anticipation."

"You speak like an Edolasian. This will be a fight to please the Mother Goddess, one we will drink to after."

Seems she will try her best not to kill me. What a nice change of pace, Serein thought.

The auburn call of the horn signaled the end of the archery competition, and the riders gathered in the center of the arena. A stocky man carried a wreath of red acacia flowers in his hands.

"The winner is our Amir Rameses!" he shouted, his dark sienna voice carrying across the sands.

He laid the wreath around Rameses' neck and thunderous applause poured a cacophony of colors into the arena. Rameses waved as he rode toward the gates, guards stepping out to remove the targets so the field could be cleared.

"Seems the prince has some skills. He's not as soft as he appears," Salveig said.

"Thinking about courting him too?" Serein asked. *Rameses might get his wish to experience an Edolasian lover.*

"That would cause too many diplomatic issues. Besides, I prefer my men with a lot more muscle. He's too lithe for me," Salveig replied with a wink. "May the Mother Goddess smile upon us, *palaúlfa.*"

Salveig slapped Serein's back as they stepped out into the arena. The battleaxe shone on Salveig's back, its handle carved with Edolasian runes and a yellow ribbon wrapped around it. She unstrapped the axe as she faced Serein.

This won't be an easy fight, Serein thought as the matchkeeper inspected their weapons. *Specializes in heavy swings and offensive attacks. As deadly with hand-to-hand combat as she is with a weapon. She has height and reach. Quick and agile, favors her right side.*

The matchkeeper left, and Serein unsheathed the daggers as the bell rang out with its familiar peach tolling. With a red battle cry, Salveig swung her weapon. The Twins arced up, the flat of the blades stopping the axe with orange sparks. Jarring force ran through her bones. Serein rolled to the right as the axe came at her left.

Salveig changed her stance, shoulders squaring as the muscles in her arms bulged. Flipping the blades around, hilts facing outwards, Serein slashed at Salveig's thigh. The handle of the axe blocked the attack as Salveig brought her weapon around.

This is the strength of an Edolasian warrior, Serein thought, yanking the blade free from the wood. *The woman with a thousand horses.*

Salveig's fist struck Serein's forearm as she moved to shield her face. Dropping the dagger in her right hand, Serein grabbed the axe handle and swung her body upward. Her foot connected with Salveig's eye, knocking her back. Laughing, Salveig twisted away. Sunlight bounced off the axe head, and Serein dropped low to avoid it. Serein skirted to the left, kicking at the Edolasian's side. Salveig grunted as she charged forward.

Solid stance. Not easy to break. Used to taking hard hits. I'll have to disable her. When she brings the axe down, there's a brief opening. I have the advantage of speed if I can get in close enough. Her swings will be slower with the battleaxe.

Salveig roared, cleaving the axe downward through the apple red cloud. The blade thudded in the ground as Serein dodged, stepping on the back of the axe before slamming her fist into Salveig's chin. Pain smarted through her knuckles, and the Edolasian staggered, blood spurting out the corner of her mouth. Serein grabbed the edges of the lamellar armor and rammed her fist into Salveig's nose, the cartilage crunching. The Edolasian cursed, slamming her weight against Serein. The force sent Serein back.

Salveig wiped the blood from her nose, smile smeared crimson. "First blood. The Goddess rewards the pain of her warriors!" she exclaimed, leaving the battleaxe in the sand.

The Edolasian charged, fists swinging. Serein wove and darted as Salveig kicked at her. *Skilled in Edolasian military martial arts. Strong strikes and stance-breaking lunges,* Serein thought.

Serein whirled around, leg hitting Salveig's shoulder. The Edolasian grabbed Serein's ankle and slammed her onto the ground. Serein tensed her stomach as Salveig rammed a fist into her gut. The pain radiated along her torso, the stitches on her side splitting. Serein rolled to her feet as Salveig reached for her hand axe.

Groaning, Serein rushed at her, trying to land a blow. The Edolasian wove and ducked, braid whipping behind her. She changed direction and surged forward as she swung with her right, knuckles skimming Serein's nose. Salveig's knee connected with Serein's injured side, pain needling through the burned scar tissue.

Serein winced, pale yellow breath hissing through her teeth. She flipped backward, boot passing close to Salveig's face as she kicked out. She dug her hands into the ground as she landed, pulse racing through her veins like fire. Serein avoided Salveig's axe and aimed her dagger at the Edolasian's side. The blade cut the lower straps of Salveig's armor as Serein dove past, circling behind her. Salveig whirled around, her armor flapping like metal wings.

Now she has openings, Serein thought, glancing at her blade half hidden in the sands.

Serein jabbed the blade at her, and it was smacked away by the smaller axe. Wiping blood from her mouth, Salveig whirled around and grabbed her battleaxe, hefting it with one hand. She advanced to bring it down with limb-severing force.

Serein sidestepped and dug her foot into the sands, kicking up her fallen dagger. Salveig's gaze went to the twirling blade, eyes widening. Serein caught it and ducked as Salveig swung the hand axe. Sarlyrian steel kissed the Edolasian's throat, sweat collecting on the sharp edge while she pointed the other dagger at her side.

Serein crouched as warm blood seeped down her side. Red laughter rippled through Salveig's shoulders as she backed away, hands raised. Serein rose, sunlight glinting off the rippled steel.

"I concede defeat. The Goddess has smiled upon you," Salveig said with a red-toothed smile.

The faint bronze rumble of thunder rolled through the clouds overhead. *I made it out relatively unscathed,* Serein thought and lowered her blades as the bell rang out.

"I'd enjoy fighting with you again," the Edolasian told her, holding her arm out.

Serein sheathed the daggers, clasping Salveig's muscular arm. "Perhaps someday."

Their grins mirrored each other as the first cool drops of rain fell from the sky. "I look forward to it, *palaúlfa.*"

Chapter Fifty
Intertwined Threads

THE FRESH SCENT OF RAIN DRIFTED THROUGH THE OPEN BALCONY doors, laced with jasmine and orange blossoms. The rhythmic murmur of opaque purple pattering fell through the night as trails of white lightning sliced through the sky, illuminating the clouds. The storm had unleashed its torrents over Oyon. Nala growled softly at the rain as she hunched down behind Serein.

The drops danced like tiny purple sunbursts as they pattered against the palace. *I didn't think I'd ever miss rain so much,* Serein thought, the cool droplets collecting in her palms.

A memory rose with the smell of water, her mother taking her to gather herbs in the forest before the concept of war had ever formed in her mind. A drizzle came through the openings between the trees, the sky cloudless. The edges of the world were softer, the rain cool as she danced in it.

Serein. My soft rain, her mother had said, turquoise voice sparkling like gems. *What colors do you see in the sound of the rainfall? Your grandmother saw green.*

Serein smiled, letting the water pour from her hands. She closed the balcony doors and locked them, drying her hands on a towel in the bathing chamber. Nala padded after her, the lanterns bright against the dim clinging to the corners.

Only Fang and I remain. He'll want to kill me, so I'll have to cut him down first, Serein thought, sighing. *Rizwana has the letter. If anything happens, Uriah will know how to find my children.*

Serein sank onto the cushions of the majlis, a dull pain spreading through her side. She had restitched the wound at her side, coating it in a poultice mixed with honey. The blows she'd received from Salveig ached, slowly turning into bruises. Nala leapt up onto Serein's lap, paws digging into her chest.

"How much more of a handful will you be when you get older?" Serein muttered as Nala chewed on her hand. "Will I be able to take you with me when I leave here?" *Luca and Astra might enjoy having a pet tiger,* she thought, a pang of sadness creeping in. *There will be many things I won't be able to take with me when I leave.*

You've intertwined yourself with these people, and those bonds will only cut you. You could have left it burning in your wake without a second glance. Now you've become attached, Xansas said, sneering. *You've shown* affection *for these people. What will happen when they figure out what you're hiding?*

Serein scratched Nala underneath her chin, the tiger stretching out across the cushions. *Only Sethos has to die. And then I'll kill you, Xansas. You won't hurt anyone else.*

The white laughter cut deeper. *What do you think these people can do for you? A thread can be cut, and then what will you have? Pain. How long do you think it'll take before you have to choose between returning to your children and killing those who stand in your way?*

I won't raise a hand to Rasima or Rizwana, she thought, hand tightening into a fist.

You won't be able to take your vengeance if you can't set aside these sentiments. They will end up strangling you.

Serein sat up, staring into the melting night. The door swung open, and Rizwana stepped through the teal creak. She balanced a tray with glasses and a teapot on her hip.

"His Highness is here," Rizwana said, lapis voice hurried as she set the tray on the table.

Nala turned her head as Serein rose. Orange footsteps filled the doorway as Rameses entered. "Did you think I would let you spend tonight by yourself, eating a simple meal?" Rameses said, gold words curling with his grin. "We have victories to celebrate!"

"I don't know if I can handle any more celebrations. Salveig already toasted to my victory," Serein told him. "I thought you'd still be wearing that flower garland or showing off that golden arrow you won."

Dark locks of hair curled against Rameses' forehead. Peach chimes settled on the shoulders of his blue qamis as he pulled over a cushion. "It clashed with my outfit," he said. "The golden arrow isn't practical, but it looks nice on a shelf."

"And all I got was a few bruises. Although Salveig and some other Edolasians bought me drinks and food to celebrate my victory, so I suppose that's something."

Servants came in with trays of food. The smell of warm spices and sizzling meats filled the room. Lamb chunks coated in yogurt, dill, and za'atar were laid next to bowls of pickles, hummus, and golden couscous. A whole grilled peacock with apricots, orange slices, and chunks of squash rested on a bed of rice. Baskets of msemen bread and meat-stuffed maaqouda glistened with butter.

"They took you out to a tavern to celebrate? Even after you defeated her?" Rameses asked.

Serein crossed her legs as she sat. "They find honor in defeat as much as they do in victory. Both are learning opportunities," Serein replied.

"Edolasians. Strange people. At least you seem to get along with them unlike that woman you fought yesterday whose throat you cut..." He poured himself a glass of wine. "You seemed to really dislike her."

"She caught me in a bad mood." *Xansas hasn't killed Mayte yet and no one's connected her to me so far,* Serein thought. *It feels like another blade hovering over me, waiting to fall.*

She filled her plate as Nala got off the majlis. A paw reached for the food. A sharp yellow whistle made the tiger stop and sit next to her. Serein pulled off a piece of roasted peacock and held it out to the tiger. Nala devoured it.

Rameses set his cup down, clearing his throat. "What did you think of the archery competition?" he asked.

"It was impressive. You live up to your boasting," Serein said and smeared hummus on msemen bread. "Salveig said your demonstration almost made her consider pursuing you."

The corners of Rameses' mouth curled behind the rim of his glass. "Oh? Does that mean Uriah has competition?"

"You're not muscular enough for her liking," Serein replied.

Rameses shrugged, feigning a look of disappointment. "Seems even I fall short in some areas."

She stared at him, chewing on the bread. "Did you come here just for compliments?"

"No. I simply wanted to celebrate our shared victories," Rameses told her, nibbling on a piece of lamb dipped in yogurt. "Tomorrow, everything will change."

The rain continued to hit the window in opaque purple drops. "Winning is the easiest step. The rest is still uncertain," Serein said quietly. "Your father will have a long list of people for me to kill. Many could have useful information." *He'll use me to silence those who hold answers, whether they're traitors or not.*

Rameses' expression darkened. "I never knew who my father sent the Jackals to kill...Now I will. Their lives will be on my conscience. This is a risk for you, but could you spare those my father sends you to kill?" he asked.

"Who would you have me spare? How will you decide who lives? Those who have the most use? Ones who are the most morally upstanding? That means someone else has to take their place. Then there's the matter of making sure those who are supposed to be dead aren't seen or recognized again. Faking the deaths won't be a simple task."

"But it could be done?" Rameses' voice lifted a bit.

Serein sighed. "With difficulty and careful planning and similar corpses," she replied. "Are you asking because you're trying to figure out if your father possibly staged your uncle's death? You haven't spoken about the other night in the catacombs." *Being face-to-face with dead relatives probably gave him nightmares.*

Rameses worried his lower lip. "I was trying to put most of that evening out of my mind..." he said, swirling the wine around in the goblet. "I finally stopped smelling rot and dreaming that rats were crawling over me."

"That's not what I meant. Your uncle's body isn't in his tomb, and your father kept something there that he removed. Your aunt and cousins were in their crypts, which makes me think that whatever happened is mainly connected to the former malik."

"You went and examined the tombs," Rameses said, grimacing.

"Before dawn. It didn't seem like an excursion you wanted to partake in."

Rameses took a long sip of wine. "No. I don't think I will be down there for a very long time. I have not been that afraid of the catacombs since Uriah and I dared each other to go and sit in the dark overnight. We only lasted an hour before we ran out of there, convinced we had seen a ghost."

"I did examine the bodies," Serein told him, and Rameses paled. "I was more respectful to them than your great relatives. The wounds appeared consistent with the healer's records, so I believe those bodies do belong to the malika and her children and aren't substitutes." *Why would only the uncle be missing? Did Sethos move the body to hide evidence or for some other reason?*

Worry seeped in, resting like a shadow on Rameses' face. "I don't want to believe that my father killed his brother, but I don't know why he would stage his assassination. Or maybe his body was stolen, but then why would my father hide that?" he muttered. "It still doesn't make sense. It feels like all these lies and secrets will never end…"

Green and gray footsteps mingled underneath the door crack as it swung open. Rameses straightened and turned around. Uriah stood in the doorway, Rasima hovering behind him.

"Looks like you finally finished your work. I thought I would have to go and drag you away from your desk," Rameses said, plastering a smile on his face. "Rasi, this is a surprise."

"I still have a lot of work to do," Uriah said, green voice quiet as he approached. "Rasima followed me here."

"You said Rameses was having dinner with Serein, and I wanted to come," Rasima told them as she darted past Uriah. Laia and

Karam followed, the maidservant carrying a plate of maamoul, crescent-shaped almond cookies, and honey-soaked baklava.

"Seems I cannot tell you no," Rameses said as his sister sat next to him. "At least for one night, let's not dwell on the threats around us. Oyon will still be standing in the morning."

Rameses met Serein's gaze, the unspoken words clouding the mirth in his eyes. *Xansas doesn't adhere to such sentiments,* Serein thought, trying to bury the lingering dread she felt encroaching.

Uriah sat next to Serein, tugging at the long sleeves of his gray tunic. He took in her bruises as he cleaned his hands in the bowl of water. He looked away and dried his hands.

Rasima pushed back her blue veil and adjusted her rose-colored abaya embroidered with white flowers. She called Nala over, rubbing the tiger behind the ears.

"Are you nervous for tomorrow?" Rasima asked, violet words falling like bright petals.

"Not particularly," Serein replied.

"Rameses has been telling me about your fights since I'm no longer allowed to go there after my mother found out I went," Rasima said, giving her brother a pouting look. "You will have to tell me how your fight goes."

He must be leaving out the bloodier details. Like how I slashed a woman's throat and broke her arm.

"Everyone will be talking about a woman winning the Aikhtiar. You will be making history," Rasima went on, excitement glowing on her face. "I will be praying for your victory."

Serein smiled, pulling Nala back from the table. "Between you and your brother, I should be well protected with prayers." *Maybe the Lights will hear me.*

"You should still be careful," Uriah said, scooping up couscous with a piece of msemen bread.

"You're much kinder when you're not wearing armor. Who knew you had a heart underneath all those *hard* layers?" Serein asked, glancing at him with a sharp grin.

Uriah coughed, nearly choking on his food as he reached for a glass of tea. He sucked in a breath, hand covering his mouth.

"Everything all right, Uriah?" Rameses asked.

Uriah kept his eyes on his plate, ears reddening. "I'm fine," he muttered.

Still embarrassed about me seeing him naked, Serein thought, sipping her tea. *Wonder how long that will last.*

"Will you have to kill people when you become my father's muharib?" Rasima asked, and three sets of eyes snapped to her.

"Rasi..." Rameses said.

Serein tilted her head, nudging Nala's paw off the table. "Yes," she replied, ignoring the startled looks from Uriah and Rameses.

Rasima nibbled on a square of msemen bread. "Is that what you really want to do?"

"We all have to do things we don't want to achieve the things we want. I'm an assassin. I'm used to having blood on my hands." *These next few years won't be easy, but it'll be worth it if I can return to you, my Sun and Stars.*

"What do you want to do?"

"I want to live in a house in the woods where it's quiet." *No more blood. No more danger. No more killing. A place where my children can grow up smiling.*

"What will you do there?" Rasima asked.

"I suggested that she either be a traveling bard or a painter, but she seems to want to farm," Rameses said. "I find it hard to picture Serein milking cows or planting seeds."

"My goals aren't as grand as yours, Rameses. Sometimes it's enough to find contentment in the small things," Serein told him.

"I think living in a forest sounds nice. Like a fairy tale," Rasima said, reaching for a maamoul cookie. Rameses looked at her, an eyebrow raised. "I'm not just eating sweets, akhun."

"I was not saying that, Rasi," Rameses replied, reaching for a piece of baklava. "Just maybe save some for the rest of us."

Rasima rolled her eyes, powdered sugar dusting her mouth. "I brought the desserts, so I think I can eat as many as I want. Serein doesn't eat them anyway."

"Perhaps you should consider studying debate and philosophy when you enroll in the House of Knowledge since you make such compelling arguments," Rameses said.

"Maybe I will, or maybe I will study how to make an argument with a sword," Rasima replied. "Like the amirahs of old."

Rameses' gaze slid over to Serein, brow creasing a bit. "Then you might need those debate courses to make a compelling argument to Mother and Father."

He's giving me a look like this is my doing. I didn't tell her to follow my life, Serein thought as she took a bite of the roasted peacock.

She saw Rasima's soft hands grow callused from holding a weapon. Bright eyes that hardened, smooth skin becoming scarred. The image of a younger Serein overlapped with Rasima, making her heart twist.

"There are other ways to fight without a sword," Serein said, and Rasima turned to her. "You have an unyieldingness to back down, and that can be sharpened into an effective weapon. A well-placed word can be a good defense as easily as it can be an offense."

"Oh," Rasima muttered, pink flushing her cheeks, fidgeting with the hem of her abaya as she looked at her lap.

"How come you never say such nice things about me?" Rameses asked.

Serein gave him a pointed look. "Because a larger ego is the last thing you need."

Rameses laughed. "Well, here's to your victory tomorrow, Serein. May the Saints protect you and grant you favor," he said, raising his cup. "Tomorrow night, we will celebrate you becoming the next muharib."

"*Pob hwyl i ti,*" Uriah muttered as he lifted his cup to her.

Rasima grinned as she took Serein's hand. "I know you will win," she said.

Serein watched the violet, green, and gold voices swirling across the table, colored threads intertwining. The rain continued to fall, the peals of bronze thunder distant.

Can I hold happiness again? Is it possible to have a brief moment not marked by death and darkness, my Sun and Stars? Serein thought. *Or will it cause me pain when it's eventually taken from me?*

Chapter Fifty-One
Blood on the Sands

THE HEAT OF THE ARENA SHIMMERED AROUND SEREIN, THE CLEAR sky filled with the colors of roaring shouts. Sweat beaded across her skin, the air buzzing with excitement. Traces of the previous night's rain had evaporated, and a thin layer of humidity hung over Oyon.

Fang's curved dao glinted in the sun. The three emei piercers were like metal claws extending from his left hand. Scale armor was strapped over his yellow and green deel, leather bracers with brass studs.

Serein's hands tightened around her daggers. *Everything hangs on the edge of a blade,* she thought.

The dark peach ringing broke out, and Fang charged. She shifted as their blades grated orange against each other.

"I'll rip those blue eyes out of your skull!" Fang said between his teeth as she deflected the attack. His opaque blue voice became a sharp blade as it cut through the space between them.

Serein's mouth curled into a grin. The emei piercers swiped from the left, and she dodged, kicking at the back of Fang's knee. His leg buckled as he angled the sword at her torso, changing the trajectory mid-strike to arc up at her arm. She parried with her right dagger, the left blade slashing at the inside of his unprotected arm. The red dragon appeared through the sliced fabric, blood running across the inked scales. Cursing, Fang slashed the metal claws at Serein's face, and she backed away, ducking low.

As she prepared to lunge for the opening on his left side, a pale figure in the stands caught her eye. Xansas' shadowed face stood out in the middle of the spectators, smiling at her.

Serein's heart tripped over itself, her gaze locked onto him. *Did you think I wouldn't be here to watch you,* volchitsa? she almost heard him say.

Fang lashed out with the emei piercers, and Serein pulled back a second too late as one of the piercers scratched her cheek. Blood welled from the gash, pain digging under the torn flap of skin. Serein looped her arm around Fang's, ramming the end of the dagger hilt into the crook of his elbow. Anger burned in Fang's eyes as he cried out. Serein jabbed her dagger at the gap between his armor. She backed up to avoid a low sweep from his dao sword.

Her eyes darted back to the stands, but Xansas had vanished. *He's taunting me. He's not worried about guards, and he wants me to know it,* Serein thought, raising the Twins as her attention snapped back to Fang.

The ground shifted beneath her, her vision doubling as an unseen force slammed into her skull. She blinked as Fang whispered into his hand, a streak of blood on his finger. Opalescent threads swirled around him with a heavy timbre, snaking from his left palm toward her.

Serein sucked in a gulp of air, stomach roiling. *Something's wrong. What's happening?*

Fang swung, and Serein staggered back, the attack missing her arm. The sky spun, and dryness spread through her mouth. Fang swept Serein's feet out from under her, knee connecting with her nose as she fell. White stars punctured her vision as pain traveled behind her eyes. Blood poured across Serein's lips, warm and sticky. Fang sang low in a language she didn't recognize, the opaque blue words heavy and twisted.

Serein rolled onto her side, spitting red saliva onto the sand. "What's the matter, little blue eyes?" Fang asked, standing over her.

She scrambled up as he kicked at her. Fang whispered another unfamiliar word, and the opalescent strands pulsed brighter, coiling around her body.

He's using magic?! How? That shouldn't be possible, she thought. *What's happening to me?* A flash of metal in Fang's hand caught her eye, and pain shot through her skull, making her double over. *Bottled magic. He's using a spell?*

Serein smashed into Fang's side. Her dagger carved through the air and nicked his face. Fang swiped at her, two swords appearing as the image doubled. She ducked, each movement tightening around her bones and locking her limbs.

Fang's sword arced toward her, and Serein jumped back. The world spun, colors seeping together as the white ringing overtook her vision like a snowstorm. Her legs seized, and she crashed to her knees. Acid burned Serein's throat as she retched into the sand. Chills spread as a cold sweat broke out across her skin.

Against the arena wall stood Death. His papery skin and ageless face appeared translucent in the sunlight. He clutched a piece of silver wood in his hand.

Go away! Serein hissed as she stumbled up.

I'm always here. I have always been here, Death told her, his pale silver voice rolling across the sands. *I won't leave you.*

Fang swung his dao upward, cutting Serein's left cheek and eyelid. She staggered back, red clogging her vision and pain streaming down her face. The sunlight burned Serein's eyes, sharpening the edges of the world as white-hot stakes pierced her skull.

Eyes closed, Serein listened for Fang's movements. His orchid-colored footsteps and opaque blue breaths broke through the bombardment of colors from the crowds. The smell of sweat, leather armor, and the oil in Fang's hair preceded the orange hiss of a weapon cutting through the air. Serein brought her left dagger up, feeling it connect with the soft flesh of Fang's arm. His enraged yell cut through the blackness like an ocean wave.

She tried to dodge as the whistling blade neared, but she stumbled. Fang's knee struck her in the gut, knocking the wind from her lungs. The sounds of the crowd became incoherent chaos as the thick white ringing sound grew louder.

Fang grabbed Serein's throat, forcing her to her knees. He cut the straps of her armor and wrenched away the front piece before the metal piercers sunk into her abdomen. Serein's eyes flew open as she thrashed in his grip, blinded by the intense light and pain. Fang twisted his clawed hand, and a yellow scream tore from her mouth.

Blood splashed onto the sand. One of the daggers slipped from her grip. Fang wrenched the emei piercers out of Serein's stomach, and she slumped to the ground. The sand smelled of baked sunlight and metal, growing sharper with each breath.

Death waltzed across the arena, his footsteps silent as he approached. *My Sun and Stars...*Serein thought, meeting his gaze. *Is this how I die? I thought I had more time.*

Get up, a dark voice rumbled. *Get up!*

Serein's vision blackened. She clutched her wound as she stood, teeth gritted against the pain. The burning heat of adrenaline numbed the pain. Blood seeped past her fingers, the tendrils of magic growing fainter around her.

Don't let him live. Rip him apart. Inky blackness moved clawed her insides as the black beast's eyes opened.

Fang brought the blade down at Serein's head. She shouted, the black beast's roar mixing with her own. She knocked Fang's sword away, burying her dagger deep in his thigh as she dove past him. He screamed, sinking to a knee. A smile cracked Serein's face as she turned and slashed at Fang's fingers wrapped around the sword until he released the weapon.

The dagger arced through the air, and Fang sprang up, face contorted. He slipped a hidden blade out of his vambrace and lunged. The blade sunk into her right palm, the metal tip poking out through the other side as her fingers closed around Fang's hand.

Break him. Let him know agony.

Serein twisted Fang's wrist around and slammed the hilt of her dagger against it, bones snapping. Taking the knife embedded in her hand, she stuck it in his arm as he tried to pull away. His blue scream sounded distant. Wheezing, Fang scrambled for his sword, broken wrist clutched to his chest.

Serein dug her boot into the sand, kicking up the hidden dagger. It glinted between them, separating two lives with a blade. Fang's brown eyes followed the dagger flashing through the air as she grabbed it in midair.

Red gushed from the thin smile Serein carved across Fang's throat, blood splattering her face. A blue gurgle bubbled past his lips. The sword fell, and Fang collapsed.

Serein grabbed Fang's sword and cleaved it into his chest, hacking at the ribs and flesh until it split open. She cut out his heart, slick tissue squelching between her fingers, and tossed it onto the sands. Slathered in blood, she grabbed Fang's head and hacked at his neck until the bones separated from his spine.

No head, no heart. Roam the Void for all eternity, the dark voice growled.

Serein threw her head back and screamed. In the distance, the peach tolls of the bell hit the arena ground like wilted flowers. The yellow sound died, leaving her throat raw.

Serein turned her gaze to Sethos, his form going in and out of focus. *You're next,* the beast growled, the sound carving along her scars.

She saw a metal vial in the sands, thin opalescent strands squirming around it. Serein picked it up, sand sticking to her bloody fingers, and limped away. The blackness subsided, leaving the world muted.

Death lingered close by, silent steps keeping pace with her. He collected Fang's blue soul, holding it in his smooth hand.

You got your sacrifice, Serein said.

You can't make sacrifices to send me away. I'm always here. You can't escape me, child, Death replied.

Serein pressed her hand against her bleeding stomach. Darkness ate away the edges of her vision, the white ringing in her ears growing louder.

She passed through the coliseum gate, slumping against the hot bricks. *My Sun and Stars...It can't end like this.* Lights danced across her eyes as she fell, weapons dropping into the sands.

"Serein!" The spinning, forest-green canopy mixed with the red in her eyes. "Can you hear me?"

She gripped the front of Uriah's armor as his blurry face hovered over her. Death crouched beside her, stroking her cheek. "He used magic," Serein whispered, choking on the bloody words. "My Sun and Stars. Rizwana has a letter...Xansas is here."

The world faded as Uriah shouted something, colors dissolving into blackness.

Chapter Fifty-Two
Hanging by a Thread

Uriah sat by Serein's bedside, staring at the dull pallor of her skin. Her rattling breath passed her chapped lips. Her injuries had been cleaned and stitched, leaving behind the sharp smell of poultices in the infirmary. Healers checked the bandages every hour as they had for the past five days. Despite their best efforts, their outlook remained grim.

The Aikhtiar ended with no decided victor, the announcement held off at the urgings of Rameses as the allegation of magic being used was investigated. Rasima often came to hold Serein's hand and pray. When Rameses appeared, he often wore a dark grimace, preferring to linger in the doorway of the sick chamber.

She said Fang used magic, but no one saw anything besides when she started acting strange, Uriah thought, remembering the small, metal vial Serein shoved into his hands before passing out. *If it was bottled magic, where would Fang have gotten it? He didn't appear to be a magic user. Could he have smuggled it in from Zhao?*

Rizwana found Uriah two days after Serein's fight, quiet as she handed him a sealed letter with instructions from Serein. Uriah kept it in the secret compartment in his desk, its presence heavy in his chambers.

Why would she write me a letter? Uriah squeezed the chunk of tourmaline around his neck. *Should I read it? Rizwana said it was meant for me if anything happened to Serein, but to open it now...She's not dead.*

Uriah studied the scars along her face, the harshness softened by sleep. He looked at his hands, remembering the blood running down his fingers. Serein's pale, gore-streaked face, wild eyes, and hands coated in crimson as she whispered to him to find her children. The heart in her hands and her vermilion smile haunted his nightmares.

I've never seen anyone do that to another person. When she talks about her children, she's so different...She smiles. Uriah raked his fingers through his hair. *How could she have that kind of brutality also?*

Feverish moaning slipped past Serein's lips. He caught a few of the Sarlyrian words. *My children. I'm sorry. Run.*

Serein's body went rigid, face contorted in pain. Her knuckles whitened, and fingers gripped the sheets, a sheen of sweat coating her forehead.

Uriah jumped up, grabbing her hand. "Serein," he said. "They're safe. Your children—they're fine."

He reached for the pitcher of poppy milk on the bedside table and forced the liquid past her lips. Serein's hands unclenched, and she sank into the pillows. Uriah wiped the corner of her mouth with the edge of the sheet. Serein's uninjured hand remained in his, limp and cold.

"You really should get some rest. I'm worried that those shadows under your eyes will become permanent, sadiqi."

Uriah released Serein's hand as Rameses stepped into the room. Worry shadowed the Amir's features as he twisted the ring on his finger.

"I can't seem to sleep much as of late," Uriah muttered.

Rameses gave him a knowing look, placing his hand on his shoulder. "How is she doing?" he asked.

"The healers came earlier to change the dressings. She has an infection and a fever, but they have been giving her medicine," Uriah told him.

Sitting on the stool, Rameses rested his arms on his knees. "You have been here every day."

Uriah rubbed his neck, hiding his twitching finger. "I...I felt like I should." *Xansas could try and come for her. Mayte escaped three days ago after killing a guard and a healer, and we have no idea where she is. She's a danger too. I promised I'd help Serein get back to her children, but I failed to do that.*

"If anyone should feel guilty for what happened, it should be me," Rameses said. "I set her down this path. She warned me it would end in death, and I didn't listen."

"It's not your fault," Uriah told him with a sigh.

"Whenever someone says that, it usually has the opposite effect."

"I'm sorry." Uriah looked at his boots. "I thought I would—"
Rameses chuckled. "Don't laugh."

"You're not one for many words, Uriah." Rameses fell silent for a moment. "I didn't think a person could have such...cruelty I cannot erase that look she had on her face when she killed Fang. It's been keeping me up. All that blood and her scream..."

Bloody fingers, her scream, the heart in her hand, the color draining from her face. The iron smell of blood clogged Uriah's nose, the sound of a rushing river roaring in his ears.

"She's not going to die after coming this far, Rameses," Uriah said, swallowing.

"Do you think she can hear us?" Rameses asked.

Uriah stared at Serein's ashen face. "The healers say it's possible." *She'd probably roll her eyes and make a sarcastic comment about us worrying at her bedside.*

"Serein's tiger must miss her," Rameses muttered as he stood, hands clenching and unclenching at his sides.

"Rizwana and I have been checking on the tiger and letting her out. Sometimes she tries to follow me," Uriah told him.

A thin smile appeared on Rameses' face. "Seems you attract all the ladies. Must be your sunny disposition."

Uriah sighed, reaching into his pocket for the rock. "Is this really the time for this?"

"I don't know what else to do in this situation. Humor keeps me from sinking into a dark pit of despair." Rameses smoothed out the front of his qamis. "Let's get a drink. I cannot think of a better time for one."

"The last time I went anywhere near alcohol, I ended up with a concussion."

"I think the riad should be safe enough. We will bring the tiger with us just to be safe," Rameses told him. Uriah glanced at Serein. "You seem worried, sadiqi."

"I'm not worried," Uriah said.

Rameses' features softened. "Your face says otherwise, and you look like you're going to crush that rock of yours to dust."

A healer appeared in the doorway, bowing. "I heard commotion in here, Your Highness. Is everything all right?" she asked.

"I think so, but Serein started thrashing a few minutes ago," Uriah told her. "She's calm now. I gave her some of the poppy milk."

The healer's eyes went to Serein, coming over to check her pulse. The woman touched Serein's brow, hands moving down her neck.

Rameses put his arm on Uriah's shoulder. "There doesn't seem to be anything else we can do here. She's in good hands," he said quietly.

Uriah hesitated, watching as the healer bent over Serein. He turned away and followed Rameses, the sound of Serein's breathing growing fainter behind him. A stab of fear needled between his ribs at the thought of her breath ceasing, leaving him in deafening silence.

Drops of sound hit the black expanse, sending colored ripples across the ground. Time unraveled as Serein drifted. Minutes branched into days, days stretching onto eternity.

"Who are you?" the darkness asked.

"No one," a pale yellow echo answered.

A child stood with her back to Serein, turning around as she approached. A bloody X seeped through the front of her shirt, blue eyes staring at her. "Who are you?" the girl asked.

"No one," Serein replied.

The child's body fissured and crumpled. "We are no one. We are wind, bone, ash, soil. We are nothing," a disembodied voice whispered.

Two lights danced before Serein in glowing blue and orange. Serein ran toward them, feet splashing through the blackness. Children's laughter sparkled around her, the familiar sound drawing her closer. Tears leaked out from her cracked heart.

Her hands closed around the twin lights, hands shaking. "My Sun and Stars," Serein whispered, throat tight as warmth spread through the cold nothingness.

"You shouldn't touch them with your hands, volchitsa,*" a white voice said in her ear. "Your hands aren't clean."*

Cracks ran along Serein's fingers, and the lights escaped. She rushed after them. Blood sloshed against her knees. Bodies with slit throats and red smiles floated in the dark lake, eyes black sockets and innards floating like glistening worms.

Cold hands gripped her shoulders. "You're not meant to hold onto anything. Don't you see how deadly your touch is?" the white voice asked as Serein strained forward.

Fingers wrapped around her throat, pulling her back. The laughing lights became two pinpricks against the stretching infinity.

"You belong to me." Xansas' voice solidified beside her. "No kingdom, no prince, no prison nothing can take you from me. I won't let them."

The blood rose to Serein's chest, hands reaching out. Her stomach opened, and burning pain spilled out. One by one, every scar unstitched until Serein felt herself falling apart. The brand on her shoulder ripped itself free and slithered across her skin.

"Perhaps you need to be reminded that it's pointless to hope," Xansas said, lips trailing down her neck. "Will those children still love you when they know what you are? Will you be able to listen to their screams when they see what you really are?"

The crimson waters lapped against Serein's throat, opening their jaws. Xansas laughed, lips curling into a smile. "How about I kill them and save you the heartbreak of watching them run away from you?" Xansas crooned. "My dear volchitsa"—he flicked out a knife and carved deep lines along her arm, forming a red word—"don't cry. You won't be alone. I'll take you back. This time, you'll never escape."

Hands ripped her stomach open and pulled out chunks of her until she was left empty. The darkness swallowed up the blue and orange lights, dragging Serein into the endless depths.

Epilogue
Stirrings in the Dark

Soron's warm summer breeze traveled through the palace courtyard, sending ripples across a pool. A white flower swayed in the middle of the water, petals gleaming under the starlight. Waterfalls tumbled down the rocky cliffs of the valley where they twisted into rivers, flowing past the palace with latticed arches and silver stone towers. Lights from the houses sparkled below.

A man stood on the balcony, his eyes closed. The wind pulled at his hair, the light strands falling across his black and silver robes. Magic thrummed through the earth, safe within the thick Fog that surrounded the Silver Shores and the rest of Bar Elenion.

The magic shifted, bristling with agitation. Fire roared behind the man's eyes, harboring dark shadows and glinting steel. Screams dug into his ears as blood ran across the land. Thirteen men marched over the valley, consuming everything in a malevolent presence he hadn't felt in over three millennia.

His eyes flew open, and he inhaled the crisp air of the dale. He gripped the railing, the white stone ring on his finger glittering with starlight.

The visions are growing stronger. The corruption is spreading, and I do not know how to stop it, he thought. *Aella...I could not protect you.* He touched the three crystals hanging from a silver chain around his neck, their cool surfaces bringing a fresh wave of grief.

He remembered the plague that had claimed thousands of lives, survivors fleeing as magic abandoned them. Caew-im-dwinath and the Immortal Kings had stood for over a thousand years, falling before one human king with darkness in his wake. Loss and devastation scarred Sarlyria, those who escaped to Bar Elenion feeling the screams of dying magic behind them.

"Something wrong, hîr vuin?"

A young man approached, silent as he strode past two armor-clad guards. A single braid hung from the left side of his platinum hair. He knelt into a bow. Two swords were strapped to his back along with a longbow and a quiver of arrows with blue and silver fletching. His jerkin bore the design of an embossed silver tree with twelve branches, the sigil of the House of Gwae.

King Melcinítan turned his gaze to the stars, the moon hidden from sight. "Vanya has hidden herself tonight," he said. "What news does your maqua bring, Caladon?"

"I am afraid I bring unsettling news, Uncle," Caladon replied, rising. "Things are stirring in the south, according to our rebel connections. Sethos has been attempting to send ships to the Wastes beyond the Wild Moors, and his Jackals have been sighted in Zhao, meeting with leaders of the various clans. There has also been a rumor that something has entered the Black Fells."

Melcinítan turned. "How has this rumor come to you?"

"One of our patrols caught a witch near the Fells. She was with a group of Fae and mercenaries," Caladon replied. "The report is that her final words were, 'Rúcarëgoth will rise again. It's already begun.'"

"The children of Rúcarëgoth still carry out their defeated master's will. One witch cannot break the spells on that tomb."

"She appeared to have destroyed the wards that had been set up. When we captured her, she was carrying something that was sealed in the Fells."

Caladon pulled out a wrapped item hanging from his belt. He handed it to the king. Melcinítan froze as an icy chill crept through the thick oilskin cloth, burning his skin. Thirteen shadows loomed behind him, whispering.

"A relic from one of the Thirteen…" Melcinítan's voice tapered off.

"Faeron reports that his contact in Sarddon has heard that Sethos is searching for the dark relics of Rúcarëgoth's Thirteen. There have been excavation parties sent to Sarlyria to find their tombs."

Melcinítan frowned. "Why would Sethos be searching for the relics? He is human. He does not possess magic. Such knowledge could not have come to him without the help of someone else."

"It is possible that he found a follower of Rúcarëgoth who helped him or is using him. If he is searching for more relics, he may be attempting to strike at Bar Elenion," Caladon said.

"The knowledge of the dark relics of the Thirteen has been buried for centuries. Even I do not know where they all are buried. I will send word to the High Council and the Calamor at once. Lady Silmëloth must know about this. If anyone would know about evil stirring, it would be her," Melcinítan said.

"Yes, hîr vuin," Caladon replied, touching two fingers to his heart.

"Continue to patrol the area around the Moors," the king told him. "Send a party to investigate the other known burial location in the Wilds to see if the wards are still in place. If Sethos has agents here, we need to be vigilant. May Yestarë's light guide your path."

"And yours as well, uncle," Caladon said and left.

A man with black braids tucked behind his pointed ears left his post by the doorway. "Shall I summon the rest of the maqua?" he asked as he approached the king.

Long-buried fatigue arose, and Melcinítan sighed. "No, Morcion. There is no need for that. You and Veryan will be enough. If I need the other three, I will summon them," he said.

"Hîr vuin, let me take that from you," Morcion said, dark green eyes on the sword.

Melcinítan held the sword out as Morcion took it, a great weight passing from him. Leaning against the balcony, the king turned his gaze back to the valley. "Make sure it is locked away until the High Council arrives. Set up wards and let no one know of its existence."

"As you wish," Morcion replied. "What is this foul thing?"

"A weapon from one of the Thirteen. It bears the essence of Rúcarëgoth."

"Is this for certain? I know Caladon said this was supposedly taken from the tombs of the Black Fells, but that's impossible. Those spells were forged by the Calamor. Only those mages could break them."

"The Council will decide what to do about this threat," Melcinítan said.

"And if this is indeed one of those swords from those graves?" Morcion asked.

"If so, Mirarnediad help us all." Melcinítan gripped the white stone. *A shadow that has long been slumbering is now moving,* he thought, staring at the sky. *Is that why you hide tonight, Vanya? Because you know what is coming?*

ACKNOWLEDGMENTS

This wasn't a story that was written in quaint cafes or Instagram worthy locations—well, maybe one or two. This story started a decade ago on a blank Word document back in high school and grew with snippets of nonsense on Evernote, ideas hurriedly written out on paper at 1am, paragraphs typed out during class when I should have been paying attention to the professor, and many late nights when I was too tired to spell words correctly. It has followed me through the years, across seas and state lines, refusing to stay silent until the last period was in place. Many patient hands guided and helped this story to become the one you hold now in your hands.

I'm so thankful to all my editors. Kelsey, for working so hard to help develop this story and loved my characters from the start. Tamara, for catching all the grammar and writing errors I missed. My Aunt Loureen, for always encouraged my writing over the years and who was one of my first beta readers. My writing group—Tori, Morgan, Sara, and Shannan—for being so encouraging and helping to shape the story. Thank you all for loving this cast of flawed characters as much as I do, for providing great insight into developing the story, and sharing so many writing memes. Thank you to everyone who has read this story; I couldn't have created it without your help.

You, dear reader, are now also a part of this journey. Without you, I would not be here, writing this acknowledgment to you. You took a chance, picked up this book, and read it to the end. Stories only survive in the hands of those willing to read them. I'm humbled that this book is part of whatever journey you are on, even if it's just a small part.

ABOUT THE AUTHOR

K.E.Andrews has always been an avid reader, which sparked her passion for writing at an early age. Her love of traveling has taken her to different places around the world, reminding her that there are always more stories to tell. She is often found at her desk, attempting to write, binging Netflix, or trying to complete a craft project. She currently lives in Powder Springs, Georgia.

Instagram: @k.e.andrews
Website: www.keandrews.org
Goodreads: K.E.Andrews
Facebook: @k.e.andrewsnovels

Don't forget to leave a review on Amazon or Goodreads. You can also sign up for my newsletter to learn more about new projects, upcoming books, and giveaways.